ENVY KILLS

NORMA HOPCRAFT

Envy Kills

Published by Jaguar Publishing

ISBN #978-0-9994089-7-1

For further information, please contact the author by sending an email to norma@normahopcraft.com.

Dedication

This story is dedicated to my mother, Louise Clotilda Miller Jaeger, who loved yellow roses, taught me to read, in great wisdom wouldn't let me teach my younger sister to read, regularly read aloud to us as kids, made sure we always got to the library, and was a fabulous storyteller and poet.

ALSO BY THIS AUTHOR

Numbers Count (Book I in the Tricia Maguire romantic mystery trilogy)

Why Spy? (Book III in the trilogy)

Want more romance and intrigue? Join my readers list and get a free, humorous prequel set in this world! **https://sendfox.com/nhop1234**

The Paris Writers Circle

The Traveling Writer, a photo journal with insightful captions at NormaHopcraft.com.

ACKNOWLEDGEMENTS

I want to thank all the people in my writing critique groups, when I lived in New Jersey, Paris, Barcelona, Manhattan, Brooklyn (these last two are actually two separate worlds), and Rochester, New York. Your insights helped me become a better storyteller.

Thanks to my Twelve Step groups (I'm a triple winner), my church families in all those cities, and my family of origin, which gave me my unique strengths. All of you have been great sources of support, encouragement, and wisdom.

Thanks to my Higher Power, who inspires, guides, and proves he loves me.

CHAPTER 1

I cuddled in bed at midnight, Ninja purring on my chest and blocking my view of *Pride and Prejudice*—delightful story, what my dreams were made of, Mr. Darcy and all that.

Somebody pounded on my front door.

All the fear that could rack the frame of a female who lives alone did so at that moment. I lay frozen, then summoned my courage and climbed out of bed, grabbed a robe, tiptoed to the living room, and peered out the picture window. Even with the porch light on, it was dim out there. I couldn't identify the person on my steps but could tell she was a fellow female, about my age. She was facing the street as if poised to flee.

My heart slowed a little as I figured that, by leveraging my womanly hips and butt, I could wrestle this adversary to the ground if need be. I opened the inner oak door and quickly locked the plexiglass storm door. With the lesser protection between me and the unknown, my heart was beating fast again.

At the click of the lock, the woman turned. I gasped. She had a black eye and a scab on her cheekbone.

"Tricia, it's me," she said, "Meg Palmer—Meg Rush when we were in high school …"

Memories of Meg, one of the most popular girls in my school, rushed in. She hadn't been intentionally cruel to me. It's just that, as chief editor of the school newspaper, and me only a reporter, she hadn't seemed to register my existence.

"Hi, Meg." The storm door was still shut against her. Was it lack of manners that I hesitated to open up to someone with cuts and bruises at midnight? No, it was abject fear. If I invited her in, I would be involved in her cuts and bruises, and my life would change. I liked my life the way it was.

But then the story of the good Samaritan came to mind. Meg must be desperate to have turned up at this hour, I thought. I'd been a woman newly widowed, alone and vulnerable in the world, not that long ago. Women had helped me, and now it was my turn.

Besides, as a journalist, I was curious.

At last I said, "Come in" and swung the storm door open wide. "Are you alright? What happened?" I peered behind her. Nobody lurking in the shadows as far as I could see, but I was glad to get her off the street. And worried about our safety.

As she stepped in, she touched her cheek. I closed and locked the oak door behind us. She was enviably trim, maybe too thin. Her hair was pulled back sleekly into a small bun at the nape of her neck. I noticed a hefty diamond on her left hand, and her purse flashed a dangling designer logo. It was midnight, but she was carefully made up, at least on the good eye. Except for the black eye, she was as pretty as she had been in high school, but not as confident. It was as if the inner magneto that had generated her charm and strength had lost half its power.

"I slipped and fell."

I thought to myself, of course you did. But I went along with it for the time being.

"Let me get some ice for your eye."

"Don't worry, I iced it when it first happened. But … could I use your bathroom for a minute?"

"Of course. It's right there." My house is a small Cape Cod, and it is not hard to find the bathroom. Meg disappeared, and I heard her lock the door. I waited, looking out the picture window. A car glided past, the white beams of its headlights slicing the blackness. Was that her abuser searching for her? My nerves were jumping.

When at last she emerged, her eyes were puffy and red, and the makeup on the unbruised eye was smudged.

I smiled my biggest welcome, a bit belatedly, I know, but this was all so unexpected. And it was midnight. And I was alone.

"Let me get you some herbal tea. Or something stronger?"

"Thanks, tea would be nice. Listen, I'm sorry to bother you so late."

"It's okay, as a reporter I work in the wee hours often. I'm used to it."

"I was thinking all day about calling on you and didn't make up my mind until a little while ago. Then I saw your porch light on, so I figured you were up."

"It's okay, don't worry. Come to the kitchen, we can talk there."

I could imagine the battle she had fought within herself all day, whether to ask for help or not. I knew from experience with domestic violence, and from writing about it for newspapers, that she must be confused to the point of losing all sense of social judgment, knocking on doors at midnight.

Meg followed me to the kitchen, and I was pleased the day's dishes were done, which wasn't always the case. I liked things tidy for company, even in the middle of the night.

I just hoped we wouldn't need to open the microwave.

"Please, sit down." I gestured toward the small maple table by the window. Meg was my first visitor since my concussion a few months ago. My work as a reporter had brought me into contact with some rough folks in Borough Hall, and after that incident I had resolved to steer clear of violent people. But here was violence again, one of its victims sitting at my kitchen table. What if her abuser was out looking for her? I breathed a tiny prayer for protection for both of us.

The kettle chirped, so I made a pot of mint tea and brought two mugs to the table.

"Honey or sugar?"

Meg declined both and sat hunched over the scented steam. Her fingers trembled as she wrapped them around her mug.

I desperately wanted to hear why she was knocking on my door in the middle of the night but thought that a gentle chat, using the most relaxed interviewing technique I knew—to ask about the distant past—would get the conversation started. It was non-threatening and would help create rapport. Then Meg would surely get around to telling me what was on her mind.

"I haven't seen you in ages," I said. "What have you been up to? Start with what you did after high school."

"I went to University of Chicago." She pulled her mug toward her. "I studied creative writing."

"Lucky you! I write too. I'm a reporter now, did you know? I use my maiden name."

"Yes, I looked you up yesterday in the phone book after I saw your byline in the *Central Jersey Sentinel*. 'Dateline: PASSAIC, NJ, June 1, 1992 – By Tricia Maguire.' It was impressive."

I plopped backward in my chair, pleased. "Oh really? Which story was that?"

"About the Andover Tract becoming Green Acres land. I live on Laurel Way."

With that, Meg was letting me know that she lived in a house worth at least two million dollars. His and hers walk-in closets, libraries, and three- or four-car garages were bare necessities in these homes. In short, her entry hall was bigger than my living room. Wow, Meg had done something right to end up on Laurel Way. And now something was going wrong.

"Did you get married?" Single people didn't live in palaces like that, or if they did, they ghosted around in vast spaces alone.

She nodded. "Dennis is an investment banker."

So he was at the top of the food chain, and by association, so was she. I twisted sideways in my seat, envying her. Some people were born to rule, and Meg seemed to be one of them. I, on the other hand, was one of those who seemed to be doomed to working feverishly and never getting recognized or rewarded.

"Dennis and I enjoy a lot of things together. We go to Europe every year. We were in Venice last spring." She fingered the rock on her left hand.

I felt another stab of envy. Of all the places in the world I wanted to go, that was number one, but I never had the money. The house always needed a new furnace or some other thing I considered vital. Come to think of it, buying those new living room curtains might sink Venice faster for me than the Adriatic ever would.

"Dennis is very good to me."

Yes, I thought, and sometimes he's a nasty son of a gun.

"We're going to Paris soon. We leave in two weeks."

"That's nice," I said, trying to be supportive rather than envious of her means.

"I'm very comfortable, the way I live. I don't have to work, so I volunteer. When I feel up to it."

She was reviewing her life, probably more for her benefit than mine. At this rate of confession, we would be up all night while she told me about extravagant Christmas presents from Dennis: the furs, the cars, the jewels, ad nauseum. I couldn't help it, I wanted to get down to the nitty gritty. But again, exhibiting patience was the priority.

"Dennis is on the board of directors of the Museum of Modern Art. In New York City."

I felt my eyebrows arch on my forehead. He had to be a very talented and well-connected man to have a position like that.

"Wonderful," I said.

"He's a trustee at our church," she said, and I cringed. An abuser in church. Yay.

"We really have an American-dream kind of life," she said in a dull voice.

"Terrific."

But then Meg's eyes filled with tears. They ran down both cheeks and created a shiny purple path under her bruised eye.

"He's getting impatient with me." She grabbed a napkin from the holder on the table, folded it, and twisted it around her index finger. The tip turned purplish. She went silent. Admitting to cracks in the beautiful picture she had been verbally painting would add to the agony that had driven her here tonight.

She must have finally decided to trust me because she looked up at me with sea-green eyes and the words all tumbled out.

"I don't have much energy, the house is a mess, and I can't get pregnant." Her shoulders shook with a sob. "He's so disappointed."

Since Meg was my age, she too was facing her biological clock.

"He's hitting you," I said, desperate to keep any inflection of judgment out of my voice. I didn't want to lose her.

She stiffened at those words. Then she slumped, and she nodded. "He's away on business or I couldn't have come." She dropped the tightened napkin, grabbed yet another one, and twisted that one tight. "I fought with myself all day—all evening—whether to come here."

And ask for help, I finished her sentence silently. "How long has this been happening?"

She winced. Her shoulders lifted closer to her ears, and her lips tightened. She stared at the table, or maybe at nothing, then met my gaze. "About two years ago he got a big promotion. I went into the city to meet him and celebrate. He had a lot to drink, and when we got home, he saw the clutter I'd left all over the house and got so angry. He punched me in the arm. It didn't show."

"But men should never hit women. It's a fundamental law of civilization."

"I know." She stirred her tea slowly, the spoon clanking against the sides of the earthenware mug. "And since then I just haven't felt like doing much. I get up late, put the television on. I thought at this point in life I would have kids, but the house seems so empty. I just can't … pull myself together."

"Could be depression, Meg. The sleep, the lethargy—those are common symptoms. There's help for you. Why don't you see a doctor?"

She shook her head. "I don't have the money to visit a doctor. Dennis gives me grocery money, but that's it."

"What? Are you serious?" My anger at Dennis had been growing with each revelation and now was hard to conceal. "The controlling son of a—."

"—Well, I see a someone regularly—for fertility. Dennis just writes a check. I don't know what he would do if I saw another doctor without asking him first."

I was appalled. Since my husband Tommy's death, I'd been making my own decisions, pursuing my own friendships, building a career, and seeing whatever doctor I pleased. It was sad, how abuse had diminished Meg to a dependent little girl. All in the name of what? Dennis Palmer's need to control? For all her status and big house and travel, I wouldn't trade places with her.

"Meg, what you're up against, you can't handle by yourself."

Fresh tears ran down the purple path. "I know. I guess that's why I'm here. When I saw your byline and read your article, I thought to myself, Tricia's a reporter. She knows the area, the services available for people like me. I didn't know who else to turn to. My mother's dead, my sister and I aren't speaking, and my girlfriends—well, somehow I've lost touch with all but one, and she's well off and happy. I've hidden … Dennis … from her. She doesn't know."

But I could bet that the friend suspected and wasn't sure how to help.

I felt badly for Meg's isolation and figured that at her level of income and society, to admit to an abuse problem was to lose face and status. I felt sorry for her.

"Listen, I'm not an expert, but there's expert help for you. There's a battered women's shelter in the Somerset Hills. They have psychologists and resources. There's a number in the phone book. Will you call them? They can get you into a shelter. Maybe not tonight, but if they can't take you right away, you can stay here until they can."

Wait. What did I just say? Did I really want to get that involved and have an abusive husband trying to break in on us? Speaking of which …

"Meg, your life is in danger. You know that, don't you? You're caught in a deadly situation. Domestic violence always escalates."

I leaned back stiffly in my chair, tension at having no special training or skills for this situation making me ache.

Meg gave me a shy, sidelong glance. "Dennis works so hard, he faces so much competition for advancement, younger people want his job, his boss demands so much."

"All that's probably true, but it doesn't give him the right to punch you. You need to make a decision. It could save your life."

"I know we have problems. But I love him …"

I took a sip of my tea and thought of Tommy, of how lucky I'd been that he hadn't been a violent drunk—well, except for that time he smashed my car window with a pickaxe. I wasn't in the car at the time, but the abuse had rocked me. He died not long after. I was sorry but also relieved that at least he had not sunk to the point of stalking me in my own home, terrorizing me with his fists.

Meg's spoon clinked within her mug, again and again, as I waited. Finally I spoke up.

"Let's call the help line." It was a wee bit pushy of me, but then again, Meg's life was at stake.

She showed no sign of having heard me. She just stared into her tea. I could imagine the battle raging within her. Trading a king-size bed in a palace for a cot in a women's shelter was a giant step down. Going from being the wife of an investment banker to being a divorced woman alone was a long fall from grace.

But her potential as a human being—her very life—was at stake. She could hardly thrive while she cringed in fear of her husband beating her. I hoped she would find some spark, some defiance, some God-given courage to strike out on her own. I waited a full, excruciating minute, which was not easy. Then I broke the silence.

"Meg, I'm going to call the help line. Just for information's sake." She looked up at me, wary. I reached for the phone book and flipped open the cover. The number was among the crisis hotlines on the first page. I dialed. Meg looked down at her tea, or maybe at nothing at all.

"Somerset Hills Women's Help Line," said a woman's alto voice. "Is this an emergency?"

I was relieved to connect with help in this difficult situation.

"I need some information," I said. "I have a friend who's thinking of getting out of an abusive relationship. She's very scared and not sure what to do. I wondered, do you have any beds at the shelter tonight?"

"I can put you in touch with them. If they don't have room, we'll put you in another one. We never turn anyone away."

"Thanks. Can you hold a moment? I'd like to put my friend on the line."

"Yes, but just for a minute."

I covered the mouthpiece with my hand. "They have room for you."

Still Meg stared, this time down the hallway. Her earth-shattering decision, to take the first steps toward splitting up her marriage, was taking time. I couldn't tie up the line for some other woman calling for help.

"Sorry, we'll have to call you back." I hung up, feeling heavily responsible for Meg. How was I going to rest easy until she had escaped her abuser?

I took the liberty of grasping her thin hand. Her knuckles were mountains under my thumb.

"Listen, it will only get worse. You know that, don't you?" She bit her lip and nodded miserably into her mug. I dreaded what she would go home to. I felt such urgency for Meg to get free. "Save yourself! Get out while you still have some ability to plan, so you can survive."

Meg fumbled with her car keys, which clanked on the table, working on my nerves that were already stretched to a painful degree in frustration with her.

I waited, tense, worried about her life.

Finally she focused her tear-filled gaze on me. She looked at me for the longest time. Then something flickered in her eyes—she had made a decision.

She pulled her hand away. "I can't."

"Yes, you can!"

She sighed and stood up, swaying a bit, placing one hand on the table for support. She was exhausted as well as bruised.

"I really can't."

I felt frustrated with her, but I had to accept her decision. It was the worst she could have made. There was only one other thing I could do to help. "If you have no objection, I'll pray for you."

"Okay," she replied. "I don't believe in God, but ... I guess a prayer won't hurt."

"I didn't believe in him either, until I was desperate, and he was there." I reflected that the Gift of Desperation, G.O.D., about Tommy was the best gift I'd ever gotten. Like some longtimers in the Twelve Steps, I could now thank God for my problem/addict/addiction, because it had led me to my Higher Power.

She shrugged. "Well, sorry I bothered you tonight. Thanks for answering the door. I think I'll go home now." She took her mug to the sink, her shoulders sagging.

As gently as possible, feeling that I had to treat Meg gingerly, I said, "If you change your mind about going to the shelter, call me. Or call the domestic violence hotline. It's on the first page of the phone book."

She didn't answer but walked slowly toward the door. I opened it for her, feeling that I had let her down. She stepped into the night.

"Call me any time," I said. "Can I call you?"

She whirled on the porch, her eyes wide with terror. "No!" she barked. "Don't ever!" She went down the steps and turned at the bottom to tell me fiercely, "I'll call you."

And she was gone.

CHAPTER 2

I slowly turned out the lights in my little cottage, except for the reading light next to my bed. I knelt and said a prayer for Meg, then climbed in. To calm down, I read some Psalms for a while and pictured myself putting Meg into Higher Power's loving hands. He could help her where I could not. At long last I relaxed and slept.

In the morning the alarm woke me long before I felt rested. My body ached as I faced the day. I had an interview to do at the Museum of Historic Tools and Crafts in Passaic, my little village. A new curator, Samantha Scarborough, had recently been hired, and it was my job, as a journalist at the *Central Jersey Sentinel,* to find out what her vision for the museum was. It would be a fun assignment—if I woke up enough to bring some personal jazz to it.

I sat down at the dining room table to do my spiritual start for the day. But my elbows dug into the pink tablecloth while I held my head in my hands. Weariness flowed up and down my frame and saturated every part of me. Helping other people, or trying to help, took energy.

Ink splotches of every color, made by my errant pens on the tablecloth during various journal- and novel-writing sessions, accused me of carelessness as I blearily considered today's assignment.

I would have pursued it at my old job on the *Passaic Press,* but I was now working for a more prestigious paper, a daily instead of a weekly. And the *Sentinel* was owned by a national chain, so if I did well, I could move to a big city.

But what I really wanted, when I admitted my flaming ambition to myself, was to move up to *The New York Times* and tool around in the greatest city on earth, looking for stories—oh, I so loved stories—and having a coterie of friends who also worked at the *Times*. Being a peer among the best of the best, which is what my parents instilled in me—you must distinguish yourself in life. I wanted it so bad, it felt like a taut bungee cord hooked to my core, pulling me inexorably toward the city.

But then again, I wasn't sure I wanted to move to New York, which I would have to do to be a reporter there. The trains to New Jersey stopped running at midnight, but writing and editing at daily newspapers ended much later than that. How could I work in the wee hours in the city and nurture a romantic relationship here? I had one that was like a tender little seedling, just beginning to stretch toward sunlight, and I wanted to be around to nurture it.

To think more clearly about it, I went to make coffee. As I watched the dark liquid shimmer with each drip, I remembered light shimmering on Tommy as he sat in his big leather armchair one evening, waiting for me to get home from night school. He sat in a circle of light cast by a lamp standing behind his chair. I knew he had been drinking—driving home, I'd hoped he'd be unconscious by the time I got there—and I dreaded a confrontation. I simply could not help wishing he would be kind to me for once, about me studying English literature, about my dreams of becoming a writer, about distinguishing myself as my parents modelled that I do. But sight of a nearly empty bottle of bourbon, backlit by the lamp, warned me.

"Did you write the Great American Novel tonight," he said.

I felt all the joy of being in class evaporate as I tried to get past him, but he caught a chunk of my skirt. It was a favorite and I wasn't willing for it to be ripped, so I stopped. "We can talk about it in the morning."

"I'm helping you finish your degree so you can work. Not write your twaddle."

"I *do* work. I'm not freeloading on you."

"I don't mean secretary. I want you to make real money with your degree in words. Advertising, something with a big salary."

So this was why he helped me pay for night school. Nothing to do with him seeing my potential to make my dreams come true. Just for cold money. So he could retire early and drink. I felt my bruised heart close tight just as strongly as I felt his tug on my skirt. My soul was wild with resentment for his drinking, his nastiness, his sarcasm. Men don't cherish women's dreams, I thought. They don't want to help you achieve, they want to extinguish the flame. I felt alone on the planet, standing just outside the lamp's circle of light, here in the living room with my husband lit up beside me. He was against me, not for me, and I was sick of it. I would have to divorce the drunken sot as soon as school was over or be overwhelmed in his tide of abuse.

Two months after graduation Tommy was diagnosed with a terminal brain tumor. I decided to see my wedding vows through and eventually had to quit my job to be his nurse. My dreams to be a storyteller were buried in a calendar jammed with doctors and hospital stays. When he did die just months later, I saw an ad in the local paper, the *Passaic Press,* for a reporter. And my dream of finding great stories and distinguishing myself in the newspaper realm slowly resurrected itself. Ten years had gone by, and recently I'd move to the *Sentinel,* a weekly and therefore a step up. Now what about *The New York Times?*

But then I pictured the man I'd met recently. He appeared to be in the same romantic league as Jane Austen's Darcy, and I was slowly getting to know him. Justin Hardy, what a fine, manly name. After experiencing the good in marriage—though with Tommy, the duration of that period had been rather fleeting—I yearned for those benefits again: to snuggle, to romp with a man in bed, to feel that sense of closeness with another human, to share my life, to create a meaning bigger than myself. With Justin, there was potential for courtship and marriage, and I did so want to have children. Could I trade in the chance of having a family for a chance to live and work in New York City, to fulfill dreams of accomplishments? I longed for the glory of saying I was a journalist for *The New York Times* ...

But my burning ambitions were being complicated by a relationship. I didn't want to end up dangling by that bungee cord from the spire of The Times building all alone. I'd built a good life as a young widow these last ten years but feared I'd be solitary to the end of my days.

Would Justin cherish my dreams of becoming a great writer? But my experience with Tommy told me men didn't, that at worst they fought you, at best they buried a woman's ambitions in the avalanche of compromise they expected in marriage.

I opened a dining hutch drawer and pulled out the resume I'd written to get the *Sentinel* job. I had recently added to it a description of the murder I'd solved at Borough Hall. I wanted to expand that resume, list more scoops, be impressive, win accolades.

I sighed. Maybe, if Justin and I gelled, I could curtail my ambitions and just be a reporter in Central Jersey and write novels. But that thought panicked me. Don't sell out your dreams, Trish! And yet … family, babies, snuggles. I shoved the resume into my purse. Who knew what would happen? For today, I would just do my utmost as a journalist and novelist. Right here in Central Jersey. And be an interesting date. If Justin ever asked me out again.

With a fragrant mug of coffee in hand, I sat down once more at the dining room table. This time

I would do my spiritual practice. I had started going to the Twelve Steps, Al-Anon in particular, when Tommy's alcohol consumption became a problem (though it was a brain tumor that finished him off). Al-Anon is for people in relationship with someone not in recovery. At first I went to meetings hoping to save a man gone berserk with alcohol. But in the meetings I found out that I was equally crazy—I was obsessed with trying to change his behavior and attitudes. After his death I stayed in the Steps for more sanity and support in a rather insane world.

On this particular morning I acted on Step Eleven: sought through prayer and meditation to improve our conscious contact with God as we understood him, asking only for knowledge of his will for us and the power to carry it out.

I meditated on a Psalm: "You hold me by my right hand, you guide me with your counsel, and afterward you will take me into glory." These words always gave me a surge of happiness. This whole mess on earth, my achy-breaky life, widowed at 27, alone for a decade—it all meant something after all, only because of God and the joyous eternity he offers.

Then, from nowhere, the thought popped into mind that I really ought to clean my microwave.

Um. I let that thought drift away, just like you're supposed to during meditation.

I prayed for Meg's protection—for the wing of the Almighty to envelop her—and that I'd somehow be of help to her. Refreshed, energized, feeling like I'd sipped clear water at a sparkling stream, I showered, dressed, ate some cereal, and jumped in my car to head to the museum.

It hunkered just up the road from my house on Main Street, near my town's Borough Hall. I drove instead of walking because I felt in a hurry to get to the *Sentinel* afterward.

The sky sported puffy clouds moving in stately rows. They promised a lovely early-June day. I carefully checked the gardens of houses I passed and chuckled to myself, because none of them had as terrific a display of roses as my garden did.

This town, I mused, was a funny little enclave, built on what used to be farmland—we still had a Farmer's Grange, now a social center rather than a center for agricultural information. My town was not quite as fashionable as the suburbs that surrounded it, though all of us were bedroom communities for New York City. But the development of high-end homes, occupied by ambitious families, was dragging my little burg into the 90s. And when you got past appearances—big houses, high-end cars, a polished way of dressing with designer accessories—it had its share of human tragedy. Meg, for example.

I parked the car in the Borough Hall lot and walked across the street to the Museum of Historic Tools and Crafts.

The building had been designed and constructed by a financier one hundred years ago as the town's first library. He wanted to leave a legacy, and he did. Gray stone formed the walls, and arched ceilings elevated the interior into an uplifting experience. Stained glass windows commemorated science, books, and knowledge, and elaborate parquet floors invited people to wander. Just being in the beautiful building always gave me a warm feeling. This architect knew how to affirm humanity in the way he used space and light. I gave him kudos and opened the carved wooden doors.

The small reception area sported a mosaic tile floor and a wooden desk. Behind it sat a diminutive woman with silver hair and bright brown eyes behind silver wire-rimmed glasses. She looked at me over the glasses' rims and smiled.

"Hi! Would you like a tour?"

"No, thanks, at least not yet. I have an appointment with Samantha Scarborough. I'm Tricia Maguire from the *Central Jersey Sentinel.*"

"The *Sentinel?* I read the *Passaic Press.*"

Nuts! Townspeople were often loyal to the local paper. Now that I had moved up in the world, from that paper to the *Sentinel,* I had to try to recruit her as one of my readers. "Well, we cover all of Central Jersey, so there's more information about things to do in the area, coupons to area stores, and great stories about people who are doing things you'd never dream of."

She waved a hand dismissively. "Oh, I get all that from the *Press.*"

I felt defeated. This adorable woman was not going to read my stories, and that was that. Oh well.

"I'll let Samantha know you're here." She dialed a number on her phone with beautiful hands—age-spotted, yes, but with lovely long fingers tipped by manicured nails. After I heard several faint rings of a telephone in the distance, she hung up.

"I'll just go find her," she said and walked briskly around the corner. I waited, admiring the parquet floor, wondering if anybody still knew how to create such a beautiful and inviting surface. I looked up at the arches overhead, marveling at how they intersected and crisscrossed each other. This architect had fun.

What was taking that woman so long?

A hideous shriek pierced the quiet of the museum. I hustled past the base of a wrought-iron spiral staircase, and I searched for where the scream had come from. Through a doorway beyond the stairs I could see an office strewn with papers and the docent I had just met leaning over a figure whose arms were sprawled across an antique wooden desk.

"There's so much blood!" she said, distressed. "Quick, call an ambulance!"

CHAPTER 3

I entered the room, drawn by an irresistible urge to see for myself. I guess that's what makes me a reporter, but it didn't impress the silver-haired docent.

"Get an ambulance!" She shouted this time. I broke my gaze away from the woman slumped over the desk, the back of her head oozing blood, the desk blotter soaked with it. I turned and ran back to reception. At first I couldn't get an outside line. But I jabbed at buttons, cursing modern technology, and finally was able to reach 911.

"I think it's murder," I said when the dispatcher picked up. I must have sounded like a nut.

"What? Where are you?" he asked.

"The Museum—you know, Historic Tools and Crafts," I said dully, pictures of the woman's bloodied head swimming before my eyes. "Hurry. I guess there's a chance. That she's still alive, I mean." When had I lost all power to think about what I was saying? I couldn't put a sentence together.

Minutes later I heard a siren. What a relief to live in a civilized country. Though what had happened to that woman was hardly civilized.

Back at the office, the silver-haired woman still stood behind the victim.

"They're on their way," I said, and just then a policeman rushed into the room. I was stunned by what had happened, but not so stunned that I didn't notice he was all chest and shoulders, tall, and looked wonderful in a uniform. Another siren sounded outside and a minute later a short, skinny policeman came in. The contrast between the two men could not have been more stark.

The tall one slid his fingers under the woman's blood-soaked hair to check for a pulse at her neck.

"She's still alive," he said.

I looked out the office window. An ambulance parked, and three first-aid squad members in white came tumbling out. They hurried up the walk and burst in a moment later.

"Ma'am, would you wait outside," said a heavy woman in white pants—an unfortunate fashion choice—I know there are more important things, but just saying. There was nothing they were doing that I could report in the newspaper—anything I wrote about this crime scene would be ghoulish. So I complied. Reluctantly.

But not completely. I didn't go out of the building but wandered among the display cases, looking at, but not really seeing, the tools and implements that people in days past wielded to wrest a living out of the wilderness. I would have to come back another day to study the collection. Right now, my mind jumped with questions. Who had hit the woman? Would the poor soul be well enough to wake up and identify her assailant? Why would anyone do such a thing? How would her family feel? What a shock for them. Here their loved one is, working in a small New Jersey town, safe from the muggery of the big cities, and she gets clobbered anyway.

I rounded a display case full of tools having to do with shoeing horses and saw the three emergency medical technicians wheeling a stretcher away. I moved to the door of the office and poked my head in.

"Ma'am, you can't come in here. This is a crime scene," the robust policeman said.

"Ma'am, you'll have to go too," the smaller cop said to the silver-haired docent, who was standing just inside the office door, looking numb with shock. She exited and gestured to me.

"I'm all shook up. I'm going to make myself a cup of tea. Do you want one?"

I nodded and clattered after her, down a wooden spiral staircase set within a paneled alcove, into the basement. This area was finished with industrial carpet and ceiling tiles with recessed lighting. Giant display cases, the nearest one devoted to the tools of barrel making, stood tall. Set in one wall was a heavy iron door with "Vault" stenciled on it in an old-fashioned typeface with gold leaf. What did a former library need with a vault? Oh well.

The docent led me to a door marked "Employees Only" and welcomed me forward.

"I'm Virginia Hopewell, by the way," she said. "And you're—"

"Tricia Maguire. *Central Jersey Sentinel,*" I reminded her.

"We've had quite a morning. No wonder I've forgotten your name."

"Is she going to be all right?" I asked. I hoped that Virginia would be talkative, not give me the silent treatment just because I was from the press.

"The technicians said her vital signs are very low. She's just barely alive."

"I'm so sorry—hope she makes it." Then I thought of a fact I needed to confirm. "That was Samantha Scarborough, the new curator, in the office?"

"Oh yes, poor thing." Virginia poured a cup of coffee for me and a cup of tea for herself. She opened a miniature fridge and offered me milk. As I poured a dab into my coffee, reflecting on the woman's tenuous hold on life, a man in a red and black buffalo-checked shirt came in. He was also wore black jeans and lumberjack boots, like he'd just stepped out of an outdoorsmen's catalog.

"What happened?" he asked her.

"I found Samantha with her head all bloody," she answered shakily and filled him in.

"You know, there's nobody at the front desk," the man said.

She drew her breath in sharply. "Nobody guarding our treasures! Yes, I'd better get back. But first—Matt, this is Tricia Maguire, a reporter from the *Central Jersey Sentinel*. Tricia, this is Matt Morgan, our caretaker and handyman."

He looked competent, as a handyman should. My mind wandered off, as it tends to do. What credentials did a person present to get this kind of job? Did they give a tour of the interior of their own home, with everything, including doorknobs, in fine working order? I gave myself a mental shake. Trish, I said to myself, you can't ask about his credentials, and of course he won't explain. The way people don't reveal all the mysteries about themselves right away—and most likely never will—unless I were to be a bit nosy—has been a major annoyance to me for a long time.

He did not fit in at all with the polished appearance that most people in Passaic maintained. He looked rugged and outdoorsy and interesting and capable—and with wild black curly hair on top, and a wild look about his whole person—capable of anything. Intriguing. I wasn't sure where I stood with Justin exactly, among the pantheon of women who probably were bringing him, a widower, their best casseroles. So I checked this man's left hand. He brought it up to scratch his ear. No ring. But that didn't mean much.

Virginia had excused herself and hurried out of the room. Matt poured himself a cup of coffee and added two packets of sugar. He sat at a table for two, apart from me, his muscular frame commanding his chair.

As long as he was here, I'd interview him for the newspaper. Novel idea. Before I got out pen and notebook, I'd ease him into it. With that wildness, he had the air of someone who needed easing.

"Samantha's so new—had you met her yet?" I sipped my coffee.

He gave me a look of suspicion. "Are you interviewing me for the newspaper? I'd rather not." His abruptness took me back a little.

"You can get a statement from our chairman of the board, Dorothy Anderson," he added, trying to be a little helpful, I guess. "She's in the phone book. On Maple Street."

He sipped his coffee, and I thought of more questions I'd like to ask but knew I couldn't. Like, what do you do at home in the evenings? Putter? Read? Do we have books in common? I kept trying to think of something I could actually say and came up with very little, but my reporter's instincts wouldn't let me give up without digging for more.

"How long have you been working here?"

"Three years. Don't put that in the paper."

My, this guy was taciturn, bordering on rude. Maybe he wasn't potential husband material after all. I thought of Justin and felt bad that I had been unfaithful (in a tiny way) by being interested in Matt. Then I felt bad that I felt bad, that I'd felt unfaithful even though Justin and I were only in a preliminary dating phase—just a few dates so far—and all I'd done was wonder if Matt were married. And how he spent his evenings. Um, I was sinking into a weird think-soup fast. Time for a reality check.

He sipped his coffee, slurping loudly. There's reality for you, I thought, and yuck, he was definitely off my list. But then again, he could fix things … my house always needed work … I'd figure this out later. Right now I had a job to do.

"What exactly do you do for the museum?"

"Climb ladders, squeeze under sinks, fix doorknobs. Handyman. Don't put that in the paper." He cupped his mug with fingers that were thick with the strength to twist tools.

"I'm not putting it in the paper," I said. "See? No pen, no notebook." Then I gave myself a good mental thump. I might need the information later to round out a story. Yeah, Trish, like, what information? I chided myself.

What story? That there's a handyman at the museum? That's the kind of news people pay subscriptions for, sure thing, I told myself scathingly. Come on, honey, you've got to come up with more than that.

"What projects did Samantha want to start in the museum?" I asked

"I don't know. She wasn't around long enough to start anything."

"But what were her plans? Did she have a staff meeting and announce them?"

"Ask Dorothy Anderson." He abruptly sat back in his seat, and the chair squeaked in protest.

"What kind of person is Samantha?" I asked.

"She's a nice lady. Now don't quote me." This time he looked angry.

I'd had enough. Interviewing Matt Morgan was like repeatedly grazing a fender on a concrete highway divider. I would just bounce off, with new scrapes and dents each time.

"Well, enjoy your coffee," I said and headed for the wooden stairs. Spiraling upward, I glanced back. Matt was watching me ascend. Did he have a guilty conscience over the way he'd treated me, or was he admiring the view? Another mystery I'd never solve.

Emerging from the circular stairwell, I saw Samantha's office was cordoned off with crime-scene tape. Inside, people in white suits were dusting the room for fingerprints. Had I touched anything? My prints were already on file with the police because of something that happened this past winter. I prayed I wouldn't get sucked into the police investigation.

I had my own to conduct.

CHAPTER 4

Virginia Hopewell sat dutifully at her desk near the front door, though she told me she had locked it, under police orders, to keep out visitors. I hoped she'd be willing to answer questions from the press. I took out my notebook and pen to show I intended to proceed "on the record." With her peaceful air, she had the look of someone who might not mind helping a reporter.

I was dying to get to the incisive questions, tensed like a long jumper ready to lunge beyond the mark. But it behooved me, and the story I would write, to build rapport first, to begin with questions on uncontroversial topics instead of leaping to the tough questions. Virginia was not likely accustomed to being interviewed by the press. Chatting about the things on display in the museum seemed like a good way to get her to open up about the workings this place. I was eager to get to the good stuff. Patience, Trish, I admonished myself.

"What's your favorite tool here?" I asked. As I said it, my opener felt trite after what had happened to Samantha. Come on, Trish, think!

"Oh, I think it's the bark spud. It was used to separate bark from logs. We own two of them, each different, because they were forged by hand."

Well, that had actually turned out okay. But it left a question hanging.

"What do you like about them specifically?"

"Their shape. They have graceful blades on the end. And they're a symbol of how hard people had to work years ago. After they stripped the logs, they would build a house with them. Incredible."

Virginia seemed enthusiastic about the tools, which to my eye were primitive, almost as primitive as arrowheads chipped into shape by prehistoric peoples. Take the display of flatirons I'd passed, for example. Talk about crude. I was thankful nobody expected me to iron acres of a cotton skirt with a fifteen-pound hunk of metal that I had to heat on an open fire in July—and do it while wearing acres of cotton skirts and petticoats that I had to keep from catching fire and going up in flames, taking me with them.

Time for more easy questions. "Tell me about Samantha. Did she have children?"

"Well, I'm not sure. She didn't mention any, but there wasn't much reason why she should."

"Where did she live?" I was still casting about for general information, tense, biting my tongue in impatience.

"I think in Somerville. But I'm not positive. Maybe David May or Dorothy Anderson would know. David's the former curator, and Dorothy is the chairman of the Board of Trustees. She and her husband started to collect historic tools, and it somehow turned into a museum."

The phone, such an interrupter of interviews, rang just then, and Virginia picked up, said sweetly that the museum was closed for the day, then turned back to me.

"Do you have some literature about the museum's history?" I asked.

"Sure. Here's a brochure David commissioned last year," and she handed me a glossy pamphlet. "He's now on the Board of Directors. You should look him up."

"I will," I assured her. There was so much to ask her. I wanted from Virginia Hopewell what every reporter wants from a source: for her to be herself instead of posing for the press, to say quotable things that showed how unique she was, and to shed light on the situation. Except for people like Matt Morgan, I enjoyed talking with my sources and felt deeply connected to them by the time we finished an interview. I hoped the same magic happened today with Virginia.

Showing an interest in people's activities was a great way to connect with the souls I interviewed. Asking questions, listening intently to the answers, and digging deeper with follow-up questions, were the tools of my business. This jived with all my writing goals, both for my journalism and my novels: to get to know people, to explore the mystery of individuals living their lives.

Active listening was key for me to what the newspaper world called "cultivating your sources." More cynical people might call some of what I do "sucking up." It's not that, though I do admit it smacks of hidden agendas—

being attentive to get information in return. But I truly want to know each source better. If listening, and then perhaps giving a compliment—only one that I meant with whole-hearted truth—helped in that process, so much the better. It gave me a reason to look for the good in people. Which fit in nicely with my personal battle against negativity. I'm predisposed toward gloominess about the world. Making a deliberate effort to find goodness helped me fight that energy-sapping tendency.

My instincts told me that chit chat with Virginia had developed enough emotional connection between us that I could now delve deeper with this source.

"Did Samantha Scarborough hold any staff meetings yet?"

"Yes, we had one Monday," she said. "It was the beginning of her second week. She worked fast." She eyed my notebook and pen distrustfully. She'd said "we"—docents were invited?

"You were in the meeting?"

"Yes, me and Benjamin Long, the other docent. And Matt."

Well, that was neat of Samantha, to include everyone.

"Are there any other staff members or docents?"

"There's Elspeth MacIntosh, Samantha's secretary. I mean assistant."

Oooo, I had to get with her. Nobody knows a boss better than a secretary—I mean, assistant. Hmm, having endured in the humbling role of secretary, I wasn't that sympathetic to people insisting on the new nomenclature.

"Where is she today?"

"The police closed the museum by the time she got here, so she went home. We're all going home in a few minutes."

Time for the long jumper to leap. "Before you go—at that staff meeting, did Samantha talk about her vision for the museum, a change of course, new acquisitions, new marketing, any sort of change at all?"

"Well, she said the museum had been well run by her predecessor, that's David May, as I said."

Unfortunately, how the museum had been run in the past was not new news. But it was good for background. "Is she going in a new direction?"

"She said she was getting familiar with the museum's operations, and she asked for the staff's help. You should ask Matt. He was there."

"He's nowhere near as articulate as you are," I said, perhaps going a bit overboard in "cultivating my source," but not too much and in a harmless way, I thought. Especially since interviewing him was futile. "Did she mention a new marketing technique to attract visitors?"

"She talked about a crafts fair. Artists bringing things they made and displaying the tools they made them with. Then the museum would point out forerunners, early models of similar tools."

"Anything else?"

"She mentioned a direct mail campaign. I don't remember anything else. I guess things will be delayed, now that she's … been attacked."

"Yes, that's so unfortunate," I murmured. It was time to get into the nitty gritty details of running a museum. This next question would sorely test the rapport I'd sought to establish. "Could you give me all the Board members' phone numbers? And her assistant's?"

Virginia looked up at me through her silver-wire-rimmed glasses. "Anything you can do to find out why this happened would help the police, wouldn't it?" she asked, as if she were giving herself a reason to help me.

"Yes, I really think so," I assured her. She sat with her hands in her lap, and I held my breath. Then she reached into one of the desk's drawers and brought out a little red address book. I rejoiced that she was agreeable to helping me.

"I can give you their numbers," she said, "but you must absolutely promise that you will not reveal where you got them."

"I absolutely promise." I made a mental note to be put in jail rather than give up Virginia's name. I devoutly hoped it never came to that.

She read out the numbers, and I wrote them down carefully. This was no time for an attack of dyslexia. She was inclined to help me now—she might not be inclined to repeat the numbers for me later. It had happened to me before. As with most things, I had learned the hard way.

What else did I need for my story before this interview began to have the feel of an inevitable end? Think fast.

"Comments from other docents would be nice. Do you have any of their names and numbers?"

"Well, I mentioned there's only one other. We split the shift, you could say. Benjamin Long, I'll give you his number too." She hesitated in her flipping of the address book's pages. "—Well—." She paused, eyes blank, and the silence dragged on.

"What?" I prompted as gently as I could.

"Oh, I was just thinking. Nothing."

Interesting. What was going on there? I wondered. I made a note to call Benjamin. Was he a suspect? I thought, Trish, everyone is a suspect at this point. Though this sweet little docent in front of me seemed highly unlikely as a violent perpetrator.

She resumed flipping through her book and then read off another number. I was excited to be able to call and interview these people. I had my work cut out for me, contacting everyone, digging to round out the story. But I might just have a scoop—the reporter from my statewide competitor, the *Jersey Record*, hadn't shown up yet. Maybe Monica Bodinsky wasn't listening to her police scanner this morning. And I would beat the weekly *Passaic Press* by a day, since they came out on Thursdays and my story would appear in the *Sentinel* tomorrow, on Wednesday. The benefit of working for a daily.

The scent of a scoop was tantalizing, though my joy was just a bit tempered by the thought of the suffering that Samantha Scarborough and her family were enduring. But I was excited about my breaking story. It was so compelling, it was going to write itself, as writers say. And if I figured out who attacked her, I would have a new scoop. Nice.

"Virginia, thanks for your time and for the phone numbers."

"Just don't let on, okay?"

"Yes, promise. I protect my sources." I stuffed the brochure about the museum into my capacious bag and headed for my car.

CHAPTER 5

I went home instead of the newsroom because my house was closer to Dorothy Anderson's place, and I needed her comment, since she was the founder and Chairman of the Board. Plunking my notebook and a handful of pens on the dining room table so I could take notes if she wouldn't let me meet her in person, I dialed her number. After two rings, a woman with a trembly, frail-sounding voice answered.

I started to identify myself, and she interrupted.

"The police are on their way here to question me."

"Can I talk to you until they arrive?"

"I don't know. I think I should talk to them first."

"Tell you what," and I cursed myself for backing off and not being New York Times assertive, "let me call you back later." She sounded very distracted when she said, "Okay," so I wondered if she'd really talk to me. We hung up and I dialed David May, the former curator. He said I should come to his house and gave me directions. He'd already heard about Samantha, too, and I wondered who'd called him.

Turns out he lived in a mansion on at least one hundred acres in the neighboring Somerset Hills, one of the wealthiest enclaves in America—in horse country, in fact, where Jackie Onassis had a home and stables. I drove up the May's winding driveway, which was flawlessly paved and reminded me that mine was very much in need of resurfacing. And had been for years.

I continued upward, turned a corner, emerged from the woods, and saw the house, set at the top of the hill. Impressive. The mansion spread out forever, made of blond stone, with bay windows, balconies, attics, and turrets that jutted from the frame. A maid answered the front door. I was going to have to say a prayer not to be judgmental of David May. The guy must have been born to it.

Now standing in the wood-paneled entry hall, I looked up at the soaring staircase. Then I noticed a mechanized stair chair had been attached to it.

The maid, dark-haired and in her forties, was playing her role in a black uniform dress, snug over her petite figure, with a small, blindingly white frilled apron. She led me through a massive living room where two concert grand pianos stood at either end.

"Who plays?" I asked, suspecting the answer.

"Nobody, ma'am," she said. Aha! The upper classes bought two giant pianos for their huge living rooms, but nobody in the family worked at it hard enough to learn to play.

As I looked around at the luxurious furnishings, I could feel my envy mounting, my old resentment of other people's houses, careers, achievements, husbands, children, plate, glassware, silverware—well, not so much silverware, for some reason.

She led me into a sunroom, and I took quick impressions of it. There were large black and white diamond tiles on the floor. Plants in big pots stood around, though not a profusion of them—the plants were there for décor, not as the object of a passion. White wrought-iron furniture stood grouped throughout the solarium, adorned by flowered cushions in shades of pink and green—was that a Lily Pulitzer fabric I spotted? From my own hauntings of high-end fabric stores, I suspected the answer was yes. The glass walls provided a view over a downward-sloping field, some woods, and the Watchung mountains rising in the distance.

A woman was seated in an electric wheelchair, and a man, presumably David May, was dressed in khakis, a blue button-down cotton shirt, and deck shoes but no socks—like a preppie. I wondered if the arrogance that so often seemed to go with preppie money was going to show up in this interview.

Yes, I do admit that I get envious of those who are born to family wealth and have no struggles with earning money. I could write novels all day if I were one of them.

But let's get one thing straight. What bothers me by far the most is their attitude. So many of them look down on people who must work for a living. They act like they've done something clever to end up in their position, and they haven't. The money is an accident of birth, a total gift, but they don't look at it that way. They think they've excelled and are better people for having money. I haven't found them to be more excellent, usually less so: likely to be alcoholic, cheating on their wives, arrogant, unproductive, and very ready to enjoy snubbing people born to fewer advantages.

The woman nudged her wheelchair's joystick with the back of her fingers to turn towards me. The man stood and stepped forward.

"Thank you, Anita," he said to the maid. "Would you bring coffee?" She nodded and left.

He extended his hand to me. "Hello, I'm David May," he said graciously, "and I'd like you to meet my wife, Kiki." If ever I heard a French finishing school nickname (I was jealous), it was then. She slowly lifted her head, with great effort, and looked me in the eye as a way of greeting me.

"How do you do—" I started to say and caught myself, because the answer to that question was obviously, "not well."

I quickly switched to "—How nice to meet you" and made no move to shake her hand, which now rested limply in her lap.

"My wife is interested in the museum too," he said as he gestured graciously to a wrought iron/Lily Pulitzer settee for me, and sat himself. Was Kiki's interest that of a wife in her husband's job? Or her own personal fascination? A mystery.

Kiki was strapped into her chair with a band across her chest, and she was leaning forward against it. Multiple sclerosis? Lou Gehrig's? It sank in on me with new clarity that money can't protect anyone from calamity. Of course, money could pay for nurses and electrified wheelchairs and vans with lifts. Many handicapped people had to struggle much harder without those amenities. But it appeared that no amount of gold could get Kiki up and standing and walking and talking easily, things I could do that I keenly appreciated.

"Virginia Hopewell called me and told me what happened," he said. "We just can't believe it. We want Samantha Scarborough to recover completely and tell us who did this. Don't we, Kiki?" She lifted her head and met his gaze but didn't blink or nod.

I had been a bit overawed by my surroundings—awe seems to be the intent of much upper-class decorating—and had forgotten to get my notebook out. I dug for it in my leather bag at that point, noting that the bag had worn spots on the corners. I didn't normally notice or worry about that, but in these surroundings, my bag's lack of freshness leapt to my attention. I set the bag on the floor to hide the frayed spots and quickly wrote down his comments. Surely he had enough experience with the press, in his role as curator of the town's only museum, to realize that he was going to be on the record. I sought to build rapport with softball questions first.

"You were curator until recently, when Samantha was hired," I said.

"Yes, I decided to retire, to spend more time with my wife."

Well, that was certainly noble of him. If it was the real reason.

"When did you first meet Samantha?"

"When she held her first Board meeting, end of May."

"What's your opinion of the changes that Samantha has begun," I said, not knowing what those were but fishing for them in David's brain with the best lure I could come up with, which was a question. Amazing the fish that a question could hook.

"I'm sure whatever Samantha has planned will work out beautifully," he said, his diplomacy annoying me because it wasn't going to look as interesting in print as meaty facts—or a snide comment. I hoped the lifelong training in diplomacy that elite boarding schools and upper-class parents had instilled in him (to be used only when diplomacy served their patrician purposes) didn't prevent him from saying something controversial.

I tried another lure.

"What is the museum's mission?" I asked, hoping to get him to talk, then gain momentum, and keep rattling on until I found something quotable in what he said.

"Now, my definition of it is completely unimportant. It's Samantha's that must prevail."

So annoyingly diplomatic.

"But a museum given to old tools—what's the importance of that?"

This time he bit. "These old tools, as you call them, were once held in the hands of men and women whose hard work, sweat, and tears created the bounty we now enjoy in this country. We can't forget that the land originally was forest. It had to be cleared of trees, roots, stumps, rocks, boulders, and then plowed, all with tremendous effort.

"Our ancestors built the foundation for all that we enjoy today—the prosperity, the desk jobs. The way we live today is directly descended from these tools and the hands that wielded them. The tools must be preserved simply as an act of appreciation for all that the previous generations bequeathed to us through their hard labor. They remind us of our origins in this country, and the lot that might have fallen to us if we had lived two hundred or even one hundred years ago."

I wrote it down, and it was eloquent and meaningful, and I'd include some of it for my history-loving readers. He hadn't mentioned that the land that our ancestors worked so hard on was stolen from Native Americans. But David May simply was not going down controversial paths today.

Anita arrived balancing a silver tray with three translucent china cups of steaming coffee. It smelled and tasted delicious.

"What else should I know about the museum?"

"It's really there to serve the public, to educate people about our country's industrious past. I'm deeply saddened by the attack on our new curator and hope for her full recovery."

I reluctantly admitted to myself that this aristocrat had been quotable again, and that I sensed strongly within me that this interview had come to a close. At least in his opinion. I gathered my middle-class forces to keep him in his talkative mode and get my money's worth out of driving all the way out here.

"What did Samantha propose in her first meeting? Changes to the museum's focus, its acquisitions, its personnel?" Lots of hooks lined up on that fishing line.

"She mentioned new efforts to fundraise. She wanted to hold a gala. I offered to chair that committee."

That was noble of him too.

"When and where would that be held?" I said. And saw my error. "Though it's delayed now that …"

"Yes, it's on hold." His tone suggested that I'd made a dumb comment.

"What do you think happened—who might have attacked her?"

"I have no idea, and I would never care to speculate and make unfounded accusations."

But I bet he'd shared them with Kiki. I wished I knew what they were. As former curator, and now a Board member, he was in the inner circle, he knew the currents and cross-currents of power. Such as they were in a small museum in a small Central Jersey town. Yet Samantha had been attacked— there must be cross-currents aplenty. Unless the attack had been random.

I wondered idly if the plan for a gala could possibly be a motive for attacking Samantha. The staff would strain to pull it off. I rejected the idea. Didn't seem at all likely.

"Holding a gala is a huge amount of work," I said, basically just making conversation at that point, giving him a chance to complain about the work, if he was so inclined, or to expand on his ideas for the event.

"Are you suggesting that Samantha's plan triggered me—or someone else—to nearly kill her?"

He had made a leap I hadn't expected. His reaction—overreaction—was intriguing. I'd raise David May higher on my suspect list.

"No, I'm just curious about your plans. Committee members, etc." It would be a Who's Who of the Somerset Hills. It would be a new story.

"Obviously all plans are on hold." His condescending tone raised my hackles. My gut was now screaming that this interview was over. It was time to get out of there with my middle-class dignity intact.

"Okay, thanks for your time," I said and grabbed my bag with its frayed corners. We said goodbye and I left the couple in the lovely sunroom, facing their problems, I supposed. Anita met me in the living room, perhaps summoned by a bell connected to the kitchen, and she led me to the front door.

As I followed her, I noticed a giant painting over the huge mantel. It was of Kiki as a young woman, standing before the very same mantel, wearing what must have been a designer gown. Cream satin flowed to her feet. Her face was unlined, also creamy. She appeared fully comfortable in her body.

But her body had betrayed her, and she was locked in it alone. Unless she believed in God, and then he would join her in her suffering, keep her company, and help her spirit to transcend her situation. I hoped for her sake she had learned that bit of truth, along with all the others she was learning from her hardships.

CHAPTER 6

Dorothy Anderson sounded upset when I called her back.

"The police were here," she said, her voice trembling.

"Well, ma'am, I'd still like to talk to you. How about if I come to your house?" Since she was Chairman of the Board, I needed her for my story. And reporters know that in-person yields better interviews than over the phone.

"Oh, I guess so," she said distractedly. I promised myself to be very gentle with this older person.

I hopped in my Corolla, revved its four-cylinder (yet zippy) engine, and steamed off toward her home, which was in an assisted-living center. The entry was decorated with planters full of purple and yellow pansies; they nodded their benign faces to me in the light spring breeze. Inside, the hallway was carpeted with a lovely floral pattern. The upholstery on groupings of chairs complimented the carpet's colors. This place was expensive to live in, I concluded. Why did most things boil down to money? And yet the best things in life were still free. Like simply walking where I wanted to go.

I took the elevator to Dorothy's floor, found her door, and knocked. A small grapevine wreath intertwined with pale pink silk flowers hung from her peephole on a strand of thin wire. Maybe Dorothy was stretched like thin wire—ready to break. I resolved to go easy and not dig too hard; however, I ached for something snazzy and quotable for my story. Being a reporter means carrying all kinds of conflicting impulses.

Dorothy opened the door. Her white hair was pulled back in a bun, and her shoulders were stooped with age. She must have rallied in the time it took me to drive there because she had the cheek (or maybe it was spunk, at her age) to roll her eyes at the sight of me standing there looking eager with my notebook and pen. Our interview couldn't get off to a good start if she was going to adopt a cynical attitude toward the press. I had to win her over fast.

"Good afternoon," I said sweetly.

"I guess you'd better come in," she said with a sigh. There's nothing like a long sigh to make me feel welcomed.

Her furniture was prettily done in flowered fabrics. The curtains were plain gauze—no lace. The room was tidy, without a lot of knickknacks, and I was thankful because I seem to bump, unintentionally, I think, into twitchy little things.

"Mrs. Anderson, thanks for seeing me," I said in my little-old-people-soothing voice. "I won't take much of your time." Though I'd take as much as I could get.

She gestured for me to sit in a chintz-covered wing chair. She brought tea, and we settled in.

I figured my time with Dorothy was limited by her stamina, that an interview with the police and tea prep had eaten into it, and that, as the leader of the museum, she was not a newbie in dealing with the press, as Virginia quite likely had been. So this time I just dove right in.

"Could I ask: What are Samantha Scarborough's plans for the museum?" So far nobody had answered this question in any detail, and it needed answering.

Dorothy slowly crossed her ankles and sipped her tea. I coached myself not to show my impatience.

"Well, one of the high priorities is simply maintaining the collection in good order," Dorothy replied with a willing-enough attitude. "And we have a budget for a few acquisitions. We were going to make some careful purchases. Of course, that's on hold now, due to this …incident. Please put in your paper that I'm shocked, and that I'll do all that the police ask me to help find out who put Samantha in a coma."

She uncrossed her dainty feet, in their dainty pumps, and set her teacup down. I felt impatience rising again within me and was ashamed of it. I liked little old people. It was just that today I had so much still to do to write my story.

"What have they asked you to do, Mrs. Anderson?"

"To inventory every tool the museum owns."

Yes! I had a new facet to my story. I would check with the police on it later.

"They'll investigate, of course, but they told me they believe she might have been hit with a tool from our collection. An inventory will take time. We have 10,000 pieces."

"When will it start?"

"As soon as possible."

"When will that be?" Nothing like being dogged.

"I suppose it can start today or tomorrow. It's urgent." Dorothy's voice sounded strong and steady. I was relieved.

"How do you feel about all that's happened—to Samantha, I mean."

"Oh, it's dreadful." Maybe she wasn't as composed as she'd seemed because with those words she sloshed her tea into her saucer. "I can't imagine why she was attacked. The tools are valuable to me since I collected so many of them with my late husband. They're tied up with his memory. But no one piece is so valuable, at least not that I'm aware of, to warrant attacking someone to get it. We're hoping for full recovery for Samantha. She has so many good plans for the museum."

"Could you give me some examples?"

"History museums are going through a big transition. We're re-examining every display, every assumption that might have been made."

"Assumptions?"

Dorothy seemed to find new reserves as she talked about her beloved museum.

"What Samantha wants to do, as we're setting each tool in context in a display, with words to describe the tool's history and use, is to thoughtfully ask, 'Who are we supporting here? Whose stories are we telling?' Colonialism and patriarchy weren't questioned as much in the 70s, when we started out. What history museums are saying now is that there were groups of people who must have been marginalized and who should be reported."

"Like who?"

"Well, women jump to mind. Their stories are so often eclipsed by men's."

I jotted everything down quickly. "Who else?"

"Black folk. Their stories are often ignored too."

"How would you go about getting these stories?"

"Hunt for diaries, journals, letters, I suppose. Samantha knows more about it than I do. I never hunted for anything but historic tools."

Now the trembling was back in her voice. I had a new fact—the inventory—for my story, and a quote about Samantha's recovery by the Chairman of the Board, so I figured I could leave her be.

"Do you need anything, Mrs. Anderson?" I asked because it felt wrong to abandon her in her solitary apartment.

"No, no, I'll be alright."

I thanked her for her time. That's important in cultivating a source.

Then I hopped back in the Toyota and headed for the *Sentinel*. As I drove down Passaic's Main Street, with well-kept houses on both sides, except for mine which needed a new coat of stain on the shingles (I'll do it in October instead of June like I'd planned, I told myself), thoughts of the grisly attack and the museum faded and thoughts about my new job came into focus.

A daily newspaper was a professional step up from a weekly; however, my new hours were a bit of a pain. I didn't leave work until press time, one in the morning, two or three nights a week. It screwed up my sleep. But I loved my job. I'd been a waitress—I'd bet David or Kiki never had—and a babysitter, and a secretary to men who had big careers in the works. This job was by far the most fun. The freedom to drive around, visit people, and ask them questions delighted me.

Who wouldn't like being paid for being curious?

The *Sentinel*'s newsroom and printing plant was on a major Central Jersey highway, Route 22. Traffic roared along it and, when my destination came into view, I took my life into my hands to slow down enough to steer onto the offramp and then into the driveway. One person honked, as usual. This time, in light of my morning parlay with God, I resisted the urge to let that driver know, with crude urgency, what I thought of him. But I was going too fast, nearly swiped the curb. At that point I said something crude.

The reception area was quiet, and I went through a set of glass double doors into the newsroom. It smelled deliciously of ink because the huge printing presses worked in the same building. I had arrived earlier than the other reporters, and the rows of desks were empty, their monitors dark. I dropped my purse on my chair and started up my computer. The *Sentinel* had recently bought desktops—the wave of the future—for all its reporters. I thought they were difficult to work with, but strangely nobody asked for my opinion.

While the computer burbled through its start-up routine, I went to get coffee. I was intercepted.

"Good morning, Tricia," said Paul Tercell, the day editor of the *Sentinel* and my boss. He had come out of his office and now blocked my path. Big and muscular, he carried himself in that tense way of body builders. I was still busy figuring out what he expected of me as a brand-new reporter on the staff. My goal was to meet and exceed his expectations.

"Morning, Paul, big news," and I told him about the attack on the new curator.

"Page one, above the fold. Go for it," he said, and he turned from me to walk in a muscle-bound, stiff-legged way to the office of his buddy, the publisher. The good ol' boys were going to have a parlay.

I continued on my way toward the elixir of life. My hot mugful of newsroom brew actually tasted good, and I gulped it eagerly. Finally my computer flashed that it was ready, and I began typing my notes. I wouldn't finalize the story until nearly one in the morning, after I'd spoken to Chief Bognavian of the Passaic police, and to the hospital to find out Samantha Scarborough's condition at press time.

Slowly the newsroom filled up with reporters. Some said "hi" to me but most slunk to their desks as they did every day, without saying anything to anyone. If this was the camaraderie you could expect among reporters at a daily newspaper, it left a lot to be desired. Surely The New York Times would be different.

"How are you doing?" It was Gabriela passing my desk, her copper-blonde, wavy hair (jealous) brushing her waist. She had taken it upon herself to be a bit of a mentor in my new workplace. She also drove in road rallies, threading her VW Jetta between traffic cones set up challengingly in big, empty parking lots. She usually won.

"Gabi, hi," I said. "Big story today," and I told her about Samantha Scarborough.

"Sounds like a juicy one. Have you talked to the family?" She placed one hand on my desk and leaned onto it and over me. I wished she wouldn't loom like a teacher over a six-year-old. With the condescending tone of voice to match.

"I can't talk to them!" I said. "They're in distress. Besides, they're probably not available—probably at the hospital."

"I recommend that you at least try to reach them for comment and mention it in your article." Gabi had gone to journalism school (jealous), so I needed to take her suggestions to heart. Still, I couldn't think of anything more gruesome than calling that family.

"Wow, that's a tough assignment," I said with a smile, to show I hadn't rejected her idea. "What would you say to a family like that?"

She leaned back and lifted her hand from my desk. Relief. But her tone of voice was still condescending. "I'd say I was from the newspaper and ask for their comment. That's all. You at least have to try. If they won't talk, then you say in your story, 'The family had no comment.' Simple."

Simple but gruesome. "I really don't want to bother the family." I was pushing back on her advice, knowing the pushback wouldn't be welcomed.

"It's your job to bother people," she replied.

Well, that was another way to look at being paid to be curious.

I wanted her on my side and was glad to have her as a mentor, though the gift seemed to come with an annoying dash of condescension and instructions to do things I didn't want to do.

Gabi drifted off to start her day. I really didn't want to bother Samantha's family. I hoped to call their number and for there to be no answer. This was a good time to try it. Her husband (if she had one) would be at the hospital by now. I looked up Samantha's home number in my notes and dialed.

Thank God there was no answer. I quickly typed into my notes that the family couldn't be reached for comment. There, that satisfied that journalistic rule of thumb.

But the call had felt terrible. I decided then and there to never do that again. Forget Gabi with her J-school degree. Forget pleasing a mentor. I would come up with my own rules of thumb—while adhering to journalism's code of ethics—and if need be, I'd find myself some other mentor and ignore the new one when I had to.

The reporter at the desk next to me, Henry Burnham, suddenly banged his phone down and leapt to his feet.

"There's a fire at the Genpharm plant," he said, as he grabbed his notebook and headed for the door.

There were two dozen pharmaceutical firms in Central Jersey, polluting, paying taxes, attracting Ph.D.s to the area, and employing tens of thousands of people. The *Sentinel*'s readers would care what happened at a pharmaceutical plant.

I fervently hoped that the "fire" would turn out to be a bit of pink smoke coming out of a test tube.

But my story's position above the fold was in jeopardy.

CHAPTER 7

The first thing I needed to do to give myself a shot at being printed above the fold was to finish translating my notes out of shorthand and into the computer, while my memory of the conversations I'd had that morning was still fresh and I'd still be able to figure out what my squiggles meant.

Having been a secretary leant itself so well to being a reporter who could write shorthand fast enough to keep up with people's comments. I liked the way the training for the first job had dovetailed unexpectedly but brilliantly with what I needed to do in the far more interesting second. My typing too had improved in the first job. Nowadays, I much preferred typing up my own notes for stories to pounding out letters for pompous men who thought in clichés that racked my nerves: "penetrate the market," "low-hanging fruit," "paradigm shift." When I had transcribed their dictation, I would put in fresh, more specific language to say the same thing, and they would assiduously take it out and put the cliché back in.

Now I had more control over the finished product, though editors did get the final say. But they usually didn't change much, which was a great source of satisfaction.

The notes typed up, I decided to get more coffee.

In the employee kitchen I bumped into one of the more friendly reporters, a business journalist who always smiled and chatted a bit. We talked for a few minutes, and then we returned to our posts. I swiveled toward my computer, woke up the screen, and saw that the notes I had just typed were erased from its benign face. I knew in the pit of my stomach, which had contracted to a hard nut, that it was hopeless, but I checked the spot in the computer where I usually saved notes. They weren't there. I hadn't saved them. For a reasonably smart person, I sure could be an idiot. I was going to have to do penance later, perhaps eat a big bowl of chocolate ice cream, for not saving my work.

Had my computer failed? Had anyone else's? I looked around, feeling suspicious. Even if I hadn't formally saved my notes, the computer should have retained them in some form. Or so I'd been told. I did a search, but no notes appeared. Was the system failing? None of the other reporters appeared to be having a problem. Nobody was showing the slightest interest in me, and nobody had a guilty look on their face.

But had somebody sabotaged me? Maybe this was all in my rather negatively-tinted imagination. Trish, let's not go down paranoid rabbit holes unnecessarily. Time to check in with your fellow man.

"Steve," I said to a reporter at a desk nearby. "Did you see anybody here a minute ago?"

"Huh?" He looked up from the pages of the newspaper he'd been buried in. His blue eyes were huge behind thick lenses.

"I wonder: did you see anybody come around my desk just now?"

"Nah." He looked completely bewildered, and he had good reason: why would anyone care if a reporter wandered near a desk? They did that all day long.

"Well, let me know if you see anybody hanging around."

"Uh, okay." He blinked his magnified eyes and dove into the newspaper again.

I had to face it: time to retype my notes. Then I panicked. What if someone had taken my notebook? But no, here it was. I looked around the newsroom again, studying each face. It was easy for me to believe that people were against me. The reality was that these reporters were indifferent to my presence. I hoped that at The Times they would care more.

I couldn't seem to let go of it quite yet and wandered to Gabi's desk to tell her about it. She seemed surprised and dismayed and said she would keep an eye out for me. "Let me know when you leave your desk, and I can watch, at least for a while," she said.

So I had two people watching, but would they tell me what they learned, or were they themselves saboteurs? I resolved to save my work more often. And to stop skulking around thinking someone had it in for me.

I retyped the notes, saved them carefully, and then remembered that

Benjamin Long, the other docent, needed to be interviewed before wrapping up this story. And Elspeth, Samantha's assistant. It also occurred to me that I hadn't heard from Justin Hardy in three days, so I decided to pause my work and take him up on his offer to call him anytime. Yes, we were doing things the old-fashioned way. I liked it. I also would like a little reassuring chat before going out to conquer the world some more. I dialed him up.

He picked up immediately. "Justin Hardy here."

"Hi, it's Tricia," I said cheerily. Who wouldn't feel happy talking to a good-looking, fun, and apparently kind and financially successful man? Though I'd be checking those last two features out.

"Hey, Tricia. What's going on?" He sounded happy to hear from me.

"A lot." I briefly outlined the morning's events and realized how happy I felt about having a mystery to solve—or perhaps just happy to be talking to Justin.

"You sure you want to be a reporter?" he asked. "You keep running into violence in that town."

Uh-oh. "Well, it keeps my life interesting, at least," I replied and changed that subject fast. "How's Mike?" Mike was his fourteen-year-old son who, I imagined, had bonded tightly with his father since his mother's death. I hadn't met him yet. If Justin ever did introduce me, I expected to be resented. Girlfriends who'd dated men with kids had warned me.

"He's great. He just found out he's going to Disney World with his baseball team next February."

"What an honor."

"Speaking of which, would you do me the honor of having dinner with me Saturday night?"

Yay! Asked out on a date, and in a chivalrous way.

"Sure. What time?"

"I'll pick you up at about four. Dinner and a show in New York City?"

"Excellent!" I saw no point, at my age in this dating game, in being cool or reserved instead of expressing my delight.

"Okay, see you Saturday." He didn't seem to mind my cheery response.

I put the phone down beaming. We hadn't had a heart-to-heart chat, which would have been nice, but we weren't quite at that stage yet. But I had been invited on a fabulous date! Not like the guy Larry I'd dated a year ago, who had never offered more than to go out for a walk and a cup of coffee. Justin was actually spending money on me.

Was he spending too much money? That's what abusers did …

But his behavior and attitude so far had been something even my most cynical friends could not find fault with. They reminded me constantly not to get my hopes up, but my hopes were up. I was on my way to marriage, to making love again, after years of celibacy, with a man I was very attracted to, who so far had demonstrated good character and self-control. No wonder I was smiling. I giggled to myself and tried to concentrate on reading my reporter's notes. But I just couldn't do it. I had to share my happiness with somebody. I wished I could talk it over with my sister, but she hadn't been answering my calls for months now. So instead I called my mom.

"I have another date Saturday night with Justin," I said joyfully, but low so my colleagues couldn't hear me.

"Now go slow," she replied. "You have to get to know this man."

"I'm well aware of that," I said, just a bit snappishly. Why couldn't anybody just be happy with me? I was so tired of caution. I was also tired of getting hurt, of seeing egregious red flags in the man's character, of having to make the heart-wrenching decision to break up with someone who was going to drive me crazy rather than help me meet my goals.

But now Justin Hardy was dating—was it presumptuous to say courting?—me. With style. And so far the red flags that I carried in my pocket had stayed there. No condescending attitude. No scapegoating tendencies. No treating his mother like an idiot. No striving to control me; in fact, the opposite—we had disagreed recently over whether or not to develop a parcel of land in Passaic and were still dating. He was mature enough to let me have my own opinion, even when it conflicted with his profession as a developer.

I felt excited about him. To be honest—euphoric. I had to come down off the mountaintop and get to know him better. My mother was right, as usual. I asked her how my dad was doing, then gently said goodbye and went to get a glass of cold water. I had to settle down.

The thought of my professional ambitions did it. What about my passion for being a journalist in New York City? How could that possibly jive with being a wife, a stepmother and, I hoped, a mother in Central Jersey?

I took a moment to picture myself in the two different professional and family roles and once again couldn't reconcile them. They were diametrically opposed directions in life. I wanted both.

Pondering it a while, with neck, shoulders, and gut tensing up, I stopped when some Twelve-Step-originated awareness switched on: a small inner voice said, "you're obsessing." My specialty. I did not have to decide this issue today. I had dated enough to know that things could implode at any moment. No use speculating on the future.

"One day at a time," I whispered and redirected my attention to my job. My computer revealed that my notes were still there despite my sojourn into the world of worry. Back to work. I called Benjamin Long, the other volunteer at the museum. I called rather than seek an in-person interview because it was getting late in the day and I had lots to do. My notes were typed up, but they weren't shaped into a story yet. Knuckle down, Trish. I remembered Virginia's hesitation when talking about Benjamin. What did she know about his character? What if this guy was the perpetrator? Maybe I should go see him and get a feel for what he was capable of. But with my deadline looming, I let the call go through.

When he answered the phone, I introduced myself and asked for his comment on Samantha Scarborough.

"Oh, wasn't that terrible?" he said. "The poor woman! I hope she makes it. I called my church's prayer chain, and we're all praying for her." A man like Mr. Long couldn't possibly have assaulted Samantha, right? His voice was gentle. Don't make assumptions, Trish, I scolded myself. The ones with a churchy screen are the ones you have to be paranoid about.

"I heard that Dorothy Anderson is closing the museum for a while," he continued, and I jotted that down quickly. She hadn't mentioned it to me. "For one thing, the museum has to be inventoried, and for another, we can hardly stay open while Samantha is suffering." This man was going to be a great source; reactions streamed from him like water gushing from a tap.

"Mr. Long, what plans for the museum did Samantha tell you about?"

"Oh, she talked about an arts and crafts fair, and she was going to re-inventory all the artifacts because it hadn't been done in about ten years." Ten years—that was news to me too. I wrote it down quickly.

"How long have you worked there as a docent?"

"I'm starting my fifth year. I'm retired, you know, and the days got very long after my wife died. The museum keeps me busy, and it's in a good cause."

I identified with long hours alone but didn't mention it. My job was to keep him talking, not to chat about the downsides of single life. The upsides too. Freedom.

"Did you go to the museum today?" I asked.

"Yes, and I talked with Matt Morgan and Virginia Hopewell. We just can't believe it. We agree that whoever tried to kill Samantha is still out there, and we want the police to protect her in the hospital."

Great! He'd said something quotable.

"Do the police agree with you, that she's in danger?"

"We're going to reason with them, and if they won't protect her, we're going to do it ourselves."

This was great for my story! I patted myself on the back for being thorough, for asking so many different questions, for asking the same questions of different people. I had a great story now—an assault, citizen vigilantes, an inventory of historic artifacts. Fantastic!

I turned to my keyboard and pounded a first draft of the story into the computer, gaining career momentum as I typed, ending up ablaze with enthusiasm. The fact that she didn't have a degree in journalism, just one in English literature earned at night school, was not going to stop this woman from rising to the top of her profession. I was young (I thought of Gabi, in her early twenties, and amended that to "sort of young") and would make it happen.

As long as I remembered to save my work.

CHAPTER 8

I dialed Elspeth MacIntosh's number, wishing for an amiable chat with a fellow secretary, I mean assistant. I reminded myself that since I was a reporter, she'd be even more discreet than she'd be in her job. That was a shame. But the phone just rang and rang. I left a message asking her to call me.

Then I went back to Dorothy Anderson's retirement home, down the halls with floral carpeting, ringing her bell and studying the grapevine wreath on her door. I heard her voice through it. "Who's there?"

"It's Tricia Maguire from the *Sentinel*. I have just a few follow-up questions."

The door opened a crack and I saw a bit of her face and hair. "Like what?" she demanded.

"Can you confirm that you're closing the museum, and for how long?"

"Oh, all these questions. You and the police both. I'm tired of it. I don't think I want to talk to you. No, I don't have anything to say to reporters."

My main source of information on the museum was slipping away from me, pulled by riptides of anti-press sentiment, or perhaps with the instinct to hide information, or perhaps just fatigue, in the opposite direction. I had to do something.

"Mrs. Anderson, talk to me, I need you." Might as well be honest about the situation. "People are interested in the museum, and they need you," I added, trying to think of ways to persuade her to talk.

"I don't want to talk to any of the papers except the *Passaic Press*."

"I used to write for them."

"But now you don't, so no."

My old paper! I'd worked my way up and out of it and was being cut off for my efforts. That added to my frustration, but I couldn't let her know.

"All the Jersey papers will be calling you in a day or two. The curator of a museum has been attacked, after all. If you shut me out, you have to shut them out too. To be fair, that is." She had a chance now to be famous in New Jersey for fifteen minutes. Who would pass that up?

"I don't want to talk to these people, or you. It's too much for me." And she closed the door.

"Mrs. Anderson?" I called.

But she was gone.

I was under deadline and had to find a workaround fast. I tried to think who could confirm the museum's closing for me. I had the list of Board members from Virginia Hopewell. I could also try Chief Bognavian and pick his brains. I drove to Borough Hall, subdued, hoping these other sources didn't shut me out as Dorothy had. How could a reporter function with people ducking under rocks like white, sun-hating bugs? Shyness was not a good quality for Central Jersey people to cultivate. Not while I was on the beat.

Chief Bognavian was not exactly shy. Instead, he was media-savvy, a worse affliction. He had a method for handling the press, which was a very great pity. Typical of police chiefs, but a shame nonetheless. That guy knew more secrets than anybody else in the borough, but he was not going to spill them. He knew which houses were the scene of domestic violence, which teenagers were stealing TVs for kicks, which residents were regularly driving under the influence. Not one word of these truths was going to pass his lips. He controlled what he said to reporters by writing out a statement, reading it, refusing to answer follow-up questions, and sticking to the script. It was a complete travesty. But his silence on crimes by borough residents propped up Passaic property values, which the good burghers of the village wanted to protect at all costs.

I parked in Borough Hall's lot and stood in front of the magnificent Greek revival building. Another financier, even richer than the one who built the library that was now the home of the museum, had built this as a memorial to a deceased daughter. He had lavished money on granite exteriors, marble interiors, and wood paneling in the mayor's office.

But I wasn't going in the main door, made of carved oak. Instead, I walked around to the back and entered the far less glamorous police headquarters at the rear. There were a few women on the force, but the place teemed with male hormones. Here a manly trait for protectiveness was institutionalized, and I found it comforting. I liked to walk in my neighborhood in the evenings and knew it wouldn't be possible except for these servants in blue. I only disliked the police when they ticketed me for dumb things like not signing the back of my license. Other than that, I made sure that we got along great.

"Chief Bognavian, please," I said to the dispatcher behind the chin-high counter. She was an officer who, I had seen previously when she wasn't seated behind the imposing desk, had been blessed, like me, with a tendency to have, shall we say, a womanly figure? In this day of magazines idolizing emaciated women, I was uncomfortable with the curves I carried. But Justin Hardy had given me a few admiring looks, so I calmed myself down and waited to be let in. At last the buzzer sounded, and I stepped into the heart of the station. No granite and marble here, in the basement of the building. It was more like linoleum and sheetrock. Men in uniform, belts loaded with black gear, passed me in both directions. I was happy.

The chief's office was at the end of the hall. When I stepped into the doorway, he motioned me in.

"The museum, am I right?"

"Yep."

He and I had been doing the media dance for ten years now, ever since I started working at the *Press*, after Tommy died, so we sometimes talked in shorthand. Yet even though the relationship between us was good, he still never said one word more than his prepared statement. But I had to try.

"Chief, what's the latest in your investigation?"

The chief was a big man with a Marine haircut, his body just to the far side of too heavy. He had brown eyes that had seen a lot of human depravity even though he'd spent most of his career in suburban Passaic.

He smiled at me, which was a slight lifting of his sad countenance. He snapped the paper in his hand.

"Let me read you my statement," he said.

Inwardly I groaned with frustration.

"Police responded to a request for assistance at the Museum of Historic Tools and Crafts today and assisted Passaic EMTs in taking Ms. Samantha Scarborough, the curator, to the hospital to be treated for a head wound. Police will conduct a search for the weapon used to assault Ms. Scarborough, pending the doctor's report on the type of weapon used."

He sat back, satisfied with himself.

"Are you posting a twenty-four-hour guard on Samantha?" I asked.

"Yes."

Bingo! Something not in his statement. Victory. While he was dispensing information, I thought I should go for one more bit.

"Chief, are you closing the museum for the inventory?" I asked him quietly, but I felt desperate for this piece of information. I needed it to complete my scoop.

He looked at me somberly, and finally he said, "I'm going to stick to my statement."

I groaned inwardly again, and a little bit of it was audible.

"Chief, what harm would it do to confirm this for me? It's a fact about the museum closing, not a matter of national security."

"I won't say anything that might jeopardize our investigation."

"But how can confirming this jeopardize—"

"That's it, Tricia. You're getting as much as the other papers will get. You know I'm fair."

I couldn't argue with him on that, but I was still annoyed, so I tossed my reporter's notebook and pen into my purse with a sharp flick and an obvious attitude of dissatisfaction. But then I caught myself—I did not want to offend him; he was a vital source. I relented, smiled at him, thanked him, and left.

CHAPTER 9

At the *Sentinel,* I had just sat down to add new details to the draft of my story when the phone rang.

"Tricia, it's Meg." My heart jumped with gladness that she was staying in touch, a good sign that she might get away from her abuser's clutches. "I hope you don't mind me calling you at work."

"No, it's okay. It's fine. How are you?" I really wanted to help this woman escape the pounding she was taking, both emotionally and physically, and live a new life.

"I'm doing okay," Meg said. "How are you?"

Well, somebody had to go first and admit things weren't perfect, so I decided it might as well be me.

"I'm writing about something that happened at the Museum of Historic Tools and Crafts today," and I told her about it. "My top source at the museum, the director, Dorothy Anderson, has decided she won't talk to me. I need an authoritative source to confirm a detail because I want this story to cover every base, leave nothing for the bigger papers to scoop me on, and I don't know what to do. That's my big problem today."

Meg was silent for a while, and then she said, "My husband Dennis is on the Board of Directors."

"Really?" Under deadline pressure, I hadn't taken the time to acquaint myself with the list of names Virginia had given me earlier today, or I would have known that. I gave myself a mental kick.

"I'd give you his number at work, but then he would ask how you got it. You and I can't know each other."

"I have a number here." I flipped quickly through my notebook. "It's a 212 area code—New York City. His office?"

"Where'd you get that number?" She sounded panicky.

"One of the docents." I thought that was general enough to keep my promise to Virginia, not to reveal the source of these phone numbers.

There was silence as she thought. Then, "Don't let on to Dennis, or to those docents, or to anyone, that you know me."

"I promise I won't give away that we've met. It really isn't at all likely to come up in a conversation about the museum."

"And don't ever call here."

"I won't, Meg. I understand the situation you're in. I won't say or do anything that puts you in jeopardy."

Another silence. Her stress came in waves through the phone. Then she said, "I wondered if I could stop by tonight. Dennis will be away."

"I'll be home. Let's say eight o'clock?"

"That would be better than midnight, wouldn't it?"

I was pleased to hear a bit of humor in her voice in spite of her anguish. "Don't worry about that. I'll be up until one anyway, to confirm Samantha's condition with the hospital before press time. Call me or stop by whenever you need to.

"Okay."

"See you tonight?"

"Yes, eight o'clock."

We signed off, and I looked at my watch. Still hours to go in which my big story could be bumped off the premier position above the fold. Where was Henry Burnham? Still out covering the fire? The longer he was gone, the bigger the fire, the worse it was for me.

I dialed Dennis' office number with fear. What was it like to be a high-paid investment banker who had to hide the fact that he hit his wife? When Meg was safely out of his grasp, maybe I could find a way to expose him. Reporter setting the world right, making the bad guys pay. I'd like that.

After a secretary intervened with my call, Dennis Palmer picked up. I introduced myself, praying I would say nothing to give Meg away.

"Mr. Palmer, I have a few questions about the museum here in Passaic."

"How did you get my number," he said abruptly, making me even more jittery. Did he feel threatened by somebody giving out his name? Who knew with a twisted personality like this?

"One of the docents at the museum gave me your name and number."

"Which one?"

"Virginia Hopewell." Uh-oh, without thinking, I had revealed her as my source. To a reprehensible man, no less. Oh damnation, I'd broken my promise to protect her. Just awful.

"Oh." Dennis seemed mellow enough about it.

"Do you mind?" I'd stick up for Virginia if he said yes.

"No, it's public knowledge. Borough Hall has our contact info too since we rely on them for some funding." Silly me hadn't thought of that. I still felt terrible. That could never happen again. But right now, onward.

"I wondered if you could confirm for me that you—the Board of Directors—will keep the museum closed."

"Yes. We talked today on a conference call—a quorum of us—six."

"How long will you close?"

"Until the inventory is done and Samantha Scarborough's condition is stabilized."

I wrote it down, excited to have finally confirmed this fact for my sweeping, groundbreaking, scoop story about a museum curator being attacked. I had met journalism ethics! And scoops were a nice thing to bring up at job interviews for The New York Times. But as long as I had a source on the line, I jumped at the chance to pump him for more.

"What other plans did you discuss in your conference call?"

Silence. Most people can't stand a vacuum in a conversation—they rush to fill it. So I'd learned to stay silent, and I found out good stuff that way.

"Ms. Maguire?"

"Yes?"

"Could we discuss this further? I have something to tell you but can't talk now. Let's meet. Tomorrow night at the coffee bar in town?"

I wondered why he wanted to meet. To intimidate? Would I leave the café with a black eye?

Well, for stories, you had to take a risk.

"Sure. See you tomorrow at seven."

CHAPTER 10

I arrived home with more to do to finish my scoop. At one in the morning, just before press time, I would call the hospital and confirm Samantha's condition. But for now, Ninja got a can of moist food, and I scrambled some eggs for myself. That was all I was in the mood to do.

At eight o'clock my front bell rang, and Meg stood on the steps, the bruised eye still achingly purple, but every hair combed sleekly back and captured in a black cloth band. She was wearing black leggings, black ballet flats, and a royal blue cotton sweater that covered her slim hips. At her throat she had pinned a black silk rose. The edge of each petal was outlined in tiny black beads that glittered as the silk petals fluttered when she moved. Obviously she fussed over her appearance and was well groomed at all times. For my part, I had plucked my eyebrows earlier, knowing she would arrive impeccable. Except for her black eye.

"I'll make tea," I said, and led her to the kitchen. "I have to let you know that Dennis wants to meet me at the coffee shop tomorrow night."

I heard her stop midstride, and I turned and saw her frown. Then she crossed my small—I mean "intimate"—kitchen and sat in one of my hard little chairs.

"Don't give me away. It would be awful."

"We're going to talk about the museum. I'll be very careful, I promise you."

I put water on to boil, plunked two raspberry tea bags into two mugs covered with hand-painted roses near the kettle, and sat across from Meg.

"Have you been writing?" I asked, to get the conversation rolling. "I remember the high school paper—you're a good writer."

"I wrote a little this morning after Dennis left for work. I tried to be honest about what was happening."

"And?"

Meg leaned an elbow on the table, put her chin in her hand, and sighed. "It was too painful. Stopped—shredded it."

"We need to write and be rigorously honest with ourselves. Have courage! Courage is fear that's said its prayers. Put everything on paper, even if you have to get rid of the pages later."

The tea water boiled. I filled the two mugs and brought them, steaming and tartly fragrant, to the table. Meg took hers and huddled over it as she had the previous night. Silence reigned, and I let it.

"I don't think I can take any more of the pain I'm in," she said at last. "What I can't stand is the terror. Last week he said he wanted something on the grill for dinner. So I made hamburgers. When I called him to the table, he threw the hamburger down and said he wanted steak. So the next day I buy steak, make it on the grill. Call him to the table, and he pokes at it with his knife. 'I wanted T-bone, not shell steak,' he says, and walks away. Like I'm a mindreader.

That evening, I get the sense he's watching me, looking for something to complain about. He tries to pick a fight over my mother. I don't say anything to defend her because I know he's building up to an explosion. He insults her six ways to Sunday, then he says, 'What's wrong with you, don't you defend your mother? Huh?'

"And he slaps me." She fingered her cheek. "So I say, 'Stop insulting her, and stop hurting me,' and he punches me in the face, as you can see. I'm damned if I don't say anything and damned if I do. I can feel the anger and violence build in him, until it explodes, and he hits me. Then he says he's sorry, buys me flowers, we're okay for a few days, and then the anger and violence build up again and soon he picks a fight."

She began to weep in front of me, brushing tears away from her bruised cheekbone. I felt privileged and humbled that she allowed me to participate in her pain. I wanted to help her, free her from her situation, but I could only bring her a box of tissues from my bedside table. I waited a while, seeing that she was calming herself. Then I spoke.

"There's a name for what you're going through," I said. "It's called the cycle of abuse. The tension builds to an intolerable level, there's an explosion, violence, then remorse, a short period of peace, and the tension builds again. It's well documented. He's a classic abuser."

"I'm sorry," she said, wiping her face.

"Nothing to be sorry about." Unless you let this darkness take you to perdition, I thought. How could I persuade her to get away from monied, privileged, powerful Dennis? I wanted to see her happy, joyous, and free, as we talk about in the Twelve Steps.

"Dennis once told me some things about his childhood that left me very scared. I don't think he's ever healed."

"But we can't just treat others the way we've been treated. We have to break the cycle."

There was a long pause as Meg grabbed a tissue and wiped her eyes delicately.

"I know I have to forgive him—"

I saw a great danger and leapt in. "You are not obligated to forgive him and stay. Instead, get away from him. Then forgive."

"It's hard to forgive." She sat back and put her hands, cupped around each other, in her lap.

"Yes. I find that the angry thoughts keep coming back, and I have to ask my Higher Power to help me forgive, over and over, sometimes for years, until the angry thoughts lessen, and at last I feel that the person doesn't owe me anything."

Meg dropped her gaze to her mug.

"We need to forgive, for our own sanity," I said. "But that doesn't mean, when our lives are at stake, we should stand in the line of fire and be a target, over and over."

I saw her shiver.

"I think Dennis feels very vulnerable," she said at last. "He was never interested in hunting and fishing like his father. He used to beat Dennis just for the sake of 'making sure he wasn't a wimp.' No wonder he didn't want to do things with his father. He'd hit Dennis with the buckle end of his belt—for nothing. For having a shoe untied. For not being manly enough. And if tears came to Dennis' eyes during a beating, his father would rage at him and hit harder and longer. Dennis prides himself now on never crying. He has layers of hard shell over every tender part of him. If I could just reach him, tell him how much he's hurting me ..."

"What's he like when you try to talk to him?"

Meg sighed and twisted her diamond ring. "He gets so angry."

"You need to get away."

"I know." She looked up at me, her eyes moist. "But I love him. And I think maybe he'll change, if he just went into treatment."

"Let me show you something." I went quickly to the bookshelves in the living room and found a book, Domestic Violence. I had bought it to write an article two years ago. I hurried back to Meg.

"This book describes the situation you're in," I said, flipping to the introduction quickly. "'Most men agreed to enter treatment,'" I read. "'Six months after treatment, virtually all participants were again using violence toward their wives/partners.'" I flipped to another page where I had underlined some sentences. "'Thirty-five percent of murders investigated nationally are domestic related.'

"Meg, you have to do something. You'll be destroyed as a person if you stay with him."

She covered her face with her hands.

"I know I need to do something—" she said, one elbow on the table, her hand supporting her jaw.

I was scared for her. I had read a lot of the book, which described the situation battered women are in. They live in extreme terror, under the control of men who continually reverse the rules they set up, to confuse their victims and render the women incapable of independent thought. The cycle of abuse escalates to the point where the women's lives are constantly in danger. And their children are emotionally scarred, if not physically battered themselves.

Meg was crying softly again. I dearly hoped this was her epiphany, when she realized that the big house, the travel, all the treasures of this earth, were worthless in comparison to her value as a person, to the value of her potential growth and learning and accomplishment.

"Please get out. Do it before your nose is smashed in." I paused for emphasis. "Do it before you're dead."

She sat quietly, hands shading her eyes, her bruise. At last she spoke.

"I can't. I can't just yet. Please respect my decision, and it is my decision."

"I know, but why? Why not run to safety?"

"Because I'm not ready to give up. I want to help him. We might still make it." Then she looked at me defiantly, as if I'd suggested something foolish. "And what's so safe about running away? Men shoot women all the time for leaving them. He's on the boards of several agencies around here. He might know all about the safe house in Somerset Hills."

Well, that was creepy.

"I'll take you further away. To South Jersey."

"Oh yeah, like that would help."

"We'll register you under a fake name for extra protection. And there's another factor here."

"What's that?"

"I have to talk about it on a spiritual level now. Which makes sense, because moment by moment, we live and move and have our being in the spiritual realm."

Meg hesitated, then nodded the go-ahead.

"I'm asking you to take shelter with God. 'Under his wings you will find refuge.' People who work with battered women have told me they've never known that prayer to fail."

Meg looked thoughtful for a moment, then slowly rose from her seat.

"I may have to start believing in God, just to get through this."

"I encourage you to seek him. He is for you."

Meg gave a nod, then crossed to the sink and ran water in her mug.

"Don't worry about it, I'll take care of it," I said.

Her frame sagged as she leaned over the sink. Her shoulders began to shake. I waited.

"I'm sorry," she said, turning, tears dripping from her jaw. "I know what I have to do. I just don't have the strength." She wiped her damp cheeks with trembling fingers. "Yet."

"I'll pray. God will help you," I said.

She hurried through the living room to the front door and opened it jerkily. Still crying, she stepped into the June twilight.

CHAPTER 11

I sat at my desk in the newsroom the next day. The night before I had called the hospital from home at 12:45, the latest that I could revise the story before the presses ran. Samantha Scarborough was still in intensive care, the hospital had said. I had then called the night editor and told her the story could run as it was.

Now today's newspaper blackened my fingertips with ink as I basked in the glow of my story and name being in the most honored position—on the front page, above the fold. A photo of the museum that I had taken accompanied the story, and my name was in the photo credit. A home run with bases loaded.

Henry Burnham's story about the fire at the pharmaceutical plant was below the fold, mostly because it turned out to be a piddling fire. The picture that ran with his story showed a wisp of smoke escaping from a window. I blessed the editors who decide the placement of stories for agreeing with me that an assault on a prominent figure was more important than your everyday pharmaceutical fire. Even though the pharmaceutical industry employed vast numbers of people in Central Jersey.

I scanned the newsroom's copy of the Jersey Record, the statewide newspaper, and saw that my archrival Monica Bodinsky had missed the attack, the biggest happening on her beat since the mayor of Passaic had confessed a few months ago. Ha! She missed it. Yay!

As I basked in the glow of a double victory—placement above the fold and scooping the state's premier newspaper—I thought it made sense to settle down and prepare a list of questions about the museum to ask Dennis Palmer later. And to think of new angles to Samantha Scarborough's story.

Each angle could generate a new story that made my editors, my readers, and the hungry printing presses happy.

But first I deserved to relish all that was happening. The Associated Press watched regional papers for interesting stories: maybe they would be calling me to confirm the details and then send my story by wire all around the world. If it was a slow news day, maybe The New York Times would take notice.

Instead of settling down, I floated from thinking about my newspaper success to considering my upcoming date with Justin Hardy Saturday night.

After years of dating deadbeats, then raising the bar of who I would date and not having anybody to date at all, I was excited about having a man in my life with real marriage potential. Evenings and weekends together! Not having to round up friends—who so often were busy with their families—if I didn't want to be alone for the umpteenth hour over a holiday weekend.

Besides which, I still wanted children, and I was in my late thirties, thirty-seven to be exact. If I was going to bear a child before the high-risk age of forty, something would have to happen soon. I felt the pressure of time moving quickly toward a life barren of children, and it upset me. Justin Hardy represented the chance that I might not be alone the rest of my life, that children and grandchildren would surround me when I grew old.

As my mind dwelled on Justin and the uncertainties of dating, the glow of victory in the newspaper realm faded and I began to feel apprehensive. First, the problem of my professional dreams vs. potential marriage. Second, the ever-present knowledge that the relationship might not make it. Each disappointment hurt a lot, and the disappointments were growing harder and harder to bear.

At that point I turned my thoughts to my Higher Power and asked him to help me quit obsessing, and to be content in the situation I was in. Then I asked for the serenity to do something about the things I could actually change, and the wisdom to let go of the things I had no power over.

As a result, I turned to my computer to dig in its files and unearth a story I'd started last week. And the phone rang. It was a member of the Borough Council in Passaic, Patricia McGrath. We always laughed at the fact that we had the same rather unusual nickname.

"Tricia?" she said.

"Tricia! Good to hear from you. What's up?"

"You know there's an election for Borough Council the end of June."

I was afraid she was going to ask me to write a story about her local election, something I couldn't promise her would be published at my new regional paper.

"If I were still working for the *Passaic Press,* I would be doing stories on the local election, but the *Sentinel* doesn't do stories on the individual town races unless something really unusual happens."

"Oh, I know, don't worry, I'm not asking for a story about me. Not that it wouldn't be nice. But did you know that somebody's going around town ripping up my yard signs? They cost $5 a piece, and they've torn up forty of them already."

"Who could be tearing up your signs?" If she had anybody in mind, I doubted she would say. We were friendly, but she knew I was media, always looking for a story, that I was a blabbermouth by profession. Both she and I had to be careful not to make unfounded accusations.

"I don't know," she said. "But my Democratic Committee is buying a new set of signs and hiring a private detective. I'll let you know what happens."

"Thanks for the hot tip, Tricia," I said, hoping to actually get a story out of it, to satisfy the relentless printing presses, which imbued the newsroom on this side of the wall with the scent of ink.

We hung up and I made a note on my calendar to call her back in a week—in case, in the demands of a campaign, she forgot to call me.

Still hunting for a story, I called Chief Bognavian to see if he had anything interesting on the police blotter. The police were really conflicted over telling the press about things going on in town. They were well aware that the most common complaint from residents at Borough Council meetings was that police salaries were too high. So on the one hand, they wanted the public to know exactly all the horrors they were protecting residents from. On the other hand, they didn't want to reveal damaging stories about residents, for fear of embarrassing people and generating lawsuits. And bringing down property values.

As a result, the police blotter tended to be stories that focused on people from out of town trespassing on their way through Passaic.

Well, I would call him and see what he told me.

"Chief?" I said when I got him on the line. "How's the investigation at the museum coming?"

"Tricia, what a surprise that you called," he said, with good humor in his voice. He had actually made a joke.

"Have the other papers called you yet?"

"Yes, I've gotten calls. And I told them exactly what I told you."

"But now I have a new question," I said brightly, trying once again to charm some information out of him.

"I'm not big on answering questions off the cuff," he said.

Understatement. "I know," I said soothingly, "but have you found the weapon used to hit Samantha?"

"Not yet. We'll go through the inventory and search item by item at this point."

"When will you start it?"

"Dorothy Anderson told us there were 10,000 items in the collection. We figure it will take several men a couple of days to check the inventory against the master database. We can't spare that many people from the roster, so we're asking the county sheriff's office for some personnel to help us. We'll start when the team is assembled."

Wow! I had a new story. I wondered why the chief was so helpful today. I'd been charming to him for years, and he'd never given me anything extra.

"Chief, what's going on? Why are you being so good to me?"

"Nothing. I'm in the mood to help the press."

"That's great. Who are you working with at the sheriff's office," I said hurriedly, trying to milk him for information before his good mood evaporated.

"The sheriff," he said abruptly. Time was running out on his helpfulness.

"Any clues as to who attacked Samantha?"

"No, and I've got to go," he said. His bonhomie evaporated, and he signed off abruptly.

I wove my way between newsroom desks to Paul's office.

"I've got a follow-up story to the museum attack," I told him after a tap on his door.

Paul had more hair in his black eyebrows than he did on his noggin. He had been in the newspaper business since I had been in high school. He wore a cotton plaid shirt, tailored to fit his physique perfectly. He was proud of his weightlifting body.

"How many inches do you need?"

I figured I would get more information out of Dennis Palmer that night, but still the story would be short.

"Eight," I said.

"Any photos?"

I wondered if I could get Dennis to approve of a photographer going to the museum and taking a few shots of sheriff's officers and policemen counting the tools. It would take a while to arrange.

"Not for this story. Maybe the next one."

"You got some space—at least until the night team comes in."

I prayed for no more news in Central Jersey that day.

I fiddled around for a while with some notes for a story on the battered women's shelter in neighboring Somerset Hills. I called the shelter and made an appointment for a tour the next day. Then I went home for dinner and prepared myself mentally to meet a wife batterer.

CHAPTER 12

A
t seven o'clock sharp, just as I was sipping my decaf cappuccino, built exactly the way I like it with a mountain of whipped cream on top, the door of the café was flung open and a successful-looking, energetic man came in. Somehow I knew this was Dennis.

His short dark hair was neatly combed, his windbreaker crisp and new, his chinos smartly creased. He had a narrow nose without much bulb on the end, which gave him an aristocratic look. His brown eyes were fringed with long dark lashes. But could I see signs of emotional aberration, of cruelty?

I waved to him from my seat by the plate glass window. He dodged chairs and tables.

"Dennis Palmer," he said, extending his hand, exuding charm.

"Tricia Maguire," I answered, feeling nowhere near as confident as he looked. I extended my own hand, felt like a traitor to womankind for doing so, and reminded myself I could say or do nothing to give him a clue that I knew he was abusing his wife. We shook hands, and I felt the electricity of his strength in his firm grip. His dark brown eyes looked at me in a straightforward way.

I had wondered for the last two days why he had asked to meet in person. I hoped for a breakthrough fact or insight from him. But first I mentally made a note, and physically straightened my spine, to not let him intimidate me in any way.

"I read your story in the *Sentinel* this morning," he said as he sat down. "Accurate," he added, in the same tone of voice he might have said "adequate." Maybe that was how his father spoke to him. I imagined him as a young boy being beaten by his father "to make a man of him." I felt sympathetic to that wounded little boy, who still lived inside of this grown man. However, I wasn't sympathetic to him wounding his wife in turn. Or to him damning me with his faint praise.

He may have realized that his comment hadn't made a positive impression. He seemed to start over.

"I know you're going to be interested in the museum until Samantha's attacker is discovered. The family told me an hour ago that her condition has worsened. If she dies, it becomes murder. I want to tell you, since you're a member of the press, what I feel the limitations are on your inquiries."

As far as I was concerned, there were no limits. I would ask questions of everyone I could think of that had any connection with the museum—Board members, volunteers, any patrons I could find. I didn't see any need to alert him to these tactics. Why tell the enemy what you plan to do? I waited in silence.

"I want you to talk just to me, not the other Board members. I've told them I want to be the spokesperson, and they've agreed."

What were they covering up? Well, I'd call them anyway, in case they would talk to me anyway. Maybe they weren't scared by Dennis Palmer, like Meg was. And would let something slip. I could only hope.

Before I challenged the limitations he'd imposed, while things were still relatively peaceful between us, I wanted to get a quote for my follow-up story.

"Chief Bognavian said today that the sheriff's office will provide some manpower for the inventory project. How many men would that be, and how many will Passaic provide?"

Dennis frowned and looked worried.

"I would have preferred the chief hadn't said anything until the Board was ready to announce it," he said.

Yikes, he wanted to control the police chief?

"Are you doing a story on this?" he asked. I nodded.

He sighed, seemed to resign himself to not having total control and said, "The sheriff's department will provide two people and the borough two. It's just been arranged tonight, and they start tomorrow first thing. This is an attempted murder investigation, after all." He seemed to know I would want more information from him, because he said, "The museum's Board of Directors wants to help the police in every way to find out who attacked Samantha Scarborough and bring that person to justice. If we have to gather DNA from the dust in the corners of the rooms, that's what we'll do."

Wow, the wife abuser was quotable. I wrote his comment down quickly in my notebook and, while I made shorthand squiggles, thought about what else to ask him.

"Can I take pictures of the inventory process?"

"Okay," he said grudgingly, "I'll tell the chief to expect you. But there's one caveat."

Uh-oh, journalists don't much like caveats. For good reason.

"What's that?" I asked. Not that I would agree to it. But let's get the facts first.

"Dorothy Anderson wants you to show your work to me before it's published."

Oh, yeah, Dorothy wants that, I thought. It's you who wants it. Coward, hiding behind her.

But Holy Moly. I now had to tell a violent man that I wouldn't go along with his plan.

"I'm afraid—" well, that was certainly true. I started again. "I'm afraid I can't do that. As a journalist, I gather the facts and report them accurately. I'm ethically bound to do so. I don't show what I've written to anybody but my own editors before publishing." I decided to strengthen my position by citing my bosses. Was I hiding behind them? "My editors would not agree with your arrangement either."

His fist, I noticed, was balled up tightly in his lap. It was frightening, after seeing the bruise under Meg's eye. Was he also the culprit who'd hit Samantha? As a Board member, he would have had opportunity. As a wife abuser, he had the propensity. Whatever. I had to stand up to this bully.

"Well." he said and shifted in his seat and rubbed his thigh wih his clubbed hand.

I waited. Sometimes silence states the case best.

"Okay, I guess I have to trust you to report accurately."

I used his own words for emphasis. "Yes, you can trust me to report accurately." I paused and asked an edgy question with total innocence in my voice.

"What specifically is the Board doing now to help find out who hurt Samantha?"

He gazed at me with squinted eyes. Both his fists were clenched, in full view on the table. I had stopped breathing but commanded myself to be brave and take in air. My cheekbones were within easy reach of his big, white knuckles and powerful arms, with the strength of his shoulders and torso behind them. Breathe! I commanded myself. And gazed right back at him.

He seemed to come to a decision and sat back, his fists still tight but now on his thighs. "We're in close touch with the police," he said, "responding to their requests, meeting with each other by conference call once a day to brainstorm on any other way we can help the investigation. Why, Ms. Maguire, do you, as a member of the press, think that there's something else we should be doing?" His voice now had edge in it—sarcastic edge. I looked up from my notes and saw his frown.

"I'm just asking what you're doing," I said as innocently as possible, trying to defuse the situation further.

His face smoothed over as he slipped back into his charming self.

"You know, I've had experience with the press before, as a member of the Board of Directors of the Museum of Modern Art in New York City." He paused to see the effect his credentials had on me. I just nodded, not willing to show that I was impressed, which I was. "I've explained the facts, I've given you a quote. You should be happy now." He smiled with these last words. If I hadn't seen him get angry, I might not have noticed the edge in his voice. Mostly he was charming. In fact, the thought crossed my mind that maybe Meg was making it all up. The impulse to doubt women as witnesses, first recorded by Moses thousands of years earlier, is still with us.

"Well, is that all you need?" he said.

"You said, when we talked on the phone yesterday, that you had something you wanted to tell me. I'm wondering what that was."

"Well, it's what we talked about tonight. That you come to me for news, not other Board members."

Well, that was a disappointment. I'd had my hopes up for something more newsworthy than that. Bummer. But keep going. Dig for more.

"You're on the Board of one of the most famous museums in the world. Why are you on the Board of this little one?"

"I like to have my finger on the pulse of my community."

Uh-oh, did that mean he knew the location of the battered women's shelter? Did he know where I lived? Courage, Trish, I thought. One more question.

"I'd like to stay up to speed on events at the museum. Will you help me?"

He nodded. "Call me and only me for news. Good night, Ms. Maguire."

He strode with the grace of strength to the door, yanked it open, and was gone.

I felt confused. Meg said he abused her, yet he seemed more pleasant than most people. Except for that one moment … or two … Yes, both his charm and his lapses sharpened my suspicions.

CHAPTER 13

T hat night before bed, I prayed for wisdom and discernment and for protection for Meg. I nearly always prayed on my knees morning and night, and had received many answers. Like ideas for stories for my job. They were hard to find, but if I prayed for them, I found them daily. God and I were a creative team.

The next morning I drove to the Somerset Hills battered women's shelter to do interviews for a story and to see what kind of place Meg might end up in. Next to the parking lot was a hedge of roses whose blossoms nodded and wafted rosy scent in the June breeze. Walking to the front door, I prayed to be of service with my pen to women suffering abuse.

A blonde woman in a blue zipped sweatshirt and jeans answered my knock. Her face had deep creases from the corners of her nose to the corners of her mouth, as if the hair-raising stories she had heard had etched marks in her face. I told her who I was, and she let me in the door.

"I'm Noelle, the senior social worker on duty," she said. She led me through a big living room, in which three women sat talking while children played quietly at their feet. One woman had a lump, black and blue, on her jaw. The women looked at me as if they were suspicious of me, as well they might be of anyone who entered their sanctuary. Noelle led me to a small office, windowless, the floor covered in piles of ragged files. The desk nearly filled the room.

"I won't reveal any last names today, and you must change the first names to protect anonymity," she said, tucking her hair behind her ear as she threaded her way behind her desk. I wondered how anybody could be so calm who daily dealt with the victims, both women and children, of scathing human evil.

"You must be wondering how women wind up here," she said, seating herself in a chair that creaked and gesturing to the one chair that could fit in the claustrophobic space. I gingerly moved two piles to the floor and sat down. "Some of these women watched their mothers being abused when they were children, and they marry an abuser desperately seeking, without realizing it, to heal their father."

Noelle put her elbows on her desk and leaned toward me. "The best prevention is to be aware of that tendency in yourself, if you witnessed abuse as a child, and to educate yourself on the red flags of an abuser. You can spot them when you date if you know what to look for. Anyone with overdone flattery, offering a life that sounds too good to be true, should be avoided. They make grandiose gestures—gifts of jewelry, expensive bouquets, anything done to excess, intending to dazzle. That's a tip-off."

Uh-oh, were Justin's dates in New York City a tip-off?

She told me that women should listen to the compliments these future abusers lavish. "The wise person will hear the criticisms that soon follow. He says he loves your hair, but then adds that the bangs are too long. When you shorten your bangs, he says that's lovely but you should have adopted the neighbor's swept-back hairstyle."

No, Justin hadn't done anything like that. Yet. And my dad had been a good man, for the most part, I didn't think I had a hidden, festering wound that I felt compelled to heal by marrying an abusive man. Tommy had started out okay; it was alcohol that changed him into an abuser.

"He soon begins criticizing and ridiculing the woman, and her neighbors, friends, and family, seeking to isolate her and remove her from any other influences." Swiftly, she tucked her dark hair behind her ear again.

"He is seeking to make himself totally central to his victim's life. He's charming to the outside world"—I thought of Dennis Palmer last night—"but once married, his Jekyll and Hyde personality will really emerge. He plays relentless mind games at home. He may hide things on his spouse, like her watch, then threaten to kill her if she's late to meet him. He will tell her to make the beds one way one week, then criticize her for doing it that way the next week. He displays an explosive temper, and his insults increase."

Noelle shifted a manila folder from a pile in the corner to the center of her desk. "Through it all, he denies he is the problem. He blames all difficulties on his wife or on other people or on external circumstances. If he becomes physically violent, as most eventually do, he will say the woman provoked him. There will be a period of contrition, of pretending to be sorry. Then he builds the tension again."

Noelle was talking steadily, without me prompting her with questions. I just scribbled shorthand notes as fast as I could, trying to keep up.

"Every eighteen seconds a woman is being battered in the United States, according to a Senate Judiciary Committee study," she continued. "Domestic violence is the most common source of women's injuries, and it occurs more often than auto accidents, rapes, and muggings combined, according to another study published by the American Medical Association. That's the physical abuse. What can sometimes take an even greater toll on women is the emotional abuse. Here's a checklist. You should publish it in your paper."

She opened a desk drawer with a quick snatch and handed me a pamphlet. "This lists the characteristics of an abuser."

I skimmed the bullet point list, with the title: "You are being emotionally abused if your partner". A few jumped out at me:

. "frequently blames, criticizes, or ridicules you, or women as a group

. harasses you about your past

. harasses you about affairs he imagines you are having

. checks on you (listens to phone calls, looks at phone bills, checks mileage, checks who calls on caller I.D.)

. interferes with your going to work or school (provoking a fight in the morning, calling to harass you at work)."

Did Justin Hardy do any of these things? Not yet, but I would watch, because I was terrified of ending up like these women, beaten down, afraid for their lives, starting over with nothing.

"It's hard to judge the number of abuse cases in the country," Noelle continued, "because even the American Medical Association admits that doctors don't report all the suspected abuse cases they see in emergency rooms, even though they're required to do so by law. But half of all American women will be physically abused at least once by the men they live with, according to the FBI."

I wrote it down, saddened by these facts.

"Over time, as emotional and physical abuse continue, the woman becomes a hostage to the abusing husband and suffers from Stockholm syndrome—she aligns with him emotionally and tries to be even nicer in hopes that the abuse will stop." I could imagine that this was the stage Meg was in, making it harder for her to break away.

Noelle opened the manila file she had placed in the center of her desk, studied it a moment, then closed it again. "The abuser will often resort to a system of rewards and punishments, then arbitrarily switch the rewards and punishments, destroying the woman's ability to think independently. Abuse is the destruction of a person."

"Wow," I said, thinking of the women sitting in the living room. "That's a lot to recover from. How much time do the women have to recuperate here?"

"The maximum stay is three months."

"Three months to recover from all that abuse?"

Noelle scootched her chair closer to her desk. "The first week they just decompress, talk to each other, talk to professional counselors. Then we begin to explore their options for housing, jobs, schools for the kids. Speaking of the kids, they come here with intense needs. They've been just as traumatized by the evil in the home as the women. We have counselors who deal strictly with them. We have a playroom in the basement. I'll show you later."

"Do you think I could interview some of the women?"

"I'll ask, but you must protect anonymity. And if no one volunteers, you must respect that and not seek to persuade anybody."

"Promise. Listen, do any of them go back? After being here and receiving care?"

"Some do, I regret to say. But it's the woman's choice, and we never coerce. I think the prospect of being alone overwhelms some of the women. It takes a lot of courage to break free."

"Maybe they forget to live one day at a time," I said.

Noelle smiled. "That's an important thing to remember—for me too," she said. "Let's take a tour."

CHAPTER 14

Noelle showed me the kitchen, which had a cast-iron stove with eight burners and a long, dark wooden table with a hodge-podge of unmatched chairs around it.

"The women rotate cooking, shopping, and clean-up," she said. "This is where a lot of healing takes place, after a day's work, while the kids play in the basement. They sit and talk and encourage each other to stick with it."

I took some quick notes and followed her down a flight of steps to a room with a television, an electronic game hooked to it, and shelves with toys, puzzles, and books.

"Here's our playroom. The children are in crisis when they come here, and they have their own needs that must be dealt with. They need help to learn that their father's abusive behavior and their parents' separation are not their fault. They need help with all their emotions. They feel anger at the parents, fear of abandonment by the caretaking parent, shame about the abuse in their home, guilt that they couldn't make it stop, fear that they might be hurt. If untreated, behavior problems set in—aggression, acting out, or too much passivity."

Noelle's hand moved up to her hair, which had loosened again. A swift tuck behind the ear. "We provide emotional support for the children, art therapy. The mothers can attend a parenting support group. And counseling continues free after the family leaves the shelter, if the mother chooses it."

Once again, I scribbled everything down, excited that my story, appearing in the newspaper, might draw some women and children out of abusive situations. When these women learned about all the help that was available for them and their little ones, maybe they would make a break for it. Maybe women who were dating an abuser would be able to spot the trouble coming their way before they were overwhelmed by it.

We went back upstairs, and Noelle took me to a new wing, off the kitchen.

"We have four new bedrooms back here." She opened one door to a large bedroom, with three cots neatly made up with gray wool blankets and contrasting white sheets, and a crib along one wall.

"We are often full to capacity, but no one over gets turned away," she said. "If we can't take a new family, we call until we find a shelter that can. If a woman needs a ride, we pick her up at any time of the day or night, it doesn't matter."

"Do you ask the police to go with you, if you go to these women's homes?" I asked as we walked back to her office.

"Yes, sometimes. Now you wait here while I go ask the residents if anyone is willing to talk with you."

I sat among the files that were teetering on top of each other, tempted to open one, to see what kind of story was inside. But I resisted the urge. Being a reporter and digging for the truth was one thing. Respecting these battered people's privacy ought to take precedence.

Noelle reappeared.

"Maritza is willing to talk with you but doesn't want her picture taken," she said. "Follow me." She led me to the kitchen, where the woman I had seen with a purple bump on her jaw was seated. Her elbows stood on the table, her chin cupped in one hand, opposite her bruise. She looked so vulnerable, so sad, when she stood to shake my hand.

"Thanks for speaking with me," I said, as Noelle left us alone. I gave her a brief summary of my personal story, so she could know we shared some common experience. "My husband, who's now dead, became abusive the more he drank," I said. "I had to start over alone."

Maritza nodded, and I could see her shoulders relax.

"Can you tell me a little of your story?" I said quietly.

"I couldn't think straight at home," she said, "so I came here. Sal was in and out of psychiatric hospitals, and things were always going downhill. I tried to save money by skimping on things. He took the money to buy guns. He kept playing mind games until I didn't know what he was capable of. I was so confused. Him sitting at the kitchen table playing with guns made the tension so unbearable, I thought I would have to be hospitalized. I needed a place of refuge to put my thoughts together."

I jotted notes quickly.

"My parents didn't want me to marry him. They saw through him right away. But I refused to believe there wasn't any hope for this man. Now I know different. He threatened to shoot my mother. He may go to jail. If he's in jail, then he's no threat to me and my family, but he can't provide child support. If he's out of jail, he still won't provide much child support. So I hope he goes to jail."

I wrote it all down, feeling unutterably sad.

"I'm a religious person who doesn't believe in divorce," Maritza went on. "I home-schooled my children. Now I have to put my toddler in daycare so I can work. I'll give my child to other people to raise." I could feel her wrenching pain.

Just then another woman came in the door, small, with dark hair parted in the middle and pulled back into a long ponytail.

"Here's Karen," Maritza said, introducing us. "Tell Tricia what he did."

"I'm hiding from my boyfriend, Dwight," Karen said. "He's always yelling and hitting me, even in front of the kids. I kicked him out of the apartment and got a restraining order, but I couldn't pay the rent alone, so I lost the apartment. Somebody told me about this place, so I came here."

A dreamy look came over her face. "This is my second marriage and second abuser. Dennis turned on me too. I guess I'm a slow learner."

At that, my investigative instincts went galloping—or was it my busybody self craving—to know about this Dennis? Should I ask? I couldn't use the information in this story, so it wasn't for journalism but for nosiness. Maybe it would help Meg.

"What did he do for a living?" I asked.

She sighed. "He was an investment banker. We could have had such a nice life."

More confirmation needed.

"Was his last name Palmer? Did he work in New York City?"

She looked worried. "You know him?"

"He's giving his current wife a horrible time as we speak." Did Meg know about Dennis' previous marriage? Should I tell her? What a can of worms I'd opened!

"Well, I guess I'm glad I'm out," Karen said. She was working a factory job and looking for an affordable apartment that would take three kids. "It doesn't look too good right now," she said.

"Would you go back to Dwight, to get out of your financial jam?" I asked.

"No," firmly, but in a whisper.

We all paused at that moment and just beheld each other with sorrow. All the hopes with which we'd gone into our marriages had been destroyed. We'd all been wounded, and these women had children who had been deeply wounded too. We were silent.

Then I stirred my feet. I had to get to the newsroom and write. Thanks to Noelle and these two women, I had my story, my quotes, and my supporting facts and figures. So I said goodbye to Maritza, Karen, and Noelle, and let myself out of the house. I made sure the door locked behind me.

CHAPTER 15

I left the women's shelter feeling sad that so many women and children were being abused, and that only a few got out. So much pain. Such destruction of human potential. And when the children grew up in that environment, they so often repeated the pattern in their adult lives, either abusing or being abused, because that's what their deepest psyches were accustomed to.

As the shelter faded in my rearview mirror, aspects of my new story floated in my mind. I would weave Maritza's and Karen's stories in with the statistics and background Noelle had given me. I'd do a sidebar on the children and a sidebar on the characteristics of an abuser. Lots of women were going to be informed, and maybe saved, by my story.

I entered the newsroom hoping that I was going to be not only an ace reporter but also a champion of battered women in Central Jersey.

Gabi passed my desk just as I plunked myself down in my chair.

"I've got a good story," I said with a smile.

"What's that?" Gabi stood over me, her hands fiddling with one of my pens. As a writer, I was emotionally attached to my pens and wished she would leave them alone.

"The Somerset County Battered Women's Shelter."

"Oh, I did a piece on that a year—no, two years ago. You should look it up. It's archived on microfilm." She set my pen down and drifted away.

I felt crushed. My story, although it had been assigned by my Paul, was a recycled one. Oh well, we were both supporting a good cause. I would look up what Gabi had done and do better.

When I found her story on microfilm, I was dismayed. It was good, very good: crisp, with statistics and interviews with victims. I had my work cut out for me to write something better.

I typed up my notes—saved them—and turned my thoughts to my other big story, the attempt on Samantha Scarborough's life. I wondered what the doctors thought of her wound, whether she was expected to recover, whether the twenty-four-hour guard was in place. And I needed pictures of the inventory process. I wanted the photo credit for myself. I walked to Paul Tercell's office. He was as tense and muscle-bound as ever.

"We need photographs from the museum where the curator was almost killed," I said. "I'd like to do it."

"Our photographers are booked all day," he said. "Go ahead."

I ate half a sandwich and made a cup of soup by adding hot water to a packet of dehydrated noodles. As I sipped the reconstituted food, I thought about the attempt on Samantha's life. I needed persist in finding out who had keys to the building, who had a motive, who had the opportunity to bash her over the head.

CHAPTER 16

I saved my notes, turned off my computer, and drove to the museum in the early June sunshine. As long as Dennis and Paul had given me permission to take pictures of the inventory process, I was going to take advantage of it, before he changed his mind.

The museum's door was locked, so I knocked. Virginia Hopewell let me in, then perched behind the front desk. She was smiling a warm welcome.

"Even though the museum's closed for business, you're in today?" I asked.

"Manning the phone and the door. They're doing the inventory."

"How's that going?" I asked.

"They're in the basement right now."

"Dennis Palmer said I could take photographs," I explained, holding up my camera.

"It's down the stairs, through the coffee room," she said.

"Before I go down, could you tell me something?"

"I'll try to help you."

"When you come to work in the morning, who lets you in?"

"Oh, I have keys. So does Benjamin Long and Matt Morgan. And of course Samantha. And Elspeth. And Dorothy Anderson. I'm guessing other Board members. Why?"

"Oh, nothing. Just wondered." I waved my free hand at her and ducked out of sight, down the spiral staircase.

Her answer to my question narrowed the list of suspects to at least twelve people.

Matt was in the coffee room. I smiled at him but he turned away, back to his cup of java. Surly son of a gun. I felt bruised. If he hurt me now in these minor social ways, what would happen to me with him in a marriage? As was the case with so many men I'd met, I was better off without him.

I knocked on a door marked "Archive Room, Employees Only." When nobody answered I opened it.

The burly cop, all shoulders, was there, with the skinny policeman, both in the blue uniforms of the Passaic police force. Two other men worked with them, both in their sixties, in the gray uniform of the county sheriff's office. I nearly giggled because all four men had on white cotton gloves, the kind my mother used to buy me for Easter Sunday. But I coughed instead and smothered my grin. They were handling tools with delicate care that belied their masculine strength.

"Number 760-010," the big Passaic cop was saying to a woman seated at a computer. Then everything stopped, and they all looked at me.

"Hi!" I said, uncomfortable under the cop-like scrutiny. Had I exceeded the speed limit lately? I always exceeded the speed limit. So I felt guilty and probably blushed a little.

Nobody replied to my hello. I plunged on.

"I'm Tricia Maguire from the *Central Jersey Sentinel,* and Dennis Palmer said I could take pictures today."

"Okay," the big Passaic cop said reluctantly.

"What are your names, so I have them for the record."

Patrolman Patrick O'Grady gave me the names of the other three officers and said that Samantha's assistant, Elspeth MacIntosh, was at the computer. So here was Elspeth! At last I'd met her. She had a cute, short haircut, brown curls covering her head. Maybe ten years younger than me. She had on a black pencil skirt. Long, slim, tanned legs emerged from the skirt and ended in red toenails showcased in strappy sandals. She looked like someone I'd like to get to know. Just for herself, not just as a source.

I got back to work, double-checking the spelling of each name, then starting in.

"What's your process for doing the inventory?" I asked O'Grady.

"We open a cabinet like that one and get to work." He pointed to a floor-to-ceiling cabinet, three feet wide and jutting from the wall three feet. Its doors were open. Inside were rows of drawers, each just a few inches high. One drawer was pulled out, and in it the skinny policeman laid #760-010 back in place.

"What was that—the thing you just laid back?"

He repeated my question. "What was that, Elspeth?"

She peered at the computer screen and said, "It's an adz."

"What a great word for Scrabble!" I got five blank stares.

"So what comes next?" I said, getting back to the topic at hand.

"Each piece is numbered," O'Grady replied. He picked up the tool next to the adz. "See, the numbers are painted on each item." He showed me the tiny white numbers on the handle.

"760-011," he called out to Elspeth. She clicked on her keyboard, and another item had been inventoried.

O'Grady handed the tool to the skinny patrolman, who walked it over to a machine that looked a whole lot like a copier. He placed it on the glass, pushed a button, and a shadow of the tool moved across the ceiling, with purple light glowing around it.

"What's going on?" I asked.

"We scan, for blood, each of the items that fit the description of Samantha's head wound: any blunt put pointed object. When ultra-violet light shines on dried blood, even if the item's been washed, the hemoglobin that remains is fluorescent."

The skinny patrolman shook his head and put the tool back in the open drawer.

O'Grady interpreted that shake of the head. "No blood there." He picked up another tool from the drawer. "We have a lot to do here." He was implying that I get out of their way. But I was nothing if not dogged.

"Question: Is there an alarm on this room or these cabinets?"

"No, but talk to Elspeth about that."

She looked up from her computer screen to field my question. Her brown eyes fixed on mine. "The museum didn't think these items were valuable enough to go to that expense. These tools aren't exactly Rembrandts. People fish them out of their basements and garages. It's the collection that has value, and the way the museum researches their use and presents them to the public."

She was a good museum employee, I thought. She knew what the institution was doing.

"Here's what I'm thinking," I said to O'Grady and Elspeth. "Let me know if you disagree. The archive room was locked, and each drawer was locked. The attacker had an impulse to smack Elaine. It's not likely that he or she unlocked the door to this room, and then a cabinet, grabbed a tool, attacked Sarah, cleaned the tool, put it carefully back in its right place—or its wrong place, we shall see, I guess—and leave."

Elspeth shifted her gaze to O'Grady, looking up at him as he loomed above her.

"That sounds about right," he said, gazing down at her. Her eyes had sparks in them as she turned back to her keyboard. Did she have a crush on the broad-chested patrolman? If it weren't for Justin, I would.

Everybody had paused and looked at me. I had just pointed out to these folks that the work they were doing probably wouldn't reveal the object used to attack Samantha. But they turned back to their inventory. They were going to do it anyway. They were good workers.

"Anything unaccounted for yet?" I asked.

"Nope." And he continued his work. The others began reading off the numbers of the tools in their hands. Elspeth and the skinny patrolman who was scanning were busy keeping up with them. I took pictures, filling up the frame individually with each of the five people. Nobody paid any attention to me. There was no awe of the press in this room.

The interview seemed to be over, by majority vote. But I wasn't done yet. I screwed up my nerve and interrupted them.

"How long is this going to take?"

Work stopped, and the two sheriff's officers exchanged exasperated glances.

"We have all these cabinets to do," Officer O'Grady said, waving at the wall of them reaching the ceiling. He waved a hand at another wall of waist-high ones. "And those."

"What about the tools that are on display upstairs? Any missing from up there?"

"They're behind glass," Elspeth said. "Nobody broke in, and none are missing."

"What's this?" I said, pointing to two blue plastic milkcrates standing on the floor near her desk, each one full of dusty, rusty tools.

The officers didn't answer, so Elspeth took over.

"That's all recent acquisitions and donations," she said. "They're not catalogued yet."

"So the weapon could have been one of these, and if one was missing, we'd never know."

"They've been checked for fingerprints and for blood. None found," O'Grady said.

Well, that was frustrating. I felt impatient with this process, these people plodding through it so diligently. Why were the police spending all this time in this basement?

And where on earth was that weapon? Never mind the person who attacked with it?

I didn't want either of them anywhere near me—me with all my annoying questions.

CHAPTER 17

I said hi to Matt Morgan on the way past, still persevering in getting him on my side as a potential source though he was a reject romantically.

"Got what you came for?" he said, his voice sarcastic.

What an attitude! But I remained sweet for the sake of learning more from him.

"Actually, I had a question for you."

"No, I don't know who did it, and I do not care to guess."

He was insufferable.

I walked out. I'd had enough of his attitude.

I climbed the spiral staircase without looking back and saw Virginia Hopewell still sitting at her desk.

"Virginia, hi," I said, wanting a cozy chat with her and trying to get her in the mood for one by being upbeat.

"Did you get your pictures?"

"Yes, and I was wondering, was everybody getting along with Samantha Scarborough? I know she was new, but did you hear any arguments between her and anyone on the staff?"

"No," she said slowly.

"How about David May, the former curator. Did he want to leave, really? Or was he asked to resign? Did he have trouble turning things over to Samantha?"

"Well, he wasn't pushed out. But now that you mention it, he was very upset his last day. He kept popping out of his office, which wasn't like him. I remember his hair was all disheveled, and he kept running his hands through it, like he was distressed. I don't know what that was about, but it did strike me as odd."

"What day was his last day? The same one that Samantha arrived?"

"He left on a Friday afternoon. She took over Monday morning."

"Do you know for sure if he still has his key to the museum?"

"I don't know," she said, her eyes widening. "As the curator, he did. As a new Board member, he very well might still have it. But I don't think he had anything to do with the attack."

"Why not?"

She shrugged. "Just doesn't seem likely to me, that's all."

"How about Dennis Palmer? Do you know for sure if he has a key?"

"I'm guessing yes. I don't know for sure. Why?"

"Oh, I was just wondering," I said. To divert her mind from my suspicions, I asked what she'd been up to lately.

She told me a little about grandchildren. Then I headed for the front door, hoping Virginia wouldn't tell anyone that I'd asked her about those two Board members having keys.

Just as I reached the door, it opened, and Dorothy Anderson stepped in, laden with two shopping bags full of white papers.

"Oh," she said, "it's you." She looked angry and flustered.

"Hi, I said, "How are you doing?"

She just grunted instead of replying.

"I hope you're well, Mrs. Anderson. I do have a question."

"I don't have any comment for you." She bustled past, set down the bags, and turned back to me. "And what's more," she said, one arm waving a giant "no," "I don't want you coming into the museum and asking questions. Is that clear?"

I had to fight for access to the museum. This was one door that just couldn't close on me.

"Mrs. Anderson, the museum accepts public funds, and I'm a taxpayer, so I have every right to be here."

"You may have every right, but I still don't want you here, bugging the staff and volunteers and distracting them from their jobs. Please go. And don't come back," she called to my departing back.

I could now add to my short list of claims to fame the fact that I had been thrown out of the Museum of Historic Tools and Crafts in Passaic, New Jersey. I would have to write it in my journal, a milestone my descendants—if I ever had any—would read.

I drove to the *Sentinel* wondering how to gain access to stories on the attempted murder. Dorothy Anderson's embargo meant I was going to have to put extra effort into keeping Dennis Palmer as a source, which raised the risk of making a mistake and betraying Meg.

When I got to the newsroom, I waved to Gabi, then threw myself in my chair. I found Dennis's address at work and called.

"Hi, Mr. Palmer—" he might be a bit younger than me, but loading on the respectful honorifics wouldn't hurt "—I wondered, what have you learned about Samantha Scarborough?"

"I've just phoned her husband. He told me she's still in intensive care."

I could find that out for myself calling the hospital. What I wanted was information inaccessible to me. "What was she hit with?"

"The doctors didn't say for sure yet, but it looks like it would have been something pointed but blunt, not sharpened like an axe. Made of iron. There were flakes of what looks like rust in the wound."

Good, a new fact. But how sad. "Poor woman." Though how he could join me in sympathizing with wounded women, I didn't know.

"They still have a twenty-four-hour guard over her." He paused. "Well, I've got to go."

"Okay, thank you."

That was interesting. Something made of iron. I thought of the two milkcrates of uncatalogued tools. Though they'd been checked for blood and none found.

As I sat there musing, or maybe just staring at nothing much, the phone on my desk rang. It turned out to be my mother.

"Darling, I'm worried about your sister. She never calls me, so I called her Monday, and she whispered in the phone, 'Mom, don't call here.' And she hung up. So I let a few days pass, and I called again a few minutes ago. This time she says, in a tight little voice, 'Mom, don't call me ever again.' What's going on?"

My heart began to hurt as I remembered all I'd learned from Noelle at the women's shelter.

"Mom, I don't know for sure, but I can guess that she's being abused."

"Oh dear God, no."

I told her how abusers isolate their victims from family and friends, how the women begin to lose themselves. Then I thought, I shouldn't have said all that to Mom. She'll worry even more.

"We've got to help her," she said. "What can we do?"

"I'll take a personal day tomorrow and go to the city to see her." I had just started this job a few weeks before, I was still on probation, and I was afraid to ask for a day off.

But she was my sister. Abuse would explain why I hadn't been able to get in touch with her for months. I'd been complacent, wrapped up in my job and in Justin, unaware while my sister was possibly suffering. Anger at myself felt like a blunt iron tool pounding on my heart.

I'd go to Susan's tomorrow. I prayed for a good outcome, and for help forgiving myself for not acting sooner. Then I turned back to my work.

CHAPTER 18

F riday morning I knocked on my sister's door on West 14th Street at eleven o'clock. The door was nicked and scarred; the hallway was painted a depressing shade of green. My brother-in-law Robert had selected an average neighborhood in which to live, though is anything average in New York City? The hallway was dreary, but when my sister opened the door, she revealed a different world.

Robert had bought two apartments and knocked out walls to create one spacious home. Not just spacious, but beautifully and formally decorated: oriental carpets, dark polished furniture upholstered in luxurious fabrics, floor to ceiling velvet curtains on the windows tied back with ropes. The tassels on the ends were thick and a foot long. A brass candelabra stood on the baby grand piano, and a painting over the mantel was by an Impressionist, or so Robert had claimed, back when he was still visiting us occasionally in Central Jersey. I had never heard of the artist, but then again, I hadn't studied art history.

Susan was elegantly dressed—overdressed for a weekday, I thought. She was in a beige knit silk pants outfit that had to have cost more than $500. A gold chain hung around her neck with a chunk of gold dangling from it, and she sported a chunk of gold on each earlobe. She had married a man whose family had money, and in addition to that he worked as a business consultant for a prominent firm and made a tremendous salary. My parents and I had never liked him but that didn't mean he didn't spend lavishly to have a well-dressed wife. For her part, Susan looked weary and frightened.

"Tricia, you shouldn't have come without calling. I mean—." She seemed to realize that sounded a bit rude. "How nice to see you. But I can't talk to you. I'm home schooling the kids, and we're behind in the lessons."

Two small children appeared in the doorway to the family room. Nathaniel was five and Louise three. They stayed where they were. They hadn't seen me in nine months, since Labor Day, the last time Susan had been with me at Mom and Dad's house. She had made excuses at Thanksgiving, Christmas, and Easter, saying she was spending them with Robert's family. In short, her kids didn't know me, and I wasn't the adorable Aunt Trish that I wished I could be to them.

"You really can't stay," she whispered.

The way she looked at me, terrified, and the way the kids hung back, cowering, said to me that a pattern of abuse could very well be happening. In fact, I was so strongly suspicious that I did something surprising, even to me. I grabbed Susan's left wrist and pushed her sleeve up. Because it was loosely flowing, I could push it up to her shoulder.

She had ugly bruises, some fading into yellow, some angry and fully developed to purple, some new. They touched and collided and overlapped each other, making her arm a solid mass of pain. She twisted away from me.

"How dare you! You have to leave," she said imperiously.

"Sue, you're being abused, and your kids are watching. Think of the effect it's having on them."

"I'm not talking about it with you."

"Talk about it with somebody. Do you need money for a therapist? I'll get money to you." As in Meg's and Dennis's case, I could guess that Robert watched Susan's expenditures like a bank manager watching a novice teller.

"I don't need your help or anyone else's," she hissed. "Now go." She looked at me and some of her defiance cracked. "Please, Trish."

I couldn't bundle her off to a battered women's shelter without her cooperation. I felt infinitely frustrated with her but unsure what else to do or say.

"Tricia," she leaned over to whisper, "if Robert asks the kids if anyone was here today, they'll tell him because they are too young to know how to lie. Please go. I can't sit down with you and talk. He doesn't like people to come over, especially when he's not here."

I didn't know what else to do, and I only had a few more seconds of my sister's time, so I put the issue in the starkest possible terms.

"Sue, no amount of financial security and material things," and I gestured to the lovely room we were standing in, "and no marriage can be worth the price of your soul, and your children's souls."

I grabbed the doorknob, exasperated at her weakness, terrified for her and her children. opened the door. I stepped out of the apartment, my eyes locked on hers. She twisted her gaze away. I turned down the hallway and heard the door shut with a bang.

As the train rocked me back to New Jersey, I mourned my sister's situation. Grief turned to anger at Robert, the insufferable brother-in-law who'd always been condescending to me and who was now busy destroying members of my family. I felt deep frustration with my sister. The blunt tool was now pounding me over Susan who, it seemed to me, was trading her life, and my niece and nephew's futures, for a gold chain around her neck.

CHAPTER 19

W hen I got home, I called my mother to tell her what happened. I didn't hold back on the kids cowering or the state of Susan's arm. Maybe I should have—Mom was in distress. Then she said she would pray, get her friends to pray, and talk to her therapist about it, so we were enlisting more help.

The next morning, Saturday, I went for a walk. Having been reminded in each Twelve Step meeting I'd ever attended that I was powerless over other people, I made a mental picture of sending Susan and her children safely up to God in a hot air balloon, to be in his care. Then I did the same with Meg. The Steps also taught me to keep the focus on myself and to live as fully as I could in just this one day.

So I decided to act on something I'd heard in a meeting: "I can stop wasting the day with worry." Instead I would breathe in the scent of the blooming roses, peonies, privet hedges, and honeysuckle vines that perfumed the air of my little burg every year in early June. I tried to relinquish my worries so I could savor the strengthening spring sun and the soft moisture in the air.

As I walked, I tugged on the strings of the two hot air balloons I'd just sent up. I talked to God, asking him to reveal to both Susan and Meg that material things and social position and a husband could never be their eternal friend, but that HP could. I also asked for knowledge of how I could be of service to them. I knew at least one answer to this prayer, which was "pray." So I did, then let the hot air balloons ascend again.

Back at my little house, I lay down and tried to sleep, to be fresh and zesty on my date. But, as always, pictures of weddings and honeymoons that starred me and Justin danced in my head. I got impatient with myself, knowing better from dating experience than to waste time and energy indulging in fantasies.

I gave up trying to sleep and decided to get dressed. After half an hour's agony, I picked a black silk shell, a black skirt, a black belt with a silver buckle and a Chinese-firecracker red jacket. A small silver chain and understated silver loops in my ears completed the outfit, with black hose and pretty black heels—not too steep because we'd be walking in the city. The outfit was a bit wintery in tone, but I'd been busy and still hadn't gotten my spring clothes out of storage in my attic. Besides, it was a cool evening, and I was sure that Justin wouldn't care what I wore; I was the only one sweating these details. Despite the agony of deciding what to wear, it felt really good to be dressing up for a date with a really good candidate.

I was thankful not to have to worry about inviting him into my house after the date. I had initiated "the talk" early in our relationship, telling him I wouldn't be sleeping with him until we'd established a strong friendship. To my great relief, he had agreed that this was the best way to proceed, and so that question was settled between us. Except that immediately, my hormones popped up with the question of when the friendship would be "strong enough." I was madly attracted to him and tempted to cross my self-stated boundaries. But I wasn't going to. Of that I was pretty darn sure.

I was ready a mere hour early for my date. So I read Jane Austen for a while, noting the brilliancy and anticipating how it would all be beautifully, wittily, and satisfyingly resolved at the end. I marveled and enjoyed, and the hour passed quickly.

When Justin rang the doorbell at four o'clock, I stepped out the door, locking it behind me.

"Hello!" he said gallantly. Totally endearing. Ugh, I thought, remember that you have to be careful: was he too charming? Was this date too dazzling? I tried to rein in my galloping fear that he was a secret abuser, which would dash my hopes of marriage and children. I'd been disappointed so many times already and didn't want to go through all those hurt feelings again.

"Hello," I said, unable to trust myself to say more, and unable to trust him completely. Men were fickle in their attachments, at least in my experience. I couldn't count on anything coming of this date.

"Are you ready for a New York adventure?" he asked.

"Yes, I love the city," I said with a smile, determined to enjoy myself even if I did have to watch for red flags. He held the door for me as I climbed into his company Jeep. He never drove his Jaguar into the city, he had told me on a previous date.

He climbed in on the driver's side, and the Jeep dipped under his manly weight. Now began the hard part: making conversation with a relative stranger, deciding what to share and what to hold back for another time, or never. I had no children whose exploits I could brag about. I had my reading to talk about, but the world's best stories, otherwise known as classic literature, didn't interest everybody. Neither did most people seem to want to hear about my challenges with the novel or the newspaper stories I was writing. Another possible topic: Susan and Meg, but then again, domestic abuse didn't seem like a good topic for a date. I decided my best option was to talk about current events, meaning my job. I had already told Justin about the attack on Samantha Scarborough, so while he drove in his competent way, I filled him in on everything new I had learned.

"You need to check some more on David May, why he was so distressed before he left," Justin said. I was already well aware of that but didn't say so, thinking it best to hold my tongue.

"And why was the Chief so willing to cooperate that day? That would be good to know."

It felt great that he was showing an interest in my job—maybe showing he cared about me?

"Yes, good to know," I said. "Any ideas on how to find out why?"

"I don't have much experience with chiefs of police but plenty of experience with your average patrolman." And for the rest of the trip into the city, he regaled me with stories from his college days. Like the time he was drinking beer on the porch of a frat house, stepped off the porch onto the public sidewalk, and was given a summons for underage drinking by two patrolmen who were watching the party. He hadn't gone to the required court date, and a warrant for his arrest had been issued. He had gone to pay the bail, fearful of being arrested before he reached the courthouse. "That was the last time I procrastinated on anything having to do with the law," he said. "I pay parking tickets on time now. And I don't get many parking tickets either," he said, looking at me sidelong. "I've come to a new understanding about life, and I don't flout the rules anymore. And I don't drink much anymore either," he said. I had dated or observed so many men who drank too much that I was very relieved to hear him say that. If it were true.

He parked on West 57th Street, a few blocks from the restaurant. He had offered to drop me at the door, but I declined. So we walked together in the cool evening air, the lights in the windows of tall buildings filling the sky above us with rectangular stars. He didn't take my hand. After a few dates, wouldn't that have been appropriate? Friends first, I admonished myself. Yet this was obviously a very romantic date.

The restaurant had subdued lighting and décor. The chairs were each covered by a beige slipcover held in place by a darker beige bow. The tablecloths were white linen. We sat by a window. Couples went by outside, some with their arms around each other, some walking without touching. Many people went by walking alone. I took note of them with sadness. I didn't want to go the whole way, into my eighties or nineties, alone. I reminded myself that Justin had to prove himself to be a good, trustworthy man. He could still fail the test.

We both wanted sparkling water, so the waiter brought a bottle of it. It seemed that Justin wasn't hooked into alcohol, though I would keep watch. After achieving a degree of happiness as a single person, I didn't want to risk it on somebody who was dependent on booze. Tonight I was being as careful as my mother wanted me to be.

I ordered salmon, and Justin ordered flounder florentine. We each had a glass of Pinot Grigio arrive with the food. I tried to concentrate on being as entertaining as possible while learning about this man. I was curious about his job as a developer. A risky business. How was he doing? Yes, he owned a Jag, I'd been in it, but would it be repossessed next week? Careful what questions you let escape your mouth, I thought. Let's assume he's a success, you're less likely to ask something that offends.

"How did your projects go this week?" I asked.

"Well. Because I'm always alert to what could go wrong. I worry about my jobs, and it pays off—I can see where things could go off track and I jump in to prevent it."

"I do the same thing! I question myself constantly."

"What could go wrong in a reporter's job?"

How great of him to ask! It seemed he was not just on a date but interested in me, in what I was doing. "Well, for example, I could develop a relationship with a public official as a source and then get a little lost in it and find myself writing about him admiringly, burnishing him a bit in ink. Without intending to. But that would be lying to my readers."

"Interesting."

"What could go wrong on one of your projects?"

"A thousand things. I have a good crew—several of them, in fact, with foremen who have lots of experience. But I'm the one with the most at risk. It sharpens the brain."

"Can you give an example?"

"After years as the foreman of a crew, and then as the owner, I know where the pitfalls are. And new ones appear with every project."

He hadn't given an example after a direct request for one. He didn't want to talk about it. Or was I reading him wrong? I'd come back to it another time. Now to explore another issue.

"How's your son doing?" I asked.

"Mike's fine. He's on the baseball team again."

"I wish him the best. Sports are tough." At least they were in my klutzy experience.

"He's got talent. He'll do okay, at least at the junior high school level."

What I really wanted to know I couldn't ask. Would Mike accept a woman coming into his dad's life? Mike and Justin had made a tight team for a while now. Would Mike be ready to let his dad have another partner?

"I'll bet you're really proud of your athletic son."

"Oh yes, I'm pretty typical in that regard."

"Typical proud parent," I said, regretting that I sounded jealous because I didn't have offspring to be proud of.

"I see him changing. He's getting more interested in friends. He asks to be with them on Friday and Saturday nights, rather than watching a ball game with me. It bothers me," he said, smiling ruefully, and I admired him for admitting it. "It's the beginning of the end, when he will leave home to start his own life."

"The process is awesome, isn't it?" I said. "You start out completely dependent on your parents for life itself, and you end up just a few years later creating your own nest and having your own chicks." Justin was looking at me, and I suspected that he was thinking how I didn't have children. "Well, Tommy and I were having some problems, so I never tried to get pregnant. But I wouldn't mind having a child of my own." That was an understatement. I had blurted it out. It might be too soon. But then again I wanted him to know my feelings about kids. I was looking for a family man, somebody who wouldn't mind having a baby. Or two.

Justin was still looking at me. Had I lost him?

"Children are fun," he said eventually, and I took that to mean he wouldn't mind having more. I blushed a bit and wondered if that settled the issue. I probably should someday seek more clarification. But I didn't want to take the risk of appearing to belabor the topic tonight.

"Did you throw Mike in the air when he was little? Men tend to do that with babies." While women snuggled them to their breast, men tossed them around. What a world! How did men and women ever get along?

"Yeah, I was a tosser. And we played cars and trains and built towers. All the typical stuff."

I felt myself really blushing. All this talk of children was making me think about sex, which was the only way they got created. To regain my composure, I changed the subject.

"Anything of note happen last week?"

"I bought some land in Somerset Hills."

"Oh? Where?"

"From a man named David May, and his wife Kiki."

"David May? He was the former curator of the Museum of Historic Tools and Crafts, and he's on the Board of Directors now."

"Yes, must be the same people. The land is part of the tract their mansion is on. I'm going to build two big homes, my favorite thing."

"I wonder if he needs money."

"Doesn't everybody?"

"He's a trust fund baby, I'm quite sure of it."

"He might have expensive tastes. He might have a profligate son that he maintains in the style to which he's accustomed. He might have a mistress, an expensive one."

Now why did Justin mention that? If he thought I'd tolerate his having a mistress for one second, he was quite mistaken. He hadn't taken the spirit of this particular woman into account if he thought he could get away with that. Then I realized it hadn't happened, his comment didn't mean much, and once again I was way ahead of myself. Time to get back to the topic at hand.

"I wonder why he sold that land."

"Why don't you ask him?"

"Heavens, no!" Then again, why not? But I didn't want Justin to think I was a busybody. There was that issue popping up again. "It's none of my business," I said firmly.

"If he's a suspect in that attack, you ought to ask him. Maybe there's a motive there. No other way to find out."

That was certainly true. Perhaps I could screw up the nerve to ask. After all, I asked people questions for a living. Note to self: call David May on Monday.

It was time to go to the theater. We walked the six blocks, talking all the way, but again he didn't take my hand. I was disappointed.

The play was marvelous, and it gave us something to talk about for most of the trip out of the city. When we got to the edge of my suburb, we both fell silent as he drove. I was thinking about how the evening might end. A kiss? That would certainly be nice. Though it complicated the friends thing. I wondered if he'd ask me out again. I wished so mightily. Oh, I hated dating, not knowing where I stood. Did he like me? How much did he like me? On a scale of one to ten, was I a three? An eight? That was the end of the scale I wanted to be on for him. He was certainly there for me. This was agony.

He pulled into my driveway and left the engine running. Okay, that meant no more than a quick kiss. I waited for a signal from him, in order to know what to do, and he reached over the gear shift to offer me a hug. I kissed his cheek because that was the only part of him available. He smelled marvelous. I said softly, "Thank you for a beautiful evening."

"My pleasure," he replied and released me. Was that all I was going to get? Oh, well. Time to push on. Friends, friends. But I moved slowly, hoping it gave him time to ask for another date.

"Good night, Tricia," was all he said, and he waited in his car until I had the front door unlocked. I waved from the doorway. He beeped as he pulled away into the night. That beep sounded friendly and made me feel hopeful. But he hadn't asked me out again. That plunged me into despair.

Ninja came down the stairs and meowed.

"Ninja, I don't know how this is going," I said to my little beastie, "and I wish, really wish, that everything was settled already. I'd like to be snuggling with him at this very moment." I scooped Ninja up. "You're the only critter I'll be snuggling tonight," and I trudged off to the bedroom with the only male creature who had seen me naked in quite a while.

CHAPTER 20

Sunday morning I went to church. After scrambling all week alone in an indifferent world, I needed the hour to sit with my church family and hear that God loved us very much, in spite of ourselves.

Church brought other beauties into my life too. The sun was shining, and a breeze made leaves dance outside a stained glass window. The leaves' shadows made the window's colors dance and sparkle along with the music.

But I got caught up in worry. The choir sang while I thought about Justin, and my long-suffering rector gave his homily while I thought about him some more. During prayers, I was on my knees asking for guidance about him, to know whether the relationship had a future or not, and to know soon, before I got any more emotionally involved. God had answered this prayer many times in the past, helping me to be honest with myself about red flags in the character of the men I was dating. Justin could be one more dead-end, and I knew my hopes for marriage and children could be easily crumpled by one more phone call, one more date. Or lack thereof. Why hadn't he asked me out again? Didn't he enjoy himself with me? Had he decided he actually did not like my boundaries? What was going on in his mind? I was completely frustrated with the whole thing.

I realized I was obsessing just a tiny bit. Time to let go. Time to focus on myself, on what I needed to do, and on God's love for me, which would be unconditional whether I felt it every moment or not. I would be fine on my own, without Justin. Though I'd prefer to have the companionship, the sex, and the children …

It wasn't until communion started that I participated in the service. As the rector raised the unleavened bread and broke it, I was homing in on the beauty and mystery being celebrated—the grace of God—the love, forgiveness, mercy. I was forgiven of things done and left undone.

Then, at that point, I thought of the dust bunnies reproducing not just under my sofa where nobody could see them but under the chairs where they could drift out—or leap out, if so inspired—and attach themselves to people's shoes.

I pushed that thought away and left the stone building, feeling refreshed in spite of my ghastly dust bunnies.

CHAPTER 21

Monday morning I called David May, both happy and scared to flout Dennis Palmer's instructions to call only him, and asked to see David again. I didn't know how to actually ask the money question Justin had suggested Saturday night, but I was at least going to try. David sounded surprised at my request to talk with him again, then said he could see me that afternoon.

As I drove up his driveway, I pictured Justin striding over this hillside in a hardhat, directing the manner in which his top-end houses should be built. I loved a commanding man. In bed, that is, not telling me how to do the dishes. I could just see Justin telling his crews where to build and how to build. Of course, if he started bossing me around in my own kitchen, he would learn there were limits. But I could teach him that gently ... I yanked my thoughts back to David May and the interview ahead.

The same maid answered the door and led me through the living room toward the sunroom. This time I tried to see if the furniture was super special—if an expensive antiquing habit was why David May was selling some land. My untrained eye couldn't tell. But I could tell I envied the means that could create a room, presumably a house, full of lovely chairs, curtains, rugs, sofas, that worked together to provide a sense of richness, elegance, beauty.

I stepped into the sunroom and blinked in the bright light.

"Hello, Tricia, would you like some coffee, or tea?" David asked as he stood up from a wrought-iron chair.

"No, thank you, I just have a few questions." Two that I could think of, though I hoped to think of more, to make it worth the trip. Should have worked harder at developing a list of questions.

"Have a seat then, and fire away," he said pleasantly. I glanced around for his wife, and he seemed to discern my thoughts.

"My wife's resting this time of day," he said. I wondered if he'd scheduled this interview purposely for when his wife would be in bed.

"Well, Mr. May, I've been asking questions about Samantha Scarborough's attack, and one person mentioned that on your last day in the office—well, this person said you seemed highly strung that day, very nervous. Distraught was the word they used." I paused to give those words a chance to land with him. "I wondered why."

David didn't answer at first, and I couldn't guess a darn thing from his expression. Wouldn't want to play him in poker—not a clue emanated from his impassive face.

"I wouldn't say I was distraught. A bit distracted, maybe that's what the person meant. I had a lot to do to turn the office over to Samantha in good shape. Clean out the desk, the bookcases, my files. And I got a late start that day, because my wife had been especially ill that morning." Was there a hesitation before this mention of his wife? Was he lying? Using her to hide?

"The person said you kept running your hands through your hair." I wasn't willing to let him off the hook.

"I certainly don't remember doing that. The person—I guess you mean Virginia Hopewell or Elspeth MacIntosh—must have an unclear memory. I was busy but not distraught."

That was not a straight answer, I didn't think, but what else had I expected? A full explanation? This was a mystery I'd like to solve, but it didn't look like it would be today.

"I see," I said, though I didn't see. Swiveling around on my wrought-iron chair, I let him see me obviously admiring the sunroom. I was laying some groundwork for the second question. "This is such a lovely house. And beautiful grounds." I waved toward the view over the Watchung mountains. I was gearing up to be nosy, and even impudent. Was I asking this question just to make Justin happy? He had urged me ... Well, I was a journalist. I was paid to be curious. And I wanted to find Samantha's attacker, who was still prowling around. On the other hand I'd also been raised by my mother to mind my own business.

Oh well, here goes.

"Mr. May, why are you selling some of your land?"

He froze, and so did I. Wow, the nerve of me to ask such a question!

The silence dragged on. It was so quiet, I heard the rattle of a teacup in the far-away kitchen.

"That's none of your business." He said it with the toughness and arrogance that only an aristocrat with old, old money could summon. "If you keep it up with these impertinent questions, you will find that the editors of the *Central Jersey Sentinel* don't need your services anymore. Do I make myself clear?"

He had the publisher of my newspaper in his pocket? Wouldn't I like to know more about that! For now it was best to simply exit with all the dignity a middle-class American could summon in the face of all this aristocratic haughtiness.

"I'm going to get to the bottom of this, Mr. May," I said, and turned on my heel and marched out, hoping to have the last word.

"Drop it," I heard him fire back. I didn't deign to reply. Even as I regretted what I'd done, alienating him as a source, my pride surged. I'd show him what someone who has no old money but lots of chutzpah could do!

CHAPTER 22

When I got back into my car, I had to admit to myself that I was a little shook up by my own nosiness and by David May's threat of unemployment. What an abuse of power it would be, if he actually carried it through.

But that would be scant comfort for me if I had no job. My former position at the *Passaic Press* had already been filled by a young mother with two small children. I had no job to go back to. My husband Tommy's life insurance policy had paid off the mortgage, but I still needed my reporter's income, scanty as it was, to make ends meet. I could be a waitress, I supposed, but I wanted to be a journalist and to grow in my skill, in my career.

I wondered what Justin would make of my interview with David May, but I didn't feel free to call him and tell him about it. No return kiss Saturday night and no request for another date. I didn't feel on firm ground. Maybe I should have shown my feelings more, kissed his cheek more passionately. Oh boy, more anxiety about dating flooded over me.

No matter what went on in my murder investigation, or my love life, I had been hired to continually feed the printing presses at the *Sentinel* with stories. I had lined up an interview with a local artist named Cindy Pierson. She had written and illustrated a children's book that won a Caldecott medal.

I drove to the town library to read the book before the interview. It was lovely, and I felt envy gripping my heart for her talent and the recognition she'd gained. Doubt assailed me that I was talented enough, as a novelist and as a journalist, to make it in the bigtime.

When I saw her house—in pristine condition, a landscaper just finishing trimming the grass near the front steps—I envied her even more. The bushes along the foundation were just the right height and shape, dark mulch had been spread to make a distinct line between plantings and grass, and a blooming Korean dogwood stood at the corner of the house looking glorious and sharing its glory with her garden.

My own landscaping needed work, and mine were the only hands that I could afford to have do it. But I couldn't afford the time. I had stories to hunt and write.

Cindy Pierson answered my knock in a form-fitting black silk tunic, with leggings underneath. Her outfit was free of any hint of paint. She kept her clothes neat and tidy, just like the artist Kandinsky had. I'd seen a photo of him in a beautiful, paint-free, three-piece tweed suit, brush in hand, back when I was exploring his work and his writings. Unless he had changed his clothes for the photo. Maybe Cindy had too, for this interview. Her hand, which she extended to shake mine, had only one splotch, of carmine red, on the thumb.

I liked her instantly—she had hazel eyes that latched onto mine the way you'd expect an artist's would, as the world caught her attention and spun her into speculation on the mysteries being beheld. The same way my eyes worked as a novelist and journalist.

"Come in," she said. I glanced around the living area—furnished comfortably but not upholstered in the newest of fabrics, like Kiki and David's living room. A picture window opposite the front door revealed a garden out back where peonies thrived.

She led me toward her studio with strong steps, planted with sureness, as if she were an experienced hiker on a rough path. I followed her down a hallway into a bedroom that also overlooked the garden. This picture window revealed a border jammed with late irises and peonies.

"This is my studio. Welcome to my world," she said.

Three easels with canvases on them stood in three corners, and a shelf that ran the length of one wall supported jars of brushes and tubes of paint. A drafting table faced the garden with a large sheet of paper taped to it with blue housepainter's tape. Rows of canvases leaned against the wall, on which others hung at all heights. The room smelled of linseed oil.

"Have a seat," and she waved toward two paint-splattered wooden chairs. She was less careful with the furniture than she was with her clothes. "Don't worry, the paint's dry."

I sat gingerly, hoping that what she said was true. She was still standing.

"Coffee? Tea? Water?" she asked, and I shook my head. She sat in a smooth motion, and we looked at each other solemnly for a moment. Her gaze was taking everything in, it seemed to me, and I hoped mine was too.

"Nice garden," I said. "Tell me, do you see your work in your garden informing or inspiring your art?"

"Oh, that's my husband's pastime," she said, crossing her legs. "I just enjoy it—I paint it occasionally. There's one on that easel." She pointed with the carmine-splotched hand to an impression of a vase of peonies. It stood on the easel in the farthest corner.

Well, she'd reminded me with a thud that I ought not to take a single thing for granted. She was not Monet, working in his garden, but her own artist who found her own inspirations, and I needed to stay aware of that and probe it.

"What else do you take inspiration from?"

She clasped her knee with her strong-looking hands and blunt fingers.

"I go to local shows, I go to museums, I have an artist's group that meets once a week and we bring a canvas or two to discuss. I look at my books of great art—" she waved with a quick flick of her hand at a bookcase I hadn't noticed until then. Huge tomes were stacked on every shelf. I could read "Renoir" and "Matisse" on two spines before she continued and I had to look back at my note-taking.

"Mostly I encourage myself to notice everything around me—people, places, and things. A glass of water can be an inspiration if you look at it deeply. I ponder."

I love to ponder, but nobody gives me Caldecotts, I thought, bugged at the difference between her success and mine. Now that's ungracious of you, I chided myself. Please concentrate on the task at hand.

"What were you pondering when I rang your bell?" I asked with my best smile. I wouldn't antagonize this source. What was she going to reveal to me—on the record, with my pen poised above a reporter's notebook?

"I was looking out the window at the shadows, the way they shift and move—dance—when there's a breeze. I was thinking of Gerard Manley Hopkins' poem, with the line 'Praise for dappled things.'"

I thought of the dappled stained glass at church on Sunday. Maybe I was a visual artist too. I wanted to be an artist of stories.

"What are you working on these days?" I asked.

"I'm deep in watercolor illustrations for the next book. Will it win an award? It's hard to have that pressure on me—people's expectations, my agent and my publisher holding their breath. It's impossible to work toward winning an award. Judges are fickle, the public's tastes change. Winning an award can't be the goal. Instead I let go of that as an outcome and just work toward making this book more true, more me, more of a vessel of my love for my children and grandchildren."

Another pang of envy. She had a great house, great garden, presumably great husband, a gift for art that she was set up in this house to develop, including the dedicated space, and on top of all that—children and grandchildren. I, on the other hand, struggled with my aloneness, my uncertainty about Justin, not knowing whether I'd ever have children to enjoy. I struggled to make time for my novel writing and didn't have a dedicated space for it, just my dining room table.

I wrenched my attention back to my job.

"How did it feel to learn you'd won the Caldecott? What happened that day?"

"I was puttering in here," and Cindy waved her hand to signify her studio, "when the phone rang. My husband answered it, and then he called me to the phone. I would have been bugged at the interruption—I protect my painting time vigorously—but there was a tone in his voice that told me something special was happening. I had no idea what it was though. I put down my brushes—rested them in linseed oil, actually, which means I suspected that something big was happening, that it would take some time, and that I had to keep the paint from drying on the brushes."

She took a sip of water from a glass that had fingerprints in every shade of red, yellow, and blue on it.

"I went to the phone, and a woman's voice asked if I were indeed me, then said she was pleased to tell me my book won this year's Caldecott Award. That's an award for illustration, by the way, though I both wrote and illustrated The Red Car."

Cindy lifted a hand to brush a wisp of hair from her lips, where it had gotten entangled with moisture from her drink.

"I was thrilled. I was thrilled for days. I was so thrilled, I couldn't talk about it. I said 'Caldecott award' to my husband and that I couldn't talk about it. I was afraid that if I did discuss it with him, if I told family and friends, the joy would dissipate as the words left my lips. He was great about it, and I just walked around in a state of euphoria.

"Like any emotion, it did finally dissipate, and then I began to tell people. My family threw a party, the library invited me to speak, I've talked to a few reporters. Lately it's starting to be 'in the rearview mirror,' as the cliché goes."

"But it's a nice credential to have," I chimed in. Flattery gets you everywhere, a cliché with undeniable truth to it.

"Yes, the medallion will go on the next printing of the book. Mention of the award will go on the cover my new book, and any future ones. In a way, I'm surprised I won. The award goes to the most universal books, usually, that reflect the lives of the greatest number of children, so that would be economically disadvantaged city dwellers. The family in The Red Car in fact own a car, not something the majority of the world's children have in their lives. But the family goes on adventures together, so that theme, I hope, is universal."

She leaned forward and again clasped her hands around a knee.

"Tell me, what are you up to?" she asked.

I gave her high points for being interested in her interviewer.

"I'm writing a novel. And I'm a photographer," I said. "I used to take all my own photographs when I was with the *Passaic Press*. The *Sentinel* assigns photographers to my stories now. I wish they wouldn't. I like to get that photo credit. But my stuff has to be better than theirs."

"I recommend that you find a photography group. They're great for improving your eye," she said. "Walking with other photographers, you'll see things you never noticed before. They'll wake you up to their world, their way of seeing."

"That's what I'm hoping," I replied. I would ask my friend Catherine to do a photo shoot with me. She had a good eye.

Time was short, I had to get more from Cindy to be able to write a story about her. So I launched a new thread of questions.

"Tell me about your artistic process. What was the seminal idea for writing The Red Car?"

"Well, I find my ideas all over the place, as we talked about: in my husband's garden, in the local parks—I love the Great Swamp. I also look at the architectural details on an elegant old building and wonder who designed them, what his—or her, wouldn't that have been nice—life was like, what their children liked to read growing up. My children loved the Chronicles of Narnia and the Little House on the Prairie series. I grab inspiration from everywhere."

But she hadn't answered my question about the seed, and I thought my readers would like to know, as I certainly did.

"What was the inspiration, or inspirations plural, for this book?" Asked differently, she might give me an answer this time.

"I've gotten into black and white photography, which is quite different from color. It tunes your eye to shape and structure and form and contrast and shades of gray."

I thought she was wandering off topic again. I tried to be patient. Maybe she was leading toward her answer.

"Adults like shades of gray," she said. "I wondered if kids wouldn't go for that too. So I set the book in winter, with black leafless trees silhouetted against the sky, which is in shades of gray. The only color is red, the car that takes the family on an adventure. I went for subtlety in the background colors and poetry in the words. Turns out kids like that, and there's something in it for adults too." She smiled.

"Has the award helped sales?" I was curious and figured my readers would be too.

"I won't know until my royalty check comes in—it's always two months behind actual sales. But let's be honest, yes, it ought to help. There are 17,000 public libraries in the United States and 105,000 school libraries— many of them, I hope, will buy my book."

"As well as parents who want great stories for their children," I said. "That's wonderful, Cindy. Thanks for your time." I was now totally envious of her success. She was making money with her art form, she had a husband so she could do her art fulltime, she shared a house and garden and life and bed with him, she had several published books, and this one was award-winning—she had recognition. It seemed she had everything I wanted.

With a pang, I wished her well with as much sincerity as I could muster. "Would you let me take your picture? The *Sentinel* will send a photographer, but maybe my photo will be better." I smiled a big cheesy smile.

"Sure."

I took a set of photos with her standing next to an easel, her work propped on it. Then with those strong footsteps of hers, she led me out the kitchen door to the back yard. I took her picture against the backdrop of a blooming spirea bush, taller than her, spilling white blossoms in graceful abundance.

I got shots of her both smiling and serious, and when I had enough, I was careful to advance my film, always seeking to be ready for the next photojournalism opportunity.

She walked me back to my car. We paused next to my Corolla.

"Well, it's been a pleasure," she said, and I felt happy. Maybe I'd conducted a very good interview. "Enjoy your photography and writing," she added as we shook hands.

"Enjoy your studio, your painting," I said. And all the other blessings in your life and not in mine. "Thank you for your time."

I could make a studio for writing in my own little house, I thought, as I drove to the newsroom. Or put in a darkroom and learn how to process my own film. I'd been postponing converting a spare bedroom into creative space ever since Tommy died. It was time to work—or play, as an artist might say—in a place other than at the dining room table, where the pink tablecloth was stained with ink spots from the blue, black, purple, turquoise, red, green, and even pink pens that I used to write in my journal and novel. But I hesitated because I didn't think I'd like to be upstairs in one of the bedrooms, no window facing the street, too far from the doors in case a vandal broke in and I needed to escape.

A husband is a good thing to have around, I thought, to dispel the fear of vandals, a fear that had arisen in me as soon as Tommy had died. A few nights after his death, spooked at being alone, I'd called the police because I thought I heard rustling in the bushes outside my bedroom window. They came, looked around, and very kindly explained that they had not found anyone or anything. But fear of being alone at night had persisted for a long time.

Cindy Pierson didn't have that problem. She was enjoying even more good fortune than I'd originally thought.

CHAPTER 23

Because the *Sentinel* hadn't commissioned me to take Cindy's picture, I had to develop my shots of her at my expense. I didn't know how to do darkroom stuff—note to self, do something about that—and I couldn't ask the paper's staff to do it since they'd have to do it under the table. Asking someone to do something Nefarious is Not Nice!

I finished the roll of film later that day by taking pictures of flowers in gardens and of architectural details adorning the Victorian houses downtown. Which made me think of Margaret Bourke-White, famous photojournalist whose work I'd poured over, who, speaking of architectural details, was enamored of the bronze eagle gargoyles projecting from the top of the Chrysler Building in New York City. I'd seen a famous photo of her perched on one of the eagles, hundreds of feet in the air, camera to her eye. I was going to be a photojournalist a little closer to earth today.

I dropped the film off at the camera store on Main Street. I would pick the photos up tomorrow, before I turned in the Cindy Pierson story, and maybe my photo of her would be better than the staff photographer's. I'd get the photo credit, yay, an outcome much to be desired. A little glory to accumulate to me, though it was much less glory than had accumulated to Cindy Pierson lately.

Per the usual, that evening I got myself to a Twelve Step meeting, this one for the families of addicted people. These days I went for my own sake, to help untangle myself from a Sargasso Sea of negativity, both in the way I thought about the world and about myself.

Catherine was at the meeting—so glad to see her. She had escaped from a husband who also was abusive and threatening—she ran for her life, moved three states away, and came to the Twelve Steps to recover. That was a while ago.

Tonight, as usual, she looked contented and relaxed. Her Irish background gave her red hair, gold freckles across her nose, and blue eyes that opened straight into her soul. She waved when she saw me approach the circle of chairs.

"Hey, how's it going?" I plopped next to her.

"Good—"

The meeting's leader began to read the introduction. Catherine whispered, "Want to do a photo walk Saturday?"

I nodded with a smile.

The theme of this meeting was "Let go and let God," always a useful tool when I was obsessing over people, places, and things I had no control over. I didn't think I was obsessed with anyone at that particular moment. Well, let's be honest, how about Cindy Pierson and her success? So I'd listen tonight, content to be in a community of fellow Higher Power enthusiasts, looking for tools to deal with life, with myself. The meetings, like church, always refreshed my sense that all things are possible with HP.

As I looked around the circle of people from all walks of life (how comforting that most of them were HP people, and the ones who weren't were experiencing some recovery too, by some mysterious miracle), I mused over what I'd seen happen many times at meetings. People would walk in beautifully dressed, manicured, and coiffed, looking like they had everything marching in their favor. Then they'd share about their husbands', sons', or daughters' drinking and drugging, and I'd learn what hidden heartaches they lived with. Without the anonymity of a Twelve Step meeting, which gives people the safety to be open about what's really going on, I never could have guessed. The honesty led to so much relief and healing.

I felt that I too would like to benefit from being open and raised my hand to share. Everyone's attention shifted to me. My throat constricted under people's gaze on me. Though I adored having my stories front page above the fold, I preferred not to be in the limelight. But the non-judgmentalism and grace of the atmosphere gave me courage to speak honestly.

"I met an artist today who has everything I want in life—a supportive husband, a beautiful house, a lovely garden, a studio all set up in a spare bedroom, no job so she can do her art fulltime, and now she's received professional recognition by winning a prestigious award for her recent book."

I was being too serious; it was time to make a joke.

"At least I *think* her husband is supportive. He grows flowers for her to paint, that's why I think so."

A few people chuckled.

"I'm trying to be content single, but I have these ambitions, these dreams for more. I'm working to make my dreams come true, I don't expect them to materialize without working for them, but it does seem at times that many people have so much more, just because they're married and have that partner, that extra earning power—and that companionship and sex life, of course."

I remembered that I was saying all this to two women in the group who had husbands who drank relentlessly. Not much companionship there.

"I guess the Steps say to do a gratitude list for what I do have. I guess the answer is to do my best and let go and let God handle the outcome." Then my thoughts started meandering, and I decided to wrap it up quick. Nobody seemed to mind.

People continued to share, and my mind drifted. I wondered what hidden heartaches Cindy Pierson lived with. Mine I was familiar with—watching Tommy descend into madness, first with alcohol, then with a brain tumor; after his death the mourning and pining for how things might have been. Now I wanted to be remarried—being single after having been married is tough. It's a different, harder ballgame than the singleness during and after college because I had experienced the togetherness. I missed the companionship, the peaceful times and shared meals that Tommy and I had enjoyed, though only at the beginning, before alcohol ruined everything. To once again have that camaraderie was a constant tug at my heart. And it was tough to be a young woman at the peak of her desire for sexual expression—it was painful how strong the urge to merge was—and yet have nowhere to go with it. And it was a heartache not having children. When was this situation going to change? Until I had met Justin, I'd only met guys who didn't exhibit enough character to be worth marrying.

The meeting was over on the dot of the hour, as usual. I finalized plans with Catherine for a photoshoot on Saturday, then drove home and went for a walk to do a Tenth Step: taking a moment to reflect on my day, seeing where I might not have been a great human being, and praying for HP to help me make amends—to myself or to others, whatever was needed. It kept my life from becoming seriously derailed.

As I strolled in the early June evening light, I stopped to sniff roses and peonies in people's gardens bordering the sidewalk—no, I did not trespass, unless one foot on people's grass was wrong of me. With my nose deep in a fragrant, pink-velvet rose, having checked first for bees, I pictured myself at Cindy Pierson's house feeling so envious of all she was enjoying, particularly her husband's company, and that she'd had children, and maybe hating her, and myself, because she had so much more than I had in life. I had focused on the obvious things Cindy had while I had no knowledge of what hidden heartaches she had experienced in life, or that she might face in the future.

Breathing in the night air, perfumed with the scent of honeysuckle and wild roses growing in the untended places and privet, roses and peonies in gardens—wished I could bottle the scent—I mused that there were bound to be problems in Cindy's life too. But it sure looked good from my perspective.

"What do I need to do?" I whispered to my HP, hoping no people in passing cars saw my lips move. We needn't add being perceived as a nut to our problems.

Oh yeah, I could do a gratitude list. I stopped to sniff the roses in my own garden. Nice.

In the fading light I stared into a half-unfurled rose and thought about how I wanted my life to open up and unfurl. I wanted to commit, at a new level, to pursuing God and journalism and uncovering the truth about the powers that be, and to use photography to nail down the truth in my stories. And I'd follow in the footsteps of my favorite women photojournalists—hey, carve my own new path. And then I'd move to *The New York Times*.

But what about Justin? The scent in the air evaporated as my anxious thoughts began to race.

"Help," I asked HP. "I'm once again ruining the present by thinking negatively about the future. Help?"

CHAPTER 24

Catherine turned up at my house Saturday for our photo walk at the appointed time, thank God, because I have a hard time waiting for people, even dear friends. She was wearing shorts and a flowing top in shades of red, orange, and blue, colors that set off her red hair and blue eyes to advantage. We neither of us were slouches anymore in taking care of ourselves by wearing clothes that did something for us.

I knew I needed to follow this bit of ancillary guidance from the Twelve Steps ("to keep our voices low and dress becomingly") because before the Steps I had thrown on any old thing while I devoted my entire personhood to trying to keep Tommy from drinking.

How did that go, one might ask.

Not at all well.

Those days were over, though I still sometimes resented Tommy's abuse, his ruin of what had started out as a very good thing. I'd struggled off and on for ten years to forgive him. I looked up at the sky—blue, cloudless. I looked down and saw that, near my feet, the familiar black hole in my path labeled Resentment was opening up. To avoid falling in, and the negative aftermath, I had to forgive. Again. When would this be over? One day at a time, Trish. Today I was with my best friend, doing something we both enjoyed.

"Ready?" she asked.

She dangled a Nikon on a strap around her neck. I wore a Canon. We never argued about it. We didn't argue about film either. I had black and white in my camera because of my job, and because I preferred it anyway. We'd heard about digital cameras coming out, but neither of us wanted to switch yet. We'd wait until the bugs were out of the newfangled devices—if not longer.

Catherine, my fellow late adopter, looked nice, and I thought a compliment might make her day.

"You look great."

"Thanks, you too."

We hugged.

"You okay today, friend?" she asked.

"Yep. Okay, thanks. You?"

She nodded.

"Want to check out the pond?" I asked. "Geese, ducks, maybe a blue heron that has stopped by?"

"Sure." We ambled together up the hill to the road that led to the pond. My town was located so near the Great Swamp Wildlife Refuge that we had lots of bugs and birds and even turtles and other critters that towns farther away from the swamp didn't have. The animals came to visit our pond. We never knew what wildlife we might find.

Catherine flipped her red ringlets over her shoulder. "So, what's new with Justin?"

That Catherine! She didn't waste a moment, did she. We hadn't talked in a while because she worked days and I worked so many evenings covering town government meetings.

I smiled. I did enjoy having a romantic interest to discuss, and sharing it with Catherine would be satisfying. "Doing my best to keep my wits about me. I really do like him, but I'm scared, watching for character flaws—especially reliance on alcohol."

We walked past a garden with clumps of lavender near the road. Catherine ran her fingertips over a clump and sniffed them. "A lot of men love to come home from work and have a beer. Or something."

"Yes, and that scares me. Alcohol slowly—or rapidly—seduces people, from what I've seen."

"If they've been doing it for years and haven't had a problem yet, don't you think you can stop worrying?"

"I don't know. You as scared of alcohol as I am?"

"Yeah, basically, but I don't want to cut every man in the world out of my realm."

Yes, Catherine *would* have a realm. She appeared to be a goddess in her current dating—though somehow, previously, she'd married a man who wound up threatening to kill her if she didn't obey his expectation that she quit her job and stay in the house at all times. Which is when she left. But now she didn't take any crap from men. At least that's what I gathered from her reports on the dates she'd been on.

I, on the other hand, swore to myself after Tommy's death that I would never take crap from a man again, ever. But after a few dates (and the word "date" in my parlance did not mean going to bed—I had sworn off that behavior after too many heartbreaks), what did I find myself doing? Taking crap from them. Little digs, sarcastic comments, criticisms of my body or the way I did things. One guy had criticized, among other things, my handwriting—that it was too spikey. Gheesh!

And to my everlasting exasperation with men, and with myself, I couldn't seem to find a way to stop them from continuing in that vein.

I would not undergo any more men like that, dammit! Or would I, in spite of my best resolves? Dammit!

"What do you think of Justin so far?" She gave me her sideways, curious smile, so endearing.

I dodged a bit of dog poo on the road, which was leading us gently downhill to the pond. We were surrounded by houses. I wished they hadn't been built. I liked things wild.

"I think he has a lot of good traits. Character *is* destiny, you know. Destiny for couples too. He's been nice to waitresses, a good sign, and he's kind and respectful to his mother, an even better sign. But everybody has flaws, and at least one deadly flaw. I want to know what his are. Because a husband's flaws affect the wife so deeply. I have a theory that his flaws affect her even more than hers affect him—men have so much more power in relationships. Because they care less. They are so fortunate to love less intensely."

"What?" Catherine exclaimed. "I don't believe it." She kicked a pebble ahead of her, took three steps, and kicked it again. It clattered cheerfully.

"Jane Austen talks about it in *Persuasion*. That most men recover so much more quickly from broken relationships than women. In her day they hardly mourned a year. In our day, it's three days and on to the next woman, while wives caught in divorce recover slowly—seen it lots of times."

The leaves on the trees around us stirred with a rustle of wind. It cooled the back of my neck on this warm day.

"Well, not all men are cads," Catherine said.

I thought her choice of the word "cad" to be interesting.

"Have you been reading about Wickham lately, like me?" I asked.

"Yes!" Her eyes lit up. I loved it that my best friend loved Jane Austen too. Fabulous!

"My brother has been married for ten years," she continued, "and he's good and supportive to his wife. Definitely not a cad."

"Of course, there are some good men, but they're taken, or they're off the market within three months of losing their wives, and I've never gotten there in time. No, I take it back, I did date a guy fresh out of a divorce. I met him at a church group for singles the night he'd signed the papers. I ended up being his rebound relationship. Dating is so hard. And there are so many unacceptable men at our age. The odds are long against us slightly older, slightly wiser single women."

I kicked a pebble in my path, and Catherine walked up to it and sent it even farther ahead. Kick the can for grown-ups.

"Hey, Trish, you're being a bit negative," she said. "Something good will happen. Look at Justin. How long has he been single?"

"True. It's been a year since his wife died. He's being careful of his young son, I think, not to drag him through a bunch of would-be stepmoms."

"See, there's a good man." It was her turn again to launch the stone. She gave it a shot and it tumbled into the grass by the side of the road.

Within a footstep I found another stone for us to kick. "I guess so. Except I've got to be clear about his weaknesses and how bad they might hurt me, before I commit."

"Oh, just have fun going out on dates. You could be too cautious, and he'll lose interest."

"I know. Thanks for the pressure!" I took a picture of the ripples on the pond. Yes, it was experimental. I wanted to see if the beauty of the light playing on the water's surface came through on film. "I'm determined to have a fantastic life regardless. But I'd love to have children."

Catherine looked wistful. "My brother has little kids, and a baby who's crawling now. I love to watch his little butt bounce as he scoots along. I love toddlers and their tippiness, and three-year-olds and the things they say…I love the whole shebang."

"I wish I could be with my sister's kids. I wish you and I both could have all the kids we want."

Time to change this painful topic.

"Look, Catherine, look at the geese! Watch! They fly so funny as they slow down to land." I got off a few shots of big birds with their wings curled into upside-down U's so they would drop altitude and slow down. They wobbled amusingly as they descended, and they braced their webbed feet forward as they landed, skiing on the surface for a moment and then settling on the pond.

We took photos of water lilies and Siberian irises someone had planted at the water's edge. The pond smelled of decay and mud. Too many people milled around, and we had to wait for them to move out of our shots before we could click the shutter.

It was funny: as one of us would spot something and lift our camera to our eye, the other would say, "Oh, yeah," and take the same shot. We inspired each other and helped one another see things we otherwise would have missed. Our rolls of film ended up looking alike, which made us laugh. We lazed along, soaked in sunlight, enjoyed each other's presence.

Would Justin turn out to be this companionable?

"So," Catherine said with one of her oblique looks, "do you have another date lined up?"

"Nope. He hasn't called in a couple of days."

Catherine was close to the pond's muddy edge, where she was focusing on a solitary mallard, his green head and neck iridescent. She fired off her camera, then eased herself away from the edge. I decided not to imitate that shot. I'd slipped in the smelly mud recently and didn't want to risk it again. At least not so soon.

"Can you call him?" she said from *terra firma*.

"I did call him once last week. It might not be a good idea to call so soon. He might be very traditional. And I am too. My attitude is: you want me? Then pursue me."

"So you're stuck waiting." But she said it with a smile.

"Yes. And all my old issues of 'he's not impressed, I'm not enough' are taking over my poor little brain."

"I know a remedy for that. Make of list of some affirmations."

That was something I'd read about in Twelve Step books. I liked to be sure that lots of wise people agreed with an idea before I lived by it—I am not looking to be the product of a cult. Would affirmations help? My insecurities, like everyone else's probably, ran deep.

"Let's write a list! What would be at the top?" Catherine asked. She leaned over to take a close-up of a dragonfly, its iridescent wings opening and closing on a reed.

"Are these going to be things I need to shore up my confidence in, or things I'm already pretty sure about?"

"Maybe both?" She took two more shots of the insect, giving herself two more chances to get a good photo. Developing film was expensive, and it wasn't cost-effective to take too many shots of the same thing.

My camera was idle, simply hanging from my neck because I was thinking hard about affirmations. "Okay. I'd like to think I'm a very good reporter. I find stories everywhere. Good photojournalist too—I've captured some moments, some action, really well." Of course, I wanted to be not just good but great at both. It would take a lifetime.

"I know you have. What else?"

"I'd like to think I'm creative. Finding stories takes open-mindedness and the ability to notice incongruities. Writing them up truthfully and engagingly is creative also. So's the novel writing and gardening I do."

"True. More. You have a date coming up with an attractive man. You've got to be cognizant of who you are and what you offer." We paced slowly around the pond's edge.

Yeah, I thought subversively, as though confidence like that, which had evaded me thus far in life, would happen within the next few days. But I continued.

"I persevere in life and in my profession like the most dogged climber of Mt. Everest. I dig my crampons into the ice, one after the other."

"I like that. Good image!" She gave me a thumbs up.

"I'm self-disciplined—I get things done."

"Good. One more."

I knew what I wanted to add to the list of affirmations, but I couldn't admit it to Catherine. How could that be? She was my best friend. But I was embarrassed. I couldn't be that vulnerable with her today. I held back.

"No, I think that's it."

"Good. Now write it down, tape it to your mirror, and say it to yourself every morning three times out loud. That's what my therapist taught me to do, and it's helped a lot."

Maybe that's why she's a goddess in her dating life, I thought.

"I wonder," I said, "if you say it first thing, before your mind wakes up and takes over and tells you the same old negative stuff, would it work better?"

"Well, like so much in life, it's a mystery how it works. But psychologists have studied it, and it helps people."

"OK." I hoped it worked mightily, overnight, before Justin called again. And worked in my professional life. And later, in secret, I would add a few items.

We were at the end of our rolls of film, so we walked downtown and dropped them off in the camera shop. While there, I picked up the envelope of my Cindy Pierson photos. Then we went for lunch at a little Italian café specializing in cold cuts on freshly baked bread. We took our sandwiches outside and sat at a table in the shade of the awning. The sandwiches were neat bundles wrapped in white paper. Now, with a table to rest things on, I couldn't wait to see how my photos had turned out.

"Show me," Catherine said.

I slipped the stack out of its white envelope, careful not to scratch the negatives. Here were some surprises: shots I'd forgotten I'd taken. Close-ups of flowers, the petals tight and fresh against each other. Architectural details on people's houses, stark and bold in black and white. I thought glumly that these photos wouldn't bring me the acclaim that Margaret Bourke-White gained for her shots of architectural details. Like earth dams and power stations.

And there was Cindy Pierson, her eyes luminous, her bearing confident, a small smile on her lips as if she felt that being photographed was amusing. I thought I'd caught an essence: of the woman, the artist, the human being. I'd get these over to the *Sentinel* office after lunch—maybe I could forestall the editors from sending a photographer to Cindy's place. And if I couldn't, two or three of these photos would stand up well against anybody else's.

"Terrific shots," Catherine said. "But don't you miss color film?"

What a pleasure to talk with a friend who cared about such things with me. "Sometimes, yes." I slipped the photos into my bag, to keep them out of reach of oil and vinegar. I reached for my tightly rolled-up sandwich and pried loose the bit of tape that held the paper shut. I said to myself, we are not thinking about calories right now. "I like color. But black and white, which I need for the newspaper, forces me to notice shapes and shadows more than just the color of things. I'm glad my journalism work makes me use it. It's good for a photographer's eye."

We talked about Catherine's job a while. She had colleagues in her lab who shared their personal lives perhaps a bit more openly than was wise in a workplace. But it made for interesting lunch talk for us. Then she asked about my job. Dear Catherine, she always showed an interest in me.

I filled her in on the newest details I'd learned about the attack at the museum. "I'd like to help solve it because whoever did it is still walking among us."

"Listen, avoid that place. There's too many tools lying around in there that could beat a human's brains in. I've been there, I've seen 'em." She rolled up the remains of her sandwich, sat back in her café chair, and looked at me with concern in her eyes.

"Yes," I said, "but that's where the solution is. It's probably among the staff, the collection, the displays." Catherine couldn't dissuade me—I was resolved. Crampons into ice.

And I resolved to find and write more stories for next week's editions of the *Sentinel*. It was going to be quite a week.

CHAPTER 25

Catherine had to do her Saturday chores, so we walked from the café to my little cottage and she drove away. I hopped in my car too and blasted off to the Great Swamp. Time to get away from houses and people and get into the wild—at least as wild as densely populated New Jersey could ever be—where I would reflect on the week just past, and the week ahead, without people swerving and darting around me like they had at the pond. Taking time to reflect on my life without distractions was key to my success. Such as it was. I had recently moved up from a weekly to a daily newspaper, so I'd had some success. But it wasn't enough.

Driving to the swamp, which lurked on the far side of the mountain, resplendent in fresh spring leaves on its trees, I considered the list of affirmations I'd shared with Catherine. They'd been mostly professional. Time to get personal.

I wanted to feel that I was beautiful. A quick glance in the rearview mirror showed my blue eyes looking inquiringly back at me. No, I wasn't Hollywood, and I was keenly aware of my figure flaws—too much of a butt and breadbasket. I hoped that by affirming that I was beautiful—in my own unique way—I could heal my negative self-image. Before my next call from Justin. If he called. And if he didn't, the hell with him. No, I didn't mean that.

Could I also credit myself with some inner beauty? That would make the use of the word beautiful even more true. I had a benevolent heart—not always, obviously. I only had whatever benevolence I had because I sought my HP's presence almost every morning, praying C.S. Lewis's prayer: "May the real me pray to the real you." I dug into the Psalms, Gospels, and Twelve

Steps, and I apologized when I was at fault. I asked my Creator to make changes in me, that I be more patient, kind, generous.

As I turned the car onto the gravel road to the swamp, doubts arose in my mind that rattled against my soul's undercarriage like the small stones being kicked up by my tires. I had to admit my insides weren't always that great. Look at how I sometimes (often) resented other people's success. I pictured all that Cindy Pierson had, and my heart clenched.

I pulled into the parking lot for the Great Swamp trails. There were only two other cars. In 8,000 acres, maybe I wouldn't have to encounter any other humans. I liked it that way on these sojourns.

After parking, I crunched down a gravel path between two ponds and soon plunged into the woods. They smelled of leaf mold and of oxygen and of the mysteries of swampy woodlands.

I had not brought my camera. Margaret Bourke-White, one of the best photographers of the 20th century, whose published work I'd perused, probably would have had her camera with her even now.

But I wanted this walk to be time to unplug.

Surrounded by trees, some tall and stately, many short and spindly and struggling toward the light, I came to a small wooden bridge, built over a stream that was drying up after the early spring's usual flood of water. My footsteps sounded hollow on the boards.

Under the canopy of the trees, in light with a chartreuse caste, I wondered why I hadn't been able to add "beauty" to my list in front of Catherine. The answer came to me: because she was so beautiful, and I didn't want to admit my insecurities about my looks to her. She simply was not the right audience for that train of thought. Maybe HP, and no human, would be the one to know about it.

I thought of another characteristic I wanted to add to my list. "I am funny." That was also an aspirational item. I was funny when I talked to myself, or my cat, but I wanted more humor in my life, especially among friends. With Justin too. Who doesn't need to laugh? If I could help people with humor, I'd like that. Opening my heart and my mind to spot the humorous possibilities added such an element of fresh enjoyment to my life. It made an adventure out of a day.

"Let's add 'funny,'" I said aloud to HP. "And I can't do it without you." Without HP in my life, I'd felt dead, trapped in a meaningless system because it ended in death. With him, I had a compass, transcendence, and an eternal, and therefore meaningful, reason for traveling on.

A chipmunk dashed into a hole in the ground just ahead of me on the path. I loved the spotted and striped little creatures, even though they were undermining the back steps of my house.

I padded along another path, wandering with no objective. My thoughts turned to Justin. After ten years of enjoying spectacular single freedom, especially compared to the dreadful alcoholism and caregiving I'd endured, did I really want to be married—sworn for better or worse—and maybe have to do that all over again? Such a risky business, marriage.

But maybe, in Justin, I'd finally met the better man I'd hoped for. Was it possible? Maybe we could swoop and dive and fly, like the swallows that were hunting for bugs over this meadow I'd just entered. Maybe it wouldn't be too late to have the children I'd longed for, the sweet babies to fuss over, as I had over my sister's little ones when they'd first arrived, before she became isolated by her husband and shut me out of her life.

"Please help Susan," I breathed. "What can I do to help her?"

On the boardwalk over the water meadow, a different set of bugs than in the woods careened around my face, and I batted them away. My thoughts drifted on. I was starved for ravishing sex, to be caressed absolutely everywhere—including unlikely places like between my toes. My body was screaming for it. Did the water striders darting on the tepid water beneath my feet feel that way? I longed for an equitable relationship with a great man; and I longed for babies. But I'd learned young that with marriage, my life—physical, intellectual, spiritual—was at stake. Susan and Meg were perfect illustrations of that truth. I gave a breath of a prayer for them both and wondered if I'd ever know what happened to them.

I needed to be wise about men, yet wouldn't it be nice to just melt in Justin's arms...? Maybe I'd end up with everything Cindy had...?

Back under the cover of trees, a squirrel scampered along a fallen log. I directed my mind onto what I could do in the following week to move everything forward.

Then I just strolled, nearly empty-headed finally, and noticed wildflowers along the path between the ponds. The geese honked contentedly on the rippling water.

I followed the gravel path around a bend and saw something writhe near my feet. I screamed and jumped a mile. It was a snake with its jaw grotesquely wide open, teeth clamped onto a frog. The frog was alive, being swallowed from back to front, its webbed feet scrabbling for purchase on the gravel path, desperate to leap forward to freedom.

After all the sweet woodland creatures I'd seen today, chipmunks and squirrels, I was loathe to witness this brutal scene. I wished Justin was with me to do something to intervene. Where was a man when you needed him?

I was totally on the side of the victim, the frog. But there was nothing I could do to help the poor frog other than to kill the snake. Which creature should die? I couldn't answer that question, so I stepped gingerly around the scene of nature taking its course. The picture of that snake's mouth gripping, and the frog trapped, was seared into my mind.

CHAPTER 26

My heart still pounding, I jumped into my car, wishing I'd never seen such a sight. To make the mental image fade, I decided to do one concrete thing: take my photographs of Cindy Pierson to the weekend editor at the *Sentinel*.

I avoided getting into an accident anywhere on Route 22, always an achievement, and arrived safely at the *Sentinel's* newsroom and printing plant. The building hulked on higher ground at the end of a ramp off the highway's high-speed westbound lane. As my car swept up the driveway to the parking lot, I thanked God I was a journalist and not a—well, just about anything else you cared to name. What if I had to work in a plumbing supply store and deal with PVC pipe all day? Or worked in a zoo and fed live animals to the snakes? I couldn't bear it. Instead I got paid to be curious and ask people, all sorts of people, questions. It could not be improved upon.

The glass door between the lobby and newsroom swung toward me with its usual burble, and I was in the inner sanctum, where reporters wrote the news that kept Americans free and politicians honest, or at least more honest than they'd otherwise be if there were no vigorous press to question and expose them.

As a reporter, I felt like Superman—a defender of the American Way. I loved the role and tried to live up to the concept while sitting through meetings of city councils, planning and zoning boards, and boards of education on my beat. I also tried to live up to my ideal when pursuing officials afterward, asking follow-up questions and digging deeper until satisfied that I'd gotten to the bottom of things. Or as nearly as I could get to the real issues while being a person who wasn't allowed to sit in on "executive sessions," where decisions about the salaries of public servants—and who knows what else—were made in private.

The newsroom was quiet on a Saturday afternoon. A few heads were intent over computer screens, but most desks were empty. I spotted the weekend editor, Christine Markham, at her desk at the end of a row of reporters' desks. Perhaps that meant she was first among equals? But she wielded all kinds of editorial power. She deserved an office. However, since she was a she, it didn't look as though she was going to get one. I might be idealistic about the role of journalism in American life, but the same sexist attitudes were prevalent in these corridors as in the rest of the world. I couldn't take on that battle, not yet, especially as a new hire. Christine was going to have to stand up for herself. Or not.

"Hi," I said, "how's it going?"

"Good. Quiet. I'm grateful for that. I want to get out of here at six and go to a family picnic, so no fires, no break-ins, no big accidents, please." Her deep alto voice resonated through the newsroom.

"I wish you luck." I hefted my bag onto a corner of her desk and pulled out the packet of photos of Cindy Pierson. "I'm turning in a story on Monday about the artist and writer who won the Caldecott medal. I have some photos I took of her. Want to see?"

She nodded, so I took the two best and placed them in front of her.

"Hey, these are good. Nice work."

"Maybe the paper doesn't have to spend the money to send a photographer to her place." I hoped my voice didn't betray how badly I wanted to get the photo credit.

"I have the log here," she said, and opened a notebook. "Looks like it was assigned to Brad for Monday. We probably should keep that on the books."

Nuts, I thought. My hopes of my name on the photo—of showing *The New York Times* that I could do it all—plummeted. But my affirmation, "I am perseverant," came to mind. I was persuasive too, another word that started with "p.e.r.s." How many others were there? Perspicacious. Oops, better focus.

"I think I captured her at her best," I ventured. Christine's lips twitched, and I saw that I'd been nailed for praising my own work.

"It sure would save the photographer time," I said.

She twisted a bit in her chair.

"And save the newspaper money," I added.

She ran her fingertips nervously over the keys. They were loose and rattled.

"Okay, yeah, I can cancel it. We'll use yours."

I knew it was within her authority to do so and exulted.

I watched as she changed the log. Then I dug into the envelope again.

"Here's the negatives for the darkroom." I handed her two strips, and with a china pencil she marked the negative that went with each of the two best photos. She gathered the whole collection up into a white envelope, put that in an interoffice envelope, and marked it "darkroom."

Things were going my way—this affirmation business Catherine had given me might help me—but I had to make sure of something else.

"I'd like the photo credit." I kept clippings of the stories I published in newspapers—I had a cardboard box of them under my bed. It was nearly stuffed. Dust bunnies hugged the corners. Maybe that was a better fate than being placed under a cockatoo.

"When you file your story, mention that the photo is yours. That should do it."

"Great! Thanks." I wanted to get away—it was my day off—but had to do it gracefully. "Only an hour to go until you're home free."

"Fingers crossed."

"Enjoy your evening!"

And I sailed out, anticipating this bit of upcoming success. Sailed home on it too. And found the light on my answering machine blinking.

CHAPTER 27

I tried to be nonchalant about the message waiting for me. Then I gave up on that.

"Maybe it's Justin!" I said to Ninja, as he stropped himself against my calves. I got his can of food ready for him and put it down. He nibbled at it in his dignified way.

"Wish me luck, Ninja." I prepared myself for the call to have been from a telemarketer and pushed the play button.

Justin's baritone filled the room.

"Hi! Would you like to grab a bite to eat with me tonight? Mike at the last minute decided to go to his grandmother's for the night, and suddenly I have the evening free. Want to say seven? Let me know."

There was a long pause. What was he thinking but not saying in that pause, I wondered.

"Bye for now."

Respectful tone of voice. A bit sudden for a date—did this mean he expected me in future to always be available at a moment's notice? I'd dated someone like that—it was an oft-repeated form of lack of consideration for my life, I'd decided, and for that and a few other urgent reasons I'd broken it off.

I wanted to keep Justin in my life, not break up with him. This longing and thinking and caution were a pain in the tush. Would I ever be relaxed and trustful with him? I had all the angst in the early stages to get through first.

I called him back. At the risk of being too available, that old game, I told him that I could go. I heard the smile in my own voice. We picked the local pub at seven o'clock, and I hung up happy.

"If any more good things happen today, I will float away." Ninja regarded me with skepticism.

CHAPTER 28

J ustin knocked just before seven on Saturday night. I opened the front
door and marveled at how good it felt to be pursued by a handsome man,
dressed nicely, apparently in his right mind. So many men I'd dated
hadn't met some of those qualifications. My mother had said to give men
more of a chance, so I did and found that my first instinct—this is not a
romantic interest for me—had been correct. But Justin was one, no doubts
there.

He drove me to the pub in his Jaguar. Very high marks because it
appeared he was also financially solvent enough to own a high-end car.

Why was a man this cool interested in me? He could have any woman.
Why did he keep asking me out?

He opened the door of the Jag for me—Tommy would not have, even
in our best, early days. Justin also held the door of the pub. I felt like a
princess. Where was the pea?

We enjoyed a surprise. The best booth in the pub, in an alcove next to
the front door, was open and nobody else was in line for it. We could be
together in a quiet, intimate spot but still enjoy the good cheer of the pub's
ambience.

After we had each ordered a cheeseburger, with a glass of beer in front
of him—I'd be alert to how quickly he drank it—and a glass of cab sav in
front of me, he asked,

"What's been happening?"

I was astounded and pleased. He looked interested, ready to listen. Was
he really? I was determined to be alert and not get swept away.

"Went on a photo shoot with my friend Catherine. Got some great shots." Did photos of loopy-looking geese count as great shots? I thought I wouldn't backpedal and would let my statement stand. With qualification. "I think. I'll find out when I pick up the prints."

He nodded. I took that as a sign to continue.

"I attended some planning and zoning meetings on my beat last week. Each time, I found the story, which isn't easy to do in the sea of facts that developers toss around in those meetings. I nailed the stories, in my opinion."

"I read those—they were great stories, with a problem and at least a proposed solution. Way to go."

"You read my stories?" I was dazed. Nobody I'd ever dated before had bothered.

"Sure. You're my favorite reporter. Plus I want to know what my competition is up to."

Wow. I couldn't take it all in.

"What else last week?" he asked.

His eyes hadn't glazed over yet, as those of so many men had while listening to me describe, in as few words as I could, what I'd been up to. Before they launched into an hour-long account of their day.

"I interviewed a marvelous artist who won a national award, who lives right here in Passaic. Can you believe all the talent in this little town?"

He smiled, with that pirate twinkle in his eye that so thrills me.

"Yes, I believe it," he said.

I couldn't talk. I was blushing, I was gasping for air figuratively. Was he saying he wanted to be with me because he thought I was a talented human being? Maybe not just in bed, which is what men seemed to focus on first, but because being with a talented person is more interesting, fun? Maybe that's why he was dating me? Instead of feeling threatened by me and my development of my gifts, he relished it? How marvelous could one man be?

I struggled to get myself back on track. I'd get him to do some talking so I'd have time to regain my equilibrium. It was nice to feel this attracted.

"How was your week?" I asked.

"I submitted plans for a development to a Planning Board in South Jersey. It's a strip mall, not my favorite project, which is big houses. But my new partner wants to do it, so ..."

When he spoke, he didn't get white saliva in the corner of his mouth, as one of my previous dates had. He spoke in full sentences, he cooperated with his partner. Would he cooperate with a wife? I'd learned that I couldn't assume that. Even men who had daughters that they presumably wanted to do well in life could be nasty toward their female partners.

The food arrived, smelling and looking great. Like Justin, I thought. I found I wasn't too hungry, with my stomach all aflutter with possibilities. Maybe we could share life …

Slow down, I cautioned myself.

Justin was eating his burger with gusto yet not getting ketchup all over himself. Another plus. But always hovering in my mind was the great profit and loss statement of marriage: gain companion, sex, children. Lose freedom, independence, come under the sway of another's flaws and limitations. I wondered what both his business and personal asset and liability sheets said. Debt? Was that Jag going to be repo'd? Even so, the sex would be great!

I was still rattled by that twinkle in Justin's eyes and hadn't come up with anything to say for a while, because my thoughts were unacceptable to be said out loud. The lull in our conversation kind of freaked me out. I tried to be Native American about it and tell myself that not every moment has to be filled with talk. But it didn't work, and I said the first thing that came into my head.

"Speaking of strip malls, I saw a new one going up in Fanwood last week. Quite the disaster architecturally—no room for a tree or a flower box or anything except cars."

Justin's face froze.

Oops. I had insulted strip malls. I had broken the first rule of establishing a future with a man. It's unfortunate, but a fact of life for my generation, that she who holds her tongue will get her man. And here I'd gone and insulted his line of work. Once safely married and pregnant, I could criticize strip malls to my heart's content. Though that would hardly be fair to him, since he'd be expecting a wife who admired every hut he put up.

"But I'm sure it will be useful," I said, backpedaling. "I use the shops in strip malls all the time myself, to get through life. We need 'em, that's for sure."

Oh damn. Justin was still looking at me with a serious expression. I've insulted him, I thought, it's over. He tossed back some beer and set the mug down. I was frozen in silence.

"How does space for six blooming trees and flower planters sound?"

Were they already built into the plan, or was he adjusting his plan for me? I was a journalist and wanted to know. Both would be good but already built into the plan would be better. Could I find out without further offending?

"That's in the plans?" I asked.

"From the start." And he smiled and threw himself back, relaxing in his chair.

I laughed with relief. He had forgiven me, and he was designing green. Sort of.

"I'm glad!" I said, though secretly I wished all strip malls would be stripped from the earth. I'm nothing if not a hypocrite.

With that potential disaster disarmed, the mellow atmosphere of the pub finally soothed me, or maybe it was the cabernet. We talked about his son Mike (age fourteen but not a problem, his father said [not yet anyway, I thought]); about the Yankees (in whom I had little interest, but I listened and asked follow-up questions); about journalism (he thought most newspapers supported liberal viewpoints and derided conservative thinking too much, and I only partially agreed but managed not to be strident about it); and then the weather.

Justin paid the check, a custom I wasn't entirely comfortable with since it seemed to put the woman under obligation, but I let it go. I didn't want to be the one woman he dated who insisted on paying her own way. It would make me one of a kind—I would stand out in his mind—but possibly in a bad way, as being too unconventional.

I noted that he had drunk only the one beer and had even left an inch. He was not an alcoholic. Not yet anyway.

He drove me home. I was in a sweat about kissing goodnight. Would he make the move? Would things escalate too rapidly? Was I going to have to be stronger than I wanted to be?

He parked in my driveway, and we embraced in the front seat for a moment. Then he broke it off and walked me to my door.

"I had a nice evening," he said.

"Me too, very much so." I wanted to kiss him, but he didn't initiate so I didn't, which kept things cooler, which was good.

Ninja hovered by the front door as I opened it. I waved to Justin through the storm door as he backed out of the driveway and headed down the street.

"I like him very much," I cooed to Ninja as I closed the big oak door. "And I think you're a honey too!" I scooped him up and kissed him as Justin's elegant taillights disappeared from view through my picture window.

CHAPTER 29

I walked in town Monday morning, stretching my legs because I had an evening meeting to cover and I would be sitting, in the council chambers and then at the newsroom, for hours—until midnight at least.

I passed a playground. Young mothers pushed babies in bucket swings. Toddlers played in the sandbox or lurched adorably across the grass to their mothers on park benches. Wow, miniature humans are winsome! I wanted a couple of these little people of my own to welcome into my arms, to call me 'mama' in piping little voices. Oh yes. My body was a swamp of desire for babies, for procreation, for small noggins to kiss and cheeks to caress as I'd seen my sister Susan do to my niece and nephew.

I thought of the deep trouble my sister was in, and Meg too, and said a prayer for them.

Pulling my eyes away from the littles because I didn't want to look like a crazy person who stares at children on playgrounds, I marched along in the June sunshine. At home, I worked on my novel for a while, ate lunch, packed some dinner, and drove to the *Sentinel*.

Arriving without crashing or being crashed into on Route 22, certainly an outcome to be desired, I marched to my desk and tossed my purse into an empty drawer. I looked around—too early for most of the staff to be there, except for the three journalists who wrote for the business section. Their jobs tended to be more nine to five. Lucky them. I wouldn't work on that section of the newspaper if you paid me. Dullsville.

I noticed the darkroom door was shut, though the red light was off. Those guys breathed entirely too many chemicals, in my opinion. I knocked on the door so they'd open it and breathe some normal air, which in Central Jersey, with all its oil refineries and pharma, isn't saying much.

Mike, my favorite darkroom guy, opened the door. He was lurchingly adorable, like the toddlers in the park, only he was six-foot-five inches or so, like Lurch on the *Addams Family*. He was also ten years younger than me. And had a wife. Oh well.

"Hey, Trish. What's up?"

"Hey, Mike. I'm just making sure you got an envelope with pictures and negatives of Cindy Pierson."

"Who?"

I began to get a sinking feeling.

"Christine put them in an interoffice envelope on Saturday afternoon."

"I didn't get an envelope with my name on it."

"She addressed it to the darkroom."

"No interoffice envelopes at all."

"Yikes, it had my negatives in it."

"Come on in and we'll look for it."

We searched for fifteen minutes, in the darkroom and then the mailroom and then we took it upon ourselves to look in Christine's inbox and outbox. I also riffled over the stuff on top of her desk—did it tastefully.

It became evident that it was hopeless.

"Mike, they were great photos," I wailed. "I captured a great expression on her face. This is just awful."

"I'm really sorry. But you're good, Tricia, I bet you can get good photos again."

I debated telling him about the other sabotage I suspected had been directed at me in the newsroom. Should I enlist another pair of eyes to watch for the culprit? Yes, I decided. We had enough fellow feeling between us, as photography buffs, that I could be pretty sure he'd be on my side. Unless he were the saboteur. Oh no, don't let this make you paranoid, Trish, I thought.

"Come here, Mike," and I led him back into the darkroom. We could talk more privately there. I closed the door behind him. Let everyone in the newsroom smirk at us. I hoped no one called his wife with a baseless allegation. A low white light was the only illumination. The chemical smell was strong but not unpleasant.

Mike towered over me, then leaned against a countertop. Which meant he still towered.

My goodness, I do like tall men! And around us it was dark, wasn't that suggestive? I remembered the pain of mourning the loss of Tommy. I wouldn't put a fellow woman through that by fooling around with her man. But oh my goodness. Well.

"I think somebody is sabotaging me here in the newsroom." I told him about the notes that I was quite sure had been deleted from my computer, and now this, the photos.

"Whoa, that's serious." Mike continued to lean but crossed one leg over the other. That was a lot of long, slim leg. His wife was a lucky woman to have all that to kiss.

"Would you watch with me? If you see someone approach my desk, would you let me know?" If Mike was the saboteur, he'd be warned by what I was saying, and that worked for me too.

"Sure. But I work with the door closed a lot of the time."

"Yes, I know, but still."

"Will do. How's it going otherwise?"

What a wonderful thing for a man to ask a woman! To ask such a question, he couldn't possibly be the saboteur. His wife was super lucky.

"Things are okay." I wasn't going to delve into my dating or Twelve-Step life with him. Let's stick to photography. "Went on a photo shoot Saturday."

"Yeah, I do those too."

We chatted a while about f stops and such. He had some pointers for me, and I had one for him. He showed me a few of his photos. They were strong and good. I told him so.

"You've had some good shots too, Tricia. Keep up the good work."

I opened the door and glanced around the newsroom. Nobody was paying the slightest attention, as far as I could tell. It was creepy to think that someone among my colleagues, writing at their various island desks in the sea of office furniture, had malevolent feelings about me.

Could I be so sure? I called Christine Markham at home to find out if she'd taken the envelope home with her. She hadn't. She didn't seem very concerned about what might have happened to my photos. They were just great photos in my life's body of work, that's all.

But I had a thought.

"Christine, do you remember who was in the office when I was with you on Saturday afternoon?"

"Why, you suspect somebody?"

Oops. I didn't want to be labeled as a paranoid, problem employee. Christine saved me.

"Well, I guess there aren't too many other explanations for it."

She gave me a list of people she'd seen in the office over the weekend, while she was in charge. But she pointed out that the night editor would have seen other people.

I thanked her for her help, trying to project that I was sane rather than paranoid, and called the night editor to ask the same question in a reasonable way. He gave me a list too.

Now I had a foundation to work from. I knocked on Mike's door again and gave him the list of number one suspects—a dozen people who were in the newsroom over the weekend *and* when my notes had been erased. I thanked him for any watching he could do.

I went to my weekday editor, Paul Tercell, ensconced in his corner office as befits a man, and told him my photos and negatives had disappeared from the mail system—it wouldn't hurt for him to know that—and asked if I could be assigned to retake pictures of Cindy Pierson. He said yes, so I phoned her and made an appointment for later that afternoon.

When I turned up at her door, she was wearing a white, paint-spattered man's big shirt and black leggings. So she *had* dressed up for our first interview.

"Come on in," she said, and once again walked down the hall like a hiker accustomed to traversing rough terrain—strong and steady footsteps, firmly planted.

"I have nice news you can add to your story," she said, sitting on a low-slung Danish chair and gesturing me to another.

"Yes? What's up?"

"Something wonderful has happened." She brought her strong-looking artist's hands together, fingertips touching, fingers stubby. Then she interlaced them. "I was contacted by ABC's *Good Morning America* to be interviewed on their show!"

"That's wonderful news," I said. Holy moly, I thought, the blessings keep rolling in for her.

"I'm very excited to be on national TV. It's quite the honor."

Will you wear clothes with no paint for *that* interview, my mean mind asked.

"When does this happen?" I said. "I'll try to get your story into the paper in time, so people can watch it." Though was that what I really wanted? Now, now, Trish, professionalism, I coached myself.

"Tuesday. My interview will take place at 8:50 a.m. exactly, they said."

"I'll include that in my story. Congratulations!"

Congratulate her on what that means for her book sales, the itty bitty shitty committee told me. You, by contrast, will never be on national TV. You'll never even be on the local station. Face it, she's got star power and you don't.

I was swimming in envy at that point, though I was fighting to do a good interview and to connect emotionally so that I'd get a good photo again. Like I'd had to do in the corporate world, before Tommy died and I switched careers to work as a reporter, I was acting like a duck—looking calm and collected on the surface and paddling for dear life underneath. Unfortunately, today my feet were caught in the Sargasso Sea's tangle of negativity. And the sharks were lurking.

I had to be a professional and draw her out to make the story I wrote more interesting. "Tell me how you found out about this great news."

"It was just like the phone call about the Caldecott medal. It was completely unexpected. I was in here working. I left a smear of cerulean blue paint on the telephone because my husband's voice, when he told me there was a phone call for me, was so excited that I didn't take time to wipe my hands."

"Who called you?" I wondered if it had been one of the stars of the show.

"It was someone on the staff, asking if I'd come in for a live interview. Of course, it was wildly exciting. I never imagined."

"How are you going to celebrate?" I thought readers would like to know.

Cindy blushed a bit. I could guess one means of celebration.

"Well, we've booked a flight to Aruba. We're taking our kids too."

Blessing upon blessing was pouring into her life. A husband and children to celebrate it all with. My heart felt sour. The thought popped in my head: I'll stop being so careful about going to bed with Justin, see if he doesn't marry me. I'll take a shortcut to getting the husband, the house, the children, the celebrations.

My deepest gut told me that something about it wasn't good. But I stifled it.

I couldn't bring myself to ask her any more questions. I just didn't want to hear any more about her success. Feeling morose, but projecting good cheer, I hoped, I asked to retake her picture. She asked if she should take off her smock, and I said no. She posed next to an easel and in her garden, as she had the first time.

A cloud of self-criticism descended on me. With my inner turmoil, was I connecting with Cindy well enough to get a good photo? Was I getting her at her best, full of feeling and expression? I wasn't sure.

Glum inside, I smiled and thanked her for her time and drove away, all kinds of envy eating away at my insides.

CHAPTER 30

Next day, I was low on local story ideas, so I phoned the police station to check their blotter. The sergeant in charge of which information got released answered. I had met him in person and knew that he happened to be a hunk. I could not get over the breadth of his chest. I tried to get my mind back on the topic at hand. But my body, as usual, was screaming to be ravished.

He gave me the biggest news first. "Samantha Scarborough died last night. So we're looking at murder, not just assault."

Suddenly my attention was focused. "I'm so sorry to hear that." The stakes of solving the mystery of who attacked the curator were now even higher. The poor woman. Her poor family. "Did she have children?"

"She leaves behind a husband and two boys in their early teens."

"Oh, that's going to be so hard for them." I thought, the father would be involved with a new woman within a few months, but the boys had lost their mother forever. I breathed a tiny prayer for these two children. The sergeant was silent too. Then I gathered myself together to ask more questions while I had him on the line—he could be called away at any moment.

"What more can you tell me?"

"The medical examiner is doing an autopsy to determine the exact cause of death. But since she was only in her forties, my guess is, and this is just my personal, unofficial guess, he'll say that she died of her injuries. Don't quote me."

"Okay." I was pleased that he trusted me enough to give his opinion—if I betrayed him and quoted him, he could be fired or disciplined. "When will you have the M.E.'s report?"

"I wasn't informed about that."

"Okay, thanks."

The sergeant always spoke to me with warmth in his voice. I was in his good graces, but only as long as I reported police activity in such a way that the men and women in blue were shown doing their jobs competently. But I couldn't lie to my readers—that was the number one rule of ethical journalism. If I saw something wrong, I was going to have to screw up my courage and report it. And maybe lose a taillight to a baton at a pretend traffic stop. I'd heard other reporters talk about it.

"I'll wait for the M.E.'s report," I said. And I didn't say: I won't quote you because I don't need an enemy in the police department. And I admire your bravery as someone who goes into unknown situations to protect people from each other. And I like you too. But if the police screw up, don't cause me any trouble for reporting it. Because my newspaper would back me up in revealing the truth.

As they say, sergeant, don't mess with someone who buys ink by the pound.

CHAPTER 31

I drove to the museum. Dorothy Anderson had banned me from going in, but she hadn't said anything about the parking lot, which is where I planned to wait for the two volunteers, Virginia and Benjamin, whoever appeared first. I needed their comment on Samantha's death for my story, since they were people who worked at the museum. If I didn't get the comments of people involved in the museum, my editor, Paul, would consider the story insufficient. That was unacceptable to me. But I was not calling Samantha's family. I gave that up for Lent.

It was nearly lunchtime, so I didn't have to wait too long before Benjamin drove up and parked to take his shift. I positioned myself between him and the walkway to the museum door, not wanting to lurk too close to his car.

He was looking at his feet, with a brown bag in his hand, as he approached me.

"Mr. Long?"

He looked up and smiled, then, perhaps as he remembered Dorothy Anderson's banishment of me, he frowned.

"I'd so much appreciate your comment on the fact that Samantha died in the hospital last night. Could you help me?"

"Well, I'm not sure." He looked at the rose bushes blooming against the museum's wall. "Actually, I don't think Dorothy would fire me. There isn't a long line of people waiting to volunteer huge chunks of time here. What do you want to ask?"

"What's your reaction to this news?"

"I'm shocked. Saddened that Samantha has died and left two young boys behind."

He paused and seemed to be groping for words. I kept my silence to give him a chance to express his thoughts.

"I hope the person responsible is locked up forever," he added. Not the type of comment that a perpetrator would make, it seemed to me. But I was still wondering why Virginia had interrupted herself when talking about him during our first interview. I had to be suspicious of everyone to the very end.

I couldn't expect much more comment from Benjamin. Paul, I thought, you'll have to be happy with this. That's it, I'm done asking this docent for comment on this painful event. "Thank you," I said.

"If you wait a moment, Virginia should be out. I'm relieving her for lunch."

"Thanks! And I'm so sorry about what's happened. This attack must be frightening for the museum staff. And for the rest of us here in Passaic."

"So true." He continued slowly up the walk. He had helped me, a real gentleman. I waited, looking at the stonework of the museum's outer walls, the architectural details under the eaves, and the stained glass windows, with sun reflecting off them. Sure enough, Virginia appeared while Benjamin was still going up the walk to the front door. When they reached each other, Benjamin put his arms around her, and she leaned into him as only a romantic partner can. Ah, so this is why she'd broken off her comment about him! A mystery solved! How nice for them, finding love.

Then they broke away and Benjamin continued up the walk. Because she was heading down a different walk, toward the shops in town, I scooted to catch up with her.

"Virginia!" I called out to her while still ten feet behind her. Startled, she spun around and tottered, losing her balance. I lunged forward to save this fragile little soul and grabbed her elbow to steady her.

"Tricia! I never expected to see you."

Well, yes, Dorothy had given me my marching orders in clear terms right in front of Virginia. But that had been inside the building and here we were, in God's great outdoors. So she should have expected me, was my thinking.

"Please, could I have a few words for my readers? How are you reacting to the news of Samantha's death?"

"Don't you think you ought to go to Dorothy, or a Board member?"

This tiny sprite was correcting my journalism method.

"I was going to call Dennis Palmer next," I said defensively. Who likes to be told by an outsider how to conduct oneself in one's profession? "And someday soon I'll approach Dorothy again. Got any ideas for me, how to get on her good side?"

"Probably not by lurking in the parking lot to interview people who come out of the museum," Virginia said. "And then quoting them in an article Dorothy's bound to read."

She had a point. And she packed a punch expressing it.

I could see I was stuck with not using Benjamin's quote and with trying to get quotes from people higher up the chain of command, who tended to be more guarded and circumspect and all those other nasty qualities, anathema to a good story. And in Dennis's case, there would be a prime nasty quality that I wanted to shout from the rooftop of Goldman Sachs' tower in New York City. Not that anybody would hear me up there on the windswept helicopter pad.

"Well, you are quite right," I said. She had saved me from making a mistake while I tried to do a Dorothy workaround. "I'll call Dennis."

But oh, how I'd rather have nothing more to do with him.

CHAPTER 32

I headed to the newsroom. My thoughts turned to Justin—the breadth of *his* chest, his smile, that twinkle in his eye—as I drove in the sunshine.

And oops, I made an error on Route 22. I was in the middle lane, and the offramp for the *Sentinel* was fast approaching off the right lane. There was a space just my Corolla's size in the speeding line of cars in that lane. In New Jersey, you put your blinker on at exactly the same moment you darted into the desired lane. If you gave people warning, they would speed up and block you. If that happened, I'd be in dire straits, having to find a U-turn, and then another, to get back into the westbound lane, taking risks with my life each time.

The Corolla had more scoot than drivers of BMWs and Audis expected, and it slotted nicely into the opening. Needless to say, my maneuver cost me—the driver behind me punished me with his supremely loud horn for an unrelenting sixty seconds. But I made it onto the desired offramp. I punished him in return, with a gesture made through my window, though he was ignorant of it, he being a mile down the road by that time. I repented of my own nastiness, though I didn't chase him to roll my window down and apologize. The whole incident had aged me a bit. Driving in New Jersey, and especially on Route 22, takes NASCAR skill and nerve. And you often arrive at your destination shaking.

I headed immediately for my desk and dialed Dennis's number in his office tower. The incident on Route 22 was already receding, being par for the course.

I reached him easily. And I wondered at that. Shouldn't he be in a meeting where hundreds of millions of dollars in profit was being discussed? Or at least be pretending to be in one? Why was he so accessible? I shook off the foreboding I felt. I thought of him hitting Meg and how warped that was. I'd much rather have stuck with Benjamin Long's comments, gathered outside the museum.

"Hello, Mr. Palmer," I said, sad that I was giving him even that much of an honorific. "I was hoping you could tell me your reaction, as a Board member, to the news about Samantha today."

"We—I'm speaking for the whole Board—are deeply saddened by this loss of a talented person who had so many good plans for the museum."

I wondered if he'd mention Samantha's family—did his mind ever run in any kind of sympathetic track?

"She was going to bring us into the modern era, and we'll miss her. And we're full of sympathy for her family." So he was capable of feeling with people. Or maybe he simply knew the social niceties to say.

"Will you continue to look for a replacement for Samantha?" Wow, in my curiosity I sounded indifferent to Samantha's death—cold, like an investment banker so busy peering into a profitable future he can't see harms being done in the present. Yet while I had him on the line, I had to ask the questions that would be on readers' minds.

"I'm sure in due course we'll resume our search for new a new curator, but that won't be right away. We need to honor Samantha and her service to the museum, even though it was cut so short."

Well said, Dennis, you scum, I thought. It was time, while he was being so pleasant, to take a risk on asking a repeat question. That's me, always digging for more.

"What do you think could be a motive for someone to hit Samantha so hard that she died from it?"

"I won't speculate. I'll leave the investigation to the police."

Well, that shut down all the fun. Though I had known before I asked that he wouldn't speculate. Not to a reporter. But it was good tactics to ask anyway.

"Who else will you be calling?" he asked.

"I want to interview Dorothy," and here I stopped to consider. Dare I present my Dorothy troubles to Dennis? Would he cut me off and never comment again, or would he help me? I decided to risk it. "But she has declared a moratorium on me and possibly all reporters. I am at a standstill there. I don't know what to do."

Did I sound a bit like a helpless woman? Well, that act worked on a lot of men.

"I'll talk to her for you," Dennis said.

Yay! I thought. "She banned me from the museum too, and I really need to visit it again. Gotta explore the exhibits, which I haven't had a chance to do." Time to tell him what was in it for him, or at least for the museum. "Please remind her that, as a reporter, I can be useful to the museum—raise its profile, generate interest in it. And since I'm with the *Sentinel,* I can reach all of Central Jersey, not just people in Passaic."

I held my breath.

"I'll mention all that to Dorothy. Hang tight. I'll let you know what happens."

If he hadn't been abusing Meg, I would have been more profuse in my thanks. But thank him I did. If it weren't for that horrendous side of him, he would truly be a great guy and not just a typical abuser who projected goodheartedness in public.

But maybe Meg was right to entertain hope for him to change. I decided to hang tight and see what happened.

CHAPTER 33

Catherine and I went to a movie Friday night. Justin hadn't called. Worrisome. It bugged me how greatly it bothered me that I hadn't heard from him. Let a man into your life and be subject to negative emotion. I'd found that not dating was so much more peaceful than dating.

Yet I was drawn to this man. I felt a bungee cord fastened to my middle, pulling me inexorably toward him. Did he feel the tug too?

At the same time that I was disappointed Justin hadn't called, I was glad to go out with a girlfriend. I had learned, when Tommy died, that married-couple friends disappear when a spouse disappears. For several months after his death, I felt desperately isolated because women from our couples' group didn't return my calls. I felt utterly alone until new friendships gelled, most of them with people in the Steps. Whether married or single, dating or not, I knew to cultivate my single female companions because they're the ones who'll see me through.

Catherine was single now, but she was so beautiful, it seemed to me she'd be remarried in pretty good order. Though it had been four years since she escaped the horror that had been her husband. What was taking so long?

We drove to the cinema to see *My Cousin Vinnie,* and we laughed with relish. Then we went to an afterhours dessert café to discuss the film, and life in general.

With a glass of Chardonnay in front of me and a virgin piña colada in front of Catherine, who didn't like the taste of alcohol, we recounted scenes from the movie.

"I love it when Marisa Tomei stamps her foot like the ticking of a clock—her biological clock," I said. "Mine is winding down while we speak."

Oh dear, I was back to that topic. I simply did not want to miss the baby experience. I would feel cheated by life if I did.

"Yeah, how's it going with Justin?" Leave it to Catherine to get to the crux of the matter.

"Had a nice date last Saturday night. I've been thinking I'll just stop being so cautious and do what everyone else is doing and fall into bed and see if we don't end up married."

"Whoa," said Catherine. "Whoa!"

"But that artist, Cindy Pierson, has it all," I protested. "I'll bet she wasn't so careful and just went with her urges. She got her man, the beautiful house and garden, the kids, the freedom to do her art."

"You don't know that, and you're not thinking clearly. Let's talk about what people in our culture don't talk about." She took a sip of her piña colada and sat back in her chair with a thunk. "Tricia, what about ethical sex?"

I went silent, and the genteel tinkling sound around me, of silverware on cake plates, increased. Then that went silent too, as I dove deeper. I would be rigorously honest with myself—a quick, personal promise. I knew in my heart of hearts what she was talking about, but I wanted what I wanted, dammit, and tomorrow wasn't soon enough. I'd read recently that women my age were at the peak of their sexual desire. It had to be true—my body was screaming day and night for a good tussle in bed.

"Ethical sex? So how do you define it?" I asked. I wanted to know what she thought and very much did not want to know. I needed to express myself sexually, and it was painful not to. I gulped my wine for fortitude.

"Don't use people. Don't use them for experiments with how it's going to work out, or your level of attraction, or what your gender proclivities are. You can figure that out better if you don't get physical, so you can see things clearly without the fog of sex. Don't use people to get your needs met briefly. That's like taking them on a roller coaster ride and throwing them off. At the top. People get deeply hurt."

Catherine sat forward and looked at me intently, a blush on her cheeks. "I have enough experience with this to know what I'm talking about." Then she flopped back in her chair.

The question of when Justin and I would have a strong enough friendship to take the next step had dogged me, but I didn't want this to be the answer. I knew what she was saying was true, deep in my bones, but I didn't want it to be true. It was too difficult to wait, to be counter-cultural. Men expected us to put out. Justin would at some point. I didn't want to be the proverbial stick in the mud. He might leave me. And besides, I was horny as hell.

"What harm? If it's consenting adults?"

"Sex is holy." Catherine flicked back her red curls. "We get knit to the core of another person. Sex without commitment to your partner's lifetime well-being is using people."

Aw, shit, I thought. This wasn't the way people lived these days. I didn't want to be an oddball. Though maybe I was already, running around finding stories instead of doing paperwork in an office. "But if people consent? Come on, Catherine, surely that's okay." It had to be okay. I couldn't do this.

"Using people is wrong. Just because two people agree to it, it's still wrong."

The waitress came by and asked if we needed anything. A great night with Justin, I thought. And soon. But you can't help me with that.

I dragged myself back to the present moment. "Sex outside of marriage is very popular. Waiting 'til marriage is not what our culture believes in."

She fiddled with her long-stem glass. "Most religions and cultures for thousands of years have encouraged people to wait until marriage. Wisdom of the ages."

"I didn't know you were quite so . . . adamant."

"I speak from experience. Open your legs and you open yourself to being used and dumped. When you say, 'not until the second ring,' you quickly sort the boys from the men, the guys who just want an affair from the men who could commit. You spare yourself a lot of unnecessary heartache—"

"—Yeah, and miss out on pleasure."

"For a few minutes. Then comes the cost. The hurt of giving everything and then he doesn't call. Ever."

Yes, I'd been in a few situations that hadn't been at all wise.

"Trish, here's what makes me strong. The number one reason to forego sex outside of marriage is that God, our beautiful Savior, asks us to. For our own happiness."

I loved Jesus. I also wanted what I wanted when I wanted it.

"It's not just spiritual. It's practical. I have a girlfriend who lived with a man who waited years—a decade—to ask her to marry him. It's a terrible way to live. For a long time she was good enough to screw but not good enough to commit to. Her self-esteem got trashed."

I twiddled my fork. I'd seen the same things. Yet the cost of bucking my culture's mores ... maybe closing the goody shop was why Catherine wasn't remarried yet.

"But sex outside of marriage is not the most important issue," Catherine said.

"Yeah? What is?" It would be relief to have a change of subject.

Catherine was sitting up, leaning toward me, her freckled cheeks pink with emotion. "Forgiveness. You gotta be forgiven by God, in the way it says in the Jesus stories, not in any old way that you come up with yourself. Writing your sins on a scrap of paper and burning it won't do it. God is holy, and you gotta get cleansed the way he says to do it if you want to live on after your body dies. And you gotta forgive others to be forgiven of your own junk." She lifted her drink to her lips and took a dainty sip. "I'm still working on forgiving my former husband. He ruined what could have been a beautiful thing."

"I know how that feels. I still resent Tommy at times, and it's been ten years."

"When I escaped Henry, I felt as if a cliff of rocks fell on me—anger and resentment pinning me down under a rockslide. I couldn't dig out in my own strength. I asked HP to help me, and I'm busting up the rocks. It's been slow. But real. 'It is for freedom that Christ has set us free.' From resentment, anger, the desire for revenge. Not to mention sin, destructive habits, guilt, shame, and all that."

Catherine flung her red curls over her shoulder. They slipped to the front again immediately. "Which brings us to what an excellent Savior he is. When we find our innermost identity in him, we're at peace."

I read the Bible and knew that. I just wasn't sure I wanted to live up to it right now.

I had only known Catherine for a year and didn't know her dating life before she'd made her decision about ethical sex. Sex without commitment might not be ethical, but how did modern dating work with that constraint? I was curious, so I brought the conversation back to a discussion that I almost didn't want to have. "How is your dating life without sex?"

"Well, I get dates, and the real men agree to those boundaries. But one of them, after a while—he whined like a baby. Off-putting. Glad I didn't marry *him.*"

Wow.

"But I met someone who I think might go the distance," she said. "We'll have to see. I'm hopeful."

"Who? Tell me!"

"I met him at church last week. He's going after his Master of Divinity. They just hired him as a youth pastor."

Men in church were as randy as other men, I'd learned, but maybe someone with a true relationship with a Higher Power could wait. Especially if he read his Bible. Not everyone in church did.

"How old is this guy?" I was picturing someone just out of college.

"About our age. He traded stocks for a while and couldn't find any meaning in it. I suspect he made a pile, though, because he can afford to be a youth pastor and go to school."

"Nice!"

"I'm hopeful he'll agree with me that the commitment comes with the second ring. With the vows before God and man. There's some dating to be done before we have that discussion. He has to earn my trust, and I'm afraid I'm a little difficult to win over, after all that's happened. But if he does, I'll talk to him about it."

And I was certain Catherine would. "You're lucky—I mean blessed—to meet a man like that."

"We'll see how it goes. But in the meantime, Tricia, don't throw caution to the wind. It's disaster for your soul."

I gave her a quick nod, that I'd heard her, and looked around the café. The lights were dim, the atmosphere romantic. Couples were sharing a drink and a piece of cake before going off to boink. I wished I were among their number. To have no sex until the second ring? Who operated like that in today's world? "Waiting is tough," I said.

"Yes, it is. But we know from bitter experience, at least I do, that we thrive best when walking with God. He doesn't want to kill the fun but to spare us from use, abuse, and unnecessary heartache. And from wasting our precious time on affairs when our clocks are ticking. We waste so much energy grieving these fly-by-night relationships."

I thought of guys I'd dated since Tommy died. "True."

"And when we nurture our connection to God—Step Eleven—well, it's sweeter than putting out for some guy when so many of them move on. Or life pulls the couple apart when they're more likely to stay together with a public commitment."

I knew what she was saying was true in a God-sense. But it was so difficult human-wise. Catherine was a Jesus-follower. I was too but wishing I could have extra-curricular activities. He sure expected a lot from his people.

For now, I'd take it under advisement.

CHAPTER 34

I t was Tuesday morning, and I was at the *Sentinel* when Paul Tercell stopped by to see me. As soon as he leaned against Henry Burnham's desk next to me—stiffly, in a muscle-bound way, as usual—I realized that I still hadn't turned in my Cindy Pierson story, especially with the update that she would appear on Good Morning America. This morning.

"Where does that artist's story stand?" he asked.

"I can have it to you in a few minutes," I replied. "I also got a new set of photos, since the first set disappeared. They're in the darkroom being processed."

"Okay, get it to me as soon as possible. It'll go into tonight's edition." He walked away, and I regarded his receding backside. He was married and no doubt didn't wait for the second ring. How was that going to work for me?

Then the matter at hand came crashing in on me. Oh boy, I had screwed up. I had sat on Cindy's story until it was too late to tell readers that they could see her this morning on TV. And I'd made Paul come looking for the story instead of submitting it in a timely fashion.

Why had I delayed so long? I thought about it, drilled down within myself, as the Twelve Steps had taught me to do, asked my HP to help me be rigorously honest with myself, waited for the truth to reveal itself, and realized it had been out of envy. Because I resented her success, I had cheated her out of an opportunity to gain more readers and sales. At the same time I had cheated my own readers out of information on a local artist being on TV, something that they might have really enjoyed watching.

I had done a poor job out of envy. I said a quick prayer to be forgiven.

How could I make amends? I knew what I could do: I would watch the segment and report on it.

Scooting to the newsroom's television in the far corner, I dialed in the show. Cindy was on already, looking poised, and I felt envious again. I didn't think I could handle the thought of millions of people peering at me through the camera. Was there no limit to Cindy's talents and accomplishments?

I did feel smug that the interviewer didn't ask any questions that I hadn't already. Cindy answered in much the same way as she had answered me. The segment was over in a flash and a commercial came on. I clicked the television off and wandered back toward my desk.

I thought I'd take a quick break, to think as clearly as I could about what to write regarding Cindy's TV appearance, and I opened my desk drawer for my purse.

It was gone.

CHAPTER 35

All that empty space within the drawer was very upsetting. My heart thunked. I looked quickly around the newsroom, but no one was looking at me guiltily.

My notes, my photographs, and now my purse.

I went to the doorway of the staff kitchen, leaned against the jamb with as much nonchalance as I could muster while trembling the way I was, and wrote down names of the reporters present. Then I compared it to the list I'd compiled from the two weekend editors last week.

Six names appeared on both lists. That reduced the number of suspects by half. That was progress, though I was heartsick to suspect colleagues like this. The notes might have been lost by a computer glitch, the photos by a glitch in the mail system.

But my purse proved I had an enemy.

Feeling downcast, not sure what to do next, I went to the ladies' room. When I got back, just to confirm this upsetting event, which I could hardly believe, I opened the drawer again. My pocketbook was there. Again I looked around the newsroom, mentally challenging each suspect I laid eyes on to look back at me guiltily. But nobody did. They were better at acting than I, or hardened beyond guilt. And enjoyed playing with my mind.

Saddened, I locked the desk drawer and took the short list to Mike in the darkroom. The red light was off but the door was closed, so I knocked.

"Tricia, what's up?" Mike said, standing tall in the doorway.

I went in. The odor of photography chemicals made my nose wrinkle up. I told him in a low voice what had just happened, and he once again leaned his towering body against a cabinet. Taking my list, he peered at it.

"I can't imagine any of these people harming a flea," he said.

"Me neither, but I think it had to be one of them."

"Well, as I come and go from the darkroom, I'll keep an eye out," he said. "Want to see your recent photos? Of that artist?"

He spread my second round of photos on a table. I remembered how glum I'd been the day I took her picture in the midst of all her success, and I didn't like what I saw laid out before me. I hoped he had a different opinion.

"What do you think, Mike? As good as the first set?"

He quietly examined them with all his attention, which lifted my spirits. With a long finger, he pushed three of the photos above the group. "These are the best. They're good, Tricia, no worries."

I was relieved. "Thanks, Mike. Coming from you, that means a lot."

He gave me the negatives to go with the three best, and I took them back to my desk. I finished Cindy's story, putting the news about Good Morning America in the past tense, mentally apologizing to her for denying her publicity before the event, though I was not, by journalism standards, obligated to give her timely publicity. Then I took the story and the photos to Paul Tercell. He thanked me, though he never did compliment me on either item, and I left.

CHAPTER 36

I had an hour that afternoon to walk solo in the Great Swamp; Catherine was at work, deep in a lab at a pharma plant, and wouldn't be able to walk with me and listen to me. "A mind is a terrible place to go alone," I'd heard in the Steps. But my hours at the *Sentinel* were so odd, it was usually hard to find somebody who was free at the same time I was, to air my faulty, negative thinking with. But I needed to air my brain, so I went.

It had rained last night. As I dodged muddy patches, on this path and that, I pictured my most recent interview with Cindy and how I'd reacted to her news. Envy had consumed my heart. I began to see that when I'd been at Cindy's, the itty bitty shitty committee, something else I'd learned about in the Steps, had kicked in—meaning it had heaped me with negativity—at the speed of light. Before I had been aware of it, the idea that I had no star power, that I'd never get accolades, that I would never have success in life, had found a home in my imagination. I had immediately agreed with it. Not only that, for the last several days I had been adding to the false story and embellishing it.

It was a demonstration of the power of my Magical Magnifying Mind, another idea I'd heard in the Steps. Whatever we focus on, our minds build upon.

A bug buzzed in from amongst the trees and got trapped under my glasses. I had to take them off to send the creature on its way. With the glasses off, the woods went blurry in shades of green. It was pretty.

I decided to stop playing lead violin in the shitty committee's orchestra. I once again (for the millionth time) thanked them for sharing and encouraged them to take a long road back to hell. They would return to me.

I just had to stay aware so when they chimed in I could thwart them instead of cooperating with them. In the meantime, I would use my Magical Magnifying Mind to focus on the characters in my novel, to spot stories and photo opportunities for the *Sentinel,* and to pursue them wisely. That was my Magical Magnifying Mind's proper and positive use.

That settled, I turned back and scooted home.

CHAPTER 37

Meg appeared at my house Wednesday afternoon. Was this the big day? Was she coming with her bags packed, ready to escape Dennis' abuse trap?

I directed her to the living room this time, just to shake things up. I made mint tea and brought the two mugs to the glass-topped coffee table in front of us on the sofa.

"How are you?" I said in my most neutral tone. I was afraid of saying the wrong thing; I had to be so careful. I was in a dark forest. Dense vegetation hid the path, if there was any path at all. If I set a foot wrong and offended or frightened Meg away, Dennis's trap would close on her.

"Okay, I guess. I read your story about that artist, Cindy Pierson, this morning. I wanted to tell you that I see real growth in your work as a journalist."

Growth? How would *she* know? She'd said she'd read my story on Laurel Way the first time she came to my house. But seeing "real growth? This called for some investigative journalism.

"You've been reading my stuff?"

"Yeah, I've been reading your stories ever since you started at the *Passaic Press*."

That was ten years ago, right after Tommy died.

"You've been following me that long?" I was stunned, and very pleased.

"Yes. And I think you're asking better questions, getting at deeper issues, as time goes on. And as you write, your stories are getting more concise, more interesting, more pithy."

She sounded so sure, like she was not making it up. It was a sincere compliment.

"Well, thank you so much." I was flabbergasted. Someone had been following my work through all those years of hunting for and writing local stories. All those stories had seemed to float away on a gentle river of everybody's forgetfulness. It felt good to know that someone had been paying attention, taking note.

Ninja came in to say hello and consented to be stroked by Meg. Then he leapt up next to me and snuggled.

I decided to ask Meg about what I'd learned about Dennis at the women's shelter. Nosy me or helpful me?

"I met a woman, while doing interviews at a battered women's shelter, who had been married to a Dennis Palmer, an investment banker in New York City. She divorced him for abuse."

Meg stared at me, mug of tea halted halfway to her lips. Dust motes floated in a sunbeam through the picture window. Finally she stirred herself. "I knew he had a first marriage, but he said he'd divorced because she was cheating."

Add "liar" to his resume, I thought.

"I'm sorry," I said, and gently added, "I would believe the woman's testimony about it, not his."

Meg sighed. "Me, too." She was silent and the dust motes danced like mayflies. Wished I could afford a cleaning woman, like Meg and Dennis. But there wasn't too much that was enviable in that relationship.

"I'm going to ask him about it," she said, flinching, a tremor in her voice. I'd be terrified too.

"I hope I did the right thing, telling you about it." Here I was, looking for reassurance from her.

"I'm glad to know. One more black mark on him that will help me—I hope—make some changes."

There, maybe my nosiness would benefit her. Time to change the subject.

"What have you been up to?" I asked. "Have you been writing?"

And we had a conversation about keeping journals, which she'd resumed doing, and about keeping up a correspondence with friends, dashing off haiku, having a blast with writing, having a tough time writing.

"Keep up the good work," Meg said.

"You, too." I wondered how she hid her journals from Dennis. Could I ask? No, it felt like too personal a question, and my knowledge of her hiding place could put her at risk if he ever tried to beat the information out of me. But I was grateful to find she was writing again. And reading again. I sensed in her a woodsprite's way of thinking that I wanted to get to know at a deeper level. How better than to exchange information on what books we were reading?

"I'm devouring Jane Austen," I said. "This is about my twelfth time through *Pride and Prejudice.* At this point I know what the characters are going to say to each other. And yet the story still totally absorbs me. I was reading it on the subway in New York last year and missed my stop. She's so fantastic."

"I'm re-reading *Wuthering Heights.* It's like putting on an oxygen mask of excellent English, excellent storytelling."

Interesting that I was reading an Austen romance and Meg was reading about a lawless, abusive man.

"I love that book!" I said. "It makes me so glad I was born a native English speaker, to be able to consume all the Brontës' stories. But I've always wondered how the daughters of a Yorkshire clergyman could know so much about extreme dysfunction in families."

"Well, it's their brother Bramwell. He was an alcoholic, bitter about how his love life and literary life turned out. They took care of him, and he abused them, while he drank himself to death."

I hadn't known that. Sounded like my own life with Tommy. Speaking of abuse, Meg, I thought, wasn't there a parallel between Heathcliff and Dennis—that slow tightening of the noose...

I looked at her with the question on my face, and she picked up on it. She flushed a bit.

"Yes, Dennis drinks very heavily at times."

"Is he bitter about something?" Why would he be, he was making more money in a year than most Americans made in a lifetime.

"I think he really wants children."

"If he drinks heavily—"

"Just at times!"

"Still, that's not great for being a father." Neither is hitting their mother. Dare I say it? Maybe I could say it obliquely.

"My sister's husband is hitting her. I'm sure the children know—they look terrified of their own shadows. They'll be scarred for life if she stays—"

"—Don't." Meg sat forward, flushed, probably resenting my outspokenness. "We keep coming back to this topic," she said. "Couldn't we talk about other things?"

"I know, but as long as you're in danger, it's hard for me not to talk about it. It's desperately important."

"Please, let's change the subject."

"Okay," I said calmly. Inside, I was yelling at her to get the hell away from Dennis. My fingers clutched my mug's handle, tight with frustration. "Just a minute, Meg." I got up and went to the kitchen with a knot in my neck. I was mightily bugged at her, for her procrastination. I stretched a bit. Said a prayer. Turned it over to HP, which only felt partially successful. Returned to the sofa.

"Change of topic. The *Sentinel* has an opening for a stringer—a part-time reporter. Would journalism be something that interested you?"

Energy flickered across her face. "Tell me more."

"You led the school newspaper, but maybe journalism is not what you want any longer, not with your creative writing degree. I had a creative writing teacher who looked down on journalistic writing as being nothing more than 'subject followed by verb.' Not creative. But then again, the person who said that—well, I couldn't make out what she was talking about in her novel, which I bought out of curiosity. I regret the price. There's something to be said for 'subject / verb.'"

Meg gave me a sideways glance, with a smile. "I could be interested."

I saw this as a breakthrough. A sunbeam had pierced the dense forest canopy and reached the ground below. Maybe I could set my feet down without springing traps on Meg.

"The *Passaic Press* and the *Sentinel* both use stringers to start out." Then I thought of the obstacle to this plan. "Though you'd probably have to attend evening town meetings."

We had hit the solid wall of Dennis again.

Meg had been smiling while we talked. At the mention of going out to evening meetings, the smile had disappeared.

Then I thought of an alternative.

"Both papers accept editorials from local people—of course, those aren't paid."

But the light had disappeared from Meg's eyes. I wanted it to come back. She stood up, however, and grabbed her purse, its designer logo glinting.

"I should let you get on with your day," she said.

We'd had, for the most part, such a fun conversation that I just couldn't bring myself to drop any warning bombs on her. But maybe I could get her to picture a future free of Dennis.

"I could put in a word for you at the *Press* or the *Sentinel,* either one that you're interested in." I smiled.

"No, thanks." She twinkled her fingers goodbye, as if we were at lunch saying *ciao* like girlfriends.

Which, it seemed, we were becoming. That was great.

But now more than ever my body was clenched in desperate frustration for her to leave Dennis and be safe.

CHAPTER 38

Patricia McGrath, Democrat running for Borough Council, called me again a few days later. We went through our "Hello, Tricia!" and "Hi, Tricia!" dance and then got down to business.

"Well, the detective we hired has found the culprit," the candidate said.

"Oooh, tell me!"

"I can't say who to a reporter because it can't go in the newspaper. At least not yet."

Damn! And I didn't see any way to find out for myself, other than to stake out one of her yard signs all night. Wasn't going to happen. But I had to chomp on this juicy tidbit that was dangling only an inch from my lips.

"I promise not to write it if you'll tell me who."

"Do you double triple promise? You've got to."

"Yes, I do solemnly swear." That was irrevocable. Unless I got Tricia's permission at a later date. Got to stick to the journalistic ethics. Number one, never lie to your readers. Which is why a lying politician is so reprehensible to principled members of the press.

"You have to keep it to yourself, no editors, no other reporters, no friends. Agreed?"

Who could it be? I was frantic to know at this point but hated the fact I had to keep it to myself.

"Agreed," I said reluctantly.

"The new mayor."

She let that declaration hang in the air for good dramatic effect.

During that pause, I was busy wondering just how much of a nut the new mayor was. The old one had turned out to be quite deranged. I didn't want to have to deal with another bizarro.

"He's a Republican," she said, "and I think he wants a Republican in the seat I'm running for. Unfortunately, that party is known for dirty tricks."

"Watergate," I said, "and the Committee to Re-Elect the President, with the telling acronym CREEP, being classic examples."

"The unethical grab for power. And it continues to this day."

Well, I was a journalist and had to be more "above the fray" than I was being in this conversation. I adopted my neutrality cloak. Only one knee stuck out from under it.

"What are you going to do?" I asked.

"I'm kibbitzing about it with my fellow Democrats. I think we'll end up warning him privately that we know and we'll go public if he doesn't stop. That's why I have to keep control of this news—to have a carrot that gets him to cease and desist."

"I understand," I said.

"I'm relieved it's just lawn signs and not a bigger act of sabotage. Like threatening our election workers and making them fear for their lives. That would be a tragic miscarriage of democracy."

"True. Well, please keep me informed, even if it's off the record. This is fascinating. Please tell me immediately if I can go public with this news— well, you know that I'll have to call it an allegation unless there's a guilty verdict.

It was her turn to say, "Agreed."

"I'll ask my editor if I can get your position on the issues—and your opponent's—before the election. But we don't usually cover local contests, cuz we'd have to cover every race in every town in Central Jersey, so—well, I wouldn't hold my breath."

"That's okay, I'll get the story into the *Passaic Press.*"

"Oh, you know exactly how to make me miserable, Tricia," I said with a smile.

CHAPTER 39

Justin had called, and so I was waiting on a Saturday night for him to pick me up for a movie. Later we'd go to the afterhours dessert café where we could discuss the movie. And later than that?

I had been feeling good lately. I'd been doing my affirmations, and I'd been listening more carefully for the itty bitty shitty committee to pipe up. I had snipped their tape—"You're a failure"—and had replaced it with the exact opposite positive, a tool I'd learned in the Steps: "You can do it!" This affirmation had been bopping around in my head more than its opposite had been. Saturday had been a particularly good day.

I was dressed for our date, and the inner oak door was open so I'd see Justin's car pull up through the storm door—when would I finally put in the screen door? By November? I decided to put some music on while I waited. Ninja was hunkered down on the top edge of the sofa, knowing I'd be going out and not thrilled about it. I put a dance mix on the music player. And got lost in the rhythms, the melodies, the bass.

First was a slow dance, so I scooped Ninja up and rocked him, risking cat hairs sticking to my blouse. He put up with it for a few bars, then wiggled to get down. He stalked off, very dignified.

Next up was a lilting number, and then the tempo of the songs got faster. Then:

"Come on, baby, do the twist!" My flippy skirt was up around my waist as I twisted lower and lower, then slowly back up. I was in a dream state—I had arms waiting for me, admiring eyes on me. Everything was going to be great.

And the storm door opened and Justin stepped in, eyes fixed on me.

I stood mesmerized by his strength, his presence. Then I tried to collect myself and stepped to the sound system. I shook so hard, it took me three jabs at the button to turn the music off. I whirled to face him.

"I knocked," he said.

"Didn't hear you." I blushed. I was all in. I could no longer hear Catherine's "Whoa" or my own cautions or anything else but the pounding of hormones in my blood vessels. My body was wholly given over to the urge to merge joyfully with this handsome, quiet man. Right now I could take a big step toward making all my dreams come true, to live like Cindy Pierson instead of my solitary life.

In my dance-induced excitement, I threw all inhibition, all the social niceties of men making the first move, out my picture window and into the rosebed outside. I ran to Justin, pressed into him. His crisp shirt, in a quiet plaid, was stretched over his chest. I stropped my cheeks across it. I burrowed into his arms deeper. I couldn't get close enough. Then I felt his arms break away and his strong hands grasp my arms. He unlocked them from their hungry circle around him and pushed me back a step.

"You said friends first." His breath was quick.

I looked up at him, terrified that I'd made an irredeemable fool of myself.

"I agree," he said.

I stepped back further, and he released my arms.

"Keeping my distance with you is the hardest thing I've ever done," he added, swiping his hand nervously across his jaw.

Well, that seemed to be a bit of reassurance. I interpreted it to mean he was highly attracted.

"I'm sorry, I wasn't thinking," I said. "You're right—we're right—friends, right?" And I smiled up at him, desperate for a returning smile from him.

"Yes."

But he didn't smile.

CHAPTER 40

We drove to the cinema silently.

I was desperate to say something to lighten the mood in the Jaguar. That meant I couldn't mention what had just happened. Probably Justin had said enough about that. Smart Justin. He had said the exact right thing: "Friends."

He'd said the right thing, but how did he feel about me now? Would I ever feel that we were back on good footing? Would we ever chat happily again? In the stress I was feeling, I couldn't get a single conversational rocket off my launchpad. And Justin didn't help. He didn't say a thing, which I resented. Talking is your job too, Justin, I thought. You have a responsibility here too.

But instead, our little enclosed world in the Jaguar was silent, except for the sound of the engine. It didn't seem to be purring tonight.

Maybe I could tell him that I thought he had said the exact right thing. But I was frightened of drawing his attention back to the situation, of accentuating it. I hesitated.

He parked, we got our tickets, and we sat in velvet splendor to watch *Sister Act*. I heard Justin chuckle once or twice. Maybe Justin wasn't too upset, if he could laugh at the movie. But I didn't see a single humorous thing. I was locked in remorse, in self-recrimination. The itty bitty committee was chattering louder than the movie theater's sound system.

We left in the midst of a big crowd. We stood outside, under the marquee, and looked at each other.

"Tricia, I'm a bit tired. It's been a busy week. Would you mind if we skipped going for dessert?"

Of course I minded. He'd never backed out from any of our activities before.

"No, of course not, that's okay," I mumbled, my stomach tense. I was desperate to avoid any sort of conflict.

He held the car door for me, as usual. I sat in the seat, a tight ball of anxiety. Maybe we'd better talk about tonight. What could I say that wouldn't make things worse?

As he got behind the wheel, the car sagged under his weight. Think, Trish, think! You're a journalist—think of a question to ask him! But all I could think of to ask was, "Is it over?" Justin didn't seem to have a clue about my distress, and that tore me up too. He didn't glance over at me, didn't ask what I thought of the movie. He just drove.

I had a flaw to write on his character list: apparently oblivious to how I'm feeling.

The Jaguar rolled to my driveway with me anxious and still stoppered up. The date was over. I'd hesitated, and I'd lost the opportunity to talk and get us back on an even keel.

"Thanks for being understanding about the early night," he said. He got out, opened the door for me, and walked me to my front door. But there was no kiss, not even a hug.

He said good night cordially and walked down the steps to his car. I wanted to just stand there and watch him back out and drive away, perhaps never to see him again. But I figured that staring after him longingly from the front porch was not accepted behavior. So I stepped inside, waved jauntily through the storm door, and closed the oak inner door.

Ninja meowed more plaintively than usual. Yes, honey, plaintive is how I feel, I thought. I scooped him up and carried my soft, silky kitty to the back porch. I crumpled into my favorite chair in the corner. I'd gone against the wise guardrails Jesus had given me and everything felt like it had blown up.

I burst into tears.

CHAPTER 41

A few days passed. I was still reeling from Saturday night, desperate to talk with Justin. But he hadn't called. I felt desolate, abandoned. Even the June sun felt thin and desperate.

I wanted to tell him I was contrite about barreling past the boundaries we had set, that I was amazed at the fortitude, the maturity he had shown, that I admired him for it, that I wondered if he'd hold my weakness against me. What was he was thinking? Feeling? I was desperate for resolution, to feel on firm ground with him. But I didn't have the courage to call.

Despite those anxieties, that afternoon I decided to work on my novel. As a writer, I always had to plow on regardless. A professional does the work even if he or she doesn't feel like it. To shift gears into writing, I meditated on HP as described in the Psalms, both as a comfort for my soul and as an entrance to a relaxed state conducive to writing.

I was at the dining room table, having punted the ball once again on making a studio, or a darkroom, or anything much at all of the upstairs bedroom. Being in the dining room, I heard a car pull up on the driveway right outside. Through the gauzy curtains I saw Meg ease out of her Audi and plod up the front walk, shoulders rounded.

Oh no, I thought. This isn't going to be fun. And I'm almost in the zone with my writing—if I'd ever really get there with my worries about Justin. Now the flow will be interrupted. Damn! Helping people is a pain sometimes. But HP says I need to help. Maybe today will be the day she leaves that bastard.

She knocked. I answered. She had a fresh bruise on her jaw. I invited her in.

"Well, I confronted him about his lie. About his first marriage. It was horrible."

I made tea while she stood silently in the kitchen. When we were settled on the sofa, with steaming mugs on the coffee table, she tucked a wisp of hair behind her ear and said,

"I've been thinking."

"Made a decision?"

She started in her seat, and a look of dismay crossed her face.

I chastised myself. In my eagerness to make a difference in her life, I had forgotten to be patient and had jumped way ahead of her current thinking and feelings instead of just listening, as I ought. My impatience might have ruined her rescue.

"I'm sorry," I said. "Let me start over. What's been on your mind?" I was conciliatory, but it didn't work.

"I don't need you to save me." Defiance in her voice.

"Quite right." Except you *could* use some help, I thought.

"I guess I'd better go." She rose from the sofa.

"Please don't. I know I can't save you. But I'd like to be of help to you. Maybe just as a sounding board? I'll listen."

She settled down and stared out the picture window. I managed to stay silent.

"It's gotten worse," she finally said. "You predicted it. And it's here already."

She sighed.

"Besides this," and she pressed the bruise on her jaw, "which I got just for questioning the reason for his divorce, he had me up against the wall two nights ago."

I nodded for her to go on.

"Hands around my throat."

That's when I noticed the bruises on her neck. They peeked from above the edge of a scarf she wore despite the June warmth. She had put thick makeup on her face and neck, but with her statement the ugly marks on her neck became obvious.

I wanted to ask her, "What are you going to do?" But I'd rushed her once already today. I had to respond somehow, however.

"I'm sorry," I said. It sounded wobbly.

"When he went to work the next day, I opened the phone book and looked for that hotline you showed me. I just want you to know so you don't give up on me."

"I won't give up, Meg. I'm not perfect at it, but I'm waiting, hoping, praying that you break free." Why not now? I thought but didn't say.

She sighed. "You marry with so many expectations of a great life together."

"I know. I did the same thing."

"But now you're single. What's it like?"

I thought, this may be the reason she's here today, to do research. Well, I wasn't going to whitewash what happened when I mourned the death of a relationship I had invested in deeply. What should I say? I asked HP for wisdom.

"The first year was tough. I won't lie to you. Miserable. The second year was worse. And I've never stopped missing the good parts of being married. I especially feel it on Friday and Saturday nights—date nights, and at the evening meal, when I'd like to share my day."

Meg picked up her tea and cupped it with hands in her lap.

"But I'm living a great life now," I said. "It took being honest about the grief, it took tremendous effort—going out when I wasn't comfortable— prayer, inspiration, courage. I had to grow in all those qualities. But I'm so much better off now."

Meg sipped her tea. She slipped off her shoes and tucked her feet under her.

I hazarded continuing.

"I use my creativity at every moment of my single life, which I didn't do when I was married, because I was so afraid of setting Tommy off. But now imagination, innovation, and my Higher Power sustain me."

"It sounds like you're trying to sell me on being single."

I started in my chair, taken aback. Then I thought, was she right? Was I trying to recruit her to singleness? Was this a sales job? No, I thought. Actually I was trying to save her butt. I was angry at her accusation. But I coached myself to not hold a resentment against her and to speak quietly.

"No, I'm just trying to show you that you can make a great life for yourself, if you decide to. As Abraham Lincoln said, 'Most people are about as happy as they make up their minds to be.'"

"I see." Meg took another sip and then stood up. "Thanks, Tricia."

I had already warned her, but I couldn't help warning her again.

"It's only going to get worse."

"But I love him," she said, beginning to sound weepy. "Sometimes he's so nice. He says we'll go to London next. Maybe I can get him to stop the bad part."

It was harsh of me, but I said it anyway.

"There are a lot of dead women who thought the same thing about their men."

Now it was her turn to be taken aback.

"You can't judge—you don't know my situation!"

"But Meg," I said gently, "I do know a lot about it. Abusive situations have been researched and their common factors are well known. Women love the men and hope desperately that they'll change. But they don't. Even the few who willingly undergo counseling—well, most of them go back to abusing."

I was being cruel to be kind, stating harsh realities, and I was weary of it. I was ready for this visit to be over. But to save this woman's life, I had to see it to its end.

"How about we call the helpline?" I said.

She dropped her face into her hands. Her shoulders didn't shake, she wasn't crying. She was hiding, isolating, thinking, feeling, weighing her options.

At last she lifted her face.

"I'm not ready."

I could have said, with your jaw and your neck you have heightened reason to get out. You may not have another chance. You may be dead next time Dennis comes home. I could have said: What will it take to be ready?

But I held back. I'd dropped enough plainspoken bombs for one day. But then I hoped my reticence didn't kill her.

I gave her the only gift I could, besides listening. And urging.

"Praying for you." Speaking of which, I needed to pray for me. I wanted HP to help me get back on track with Justin. But what if that relationship wasn't meant to be in HP's plan? And there I was, right back to thinking about myself.

"Like I've told you," Meg said, "I'm not at all sure there is a God, or that, if he exists, he's interested in the details of my situation."

"In my extensive experience with hardships, he is." Yes, he'd been loyal through my worst times. I needed to be loyal to him and follow his guidance on sex. Oh dear.

Meg set her drink down. "We'll see. Thanks for the tea. And the prayers, I guess."

She got up, went down the front steps. I watched her climb into her sleek Audi, the four rings of its insignia gleaming on its nose in the afternoon sun.

Great car, but I could see the strings that had been attached to it by the man who'd purchased it. They were as clear as the sunbeams reflecting off its beautifully designed fenders.

A Corolla—one without strings—would do me just fine.

Though Meg's car sure was gorgeous. A real symbol of success.

As Meg drove off, envy of her car, her income—if I had her income and the freedom it bestowed, I could write novels all day!—her status as a married lady, her big spiffy house, all roiled within me. If Justin and I could just get through this friends phase, I could have all that. Or a career at the *Times*.

Oh, I groaned to myself, he's probably gone. So don't rely on anyone but yourself, your girlfriends, and your HP. And mostly HP.

CHAPTER 42

Later I called Dennis Palmer. Had to. Despite my anxiety about Justin, my craving to succeed was making itself heard. It was screaming: "Get into the museum! Solve the crime!" Dennis had said he would win that roadblock, Dorothy Anderson, over to my side. Had he?

I reached him at work, loving the twenty-five miles between me and his too-active fists, which were holed up with him in his Financial District office tower.

He answered his phone. We made social niceties. Then, "Been wondering, Mr. Palmer, if you'd had a chance to talk to Dorothy Anderson on my behalf."

"Yes, I did, and I think I've won her over. Meant to call and tell you, but work …"

Oh yes, I thought, a man's work is so much more important than helping a woman advance hers.

"So I can go back to the museum? Interview people? Ask Dorothy questions too?"

"Yes."

"Great, Mr. Palmer. I'll stop by the museum tomorrow."

"All right."

And Dennis, don't go home, I thought, and hit Meg. But the fact that I had never confronted him—was I therefore complicit in his destruction of his wife? I paused to consider. I was someone who didn't want to trigger an abuser. Who prayed for Meg to get free. Who thought it was wiser to work and pray behind the scenes. A coward? I hoped not, but I wasn't sure.

"Anything else, Ms. Maguire?"

I didn't like his sardonic tone of voice but answered sweetly cuz there's not much else a woman can do and still have access.

I said goodbye, then went for a walk in the long June twilight, wondering about all the men in my life—all of whom I was investigating in one way or another—and what I was supposed to do next about them.

CHAPTER 43

I went to the museum the next morning, an hour after it opened. Virginia was at the reception desk, and Dennis must have filled her in already this morning because she didn't refuse me entry. I was relieved I didn't have to invoke Dennis's name and Dorothy's new permission in order to browse the display cases. I hate having to explain to people, though journalism sure requires writing a lot of explanations.

"Nice to see you," Virginia said. "If you have any questions, just let me know." Judging by her gracious invitation to meander, I thought Dennis must have thoroughly prepared the ground for me, just as he must thoroughly prepare for his mergers and acquisitions. I wondered how thorough his plans were for Meg. My guess was he was operating on instinct. HP, spare me from men who obeyed their instincts. On Saturday night, Justin hadn't. That was such a good sign—but darn, he might have written me off.

I wandered through the display longing for Justin to be there with me. With his silence, his absence, the display cases seemed cold and empty, the tools meaningless. I forced myself to pay attention, to linger over the huge iron implements. All of them had been checked for Samantha Scarborough's blood. They stood behind sheets of glass in exhibits that described the settling of New Jersey in centuries past. I studied a scythe to cut wheat, and a mattock, which looked like a pickaxe except with a blunt rather than a sharp point. It was used to break up stubborn clods of soil.

Virginia poked her head around the corner of a display.

"Have any questions I can help you with?"

"Not really, just browsing. Actually, I do have a question: does the museum have any quilts?" My mother made some, and I had fond memories of wrapping myself in a red and gold cotton one on cold January nights.

"Yes, over this way."

She led me under all the arches that held up the ceiling of the museum, into another room with two quilts on display behind glass.

"Samantha put these on display within days of arriving," Virginia said. "Her overriding question, she said, was, 'Whose stories are we telling? Whose story has been marginalized, submerged, in favor of the people who wrote the history?' She wanted women represented. These are the two most intricate."

"They're lovely." One of the quilts was made of triangles and squares of flowered fabrics in smartly contrasting colors. Next to each other, the colors popped. Deeper and richer. Like I wanted to write.

"Yes. We don't have names, but women made them to keep their families warm. Many are beautiful in their own way, full of self-expression. Women realized they had to make something utilitarian, but they wanted to put themselves into it, to make art as well."

I thought about the unknown woman who had designed and built this eye-pleasing textile. When the people who had huddled under this quilt had gotten up on a winter's morning, they'd had to crack the ice on the water they washed their faces with. They'd had to work all day six days a week to have enough to eat.

We have it so much easier, I thought. Instead of raising, catching, slaughtering, plucking, cleaning, quartering, and cooking a chicken over a fire, we buy it all prepared at the store. And yet maybe life is difficult now in a different way—stress and anxiety about nuclear war, crime, the climate, and the potential collapse of the economic system. The getting ahead in careers or the enduring of jobs that were soul-dead boring. And there was the anxiety most people had to be feeling from living their lives so far away from any sort of Higher Power. Which reminded me. I needed to get to a meeting.

Matt Morgan stuck his head around the arched doorway.

"Virginia!" he said. "Been looking for you."

"I'd better get back to my post," she said and dashed away.

I sauntered after her, admiring the parquet floor and peering at a display of flatirons. My grandmother told me she had used one. They looked immensely heavy. Any one of these would be a fine murder weapon, I thought.

I rounded the arch that framed Virginia's reception area. Matt had disappeared, whatever his question for Virginia had been. It was time to ask questions, the same old ones I'd already asked. But time could loosen up information stored in people's minds. Now was the moment for me to heft a mattock and see if soil I'd already plowed might have a clod that could be broken up.

"Please tell me about Samantha's plans for the museum," I asked. "I know I've already asked you, but I'd like to ask again."

"Well, she only led one meeting before—before she was killed," Virginia said. "It's a sign of how fair she was that she brought the volunteers into the meeting."

"What changes did she say she was in favor of?"

"Come to think of it, she said she was going to save money by laying off our handyman, Matt, and bringing in a contractor on an as-needed basis. I didn't think it was a good idea—little things are going wrong in this old building all the time, and he knows its temperament well. He can fix anything."

Pay-off! Ask the same question, just like the police do when they interrogate a suspect, and wait for new information to emerge. Here was a motive for murder.

Matt was so cantankerous, I decided to see what insights Virginia had into his psyche so that maybe I wouldn't have to be subject to his refusal, once again, to talk to me.

"What did Matt think about that?"

"He doesn't say much. But I know, because he told me once, that he loves this historic building. He told me, in one of the few times that he's ever opened up to me, that its design and its quirks were engraved on his heart. It's a funny thing to say, but I'd guess he loves this building much more than he loves the museum that's housed in it."

"So to hear that he would be laid off would affect him deeply," I prompted.

Virginia sucked in her breath.

"You don't mean that he'd kill Samantha for that?"

"What do you think of that idea?"

She looked down at her hands, age-spotted and yet beautiful, with elegant, long fingers, her nails manicured with pale pink polish. She thought a moment, then looked back up at me.

"I really can't say." I felt that she had shut a door on me. I wondered what it meant. That she thought Matt capable of clobbering Samantha but would never say it?

I was at a dead-end with Virginia. I decided to screw up my fortitude and attempt an interview with the curmudgeonly handyman.

"Where is Matt, any idea?"

"He said he would be in the basement."

"Thanks."

She nodded at me but didn't say anything. I hoped I'd be able to get her to open the door to me again.

I descended the wooden circular staircase to the basement and found Matt having a cup of coffee in the employee break area. The square tiles that covered the low ceiling down here stood in contrast to the glorious arches of the main rooms upstairs.

"Hi, Matt," I said in a spritely, friendly tone. How would I ever win him over?

He replied with a nod. Well, a nod was an improvement.

"What will you be fixing today?" I asked. "I'm not reporting on it, just wondering." I hoped to pre-empt one of his caustic remarks about having no comment for journalists.

"Not fixing. Helping to oversee the work of installing an elevator."

Wow, I'd gotten a complete sentence out of him! And I had a new story!

"The museum is moving ahead with it, in spite of ... all that's happened?"

"The Board of Directors said yes. Limited availability of the architect and engineer that were already hired."

"Where will you be fitting it in?"

"We have to break through the original stonework at the back."

"Sounds like major work."

"Not wild about it. Worried about structural integrity. This is a beautiful building—hate to change it. But the engineer we hired says it will work. I have to go along with it."

Why was he willing to be civil with me today? I could only guess. But I wanted to take advantage of his talkative mood.

"You really love this building, don't you?"

He looked at me quietly. No answer. I'd lost him, hadn't I?

He picked up his mug of coffee and sipped, slowly, deliberately, insolently, it seemed to me. Then he surprised me. He spoke graciously.

"It's a special place," he conceded.

"What is special about it to you?"

"The architecture, the stained glass window with sayings about reading and books. The spiral wrought-iron staircase to the upper level. The spiral wooden staircase to the basement. The arches."

"Yes, I've noticed them and enjoyed them too," I said. "I love the parquet floors. The mosaic floor in the entry way."

"I love all that stuff."

"Do you have much fixing to do? Of the mosaic or parquet floors, for example?" I had him talking! I was excited to finally have connected with this source.

"I seem to end up changing light bulbs." He reconsidered that. "I run wires behind the plasterwork. I've fixed plumbing in the break area downstairs. I've regrouted the chimney. I do everything I can to keep this building in great condition. In fact, I've bled a little over every square inch of this place."

"So it must have been tough when Samantha announced she was planning on cutting your job."

He shoved himself back from the table and stood, looking down at me with scorn.

I'd blown it.

He grabbed his mug, slapped it into the sink with a thump, and stalked out.

I sat in self-recrimination. In my rush to investigate the murder, I'd jumped to the crux too soon. I had to learn not to shut people down. But then again, what kind of source was it that usually refused to reveal a single thing? Answer: not a very good one. I'd uncovered and developed stories about the museum without his help so far.

I'd just have to continue to do so.

With the knowledge in mind that he loved his job, and that Samantha was going to end it.

CHAPTER 44

As long as I was in the museum's basement, I thought I'd check on the progress of the inventory of artifacts being made in the workroom. I opened the door and found everybody in there, just as before. But this time they were sitting, chatting with mugs of coffee in their hands. The room felt close, literally and figuratively. The low ceiling made the space feel tight. And the bond I sensed between all the cops—camaraderie—felt tight too.

"We just finished," the burliest of the local cops said, a bit nervously, it seemed, since he began shifting from foot to foot. Maybe he cared what I thought about the fact that they weren't working.

"What did you find out?" I asked.

"We didn't find the murder weap—"

"—Hey, shut up!" The thin cop shouted him down. "That's something only the chief can talk about."

"Yeah, okay," I said, to calm everyone down. But I was going to use it in my story, just without revealing which cop said it. I'd protect him. Maybe I'd have to go to jail rather than reveal my source. Well, that was a bit overdramatic. And, I hoped, would not be necessary. When the story was published, however, the chief would drill these guys and find out who had spoken unauthorized. I felt sorry for the patrolman, but my readers had to know. Didn't they?

"How many objects did you inventory in all?" I asked Elspeth, Samantha's assistant, whose computer screen was still lit up. They literally had just finished working.

She turned back to her computer, scrolled down a bit, and gave me the number.

"Total of 11,378."

"Wow, that's a lot of old tools," I said.

"We've been collecting them since the 1970s. Word got around that we take donations, and people brought in stuff from basements, sheds, barns."

"And no murder weapon among them?"

"We're not going to discuss that," the thin cop said. "Talk to the chief."

"I see." I could certainly sense a brick wall when I had groped my way against one. "Well, thanks." There was no point in asking them how the job went. It was boring, methodical work, anybody could see that, and it wouldn't interest readers much. And this team's ranks had hardened against me. I could sense it at a deep level—they simultaneously turned their backs to straighten up their workspaces. It was time to leave them be.

I went back to the coffee room and poured myself a mug. Matt Morgan's mug still stood in the sink, accusing me of asking him key questions too soon. I sat in one of the molded plastic chairs. A few minutes later all the cops and sheriff's deputies came out, put their mugs dutifully in the dishwasher, eyed me with suspicion, nodded, and filed out. All those shoulders and chests and slim hips in form-fitting uniforms made me think—well, not *think*, actually …

Last into the break room came Elspeth. I hadn't had a chance to interview her before, and I was pleased when she poured herself coffee and plunked herself into a chair. Her face, framed with her curly brown hair,

"Well, that was a chore," she said. "It took longer than it had to, those policemen moved so slow."

"Oh," I said, taken aback by her criticism.

"Just kidding!" she said.

"Ha!" I said, though it wasn't very funny.

"I'm glad that's over. We couldn't scan all 11,000 tools for blood. But we scanned the ones that fit the description the medical examiner gave our team of a heavy, pointed but blunt object. Not sharpened like an axe. None of the tools had any trace of blood on them. And they all were in storage down here when the attack happened, locked in cabinets that were locked in the workroom. They don't seem like possible murder weapons."

"What about that bin of miscellaneous tools that hadn't been catalogued yet? Anything in there?"

"We inventoried them. No potential murder weapon."

She got a gleam in her brown eyes. "I just thought of something. That bin of tools used to be stored in that closet—" she pointed to a door in the wall of the kitchen—"not catalogued, not under lock and key. They were a recent gift from somebody."

"Who has access?" I asked.

"Well, this whole downstairs area is off-limits to visitors. So only staff." She reconsidered that. "And volunteers." She thought again. "And Board members. I've never seen them down here. They meet in the Avery room upstairs. But they would have access."

"And a visitor could sneak down here?"

She blinked. "You're right. It's only happened a few times in the time I've worked here. But it's possible. Some people love breaking the rules."

"Or they're very curious and have to see what's at the bottom of that beautiful spiral staircase." That's the kind of person I was, actually.

"That too," she said.

"As long as you're here, would you speculate on something?"

"I don't know. Try me."

"Do you think Matt Morgan might have attacked Samantha to keep from being laid off? She planned to outsource his job."

She thought a moment.

"No, I can't comment on that. I'm gonna stick to the facts. Like I gave you."

Looked as though I'd asked too awkward a question too soon again, because she ended the conversation by standing up.

I stood with her. She put her mug, and Matt Morgan's, in the dishwasher. I was glad I didn't have to wrestle with whether or not I should clean up after Matt since, post-Tommy and cleaning up his vomit, I was off of cleaning up after men. We went up the wooden spiral staircase. She undid the velvet rope that blocked off the downstairs and put it back in place after I passed through.

It wasn't much security for keeping a murderer from accessing tools that hadn't been inventoried. Nobody knew if one was missing. What a source for a murderous tool.

Very handy.

CHAPTER 45

I exited the museum, circled the building, and found the architect, engineer, and Matt Morgan around the back, looking at the stone wall they would eventually break through. Matt glared at me, but I didn't let that stop me. The architect and engineer were both willing to be pulled aside for a few minutes and be interviewed about the elevator that would make the museum wheelchair accessible. New story!

As I walked back to my car in lovely June sunshine, a cloud descended, however, one of self-criticism. I began to chastise myself with every footstep. I had done damage in the museum. I'd asked questions that had shut down the museum's receptionist and the handyman, all in one morning. Not to mention an array of board members—David May and Dorothy Anderson—previously.

It was my job to ask questions. I loved being curious and probing, as a journalist ought to be. A reporter had to get the facts of a story fast. I was very "Tell me now, now, now, don't be circumspect, don't be wise, don't think, just spill," before the chance faded, as chances always do. A source at any second could say, "I have to go pick up my kids," and disappear. Even if they gave their phone number for follow-up questions, they probably wouldn't pick up later. It had happened.

I sat in my car, the air and the bucket seat hot. The backs of my legs, exposed because I was wearing a skirt, were burning. I rolled the windows down to let heat out, and the air conditioner kicked in. But I didn't drive away just yet. Time to reflect was essential.

More patience was necessary in the interview process, more holding my killer-question instincts in abeyance—at least sometimes, with some sources.

I would have to be more discerning. Should have used more warm-up time with David May, in his solarium.

I had sabotaged myself, albeit without meaning to. Time to get smarter.

Putting the car in gear, I headed to the newsroom. The scent of wild, thorny roses and ripe honeysuckle wafted through my still-open windows.

Driving slowly, I realized I'd better get with my HP and ask for help. I needed to change. Not just to fulfill my own goals and be a better reporter but to be a better person, a better citizen of the world.

Which led to the question of building rapport with sources. I reached out to them with a smile. I encouraged them to talk by listening intently. I wanted to do it not just to get their stories for the newspaper, not just because I was curious, but also to build connection with other human beings, even if it was fleeting. Life was lonely for many people. To be listened to by another person, even if she was a reporter jotting notes, could be my gift to the world.

I drove past my little house and approached the traffic light at the corner.

What did the people I interviewed experience? What were they feeling? Certainly fear of being misquoted or of having what they said presented untruthfully, out of context. Maybe I could read back from my notes once or twice in the course of an interview to show them at the very least that I had captured every word with my shorthand, and that I respected their words. Which was true: I never changed what people said. My first newspaper editor had taught me that what was placed inside of quotation marks had to be exactly as the person said it, except for "um" or "you know." I'd never forgotten it.

I was going to need divine help to juggle all these facets.

"Help me, please," I said to HP under my breath.

Just then the person behind me at the light honked. I'd been lost in thought and the light was green. I accelerated away, annoyed at being beeped at. In New Jersey there were lots of people who drove with one hand poised over their horn. Then I admitted to myself that I would have honked too.

That night I was propped up by pillows in bed, balmy June air wafting through the open windows, Ninja snuggled alongside me. I was reading a Tony Hillerman novel about Jim Chee, a Navajo policeman on the reservation in Arizona. Chee was narrating the story, and he commented on the Navajo tradition that allowed for long silences in a conversation while people thought about what they wanted to say. White folk who interacted with the Navajo were acutely uncomfortable with the blank spaces and rushed to fill them.

What if I used silence more often as an interview technique? I'd forgotten that tool, and my HP, as a result of my prayer today, had reminded me.

I remembered using that technique once at a huge appliance store when I was shopping for a new stove. The salesman had quoted a number, and I'd been shocked into silence. I just stood there thinking, and my salesman apparently was rattled by the silence because he rushed into it to offer a lower price. I realized what was happening because of Hillerman books I'd read, and I stood silent again. The number came down again. I tried silence again, and the number came down again. At this point he called over his manager. I guessed that by now the price was barely above wholesale, or at least at their lowest threshold. The salesman and the manager were looking uncomfortable, and I figured I'd won.

I decided then and there to use the same technique to buy a high-functioning vacuum cleaner. It worked again.

Not that I wanted to make my sources uncomfortable. But silence might draw them out.

"Thank you for reminding me," I said to HP as I stroked Ninja. He blinked in contentment. He was the only male who'd been in or on my bed in a long, long time.

I'd had one prayer answered today, so I tried another.

"Help with Justin?" Huddled in bed, I realized that I'd fallen in love with him despite my efforts to check him out dispassionately first, to be friends first. Instead, I was hooked. I wanted him near me, forever.

My body and soul ached for him as I rolled to click off the light.

CHAPTER 46

By the next afternoon, Justin still hadn't called. The hole of male companionship left by Tommy's death had been so nicely filled by dating Justin. Because he hadn't called for so long, I was feeling as desolate as a waif abandoned in one of Central Jersey's vast shopping malls. I drove to the *Sentinel*. Instead of trying to write alone at my dining room table and feeling acutely lonely, I would write in the newsroom with at least a few people nearby and be just ordinarily lonely.

Having navigated Route 22 and the offramp to the newspaper without so much as a single honk being directed at me, I plunked myself into my chair and flicked on my computer. The *Sentinel*'s computer system was brand new, just recently installed, and I found it difficult as hell to work with. I'd been told all the reporter's computers were networked, whatever that meant, and I knew they all connected with a printer that spat out our stories on strips of paper. These would be laid out by hand on a mock-up newspaper by a crew at about eleven o'clock each night. A story could be lifted off and replaced by another breaking story at any moment—they used an adhesive (it smelled remarkably good) that allowed almost infinite rearranging. I was hoping to be on the front page again with my story about the elevator being installed at the museum. I prayed for nothing to happen in Central Jersey.

Except for Justin to call.

With the comforting sound of keyboards tapping around me, I typed up my notes. Then I began shaping them into a story. I'd taken a photo of the *troika* that was managing the project: architect, engineer, and Matt Morgan, who'd reluctantly joined the photo. I suspected he did so, even though he hated reporters, because he wanted credit for his role in the project. My photo would accompany the story if there was room. I'd get another photo credit. Cool.

Save your work, I told myself. Give your negatives directly to Mike in the darkroom. Keep an eye out.

After writing the article—in which I quoted the architect and engineer, Matt Morgan's thaw not extending to talking to me on the record—I hit the combination of keys for "save" and made sure I'd tucked the story in a folder where I could find it again. I went to the ladies' room and, on my way back to my desk, peered around the corner first to see if anyone was lurking near my desk. Nobody was.

I had thought of a few changes I wanted to make to the story before I submitted it to Paul Tercell. I woke up my computer and went back to the folder. The story was gone.

I double-checked myself. Where did I leave it again? But I was sure I'd put it in my "Museum" folder, and it most certainly was not there now. I checked all my other folders—I didn't have that many since I'd only been working for this newspaper for two months.

My story was not misfiled. It was gone.

Studying the newsroom, I made a list of all the people present. Gabrielle, Henry Burnham, a reporter named Nathan who specialized in education, Paul the editor, Mike in the darkroom, and two of the business reporters doing their deadly-boring day jobs.

I decided not to suspect Mike. Nobody that tall and that interested in photography was deleting my work. Nor would I suspect Paul. No way an editor would delete his journalist's stories and sabotage his own job. I knocked on the glass door to his office.

"Come in," he said.

But I paused in the doorway and surveyed the newsroom. Gabrielle and Henry were watching me. My suspect list was down to two.

Realizing that Paul expected me to come in and not just stare around the newsroom, I sat down in one of the plastic bucket chairs in front of his desk and told him what had happened.

"You're positive you didn't just misfile it?"

"I file my stories carefully so I don't lose them and have to do them over," I said. "Who wants to type do-overs? I filed it very deliberately. And I've checked all over my computer."

"Nothing?"

"It's gone."

He sighed and reached for his phone. He called for what he called "technical support." I wondered what the heck that was.

"They'll be here later today. I'll ask them to find out who might have gotten into your computer."

"I wonder how that works?"

"No idea. In the meantime, rewrite the story and send it to the printer immediately. I mean the moment you type the last period. No breaks, no phone calls, just write."

"Got it."

I went back to my desk, hating having to write the whole thing again. I was tired of the story already. That's what happens when you question and requestion every word for the truth test. But at least I'd have my notes to refer to, to make sure I got everything right.

When I got back to my desk, my reporter's notebook was gone.

CHAPTER 47

I studied Gabrielle and Henry, but they were on phone calls and
appeared nonchalant.

I went back to Paul's office and reported the new sabotage.

I was shaking with anxiety and frustration. But I forced myself to rewrite
the story. It was all still fresh enough in my mind. I wanted it to appear above
the fold in tonight's edition, to scoop the other newspapers. I was doing the
quotes from memory, but the architect had a Slavic name, and I couldn't
remember where all the s's, c's, and z's went. So I looked him up in the
Yellow Pages directory, keeping an eye on my desk. The rewritten story was
still in my computer when I got back from the reference shelf.

Out of the corner of my eye, I saw Gabrielle get up from her chair, grab
her purse, and head towards the ladies' room. Did she steal my notebook? I
sauntered over to her desk and gave its surface a quick glance. Then,
abandoning my rewritten story to its fate, I followed her to the bathroom.

Gabrielle emerged from a stall. She set her bag at her feet to wash her
hands, and it gapped open. I peered in it for my notebook, and Gabrielle
noticed that I was eyeing her bag.

"What?" she said. She didn't sound cheery, or even falsely cheery, like
she normally did.

Her question hung in the air, demanding a response. I decided not to
confront her then but to wait for the techie guys.

"I like your bag." I kicked myself for not being more confrontational,
but then again, she was a colleague who had shown an interest in me. To
unjustly accuse her would be to lose her good opinion of me forever.

I dashed into a cubicle, heard Gabrielle leave, and re-emerged to slink back to my desk. My story was still there. I sat with a sigh and began to re-read the story for errors.

Then the phone rang. Paul had commanded that I take no calls, just write and get the story to him before any more disasters struck. But this might be Justin. I debated for one more ring—what was more important: this story or love?—then picked up.

It was my mother.

The letdown felt like a plane crash into a vast Central Jersey parking lot.

"Tricia, I want you to take me into the city to see Susan and the kids," my mother said. "We have to rescue them."

"I don't think she wants to be rescued—at least not yet." I thought of my deadlines, of all the stories I was working on, of all the meetings and interviews I would miss if I went into the city for a day, especially with no guarantee Susan would leave with us.

"Honey, we're going. Tomorrow. Take the day off and meet me at the train at 8:15."

I groaned inwardly. But she was probably right. We had to take steps.

I got the next day off by hinting to Paul that a family matter of life and death was at stake, which was true. This wasn't just a mental health day.

The next morning, Ninja complained as I prepared to leave him behind.

"I know, honey, it's tough. But you just take a nap and I'll be back, maybe with company, before you know it."

I remembered with a chill that Susan's husband knew where I lived. She wouldn't be safe here. Nor would I be if she were living with me, though I hated to be thinking of myself. But I did.

CHAPTER 48

I met Mom at the train. It arrived with a screech of brakes, we clambered aboard, and it took off toward the danger zone. The car we sat in smelled of popcorn. The landscape outside the windows rushed by. Usually I'd be excited, heading into the city, with so many buildings and vistas that were used frequently in films. Today we were in a suspense movie with a violent man lurking in the shadows.

"I'm not leaving without her," my mother said, plunking her big leather handbag in her lap. "We're not taking no for an answer."

"It might not go the way you hope," I said, thinking of how long it was taking Meg to decide to leave.

"Start praying now and don't stop the whole time we're there, and it will go better," she replied.

I thought of something someone had said in a Twelve Step meeting about what she did when she was nervous, like before a job interview: "I send my Higher Power into the room ahead of me." I'd do that too. And pray for the wings of the Almighty to be over us, especially the children.

"She'll have to go to a shelter," I said. "She can't stay with us. Robert probably has our addresses written down somewhere. After the beautiful décor she's enjoyed, she's not going to much like the ambiance in a battered women's shelter."

"Fuck the décor," my mother said. I stared at her. She'd never used that language before. "This is about saving her life, and her children. I'll make her leave that nasty piece of work. They'll stay with me. I'll kill that son of a bitch if he gets anywhere near us."

We sat in silence, me thinking *good luck with that*, while the train rocked us toward the city. By 10 a.m. we were in front of Susan's building.

"You grab Nathaniel," Mom said, "I'll grab Louise. Susan will naturally follow them. And we'll be done."

"What about packing some clothes?"

"Forget clothes, forget crap. Just save them."

I thought they should each be able to at least grab their favorite toy. Surely there would be time for that tiny comfort to come with them.

There was no doorman at Susan's building. Robert had scrimped on that but let the money flow when expanding and decorating the apartment. To get in, we had to use the intercom. I buzzed Susan's apartment. Mom said not to let on that she was with me.

There was a long wait.

"Yes?" It was Susan, more tentative than ever.

"Hey, sis, it's me. Just a quick visit. Let me up."

Another long pause.

"I can't see you today. You should have called first."

"Aw, come on, I took the day off to see you, took the train, then the PATH train. I've suffered. Just let me come up and say hi to the kids."

Silence.

The door buzzed, surprising us. We dashed through before she could change her mind.

The elevator smelled of popcorn too. I didn't want this visit to turn into a horror movie.

Standing in front of Susan's door, my mother said we should pray before we knocked. So we each breathed a prayer out loud, "Help us" and "Save Susan, please, Lord, save the children." Then I knocked.

Susan opened the door a crack. She was blocking any sight of the apartment or the kids.

"You should have called first," she whispered. "He might be back any minute. He just went out for coffee."

"Let us in," I said, pushing on the door. I was running low on patience for all this cowering around Robert. I just wanted to do the rescue and get the hell away from this hell of an apartment.

The door hardly budged. Susan had her foot and leg securing it. She spotted Mom behind me.

"What? You shouldn't be here!" she cried.

I was plumb out of patience. I shoved the door mightily and it banged open. She stumbled back, revealing Nathaniel and Louise huddled in the entrance to the kitchen. The luxurious, full-length velvet drapes on the windows were all drawn shut. It was dark in the living room, the air and the atmosphere stale.

Despite the humidity of the room, Susan wore long, loose sleeves again.

My mother—I'd never seen her more fierce—plunked her big bag on the Oriental carpet, grabbed one of Susan's hands, and shoved her sleeve up. New purple bruises shone forth over the yellow, fading old bruises. She grabbed the other arm and did the same. Yellow and green skin. I couldn't bear to think of the pain. And of the children's pain as witnesses.

"Look at you," Mom said. "We're leaving. Together. Look at your children." We all turned toward them. Their faces were twisted into knots of fear.

"You can't tell me what to do!"

"Susan, you idiot, your children know what's happening. It's ruining them. You're leaving here for good. Now."

I didn't think calling Susan an idiot was going to help win her over, but it was understandable.

I was worried about Robert coming back. I had no stomach for confronting a man with no compunction about hitting women.

"Susan, let's go," I pleaded.

She looked around the spacious living room, eyes lingering on the grand piano. Maybe she was saying goodbye to precious things, the kinds of things she might not be able to buy in her single state.

"I can't afford to leave," she said, turning to Mom with big anxious eyes.

"Yes, you can. You'll do what's necessary to save your children," Mom said. "I'll mind them some. He'll pay child support. The rest you'll figure out. Get going, come on, he'll be back soon."

At this, the children whimpered.

It was time for me to be as decisive as Mom.

"Nathaniel, grab a toy," I said. He picked up the dinosaur at his feet. I picked him up. Oh my God, a five-year-old is heavy.

My mom grabbed three-year-old Louise, who had a book in her hand.

We headed toward the front door. Susan closed it on us.

"Susan, open that door," my mother panted. Three-year-olds are heavy too. "You're getting the hell out now."

"At least let me pack." She was all hunched over, in a defensive position, but I hoped that, if she wanted to pack, she might be close to being ready to go.

"He might be back any minute. We're leaving now." My mother was short of breath.

Slowly, slowly Susan straightened her spine, then her shoulders. She looked around the apartment, saying a last goodbye to beloved things, it seemed to me.

We heard a key in the lock.

The door opened and Robert strode in, paper coffee cup in hand. He was nattily dressed in sharply creased khakis and a crisp blue button-down shirt. His tanned skin shone with a light June sweat. His longish hair was slicked straight back with gel—I could see the tracks of the comb. I loathed that hairstyle.

"Susan, what the hell?" he demanded. His condescending tone of voice said everything about their relationship.

My fierce mother became even fiercer. She was not so much a mother hen brooding over her chicks as a fighting rooster ready to rake Robert's face with its spurs.

"What the hell have you been doing to my daughter!" she spat out. "And to these children! A big man like you hitting a woman. Coward!" She seemed to be searching for more names to call him but was too overwrought to come up with them.

But then she drew herself to even more height and width and advanced on him as he blocked the door to freedom.

"We're leaving now. You're done ruining these lives."

He watched her step toward the door and stagger under the weight of Louise and her big pocketbook. The look of scorn that permanently occupied his face grew more pronounced.

"I know where you live," he said, each word redolent with menace.

My mother froze, then stepped toward him with calm rage.

"I know from Susan—the one time she's called me in six months—that you're worried about your job."

His look of superiority faded. Just a bit.

My mother drove it home.

"If we so much as see your shadow, ever again, your boss—no, your CEO—will receive pictures of my daughter's arms. I'll ruin you," she said.

He swallowed.

I loved my mom for her courage. For turning the tables. Though it was a man's world, and the CEO might do nothing. I didn't think I'd ever feel safe again. How much worse it must be for Susan.

Our little troop of threatened females, plus our tender youngster Nathaniel, sidled toward the door.

"That necklace you're wearing—it belonged to my mother," Robert said. "Give it back."

Susan looked down at the heavy gold chain and the heavy knob of gold at the end of it.

"It's coming with me," she said defiantly. "You owe me at least that much."

My mother's courage was infectious! Go, Susan!

"I'll see you in court," he snarled with all his scorn firmly back in place.

Susan took Louise from my mother's arms and opened the door.

Robert threw his coffee at Susan. It drenched her sleeve—and the back of his daughter's dress. Louise shrieked, drew in a deep, deep breath, then cried piercingly.

With a fear-laden glance at her husband, Susan opened the door and left.

We dashed out after her, crowded together onto the elevator, and escaped.

CHAPTER 49

Susan assured us in the elevator that the coffee hadn't been very hot. When she sat down in the train, she fussed over Louise's wet clothes but couldn't do a thing to change them—she'd left everything behind. She then cried the rest of the way back to Passaic. Nathaniel and Louise wailed inconsolably. Mom and I cuddled the children and patted Susan's hands, careful to not touch her sore arms. We murmured reassuring words as best we could, but their grief was overwhelming. It's huge when a marriage is over, a father lost.

But that abuser's devilish control over them was broken. At least externally. It might be a long road to freedom for them internally. Their psyches had absorbed so much malevolence.

Upon arriving at my town's train station, Mom loaded us all into her car. I directed her to the Somerset battered women's shelter. Turned out they had a room. Susan scanned the decrepit living area with dismay but stayed. The kids looked around, wide-eyed. I took comfort in the fact that they all were in a secret location, being debriefed by professionals on all that had happened to them.

But would they ever heal? Especially the children. Would they become abusers themselves, since that's what the most powerful adult in their lives had modeled? Would they marry abusers instinctively, seeking at a subconscious level to heal their father? Both outcomes were so common. Susan should have left long ago. I hoped and prayed she would do everything in her power to get her children all the psychological help she could. But it might not be enough to spare their futures.

The next day I drove to work, dodging aggressive New Jersey drivers, and driving too aggressively myself, to be honest. I entered the newsroom feeling the sorrow of the damage done to my family. I scribbled page after page about the rescue into my reporter's notebook, as if it were a diary, putting the details on paper so I'd stop carrying them inside me with all the pain they gave me. Since someone kept stealing my notebooks and this was personal, family information, I tore those pages out when I was done and went to the kitchen, where I ripped them into tiny pieces and threw them in with the coffee grounds. Surely that would foil any sabotage.

When I returned to my desk, Paul was looming over it, entire body tight as usual.

"Please come to my office," he said.

Was this news about the computer sabotage, or had I done something wrong myself? Bosses saying "come to my office" always caused me overwhelming dread.

"Close the door," he said when I got to it.

He tilted himself into his chair stiffly, hardly bending at waist or knee. Normally it would have made me smile, at least inwardly, but today I was too nervous.

"Well, our tech support figured out what happened."

Had I made a mistake saving the document? Was this all my fault? Had I raised a false alarm? I felt as tense as he looked.

"They saw that Gabrielle deleted your file." He paused, considering what to say next. He pushed his glasses up with his forefinger. "They had told me to require passwords when we installed the system two months ago, but I thought it was unnecessary—that we were all working toward the same goal." He shook his head. "So I overruled that recommendation, thinking passwords were a roadblock to writing. I'm just glad worse didn't happen."

I sat there, stunned. I didn't know what to say. Into the silence, Paul leapt. Bingo!

"We fired Gabrielle just now."

I rallied my wits. "Gabrielle was always friendly toward me." Then I remembered how her advice had always been given in a patronizing tone. I'd felt condescended to.

"Well, she no longer works here."

"I see."

"When you get back to your desk, you'll see a prompt in your computer to create a password. There'll be no more sneaking into other people's work and deleting files."

"I see," I said again stupidly. I was reeling with this news. Gabrielle was such a competent reporter. Why had she risked her job to sabotage me?

As I headed back to my workstation, I saw her with a box, loading things from her desk. She finished up, hoisted the box, glanced around the newsroom contemptuously, and headed to the exit.

This was a mystery that I was going to pursue. There were so many others—who murdered Samantha? What was Justin thinking? Where was the murder weapon?—that were unresolved, but this one I was going to get to the bottom of right now. Leaving my purse and reporter's notebook unprotected on my desk, I followed Gabrielle.

Out in the parking lot, she put the box on the hood of her car and unlocked the door.

"Wait!" I called, approaching her.

She stared at me with a look of dislike, if not hatred.

"Gabrielle, why? You're such a good reporter. Why mess with my stories?" And photos, come to think of it.

"You had that great source of stories on the museum. On murder."

I just couldn't comprehend what she was talking about. "What about it?"

"You pushed me off the front page—twice. You were going to keep doing it, with a murder to write about and all." She grabbed her purse strap from off her shoulder and swung the big bag, and I stepped back because her motion seemed aggressive. "I just wish I'd read the memo about how the system kept track of who and what and when. Stupid me." She took the box off the hood and put it on the passenger seat. Then she surprised me.

"You have a big future in journalism."

"And you—envy me?" I really wanted to know her base motivation.

But that mystery didn't get solved. She turned with a flounce, strode jauntily to the driver's side, got in smoothly, and started her engine with a roar. Pulling out of her space with tires squealing, she sent her car's rear end swerving dangerously close to the taillights of my car, parked nearby. But she righted her VW Jetta with an inch to spare. She was a rally driver, she knew her stuff.

I watched her accelerate down the ramp onto Route 22. Two cars honked mightily, one high, one low, as she cut into the relentless New Jersey traffic.

I thought, there goes someone who has, or had, a big future in journalism too.

CHAPTER 50

W hen I got back from my encounter with Gabrielle, Paul approached my desk in his stiff, muscle-bound way and asked, well, told me really, to interview a man who had just been released from prison. He had written and illustrated a children's book in jail, and it had been published. He was planning to start an art school. Instead of having to beat the bushes for my next story (which might be why they call a reporter's territory a "beat"), I'd been handed an assignment.

"He's paid his debt to society. Check him out."

"Maybe we can give him some free publicity," I said. Paul nodded and lumbered back to his office, heavy shoulders tottering from side to side.

So I gathered up my reporter's notebook and several working pens, stuffed them in my shoulder sac, grabbed my camera, and scooted out to my car.

At a strip mall that graced the next town, where the art school was going to be located, I met Louis. He was a medium-sized man who had spent his time with barbells, evidently, because his cotton knit shirt was molded to a swelling chest and biceps. He had a German Shepherd with him, held by a short thick chain.

I thought, ooops. Here I am, alone with a man holding who-knows-what-temperament of a dog, a man who might have been put in prison for violent crimes. I should have asked Paul about it before agreeing to this assignment.

But I was a reporter who prided herself on getting the story. Besides, my editor assigned it, so I would do it. No way I wasn't fulfilling an assignment. And maybe this interview put me in the same league as war correspondents who conducted interviews with bombs falling around them. Heroic pursuit of the truth. That was me. And look, Louis had greeted me with a big smile that couldn't possibly have an evil ulterior motive to it. Though maybe Jack the Ripper would have too.

Louis fumbled to unlock the door of an empty storefront. Maybe he was nervous, like me, although I thought I had better reason to be. With more than a *frisson* of fear, I followed him and the dog in. The interior had gray industrial carpet throughout, a few folding chairs, and walls with scars and marks.

"I still have to turn this into an art school," he said, sitting down and indicating a chair for me to do the same. The dog paced the edges of the shop nervously, maybe like a convict in his cell. I wished Louis hadn't let go of his leash.

"You must be wondering how an ex-con can afford to do all this." He gestured around the shop.

I was relieved about one thing: this man was revealing nuts and bolts, not forcing me to ask the question. I nodded encouragement, clicked my pen, checked on the dog's whereabouts, and started scribbling.

"My church is helping me. I made some bad decisions. And paid for them. But kept in touch with my church—my wife did, really—and they're helping me. We'll make a new start."

I decided to be bold, especially since he'd been forthcoming so far, and ask him a piercing question. I approached it as gently as I could.

"Could you please tell me what you were in prison for?"

"I don't like talking about it."

I decided to be silent and see what happened.

Louis tapped his fingers on one knee. He leaned back and folded his muscular arms. The silence stretched on. I thought the technique had failed this time and mentally formed another question to ask.

"I stole high-end cars. Mercedes. Lambos and Ferraris when I could."

I was surprised. Saddened at the profound folly.

"At night. Rode them around. Then I parked them, in good shape, and found another one. Bunch of times. Got caught."

I didn't know what to say. We're all desperados, was the Bible's take on things, though *my* transgressions hadn't put me in prison. At least not one with bars on the windows. They cost me freedom in other ways.

"I'd say envy is a deadly sin," Louis said. "Just like they say in church. It's a number one reason people get in trouble, end up in prison."

Here was the topic of envy emerging yet again, I thought. Must take note—Higher Power specialized in "coincidence."

"If you envy what other people have," Louis continued, "you'll be tempted to do anything to get it."

The dog was now at his master's side. He looked at me with the same attitude that New Yorkers did on the streets of Manhattan—not caring if a person lived or died. I looked away before he'd get irritated with my gaze locking on his and leapt at my throat.

"Thank God they let me have some art supplies in jail. And I had time to think. Got some ideas for a children's book. Here it is." He reached into the satchel he was carrying and brought it out.

The cover art was very appealing. I opened the book. The other pages too had attractive illustrations.

"Congratulations on great work," I said.

"You can keep that copy."

"Thanks, I'll read it. What's it about?"

"My childhood. I was raised in the South Ward of Newark."

I had an idea that he was saying he was poor, impoverished even, schools crumbling, lacking proper textbooks. "Tell me what your childhood was like there."

"School was as dangerous as the street." He was silent. Perhaps to wait for my next question. Perhaps to give his words impact. I decided to simply wait myself.

"My friend Frankie was killed by a stray bullet in a drive-by shooting. Eight years old. His older brother was arrested for running a drug ring and been in prison ten years. All my other friends ended up junkies or in prison." He looked at me appraisingly, perhaps calculating the price of my clothes and shoes and haircut. "Where did you grow up?"

"Here in Passaic."

"Your childhood was nothing like mine. You didn't see your friends in coffins. Your best buddies could play on Saturday—they weren't visiting their Dad in prison. You and your friends all got good educations and jobs."

I didn't answer. I was too busy noticing the envy in his voice and attitude. He was frowning at me. His negativity charged the air between us.

I'd never thought my childhood was particularly enviable. But looking through his lens, I could see that the quiet, leafy suburbs might seem like paradise. A "cookies with your mom after school" sort of thing. Though much has been written about how appearances in the 'burbs mask nasty problems.

"I'm sorry it was so tough for you," I said.

He sat quietly, sorting through some thoughts, I guessed.

"Well, I got a good story out of it," he said, waving his hand toward the book in my lap. "But I gotta learn not to be envious. It's a trap."

His mood seemed to have lifted. He told me he was opening his art school in three weeks, that church members would help him paint the walls, that he was calling the school the Folsom Blues.

"I'm not hiding my past," he said. "That's why I finally told you why I was in prison. 'We will not regret the past nor wish to shut the door on it.'"

"You're quoting the Twelve Steps!" And I began to relax. This was evidently a compadre I was talking too.

"Damn right—I mean, yep."

"I'm in them too, for the stuff that's whooping me," I said.

"It's a good club to be in."

"So true. What's your specialty?" I asked.

"Alcoholics Anonymous. You?"

"I'm in Al-Anon. For people who are in relationship with people who aren't in recovery. Which is so much of the world. It helps me a lot."

"Between the Twelve Steps and Jesus, my life is transformed. I was miserable before, drinking, stealing cars. Reached bottom in prison. I'm thankful for it—it led me to my Higher Power. Confessed to my sponsor and to God the exact nature of my wrongs. Made amends where I could. I'm seven hundred pounds lighter. Now I'm bursting with energy." He slapped his chest with one hand. "New man!" He cocked his head to one side, regarding me, and then smiled a beatific smile. "Bet you were nervous to meet me!"

We laughed. Our common ground felt good. And the dog lay down and put his head on his paws. He really looked benign.

"Listen, I'll check into taking a class with you."

"Call me in three weeks, and I'll have the schedule." He handed me a business card that revealed an artist's flair, with a brush stroke of cobalt blue in one corner.

As we sat in the raw, unfinished space, enjoying our new camaraderie, he told me more about his plans for Folsom Blues. I was glad to give him a story in the *Sentinel*—free publicity—and glad to have a means of doing him a big, good turn. I hoped the story got prominent placement.

Outside the shop, I took a picture with him holding a copy of his book. A big smile lit up his face. Nobody would be scared to take an art class with this man.

We parted friends.

CHAPTER 51

As I had reflected the last few days on my recent interviewing style, I felt twinges of remorse about my conduct during my last interview with museum Board member David May. I had jumped to the hardest question—truth be told, an impudent question, his reason for selling some land—so quickly. It had been wrong of me. Impolite—though weren't reporters supposed to show some chutzpah to get a story? Yet I could hear my mother saying his personal finances were none of my business.

He had been wrong to threaten my job, but that was his stuff, not mine. I had talked it over with Catherine, since my sponsor was vacationing in Europe. She'd said to clean up my side of the street and apologize, that I would feel better. And it occurred to me that this was a good idea for another reason: it would be very wise to regain him, if I could, as a source for news and perspective on the museum.

So I called him that afternoon and asked him contritely if I could meet him. To apologize, I admitted, hoping that would convince him to say yes.

He'd sounded surprised but invited me to come to his home that afternoon.

I did chores first, to catch up with the backlog, washing a few days' worth of dishes, mopping the kitchen floor, and snagging a few dust bunnies in the living room. Then I looked out the picture window. The grass! It had taken a few leaps upward since I'd last mown it. Trudging outside in shorts, I did that too. The roses needed deadheading. Got pricked on arms and legs.

I was sweating in the June sun and had bits of chopped grass sticking to my skin, so I showered. I raced through it so I wouldn't be late. I left towels on the floor and make-up tubes on the sink. Talk about two steps forward and one back.

It was pleasant driving in David May's wealthy countryside. Each mansion was set off to advantage, far back on hills above quiet lanes. A few places had a small herd of cows lying down to chew their cud under trees. Gentleman farmers got a tax break that way. They hired people to milk and feed the beasts. The gentlemen themselves never stepped in a cowpat, that's for sure. The whole arrangement was such a cheat. The laws had been written by people from their class who, for something to do in their unpressured lives, had joined the state legislature.

Very famous people, not from the class of inherited money, bought houses here too. Mike Tyson, World Heavyweight Champion, had owned an 18,000-square-foot mansion in the Somerset Hills for two years recently. There had been accounts in the *Sentinel* about the police going to the house to break up parties turned violent. Now that was an example of a person who had made his career dreams come true—but was he bankrupt of true friends? Dear family? Deep happiness? I wished Justin would call. The bungee cord of *The New York Times* might not pull me toward the meaningful life I yearned for.

I rang David's front doorbell. The same maid in the same uniform answered and led me through the vast living room. I gave the home my sniff test. This house was *clean*. Mine, I was sure, had the scent of dust bunnies— faint, I hoped. Anita stopped outside the solarium and gestured for me to continue in. The room appeared different somehow. Then I realized the cushions for the wrought iron furniture were new. The fabric was gorgeous, leaves and vines in deep greens and blues, surely by a famous designer. $100 per yard, I could guess.

David stood when I entered the glass room and extended his hand.

"Mr. May, thank you for meeting with me."

He smiled, I thought a bit wolfishly, like he was lying in wait to enjoy watching Red Riding Hood eat crow. But it was my Twelve Step responsibility to apologize and make amends when I'd been wrong. I'd gotten a lot of wisdom for living from the Steps, so I did what was recommended.

"I'm sorry I was rude to you the last time I was here. I got carried away and asked too personal a question, and I hope you'll accept my apology." There. That was enough. Any more, and I'd be repeating myself and losing dignity.

"Accepted," he said. A bit triumphantly, it seemed to me. And I began to feel defensive. Was this the upper classes condescending to the middle class yet again?

I tried to calm myself. "Thanks." I noticed that he didn't apologize for his threat about my job. But according to the Twelve Steps, getting an apology from him for his overstepping of boundaries was none of my business.

"As long as I'm here, can I ask you a few questions about the museum?"

"Sure. But let me offer you something to drink first." He pressed a button, and the maid appeared at the door a few seconds later. "Anita, will you get us something to drink?" He turned to me. "Coffee? Tea? Soda?"

"I'll take water." I minded the manners my mother had taught me and said, "please.'

"Sparkling or plain?"

Wow! So many options in this mansion. "Sparkling would be nice, thank you."

"I'll take Indian tea," David said to the maid. No please or thank you there.

"Yes, sir," she said and disappeared.

And I felt my resentment grow. My magic magnifying mind went spinning: she probably shopped for the tea, put it away in a cabinet, took orders to make it, steeped it, brought it, took his cup away, washed it, put it away. And then cleaned the microwave.

Out the solarium window I saw a man on a tractor, mowing acre after acre. A team of laborers worked on the flowerbeds. This was a whole different way of life from mine. The owner of this house didn't get itchy bits of grass sticking to his sweaty legs. I remembered a quote I'd read somewhere, by an upper-class English writer: "Life without servants would hardly be worth living." At the time, I had choked on the sense of entitlement, the hubris. I still did.

I tried to shove the stew of envy aside, so that this time I'd have a good interview with David. I couldn't let resentment ruin this opportunity. But wisps of steam from the fetid stew kept rising. Struggling with myself, I decided to ask a softball question wrapped in a compliment—a true one. I hoped he couldn't hear the envy in my voice.

"This is such a lovely home. Have you lived here long?"

He smiled, leaned back in his chair, and crossed his long, elegant legs in their creased khaki pants. His loafers gleamed. Did he even have a valet to care for his clothes and dress him in the morning?

"My family has been in New Jersey since the early 1700s. One of my great-great—you don't need to know how many greats exactly—grandfathers was president of Princeton University." He was smug and probably intended for me to be impressed, which I was. I nodded and raised an eyebrow, to ask for more information.

Anita brought his tea and a sweating glass of fizzy water with ice on a tray. She set my drink on a nearby glass-topped table, with a cork coaster underneath.

"Thanks," I said, looking up at her to acknowledge her. She didn't meet my gaze.

David said nothing. Anita disappeared.

"That's when it was known as Princeton Seminary, of course," he said. "The Reverend John Witherspoon. Became president in 1768. He guided the seminary for twenty-six years."

All this ancient lineage. I felt at a big disadvantage. Unlike my sister, I knew my grandmothers' maiden names. But not much more than that about my family. They had been ordinary people. They did not have two-hundred-year-old portraits hanging in the president's office at Princeton University.

"That's really terrific," I said in response. A bit dully. My resolve not to be envious was being overwhelmed by all these irreproachable credentials.

"One of my great-great grandfathers helped to write the Constitution. Later ancestors of mine also served Princeton or served the state as attorney general or state treasurer, and so forth. They helped to shape this state, to shape this nation." He leaned back in his wrought-iron chair to regard me with satisfaction. "To answer your question, they built this house in the 1850s. I was raised here."

I had exhausted my supply of compliments for his house and his background—which I could imagine included a country club and tennis lessons since childhood. In fact, I was now feeling envious of his heritage as well as his cushions. And I couldn't get over how many people were working on his grounds. I had better not let him know it, I thought. This is not a good state of being. This is what Louis had been feeling about my background, envying the advantages I'd had as a middle-class person raised in a calm suburb. I mustn't ruin this opportunity for an interview with a Board member by emitting waves envy.

Also, I mustn't give David the satisfaction.

I thought it would help me if I changed the subject. I repeated a question I'd asked him before. "Tell me about Samantha's plans for the museum in that first—and only—meeting she held." I took my reporter's notebook out of my purse and opened to a clean page, to show him he was on the record. I scribbled the date at the top.

"She had the latest ideas about presenting not just men's work, but also women's and—." He stopped himself, then started again. "To tell the untold stories. She was going to revolutionize our mission, our exhibits. She would have been a breath of fresh air. It's such a sad loss."

Several days had passed since I had last asked this next question. I'd ask it and be silent and see what David May leapt into the silence to tell me. I was looking for a scoop.

"Is the Board of Trustees ready to hire another curator?"

"Funny you should ask. We met just last night. We'll begin advertising for one immediately. Dorothy Anderson is in charge of getting the notice into the magazines that museum personnel would read."

I waited. He didn't fill the silence. So I gave in and did. "You're hiring someone new not knowing who or why someone attacked Samantha?"

"We think it must have had something to do with her personal life."

That seemed like a big presumption, but I didn't want to say that to David and get kicked out again. So I countered with a different card. "Did you change the job description at all?"

"Not a word. We wanted someone to shake things up, and we still do."

He seemed subdued at that statement. Maybe he wasn't quite in favor of shaking things up.

"Perhaps several Board members didn't want things changed much?" I cocked my head, made my whole body into a question mark. I'd read that human beings can hardly resist answering a question.

"I would say most of us are all for it."

He hadn't been specific, so I thought I'd pin him down. Gently. No desire to have to make another apology.

"What did you think of her plans to change things?" I put a slight emphasis on "you."

He waved a hand vaguely. "Oh, I was all for it."

But it wasn't convincing. That gesture seemed hesitant, not confident.

I couldn't press any further.

But I had gotten my new news, that the search was on to fill Samantha's job. That was cool. Now I just had to round out the details for my new story. "Could I have a copy of the job description?"

"Sure. I'll get it." David got up in an easy, well-oiled movement and disappeared. Probably going to his cherry-paneled office, to search his priceless family-heirloom desk for the right paper. While he was gone, I quickly examined the beautiful cushion I'd been seated on. Sure enough, a tag revealed the provenance. Dior. I set it back in place and plunked myself down quickly. It wouldn't do, in polite society, to be seen reading the labels on things. That would be as gauche as asking how much he'd spent on them, which I could already guess.

Through the greenhouse's panes, I watched the man on the mower, now at the far end of the meadow. What would it be like to live like this? New curtains and fresh upholstery whenever you felt like it. People asking you deferentially to be on the boards of prestigious organizations. On the downside, people asking you for donations, and you feeling the weight of their expectation of a hefty amount. I watched a gardener watering the rose bushes. The scratches my roses had given me still stung. Yes, I could deal with this life. And look at those two Tiffany lamps. Had to be genuine. They glowed in the afternoon sun that poured through the glass walls and ceiling.

David came back and gave me the page with the job description on it. I read the first paragraph to myself—quickly, thanks to the good education I'd received in my middle-class suburb. I read: "The curator will direct the acquisition, storage, and exhibit of collections, including negotiating and authorizing the purchase, sale, exchange, or loan of collections. They also will authenticate, evaluate, and categorize the specimens in a collection."

I looked for and didn't find any sentences about providing new approaches. "This is the job you had before you resigned and joined the Board," I said. It wasn't a question: I wasn't sure what my question was. I hoped David would just talk and say something pithy.

"Yes. I studied museum management in college and served several museums. One was in New York City. The commute was crazy, then Kiki got her diagnosis. So I wanted to work near home. I brought the Museum of Historic Tools forward in its mission, I like to think. The Board has said I did. But it became time for me to be with Kiki more."

I certainly didn't envy him a sick spouse. Been there, done that.

I glanced over the job description again. "Where's the part about shaking things up?"

"That was discussed with Samantha during the interview."

"Oh." That seemed odd. "I'd want it in description if I were thinking of taking this job."

A look of annoyance crossed David's face. "As I said, we'll take care of it in the interview process."

I didn't press for more on that. I could sense that his patience was ebbing, that this interview was coming to a close.

I folded the job description and slipped it into my purse. "Who is on the search committee?" I asked. My readers may not need this information in the story I would write, but I did.

He rattled off three names. Dennis and he were both on the list.

"Is there anything else I should know?" I'd found that was a great question to conclude with. People often added footnotes to what they'd said that turned out to be very interesting.

But not this time. David shook his head a brief "no."

Time for one sticky last question, one that begged to be asked. I softballed it as well as I could, like I'd softened my question about prison to Louis.

"Mr. May," I asked deferentially, "you know the museum and its staff and Board members well." That compliment might help. "Who do you think was so upset with Samantha Scarborough that he—or she—struck her with so much force?"

He smiled coolly, not that difficult to do in the well-cooled air of the solarium. He leaned back and clasped a knee. "I don't even have a theory about that one. Do you?"

"No, not at all." I didn't much like having the question turned on me. And I sensed I could keep digging for a theory from him and would never get it. "Well, thanks. I appreciate your time. Very much."

I stuffed my reporters' notebook into my purse and stood. David rang the bell for Anita, who appeared moments later. He and I shook hands, and I followed Anita out, through the enormous living room—there stood the two glossy concert grand pianos at either end. The Mays also commanded a view of the Somerset Hills out of a huge bay window. I thought to myself, even if I wrote several *very* successful books, I'd still never be able to afford this way of life.

In the entry hall, floored with black and white marble diamonds, like the solarium, I got a whiff of what was probably dinner being started. I had to go home and start supper too. I was cook, housekeeper, valet, mower, and gardening team, all in one. What really upset me was that I'd met people like David May, from old money, who looked down on middle-class people like me for all that we had to contend with because we couldn't afford servants. I suspected David had that attitude lurking in him too. I'd seen him trot out the *hauteur*—the pride of an old family with lots of high-level connections. And tractor-trailer-loads of money in the bank. Investments all over the world.

I stepped out of the big front door onto granite steps. Anita closed the door with a firm click behind me. This place was most certainly not my world. Big planters full of cascading flowers, that a worker kept in their prime all season long, taunted me.

The stew of envy I'd been shoving down came boiling up and over.

I got in my Corolla, wondering what David May drove. But his cars were behind the four garage doors that were discreetly shut against prying eyes.

As I pulled away, I accelerated too hard by mistake/on purpose and showered a manicured foundation planting with gravel. In my rearview mirror, I could see small white rocks bouncing off the stone walls behind the bush.

I hated myself for envying the rich. It was making me miserable. And it looked like I was going to have to apologize *again*.

CHAPTER 52

I drove down David and Kiki May's long, long driveway, toward the shady, winding lane that would return me to the land of people with ordinary means.

While wrenching the wheel to make the right turn onto the road just outside the May's pillars, which were topped with two gilded, winged lions—of course they were—I could see even more clearly how upset I was. At their luxurious life and at myself. Churning up that gravel, I had been just as childish as Gabrielle putting her car into a fishtail so close to my car. That poor bush I'd just abused. Certainly it was innocent of *hauteur*.

It wasn't just the bushes. What if I had broken a window? What if I'd knocked an eye out of one of the gardeners? He would sue me, and I could very well lose my little house, my main asset. I shuddered in the June warmth.

I passed through the Mays' village and out the other side, the houses getting smaller and closer together. I thought of Louis and what he'd said about envy and what it had driven him, and so many others in prison, to do. I was scared. Envy was whooping me.

I'll talk to Catherine, I thought. But that hardly seemed like enough to purge it. I'll journal about it and call my sponsor—when did she say she was getting back from vacation?—and talk about it in the meeting tonight and call other Twelve Step people, whoever will listen. I've got to get free of this potentially disastrous defect of character.

I telephoned Catherine as soon as I got home to my neighborhood of postage-stamp yards and shoulder-to-shoulder houses. She said she'd come over right after work. That was only an hour away, so I tidied up and cleaned the bathroom while picturing Anita vacuuming and tidying and cleaning for the Mays, all day every day.

Then for a few minutes I read a novel that had been recommended. I found myself envying the writer's prose style. I could never write with that kind of imagination, I was thinking. I was bedeviled by this envy thing, I was beginning to see.

Then I heard Catherine park in the driveway. Her car's engine sounded different to me. I hurried out to the steps.

There she sat, in a periwinkle-blue convertible BMW sports car, her golden-red hair gleaming. She waved, cut the throaty engine, and popped out of the car.

"Tricia, look what I did!" She rushed to me in excitement. I came down the steps and we hugged.

"Catherine, it's beautiful! Absolutely stunning." And you make a much finer sight driving around in it than I do in my gray, hard-top Corolla.

"Come on, we're going to the Jersey Shore!"

She was beaming. I was supposed to be happy for her. But her Ph.D. in chemistry and her pharmaceutical job brought in a better income than mine—much. I'd suspected it; she'd never flaunted pricey items before, but here was dazzling proof of my suspicion.

"What on earth, Catherine? What have you done?" I sounded mean in my own ears. Wait, try again. "Wow!"

"Get your stuff. I'll tell you about it while we drive in my Brand. New. Convertible!" She danced a little jig. "Let's go!"

I put on shorts. Mid-June was too early for a swim in the Atlantic, but I'd at least get my feet wet. I grabbed a windbreaker for those evening ocean breezes, patted Ninja, who was lurking near the door, bugged at my leaving, and locked up.

"Here's sunscreen," she said, protecting her face and bare arms. "We don't want to turn into giant freckles. Take this hat or your hair will tangle." She handed me a baseball cap with "Brooklyn" emblazoned on it and captured her own hair in a messy bun with a scrunchy. I could imagine how care-free we looked, two young women—well, relatively young—tooling down the roads, drenched in sunlight. I tried to shake off the envy I felt for Catherine's buying power and to get into the spirit of the day. But I was being whooped once again.

"This is my consolation prize," Catherine said. "My youth pastor's parents had big health problems suddenly. He's moving to Florida to be near them."

I turned in my seat. Catherine was relaxed, entering the highway with just one hand on the wheel. The windshield protected us, but there sure was plenty of fresh air and sunlight milling around in our cockpit. "How do you feel about it? You miss him?"

"Yeah, I miss being asked out. I liked that a lot. But he didn't ask me to go to Florida with him. Not even a murmer." She turned her head and gave me a big smile. "Good thing we stuck to our boundaries. Makes it easier to see he just wasn't that into me, that it would've been a mistake. Makes it much less painful to let him go."

Playing devil's advocate, I said, "But you missed a chance for some pleasure. Certainly you deserve it after all you've been through."

"There's not just me to think about, Tricia, you know that. He was setting an example for his teens, for a healthy delay in sexual involvement, showing that it's important to keep yourself tidy so you can choose a marriage partner wisely. There's always more involved than just the two people circling each other."

"True."

"I was a little down about it, sure. Basically, he rejected me. But it's okay. I couldn't stand to live in a place where the bugs are as big as houses." She accelerated and passed a Mercedes easily. "My old car was making weird noises and I saw an ad for this make and model—" she rapped the dashboard smartly—"and I marched in and bought it today."

"Good for you!" I tried to sound upbeat but instead came off sounding bad-tempered in my ears. Catherine didn't seem to notice because she chatted on.

"I'm sorry he's gone, but happiness is an inside job, Tricia. Married, unmarried, no diff. People are about as happy as they decide to be. Abe Lincoln was right."

She accelerated down the ramp onto the Garden State Parkway. The car had incredible scoot. My Corolla, strangely enough, had scoot too. It could get out of its own way, as car buffs say. But nothing like this.

"I've got to talk to you," I said. "On the beach or boardwalk, though. This car is great but with all the wind, it's a little noisy."

Catherine smiled like a princess and drove, her slim white arms relaxed on the steering wheel. I, on the other hand, was struggling. I combed my memory for a Bible verse, a tool about envy, and thought of "Love doesn't envy" in I Corinthians 13, the Love Chapter, read at so many weddings. If I truly loved Catherine, I thought, I would just be happy for her good fortune. Maybe I needed to love David May enough to be happy for him too. Envy was a red flag that I wasn't loving the person enough. But to love David May? Hunh? Let's just start with loving Catherine enough to be happy for her.

I began to relax and enjoy being a passenger. We flew over a bridge that crossed an inlet, white-hulled boats in the distance tied up to pilings. We got to the exit for Ocean Grove and drove the ten minutes eastward on the road to the beach. The air suddenly had that salt tang. Delicious. We parked, got onto the beach, and removed our shoes. The surf was quiet.

"Aaaahhh," Catherine said, twirling, arms pointing skyward, feet kicking up sand. "This makes me happy too."

We walked to the water's edge and braved the initial chill of the water on our bare feet. Then we turned and headed toward Asbury Park, scuffing along in the shallows, bubbles caressing our ankles. I was on the side closest to the breaking waves.

"Catherine, I have a confession to make."

She nodded for me to go ahead.

"I'm having the worst problem. I envy other writers and what they can do with words. I envy a rich man I interviewed, his maid and all his paid help and his enormous house, decorated with gorgeous things. I envy an artist I met, her awards and her husband and children and all they do together." I stopped and turned toward her. She was so pretty in her beige linen shift that now had salt-spray spots on it. She stopped too and stood looking at me out of her blue eyes full of good humor. "I'm envious of you and your beautiful new car."

She just smiled. She didn't mind. My confession had been accepted gracefully, thanks to the Twelve Steps we both followed. A small wave of relief washed over me just as chilly Atlantic waters washed over my calves.

"Have you ever thought about *why* you experience so much envy? I think I might have an answer. Tell me if you agree." She turned toward me and took my elbow in her hands. Her fingers were icy, like the water our feet were walking in. "I have an inkling that you don't love and believe in yourself enough."

I thought about it, and it resonated with me. She might very well be right; amazingly enough, this girl had a lot of insight. For some dumb reason you wouldn't expect it from someone this pretty.

"Have you been doing those affirmations I told you about?" she said. "They work, you know—it's been studied by psychologists. It just takes a couple of weeks."

"I started, did it a few days, but then forgot and slacked off. You're right, they're necessary. My parents were stingy with praise growing up, maybe that's why. They thought my sister and I would get arrogant if they said anything about our accomplishments. I think I've been starved for affirmation for a long time."

"Remember, write them down, tape them to your mirror, say them out loud three times every morning, first thing. Give yourself in adulthood what you didn't get in childhood."

"Thanks."

She released my elbow and splashed along. "You know that envy hurts *you* the most, right? It blocks you from doing your best, it pulls you down, it eats at your self-confidence and your ability to love yourself and believe in what you can accomplish."

I thought of my novel and the hopes I had that it would be successful in the world—so maybe I could buy a sportscar too—and how my envy of Cindy had given birth to a flood of negativity about my writing. I'd been so stuck lately.

I looked down the beach toward Asbury Park. The Stone Pony, where Bruce Springsteen got his start, was just a little further up, on the edge of the sand. New Jersey had nurtured some amazing artists, I thought. Whitney Houston, Frank Sinatra. Many others. Maybe I could be one too. Already I was feeling stronger.

"Don't worry," I said, "I'm going to deal with it. I'm confessing my envy to you, I'll write about it in my journal, talk about it at meetings, do Steps Four, Five, Six, and Seven. I'm gonna do whatever it takes to get past this."

Catherine stopped so I stopped. She threw an arm across my shoulders. "Tricia. Just get with your Higher Power."

I thought about that, and my gut instinct said, Yes. Happy to. A simple, cozy relationship with Abba Father.

Simultaneously we turned and started walking again.

"Curl up with him," she said, "tell him all about it, trust him."

Relief washed over me again just as a boisterous wave flicked the hem of my shorts.

"Catherine, you're amazing! Thank you!"

"You know what I heard in the Steps recently? Don't envy other people. If we could each spread the stuff of our lives out on the grass and walk around and pick up someone else's life—the whole thing and all that happens to them—well, once we saw what burdens other people have to carry and what they have to go through, we would go back and pick up our own."

We hugged, and walked a bit farther. Suddenly another rogue wave slapped us, soaking us to our thighs this time.

"Tide's coming in," she said. "Let's go get some seafood."

So that's what we did.

CHAPTER 53

The next day I drove to the hospital where Samantha had died to interview the doctor who had cared for her. No law against it, though there probably should be. No guarantee I'd learn anything either. But luck might help me pick up a few clues as to the murderer. Clues the police weren't sharing but that might help me solve this mystery, bring her murderer to justice, and get the attention of my preferred employer, *The New York Times*.

But what about Justin? Did I want to wander around finding stories in the five boroughs of New York all alone in life? Well, not Staten Island so much, nor Queens nor the Bronx.

Manhattan or Brooklyn, yes.

Just as I would if I were at work in New York City, I had plenty of pens in my bag today, plus my reporter's notebook, which to me was a wonderful status symbol. It was half the width of a stenographer's notebook. When I'd been a secretary, before Tommy's life insurance freed me to answer an ad for a part-time reporter at the *Passaic Press,* secretaries had been at the bottom of the heap. Carrying around a stenography notebook had meant that I merely transcribed the words of the people (all male) who were rising stars.

Now I carried a reporter's notebook, which meant I jotted down the words of others, true. But I talked to all kinds of people, in all walks of life, and dug for facts. Then I dug for the story behind the people and the facts. And I presented that story as clearly as possible, so that my readers knew what was going on and could take steps, if they chose, to change the course of events.

In other words, while doing an average day's work, I was fighting for freedom and justice and the American way. Just like Superman. Loved it.

And now I was working, albeit a bit stealthily, without my boss knowing my intent, to help put a killer behind bars.

Approaching the hospital's sliding glass doors, I dug in my bag for my reporter's notebook and brought it out to carry it as a badge of honor.

A few inquiries took me to the sixth floor nurses' station in the intensive care unit for brain injuries. My heart sank—this had been Tommy's floor. A friendly nurse told me that the neurologist who had treated Samantha Scarborough, Dr. Bartlett, was on rounds and might be back soon.

While waiting impatiently, I combed through my notebook to see if there was a seed in it for a story that I had overlooked. I was distracted: I kept one eye on the nurse's station to spot the doctor before this opportunity escaped me.

The odor of the hospital's cleansing agents, the sound of people paged on the loudspeaker, the sight of people bustling in green and blue scrubs, immersed me in scenes of the last six months of Tommy's life. He'd been in and out of this ward during that intense time. His decline had been swift and terrifying. I thought to myself, it isn't normal for someone my age to have been through the final illness and death of a spouse. I was widowed at age twenty-seven. What an outlier I am. I never want to go through that again. And I don't want to go the whole way to my own death all alone either.

The hallway was busy. Wives arrived to visit husbands, and vice versa. A quarter hour passed with me steeped in dark memories, my notebook resting on my lap. Then I spotted a tall, slim woman in a white lab coat stride up to the nurses' station and plunk down a thick green binder. I hurried to catch her and introduced myself as a reporter with questions about Samantha Scarborough.

"Why should I talk to you?" she asked, drumming the binder restlessly with long, slim fingers.

"Please. I need your help."

"To do what?" She flicked her long blonde braid over her shoulder and moved her feet. It was hard to talk to someone bursting with nervous energy.

I kept trying. "To get to the bottom of what happened." I didn't add my true motivation; it probably would have sounded, to her ears, inappropriate. Because for a reporter to try and catch a killer—well, it was.

I waited, breathless, praying she would help me.

"I told the police everything that had any relevance to arresting who did it." She clicked her pen. She was beginning to annoy me.

"But they didn't share much with the press. Just death by a blow to the head. I'm sure there's more that can be said about it than that."

Again she drummed her fingers. The rat-tat-tat unnerved me. Evidently, though, she made up her mind. "Okay." She handed the thick green binder to a nurse for filing and spun on her heel. "But I have to think of what the hospital administration will say. So I'll tell you exactly what I told the police. Not a word more. Walk me to my car, I'm late for office hours."

Her long blonde braid swung wildly as she set her shoulder against a door. Now in a stairwell, we descended six floors fast and arrived in a parking garage, where she basically sprinted down a row of cars.

I could barely keep up. Digging deep for my best stamina, I panted out a question. "What can you tell me about Samantha's head wound?"

"She was hit with a pointed, but not sharp, iron object that left some flakes of rust behind. Her skull was cracked, but the wound was not too deep." Dr. Bartlett unlocked a white Mercedes and swooped gracefully in, with her long legs set off by black flats with a shiny buckle on each toe. She left the door open and looked back at me. "Anything else?"

I wasn't sure what to ask, having no training in head wounds. Silence wasn't going to work here—she would just drive away. So I repeated my useful reporter's question. "What else can you tell me?"

"I told the police this too: She was attacked the night before. My guess is nine p.m. or so. She bled to death. If she'd been found sooner, she very likely could have recovered from the head wound."

"Oh, that's tragic, it makes the whole thing worse."

"Yes, it's sad." Dr. Smith paused with both fingers wrapped around the steering wheel and seemed to be reflecting, perhaps on the sad business that happens all day long in a hospital. But she couldn't stay still long. She came back to the present and twisted the key in the ignition.

"Thanks, doctor," I called as she closed the car door. With a quick wave, she was off.

Leaving me wondering who had been in the museum with Samantha, not the morning we found her, but the evening before.

CHAPTER 54

E lspeth, Samantha's assistant, had been helpful in the past, so next I scooted my car to the museum. After swiveling my womanly hips and butt out of the car and into the reception area, I greeted Virginia, seated behind the front desk.

"Hi! Is Elspeth available perhaps?" I gave her my biggest smile. Cultivate your sources.

She smiled back and dialed an extension. A moment later Elspeth appeared.

"Let's go for coffee," she said. As I followed her down the wooden circular staircase to the basement, her filmy summer skirt, with a lettuce-leaf hem, caught the air and billowed out around her. She pushed the skirt down with both hands. When we sat together at the break table, our mugs of brew sent wisps of steam upward. I sipped appreciatively. The museum gave its employees good java.

I wanted to enlist her as a collaborator, make her part of the venture to solve the crime, not just pump her for information. She'd make a great collaborator, I suspected. Assistants know so much more than their bosses give them credit for, I had learned from my own experience. We know their quirks, moods, and true priorities so much better than they know ours, or even their own. Just like women know more about men, and minorities know more about the majority they live among, than vice versa. Survival depends on it.

Plus I wanted to cultivate a friend. You can never have too many of them, and she looked like a fun person.

She told me about her summer vacation plans for a few minutes, then we got onto the topic of careers. I offered the first tidbit—that I loved my job. I did not mention my aspirations to work for a bigger newspaper someday. I was still feeling it difficult to establish rapport with Elspeth. There was a limit to what I was going to confide.

Elspeth said she liked working in the museum but thought she might like to get into Human Resources. I felt a stab as I remembered a power play perpetrated against me in my first corporate secretarial job and the chilly attitude HR had displayed when I complained.

Then Elspeth brought up the topic of Samantha. I was glad she spared me from having to find a clever way to do it.

"I placed the Board's ad for her replacement today. In museum and philanthropy magazines." Elspeth smoothed back her bouncy curls with a beautifully manicured hand.

"I knew they were moving ahead with a new hire," I couldn't resist saying. I wanted to appear ahead of the curve, in the know, a good partner in solving a crime. "But I'm dismayed they're doing it without knowing who attacked Samantha and why."

"The Board met the other night—I'm the notetaker. Their thinking appears to be that it couldn't possibly have anything to do with her role as curator of this little museum."

Interesting that two of my three top suspects were on the Board and were saying that. I was so happy to have Elspeth's window into the Board's doings. It was time to officially enlist her. "I bet you and I can solve this crime, if we put our heads together."

She didn't look impressed, so I forged ahead with my pitch. "Let's figure out whodunnit. And if we do, I'll give you credit in the story I write, since I believe in giving credit where credit is due."

She sipped her coffee, then put the mug down and tossed her short brown curls. "It will depend on circumstance, about my name being known. Don't do it without asking me. But yeah, let's noodle on it."

"New news for you: her doctor said she was attacked the night before she was found. She probably would have survived if we'd found her sooner."

Elspeth's eyes widened at this news.

"Who do you think might have been here the night before?" I asked. "Around nine p.m., the doctor said. Did Samantha have an appointment in her agenda?"

"The police took it, so I can't check."

"Let's try another angle—who has keys to the museum?" Virginia had given me one answer, but maybe Elspeth would give another and provide a clue.

"All the docents, all the staff—including me—and all the Board members have one. It's impossible to pinpoint someone because of keys." She scratched her head with pretty, bubble-gum pink nails. "Let's think about motives. I know of one." She leaned forward.

I leaned in, loving the conspiracy.

In a low voice, she said, "What do you know about Dennis Palmer?"

I flopped back in my chair, stunned by her question, thinking about Meg's safety and how I couldn't jeopardize it by mentioning Dennis's abuse, even to my new conspirator. Besides, I'd promised Meg to keep it to myself.

"I know he's very successful in business, an investment banker. He's a trustee of the Museum of Modern Art." I wondered if my long pause after she'd asked her question had alerted Elspeth that I knew more than I was saying.

But it didn't seem to. She jumped into her next question. "Have you ever wondered why he bothers with a little museum like this one?"

"Good question! You got a theory?"

"I've watched him at Board meetings for three years now. He's a grandstander. He craves everyone's good opinion. He mentions his position on the Board of MoMA every chance he gets. David May rolls his eyes when Dennis namedrops Goldman Sachs. Why is he always bragging? Is he insecure? What's he hiding?"

I knew but couldn't say. At least not directly. "I've interviewed him a few times, in coffee shops. He has—" how to put this obliquely—"a lot of negative energy, maybe?"

"Like, give an example?" Elspeth crossed her legs, and floaty skirt settled onto her suntanned knee. I thought, what adult has time to sunbathe? She seemed to be looking forward to hearing dirt on Dennis. I didn't want a gossip-fest, I wanted to stay constructive. Investigative. But I had to give her something.

"Well, he balls his fists. While we're talking, he clenches and unclenches them, rubs them on his thighs. Makes me pretty uncomfortable. Scared even."

"I don't like him," Elspeth said and sat back in her chair. The curls all over her head bounced.

"But what motive could he have for attacking Samantha?"

Elspeth sat forward again and lowered her voice. "I know of one. A good one. Samantha announced she was going to streamline the number of Board members. She told me confidentially that she'd like to get rid of Dennis—she didn't like him either. I heard him talk to her in a condescending way. You should have met Samantha. She was very self-confident. Anyone who treated her as less than was going to get an ice pick in the eye."

"And someone like Dennis wouldn't want to be kicked off the Board—it wouldn't be good for his image. The newspapers would broadcast it all over the community." I sat with that information for a few moments, my thumb toying with the handle of my cooling mug.

"Exactly!" Elspeth exclaimed. She stabbed a finger into the air between us to make her point. "That's what's important to him—his image. His self-image. What people think of him. All of the above."

"I'll find out if he was in town the night Samantha was attacked."

Elspeth frowned. "How will you do that?"

Uh-oh. Time to tread carefully. I planned to ask Meg but didn't want Elspeth to know there was any connection there. "By setting up an interview—he insists on meeting in person, unfortunately—and working it into my questions. Somehow."

"I hope you don't get a balled fist for your trouble." Well, that was prescient of her.

"Me too. Listen, have you told the police about all these things?"

She shook her head again. Those curls were really adorable. "No, they didn't ask and I didn't think of it until today. It's mostly impressions, anyway. No proof. You couldn't get a conviction on it."

I sat and regarded her. She was very sure of herself—perhaps too sure. It was a little annoying. She didn't know what the police would do with that information. But I had a collaborator with lots of insider knowledge, so I pressed on. "What do you think of Matt Morgan as the murderer? His job was going to be cut."

She tapped a pink-tipped finger on her lips, thinking. "Yes, I can see that. He's a curmudgeon, hardly has a polite word for anyone."

"Oh, he does that to you too?"

"Sure, and he did it to Samantha. From the moment he met her. I saw it. Doesn't mean he isn't a great handyman. But he likes pipes more than people. Behind his back I saw Samantha shake her head at him, after a taste of his attitude." See, secretaries notice and know a lot.

"I wish I could find the murder weapon," I said forlornly.

Elspeth waved a glorious hand dismissively. "That's long gone. Buried in someone's garden."

Dennis, I was sure, had gardens around his Laurel Way home, and I knew for sure that David May did. Matt Morgan might very well too. Or they could have thrown the weapon into the murky brown waters of the Great Swamp. That line of inquiry was hopeless.

"How are we going to pin this on somebody?" I said. "The true killer, of course."

"We should figure it out before the Board stupidly brings in another curator," Elspeth said. "I don't want another dead boss to deal with."

"Was Samantha doing any research that you know of? Making calls? Buying books?"

Elspeth stood and put her mug in the dishwasher. "That's a good question. I have to get back now, but I'll check the phone bill and give you a call."

I fished out a card with my number at the *Sentinel* on it, then scribbled my home number.

"Would you look around her office and see if there's any books that might be related to the museum? The exhibits? Call me anytime. And thanks for your help today. It's great to work on the mystery with someone."

"Sure thing. It's in my best interests too." Giving me a little wave with her pink-tipped hands, she left me at the table and climbed up the staircase with her kicky skirt flouncing.

I was very intrigued with all she'd revealed and appreciated her collaboration.

Speaking of which, I longed to collaborate, in every possible way, with Justin. My heart had sped ahead of my intention to be friends first. I was more in love than I wanted to be and ached to talk to him.

But couldn't make myself call him. If he was letting go of me, I didn't want to know.

CHAPTER 55

I went back to the newsroom to call Dennis, to find out where he was the night Samantha was attacked and left to bleed to death. It would require the most delicate management, the most roundabout finesse, because I most certainly did not want to anger him and lose him as a source—or become a target of his ire. I just had to be smart about this.

His assistant answered and said he was on the phone and would call back. We chatted a moment, she in what was probably deluxe workplace splendor at Goldman Sachs, with art on the walls, me in this newsroom with dirty windows and dingy paint on the walls. Then we signed off.

And it dawned on me: Now I was tied to my desk, waiting for his call. I sat back in my chair with a thunk. Damn! It was June-beautiful outside, I was restless with spring fever and needed to get out to find a new story to feed to the printing presses. Outdoors I could find somebody to interview—maybe even for a moms-watching-kids-in-the-park kind of story. I'd pursue anything rather than be stuck in here.

With a sigh I decided to use the time wisely. I opened my notebook and once again poured through my shorthand notes, looking more attentively this time to see if a story nugget was buried there. It wasn't. I decided to write out a script to follow when I ever-so-delicately, yet with a neurosurgeon's accuracy, probed to find out where Dennis was that night.

Then I slapped my head. Not really—only in a figurative way. His assistant had his agenda. We were on good terms. Maybe she'd tell me what she knew, just as Dr. Smith had. I had to try.

I waited impatiently while her phone rang, my fingers and toes crossed. My interaction with her would require delicacy too.

Finally she answered. "Sorry, was ordering lunch for the boss," she said cheerfully.

All that geniality about a menial task Dennis could have done for himself, I thought. Maybe she harbors no ambition. Either that, or she wisely makes the best of the position she's in. I hoped she got her own free sandwich out of it.

We chatted about the weather for a minute—clouds were rolling into the Financial District off New York Harbor, she said, and soon the windows near her desk would be awash in tiny water droplets.

"Does it snow *up* where you are?" I asked. "I used to enjoy that, when I worked in the City. I was in midtown—does it happen downtown too?"

"Oh yeah, it's fun here," she said.

We chatted about New York City—Wall Street is a different experience than Midtown—and then I got down to business. "Listen, I'd like your help with something."

"What can I do for you today?" What a nice attitude she had! I was hopeful to get my answer from her and not have to meet Dennis in a coffee shop ever again.

"I'm writing a story about the museum here in Passaic—the Museum of Historic Tools and Crafts. Dennis, as you know, is on the Board of Directors."

"Yes."

"There was a meeting of the Board not long after the new curator was hired. In late May, I think, and I thought you might have the exact date of it, and was Dennis able to attend?"

"I'll look." Everything about this woman was crisp and professional. No wonder she worked for Goldman Sachs. I heard pages being flipped. "Here it is. Tuesday, May 26. Dennis was in the office that day, and I believe he planned to go to that meeting."

"Thanks. Did Dennis travel after that?" This was my real question, hopefully beautifully hidden behind my first questions. "I'm wondering because..."

Her helpful attitude perhaps led her to answer before I was forced to make up a reason why I was asking. "He left for Atlanta the next day and was back that Friday. And he's been around ever since," she said with her usual good cheer.

"Thank you." That meant Dennis was back in town the Tuesday night Samantha was attacked. I was going to nail that wife-abusing scum.

The secretary had graciously filled in Dennis's calendar. There was no protocol I knew of around assistants not revealing a word about their boss's whereabouts. But maybe she'd been a tiny bit more revelatory than Goldman Sachs would have liked? Well, thank goodness for that! Who was I to question?

"Thank you again—by the way, have the clouds arrived yet?"

"Yes, we're in a fog. No view for us until this blows away."

"I enjoy a good fog. You?"

"Very much so."

"Great. Thanks, and please don't tell Dennis to call me. There's no need."

"All right."

We signed off.

I was sure Dennis was in his tower in New York City because his secretary was ordering his lunch. Therefore I could go to his house and ask Meg, if she was home, where Dennis had been on the night Samantha was attacked. I drove to Laurel Way, parked in the driveway next to the gleaming Audi, and went up the immaculate herringbone brick walk to the front door. When I pushed the doorbell, chimes sounded from deep within the house. Everything was very spiffy here. Including the landscaping. A row of low, nicely shaped, dark-green yew bushes graced the foundation.

I rang the bell again. Finally the front door opened, and Meg stared at me through the storm door. This was exactly how I'd welcomed her the first time she came to my house. It didn't feel good.

She cracked the storm door open. "You shouldn't have come here. I told you not to try to reach me." Her hands grasped and regrasped the door nervously. It reminded me of how her husband clenched and unclenched his fists.

"I know that Dennis is in New York City because I just talked to his assistant. They just ordered lunch. I wouldn't have come otherwise."

The house faced south, its sandstone bricks were radiating light and heat, and I was beginning to feel overheated. So when she opened the storm door wider and beckoned me in, I was relieved.

The interior was cool—Dennis didn't stint on his air-conditioning bill. But the home displayed a state of disorder. Chaos, in fact. There was a group of baseball bats leaning against the wall—what the hell did that mean? Dennis's perpetual threat against Meg?—and next to them a pair of muddy, grassy cleats standing amongst scattered clumps of dried dirt. The center hall table had a huge pile of mail sliding off to the side, with several envelopes on the floor at the table's base. A quick glance into the living room revealed posh furnishings, plus disheveled stacks of papers, magazines, and books everywhere. This confirmed what Meg had told me about her depression, her inability to keep house to Dennis's specifications.

Meg saw me glance around and blushed.

"I'm a little behind."

She didn't appear to be willing to lead me to her kitchen and offer tea so, standing in her vaulted entry hall—which was as big as my living room, just as I had suspected that first night she visited me and I invited her into *my* kitchen—I got on with my questions.

"Listen, I'm needing your help with something."

She nodded, shoulders hunched, and grabbed her elbows.

"Can you tell me if Dennis was home the night of June 3? Can you check your calendar? It was a Tuesday night."

"Why?"

"That's the night someone attacked the museum curator. At around nine p.m."

She stared at me a good long while. Without moving a muscle, except to finally blink.

"Please, Meg, it's important."

She turned, dug through the pile on the hall table, and produced a spiral-bound agenda.

Flipping through the pages, she came to June 3. We both peered at the evening time slots.

"We had a show to go to in Morristown. But I remember, we didn't go. Dennis said he was too tired after work. But then he went out. I remember because I really wanted to see that show."

"Do you remember what time he went out?"

"It was after dinner. We eat late because of his long commute home. So it might have been around eight o'clock."

"That you ate or that he left the house?"

"That he left."

"What was he like when he got back?"

"Pretty much the same as he always is. Domineering. On edge. I wanted to talk to him, tell him I was disappointed to miss going to the show. But it was obvious that anything I said would cause a fight." She flinched. "So I just went to bed."

"Thank you, Meg! This info's important. Well, I'll get out of your hair now."

"Don't tell Dennis I told you all this!" She had a hand cupping her cheek, rubbing the yellowed bruise.

"I'll protect you, Meg, please don't worry." And I dashed back out, past the sweltering bricks and well-watered foundation plantings, back to my ordinary car.

Driving away from Laurel Way and its perfect-looking façades and luxury cars in the driveways, I wondered how to use this information. Tell the police? I guessed that I should, but I don't believe in "shoulding" on myself, as I'd heard it expressed in Twelve Step meetings. Instead I think "What do I need to do, what would I like to do?" Great, freeing tool.

So maybe I wouldn't tell the police. After all, what had they shared with me? Was there any reciprocity coming from them? None. I just got the same scraps they gave the less invested reporters.

No, I'd confront Dennis. In public. At the café. It was risky. What would Justin say about it? But where was *he*, after all? Not in a position to advise me not to do it.

Besides, this was how careers got made.

But I hurt all over thinking how he'd gone silent.

CHAPTER 56

I called Dennis's office again and arranged to meet with him at the same old coffee shop, using the same old excuse: to talk about the museum. He couldn't meet me until the following evening. That gave me time to marshal my arguments and think of a way to trap him in his guilt.

Then I walked to the museum to ask Elspeth for the minutes of the Samantha's first Board meeting, in late May. Elspeth was in a gauzy skirt again today and also seemed to not be in much of a mood to collaborate. She flounced into her chair, drew herself up close to her desk, and looked at me as if I were a stranger. Aw, Elspeth, get with the program, I thought. Help the cause of justice!

I didn't say any of that. I chatted for a while instead and worked into the conversation that she was crucial to solving a crime. Eventually she dug the minutes out of a file cabinet and copied them for me, her clothes floating around her.

I rattled the pages in my hand, impatient to see the list of those present. Yes! Dennis Palmer was there. So he couldn't claim ignorance of Samantha's plans to cut Board members.

Looking up from the minutes, I continued to schmooze Elspeth, to explore other suspects besides Dennis. David May was also of interest because—well, because he was a member of the indolent aristocracy. Because my gut instinct thought so. Just 'cuz.

"I know it's only been half a day since I asked, I'm sorry to be so eager, but did you have a chance to find out if Samantha had books on order? A research topic?"

She didn't become more conciliatory in attitude but deigned to answer.

"The library just called to find out if we had their book, *Slavery in New Jersey*. I searched her office and found it."

I was floored. Gazing at Elspeth in stupefaction, I thought, slavery in my home state? This far North? In a state that sent men to fight for the Union Army? I'd attended the public school system in this state my entire life, had talked to tons of people in government and education, and had never heard a word about slavery in New Jersey.

"Here it is," she said, handing me a book with a gray cloth cover.

Tucked into the book, perhaps marking Samantha's place, was a piece of copy paper folded in half. Putting my thumb in the book's page to preserve the spot, I read the paper, in handwriting I guessed was hers:

I want an exhibit of unheard voices.

Some stories were pushed aside, others given precedence. Our job as a museum is to find the true stories.

Sometimes the ones not told are more interesting. The stories that are not so pleasant. The people who didn't have history writers on their side.

Look at all the exhibits and how do we include ... What about the African-Americans or Caribbeans? New Jersey had a big slave population. Make sure all those stories are told.

I opened to the spot in the book that my thumb had preserved. The page contained a letter written by Barnaby, a slave (I noted he only had a first name): "Each farm around here has from one to eight slaves."

Whoa. I had always thought my home state was a haven for run-away slaves. I'd heard there were Underground Railroad stops not far away, in Morristown. But maybe they couldn't live in New Jersey—they had to keep running.

"Elspeth, would you let me take this book? I'll go to the library and pay any fine that's due and take it out for myself."

She waved her pink-tipped fingers, now in a better mood because she had one less task on her to-do list. "Sure."

"Thanks. See ya."

I hurried to the newsroom to read both the book and the minutes carefully. There were seeds for a story in these documents. The fact that there had been slavery in New Jersey was not recent news, but it might very well be new news to a lot of readers who, like me, hadn't known. I wondered idly if my editor would let me publish a story about it. He wouldn't—it was old news—but "Slavery in New Jersey" sure would make an eye-catching headline.

CHAPTER 57

I was gobbling up the museum minutes—yes, Samantha did announce her plan that the Board be reduced in numbers (Dennis's motive) and she did announce that she would be creating an exhibit on slavery in New Jersey (who would be offended by that?)—when I got a call from my mother.

"This morning, in front of the kids, Susan said she was going back to Robert."

"Oh no!" In reading about domestic abuse in order to write about it, I'd learned that that's when women get killed. But I wouldn't tell my mother that. Instead I'd pray.

"We enrolled them in school here last week, so they'll talk to the staff psychologist today. I've already called and arranged it. But this morning, when she left, they cried. They went to school broken-hearted. The poor little people."

"Don't give up hope, Mom. I bet you Susan will be back."

"When? In five years? Ten? What's it going to take to open her eyes? A smashed-in face? Ending up in the hospital? And what about her children being abandoned in the meantime?"

I couldn't answer those questions, so I asked one of my own. "Has she been looking for a job?"

"Yes, she started looking for something in statistics for neuroscience. With all these pharmas around here, she should have something soon. Why did she throw it all over? Why did she leave her children?" My mother's anguish welled up in her voice.

"People who are divorcing go through something called 'uncoupling.'

They adjust to the idea of being on their own in phases. Maybe that's what this is."

"Just pray he doesn't kill her for leaving and taking the kids." Oh, so my mom knew the danger.

"Did she hire a lawyer?"

"We got a few names last week. She called one or two."

"She's in the process, don't you think?"

"Could be." I heard a deep sigh. "I certainly pray so. Listen, there's the weekend coming up. The kids need you. I need you."

"I'll be there."

"Pray in the meantime, hon."

"Will do. Love you, Mom."

I set the phone down breathing a prayer for all the things I couldn't do but that Higher Power could, right now: protect Susan; reassure the children, in their distress; strengthen my parents.

Then, having sent my concerns up to heaven as best I could, I took a coffee break, then perused the book about slavery some more. An hour later, I read something that made me sit up with a jerk. Was this a motive to attack Samantha? Now I had grounds to confront not just one but two men.

And I couldn't overlook Matt Morgan, curmudgeon extraordinaire, whose job, fixing up an historic building he deeply loved, Samantha was going to cut.

CHAPTER 58

June evening light poured in the big windows on either side of the café's door. I bought herbal tea, claimed a table outside, and sat with a sigh.

My town's signature June scent of blooming honeysuckle, peony, privet, and wild rose perfumed the air. It was an idyllic setting, but I was feeling so much fear. I looked around. Two other tables were occupied, both with big men. I hoped they were heroic types who would step into a fight and break Dennis's grip on my throat.

I wasn't sure I was up to playing footsie and being delicate with him. I was going to have to confront him with what I knew at some point. Why not now? Why feint and dart about—why not be plainspoken?

No, finesse it, Trish. Because he's volatile, he has no compunction about hitting women, he has violence stored up in those clenching and unclenching fists that he rubbed on his thighs.

I saw a red Audi turn into the café's parking lot, and my own fists tightened with fear.

Then he appeared, waved, and dashed into the café for his drink. He came out to sit with me under the awning that rippled in the light, scented breeze.

He appeared confident. Robust. Strong. And I sensed his undercurrent of threat.

I breathed a prayer. My plans for interrogatory finesse seemed to dry up when faced with the man in person.

I dove in. "Did you ever meet with Samantha separately, outside of a Board meeting?"

He froze and gazed at me. Finally he said, "What?"

"Did you set up a private meeting with Samantha?"

"What business is it of yours?" He was rubbing his thighs again. I hated that.

"In the course of talking to people" (I kept it vague—no way I wanted Dr. Smith or Elspeth or or anybody else to lose their job)—"I've learned that she was attacked the night before, not the morning we found her." I shifted nervously in the wooden café chair, which creaked. "Somebody was with her—who more likely than a Board member?"

"Or a husband, if she was working late?" His sarcastic tone said it all— he thought I was an idiot.

I felt my hackles rise. Defensive, angry, I felt all caution about delicacy of questioning simply evaporate in the June breeze.

"Tuesday, June 3. You were free that evening."

He recoiled, and I realized too late that in rushing to pin him down, I'd said too much. His assistant could get in trouble. No worse, oh my God— Meg. My heart double-clutched into its highest gear.

Dennis was frowning. Probably the wheels of his fine, financier's mind were spinning with speculation on who had given me that information, how, when, where, and why.

"Sorry, I have to go to the ladies' room. Uh—I'll be right back." I hoped my voice sounded casual and did not betray the molten fear coursing through my heart. I tried to walk calmly into the café while remaining in his line of sight but then hustled out the back door into the parking lot. There was the red Audi, shining in a beam of pollen-gilded sunlight. The car was looking peaceful and prosperous but in actuality was the willing conveyance of a domestic terrorist. It was the only Audi in the lot. It had to be Dennis's.

I had to slow him down, buy time to protect Meg.

I didn't know what else to do but to render one tire inoperable. I wasn't up-to-date on breaking into Audi engine compartments and stealing carburetors or alternators or whatever it was that clever people did. Instead I knelt out of sight by a tire and scrabbled in my purse, past a sea of pens, for my Swiss Army knife, hands shaking, fumbling for a blade long and strong enough to slice a tire. I plunged the knife in between the treads and sawed it back and forth, hearing the hiss I hoped for. Tugging the knife out, I ran to my car, got it started, pulled onto Main Street, and headed toward Laurel Way. Dennis was still seated at the café table. Down the street I twisted to look back, and he was standing up.

Oh shit, oh shit, I had done what I'd promised Meg I wouldn't do— get her in trouble with Dennis. What would he do, now that he had realized it must have been Meg who said he was out the night Samantha was attacked? I had to rescue her.

I plunged my foot into the gas pedal, desperate to get Meg out before Dennis got there.

I parked in Meg's driveway, trembling so badly I could barely walk up the brick path. I yanked the big brass knocker up and then smashed it down. Then I jammed my thumb into the doorbell and heard the chimes play merrily. Where was she? Answer the door, Meg! Stop being such a scaredy cat. Your fear will kill you.

I gave up on being polite and twisted the knob. The door swung open. I looked back and saw a dot of a red car turning onto the street.

"Meg!" I called. I ran toward the back of the house calling her name, searching for the heart of the home, the kitchen. It was a mess, but that hardly mattered. I raced to a sliding glass door and saw Meg sitting on a lovely patio next to a pool. She was reclining in an Adirondack chair. I slid the door open and tumbled onto the patio. She sat up with a start.

"Meg, we're leaving. Now! Dennis knows you talked to me and he's on his way here. I'm sorry, but we have to go. Get up!"

She must have heard the urgency in my voice because immediately she struggled to get out of the deep chair.

"Don't go back in the house. Quick! Around the side to my car!"

Lots of credit to Meg, she was doing it without losing time demanding explanations, without insisting on going back into the house for useless things.

We rounded the corner of the garage and stepped onto the driveway.

And there was that lovely Audi, one corner sagging, riding on one rim, turning into the driveway. Bits of shredded tire were scattered on Laurel Way behind the car. Dennis parked behind my Toyota, blocking me from backing out. He leapt out of the car and strode toward us.

I grabbed Meg's elbow; it felt like she was ready to break with tension. "We'll make it," I said to her. "Lord," I breathed. Dennis was five feet away. There wasn't time to pray more.

"You stop right there," I commanded at the top of my lungs. He did stop, maybe surprised at the strength in my voice.

We all faced each other, Dennis's gaze shifting from me to Meg and back.

"We're leaving now," I said. "If you're going to be a coward and hit a woman, you're going to have to hit me too."

"That's my wife!" he shouted. "Let go of her!"

"No," I shouted back, stepping toward my car, still holding Meg's elbow.

"This is none of your business!" he yelled, his strong fingers ripping at my arm, to shake loose my grip on Meg.

"It *is* my business. It's everybody's business," and I pointed to the next-door neighbor who was standing at his mailbox, watching us.

Dennis took a step back. Proof that what people thought was more important than anything else to him.

I hustled Meg to my car's passenger door and got it open for her. Then, keeping the car between me and Dennis, I got in the driver's seat. Locked the doors. Turned the key.

My trusty Toyota was ready.

To escape I had to pull up toward the house, then back around the Audi. But Dennis was standing directly in front of my car, clenching and unclenching his fists.

I put my car into drive. In my fear, I gave it too much gas, and it surged forward and smacked Dennis's thigh. Meg gasped. Maybe she still loved him enough to care.

He limped out of the way. Oh God, he was going to sue me for that. Oh well.

As I took a split second to switch gears, Dennis limped up and pounded the roof above Meg's head with his fist. She bent over, huddled into herself, wailing. He yanked at the door, but my locks held. I was shaking but got the car into reverse and backed myself around the Audi somehow, because I could no longer see anything, I was so terrified.

On Laurel Way, I shoved the gear stick into drive and got the hell out of there.

CHAPTER 59

In the June twilight, I drove, shaking, distracted, not knowing any destination. Scenes from in front of Meg's house replayed vividly in my mind's eye.

We'd been given a crucial moment to get in the car and lock the doors—saved—because Dennis cared so deeply about what his neighbor thought of him. Then he'd forgotten himself and tried to rip Meg out of the car. But that moment had given us an advantage, a chance to protect ourselves.

Credit where credit is due. Saved by Higher Power.

I was still breathing in gulps, still trembling from head to toe. Meg was still bent at the waist, crying into her knees.

"Meg, I'm so sorry. He insulted me, and I lost my cool."

"I trusted you!" she sobbed.

I reached across to open the glove compartment and pointed to a packet of tissues. She rustled it open and pulled out two. A third fell to the floor, and she snatched it up.

"That was so stupid, Tricia! How could you?"

"You're right, Meg."

It occurred to me that we needed to talk quietly, just ourselves. We needed to decompress. So I drove to the Great Swamp. There were a dozen cars in the lot. I parked as far from the gravel road as I could. Dennis the New York City investment banker would never think of this spot—I hoped. With a glance at the phone book, he could have my home address. We were safer here than at my house.

"Let's talk, Meg. I slipped up, I'm absolutely at fault."

She bent over and wailed into the bunch of hankies in her hand.

"Please, when you can calm down a little, could we walk and talk in the woods?" I said. "It would help us both."

Meg unfolded herself, sitting up to wipe her face. She stared out the windshield for a moment, then nodded. We climbed out of the car.

We headed down the gravel path between the two ponds toward the woods. The park closed at sunset, in the near future. The low sun filtered through the leaves, which gave a greenish cast to the light. It was peaceful. My heart slowed a fraction, and I hoped the same for Meg.

We walked slowly, at Meg's pace. She was wiping her eyes often. We traversed the boardwalks over slow streams and murky waters. I recounted to her how I'd gotten flustered by Dennis's sarcasm and precipitated tonight's confrontation. "I made a huge mistake."

"I know, I get it," Meg said, sounding a wee bit calmer, her sandals clopping on the boardwalk. "But my, oh my, who can I really trust?"

"You're right to question. My answer is: Higher Power. It's simple. He doesn't make mistakes."

Even though we were walking slowly, we seemed to be outpacing the mosquitos as we moved through the greenery.

"Please, someday, forgive me."

"Oh, I guess it's okay. To be honest, I was planning on leaving him the next morning, after he went to work."

"There would have been less stress in that scenario, that's for sure."

She smiled weakly. I was relieved to see it.

Meg said she needed her pocketbook for her driver's license, cash, her passport. We assumed that within an hour the credit cards wouldn't work, thanks to Dennis being as cruel and controlling as he was. I said I'd help her. I said we'd go back in the morning, with the police, to retrieve her valuables.

We rounded the curve of one path and struck off on another.

"You know where you are?" Meg asked.

"Very much so." Then I remembered how confidently I'd assured her, just yesterday, that I knew what I was doing and wouldn't put her in harm's way with Dennis and felt a tremendous weight of remorse descend on my shoulders again. I'd already apologized. Now I needed to forgive myself.

We still had to find shelter for Meg. So I asked if we could head back, and she nodded. The trees and the saplings crowded right up to the path and seemed to embrace us.

Meg walked along quietly, perhaps thinking of all she'd left behind.

That patio. That pool. Finally she sighed. "I have work lined up. I start in a week."

"Good for you!" I exulted. Then I felt hurt that she hadn't told me as soon as she'd landed the job. Hadn't I invested in her as a friend enough for that consideration? But then again, I hadn't turned out to be such a reliable friend.

She told me she'd landed a job in corporate communications for a Central Jersey pharma. Her creative writing degree had opened the door to an entry-level job since she had minimal work experience.

She'd been an investment banker's wife, I thought, and it's not enough, not with the way things are between men and women in this broken world. A woman's got to have her own money, her own income, not just a room of her own, as Virginia Woolf put it.

Even if a woman had that, marriages still go wrong. And when they end, it's misery. Meg already suffered from depression. I had to caution her.

"Can I just say one thing?" I asked. She nodded. "The end of a marriage means a ton of grief. The process includes depression. If you need a medication to help you pull out of it, please don't hesitate."

She nodded.

We re-emerged from the woods and walked past the ponds to the car. Our drive to the Somerset Hills battered women's shelter was quiet. When the social worker let us in, Meg looked around the living room, with its worn-out furniture and threadbare carpet, and my heart went out to her as she experienced a long fall from the grace of a well-appointed home on Laurel Way.

We asked the social worker to check with other shelters for a bed because Dennis, with his connections, could find this one, in his own county, too easily.

"I know what you mean," the social worker said. "We've had to move a few women a couple of times because the men found them." Meg shivered.

After a few phone calls, the social worker sent us to a shelter in another county. Not too far, I noted with gratitude, because now it was getting late.

We drove in silence, both of us tense, though Meg was no longer accusatory toward me, I sensed with relief. I hoped that someday things would calm down enough for us to become friends. We had a lot in common: writing, husbands gone awry, no children but the longing for them. However, tonight was not the time to bring up any of that.

At the next shelter, the social worker took charge briskly. I opened my arms to offer Meg a hug goodbye, and she stepped into my embrace. We held each other tightly, having survived a natural disaster together tonight.

"I'll phone the office here tomorrow and try to reach you," I said, "and please feel free to call me. Any time." I once again gave her my *Sentinel* card after scribbling my home phone on it.

"Thanks, Trish."

"You are most welcome, and I'm sorry I let things slip so that you had to leave so suddenly, in so much danger. I feel terrible about that."

"It's okay." Meg's face looked like she was going to crumple again into tears at any moment. I tried to reassure her.

"You have a fresh start on life now. We'll get the police to meet us at the house so you can get your stuff."

"I know where I secretly put a spare key outside."

"That solves that problem."

She looked exhausted. I held her by the shoulders, searching her sad face, trying to send hope and strength into her through my hands.

"Just take it one day at a time," I said. I didn't say, "You're finally safe" because neither of us was. But I brought her to me again, then let her go.

"Bye," she whispered, eyes downcast.

CHAPTER 60

I drove home thanking HP for helping Meg and me escape with our lives this evening. I knew that sometimes women don't get to escape. But I believed prayer made a difference. I prayed for Susan and Meg as I parked my car on my backyard grass so Dennis couldn't spot it. With that thought of Dennis, I prayed the prayer for me.

I locked all my doors and windows upon entering the house and prepared to have a stuffy night. While Ninja was lapping up a fresh bowl of food, I called the police, told them what happened, and asked for extra patrols past my house for the next while. Weeks, I added. They knew my name, from my stories about arrests they'd made and their training regimens. Whether that made a difference or not, I don't know, but they said they would try. Then I called my mother, who said the children had been crying for their mommy but were now asleep.

"Help," she said. With my talkative mother saying that one word in so small, so depleted a voice, I knew the situation was dire.

"I'll be there tomorrow. Say from five o'clock on."

"I'll feed you."

With that agreement, I threw myself on the bed and went unconscious in my clothes. I should have slept lightly, or not at all, on edge for an abuser seeking revenge. But exhaustion made wakefulness impossible.

In the morning, another fine June day, I opened the windows. Sunlight slanted through the trees, a soft breeze wafted, and the scent of roses, privet, and honeysuckle enhanced each breath. I spent time with HP, meditating and praying for the strength to help the world just a little today. "I love you,

O Lord, my strength, my rock, my fortress," I read in the Psalms. I needed a fortress, and I cuddled within it.

Feeling the sparks of lightness and energy that HP gave me, I called the women's shelter and asked for Meg. She came to the phone a moment later. Her voice sounded a little stronger than it had last night.

"Some of these women have it much worse than me. They've had teeth punched out, they need dental work before they can even look for a job. I'm glad I left Dennis. Thank you for encouraging me, Tricia."

"You're welcome. Sorry I messed up last night."

"It was terrifying." She sighed. "But maybe it will all work out."

Especially after precipitating such an unorganized exit from her life with Dennis, I had to help her get a new start. I called the police and asked them to meet us at Meg's house. They said they could in half an hour. Then I picked her up and we drove to her home. Two policemen stood by the front door. Before laws were changed, the police had been known to watch and laugh while men beat their wives into cripples. But now they were trained in handling domestic violence with wisdom. For the most part.

They accepted the fact that Meg knew where to find a hidden key, under one of many pots of gorgeous caladiums standing around the pool, as sufficient proof that she lived there. While they searched the whole house, we waited in my car, for a quick get-away if a crazed Dennis emerged. Then the two officers summoned us in. Dennis had left for work, evidently, probably to save face with his boss and colleagues. I wondered if we couldn't use his concern for what people thought of him to deflect his abusiveness away from Meg in the future—to warn him we'd tell his CEO if we ever saw his face again, just as my mother had warned Robert, Susan's husband. Aw hell, that reminded me, what was Susan going through today?

While I stood in the foyer thinking all this, Meg descended the staircase twice, lugging a giant suitcase each time.

"Winter and summer clothes," she said as she let the second suitcase down with a thunk. "I guess I'll get the rest later."

"We need to confer a minute. We need to tell the police that Dennis was in town and has no alibi, at least not with you, for the night Samantha was attacked."

She studied the gleaming parquet floor at our feet.

"Yes, I suppose so." She sounded so sad. She was in the midst of the unraveling of her life.

"Are you going to press charges for his attacks on you?"

"I haven't decided yet. The evidence is fading." And she touched her cheekbone and its yellowed bruise.

"We have to take a photo of it soon. We'll need color film. Don't worry, I'll support you in court," I added, wondering where I'd find the time to do that and earn a living as a journalist. Maybe it would all work out.

"I have to go get my purse," she said, turning toward the kitchen. She came back a minute later riffling through her wallet.

"The cash and credit cards are gone," she said in a tiny voice. "How can I start a new life?"

"We'll get you sorted out," I said, wondering how on earth I could support both her and me until she got established. Well, once Dennis cooled off, I could give her my spare bedroom until she found her own place, though maybe he'd never cool off. "Is your ID there?"

She probed the wallet's pockets and came up with it.

"He forgot it!" she said, holding the white card aloft triumphantly, smiling. That's what I liked to see.

"Don't worry, he'll stop messing with your life soon. With a little luck, some other woman will be in his orbit within days and absorb his attention."

Once again Meg looked crestfallen. I had said the wrong thing. Nobody likes to think the man they'd loved for all these years could find the next woman so soon. But it was certainly the way of the world. A wealthy, good-looking man like Dennis could attract his next victim within days. And so many women aren't alert to abusers' red flags. Yikes, women trust men way too readily.

CHAPTER 61

I 'd been running around, trying to solve the crime and helping Meg, but a steady, low-grade pain in my life, like the sorrowful, underlying drone of a bagpipe, had been the question of Justin.

I wanted to walk and talk with Catherine to discuss his disappearance from my life.

Then again, the thought of men was just a little off-putting right now. My husband, Meg's, Susan's, Catherine's. How sure was I that Justin was not like them?

But I called her and asked if we could do lunch.

"I'll be at work, but we have a cafeteria. The salads are fresh."

So I left the newsroom at 12:30 and drove Route 22, risking my life as usual, to Catherine's pharma.

She was dressed in a pool blue silk blouse and white pencil skirt, and her red hair hung in soft curls to her shoulders. I saw a few men's heads turn as we bought our salads. Envy started its siren song. They're looking at her more than me, I thought. I look good but she must look fantastic to get all this attention.

We took our trays outside to picnic tables shaded by trees. Sunlight filtered through the leaves and danced on our green, leafy food as a breeze stirred the air. I shushed the voice, but it continued to yammer deep in my soul.

We asked each other how our jobs were going. Catherine said she'd been assigned to a team developing a new cancer drug. "It just happened this morning, or I'd have told you about it already. It's a dream come true," and she flipped her gleaming hair over her shoulder. It was too short to stay back there and slipped forward again. "I'll be making a real difference in many lives."

Did I make a difference in many lives with my job? I wanted so badly to help keep Americans free by reporting the truth about what those in power were doing. In between stories on the museum, I'd been chronicling what happened at local government meetings. Nobody had complimented me on my stories or thanked me for sitting on hard chairs for hours during decision-making processes. But I believed that, just because the press was present as a witness, more honest decisions were being made. I believed in a strong local press. I tried to live up to the ideals of journalism. It really made me tick. I was involved in my community—but as an outsider, an observer. How I loved being on the fringe of things! My sweet spot, as a writer.

Though my job was gratifying and challenging, and I hoped to excel in it, I also wanted to return to the comforts and joys of marriage, and to have children. I couldn't imagine how family and job at the *Times* could work together. But when I wasn't looking, I'd developed so many feelings for Justin. I burned to see him again. The immediate question was, why had Justin been silent all this time? And what to do about it?

"So, have you heard from Justin?" Catherine asked. A breeze lifted her hair. Mine was auburn but hers was a luscious, multi-hued *red*.

"No, and I have no idea what to do," I said, subdued, trying to learn my lesson, trying to love Catherine enough to be happy for her fortunate good looks.

"Maybe it's best to be free."

"Certainly to be free of madmen." I took a step out of the swamp of envy and snatched a strawberry off my salad. I savored its peak-of-the-season perfection. "Of which there seems to be quite a lot to choose from."

"I have to admit," Catherine said, "it would be lovely to have a man with a gleam in his eye who also helped with daily life—to bring groceries in from the car and put them away, perhaps. One who would put a load of laundry on. Who'd take the garbage out without having to be reminded."

"Doesn't seem to exist, in our generation at least." I munched a walnut, feeling sad about that. Another way of the world.

"You're hopeful Justin is a better man than Tommy, no?" Catherine looked at me with those big blue eyes, dappled sunlight playing on the cinnamon freckles on her nose. Maybe I needed to get me some freckles.

"Yes. He seems like a reasonable man."

"Manageable, would you say? Yet with a pirate's twinkle in his eyes?"

"Seems to be."

"So what are you going to do?"

"I wish I knew."

"You could call him."

"And say what, exactly?"

"Apologies soften hearts. Tell him you're sorry about that night. Then see what he says."

My heart quickened a beat. "That might just work." Although I'd apologized to David May and then spun gravel on his poor bushes. I needed to manage myself better, much less any sort of husband.

"You may be back on track in an instant." She smiled, happy with her own advice.

Certainly to call and apologize couldn't hurt any worse than this long silence had. I smiled at her, and we gathered up our trays to go back inside. Heads swiveled to watch Catherine again. I had resolved to love myself and her enough not to be envious. Yet here I was, in the great swamp of it again.

CHAPTER 62

I was going to think about Catherine's advice. Was it right for me and my situation? I needed to give it some time. Better yet, a few prayers for guidance. Then go with my gut. As long as my plan was moral, this method of decision-making worked.

Meanwhile, Matt Morgan had come to the fore again in my suspicions about excellent suspects. A beloved job was at stake for him. My future as an investigative journalist was at stake for me. How could I find out more from Matt? I had to do a better job of confronting him than I had with Dennis last night. Nerves of steel, that's what was needed, so I didn't blurt out the wrong thing.

Since planning what to say to Dennis hadn't worked very well, I decided to wing it with Matt. If I kept a yellow traffic light in my brain and thought hard before giving what I was thinking the green light to be spoken out loud, I'd be okay. I drove to the museum and asked Virginia, at the front desk, if he was around.

"He's outside with the architect and engineer," she said.

Excellent. Witnesses that could claw him off me.

He was standing on the grass behind the building, looking at the section of wall where the elevator was going to be installed. The architect and engineer were deep in discussion. Matt was standing to the side a bit, gazing up at the honey-colored stones of the museum. The stained glass windows honoring books and knowledge, installed back when the building was the town library, towered above us, protected by an outer layer of plexiglass from hoodlums.

"Hi, Matt."

He was startled to see me. He didn't seem too unfriendly, however. Maybe a good woman was turning him into a manageable man rather than a resentful curmudgeon. I was just glad that woman wasn't me, that I hadn't volunteered for such a heartwrenching task.

"Yes? What?" His abruptness was still evident. It meant that woman still had a long road ahead of her.

"Can you fill me in on something?" I smiled, trying to soften the question I would be asking soon.

"You being nosy again? You ought to give it up."

"Just working on all fronts to find the truth and report it, which is, actually, my job."

He appeared to back off his resentful stance. His shoulders seemed to relax a bit.

I dove in. "I've been thinking about the changes Samantha had announced she'd be making."

"Yeah, you asked me this. Did I kill her to keep my job." All the force of negativity in his personality was back on display. Which was not unreasonable considering that accusation I'd made last time we talked.

"Samantha worked late on the night before we found her. My question is: did you see anybody here? Who came in during the evening?" There, I didn't accuse him of anything except being a great employee who worked late.

"Nah, I was at my mother's that evening. I'm sick of her spaghetti," he muttered more to himself than to me. He stood thinking, then came back to the present. "I don't know who was here that night. Are we done?"

He shoved his hands straight into his pockets, arms rigid, and turned away without waiting for an answer. He strode toward the men planning to puncture the load-bearing walls of his beloved building. He had declared the interview over.

At least he'd given his alibi without me having to probe for it. It didn't appear as though he could have bashed Samantha. Was I going to try to find out his mother's name and address and ask her about his alibi? I truly did not think so. That comment he'd made about his mother's spaghetti had the ring of truth to it.

As a person, and as a reporter responsible for telling readers the truth, I loved when that happened.

But then again, maybe I was trusting a man way too readily.

CHAPTER 63

I was in the newsroom that afternoon, dingy walls bearing down on me as I struggled to come up with a new story idea. I needed a new angle on an old story to produce a new story, but my cylinders just weren't firing with anything. Nada. Yet I needed to turn in new work.

And, as so often happens in a newsroom, the phone rang.

"Tricia, it's Cindy Pierson."

"Hi." Oh dear, what further good news about her career was she going to want to have highlighted in the paper? Didn't she love herself just a little too much? Or maybe she was just a good businesswoman.

"I thought it might be a slow news day, and that you might be open to a story."

So clever of her to frame it as a benefit to me. I made a bet that she was calling to get free publicity and sell books.

"Yes, what's going on?" I spoke in my journalist voice: glad to talk to you but there are no guarantees I'll write anything about you.

"Because of my book winning the Caldecott, I'm going to be awarded a citizen's medal by the governor of New Jersey the last Saturday in October."

Damn! The yammering voice of envy was shouting once again inside my heart.

"Wow!" I said. If I had added, "Lucky you," it would have sounded as ungracious as I felt. "What great news!" I ventured.

"The ceremony will be at the governor's mansion." Her question, can the press be there, hung between us.

"I'll tell my editor about it. I don't generally work on Saturdays, but I may be there. I'll ask him."

"Great! Would you let me know what he, or she, decides?"

"I will."

"Have a great day!" And she signed off.

Was I going to have a great day? Envy of her book's success, and of all the accolades and affirmations she was garnering, darted around in my body like a prickly pinball, banging into my gut with sharp needles.

I snapped my reporter's notebook shut and went out.

CHAPTER 64

I had a deadline looming, a story to write that Paul Tercell had pressured me for earlier in the day. I had never missed a deadline and wanted to keep my great track record. On top of that, I was due at my mother's in an hour, to help comfort my niece and nephew. When I'd agreed to be there, I'd pictured snuggling with them while reading stories and then tucking them into bed. But now I didn't think I could do it. I was laid low by Cindy's news.

How was it possible for her to have so much and me so little, even though I worked so hard? Was it luck? I had thought I didn't believe in luck, just in hard work hand-in-hand with Higher Power. But maybe Cindy was proving this concept wrong. Maybe God wasn't really on my side. I wrenched the wheel around a corner, nearly clipping the curb. Higher Power, give me luck! I demanded. Why don't you help me! I was driving blindly, regretting everything in my life, overcome with demons new and old.

By some miracle, I ended up parking safely. I found myself at the town pond.

Envy prickling in my heart, I went for a walk around the pond's slippery edge. Frogs splashed from their hiding places among the grasses into the water as I approached. They lived in the muddy bottom during the winter, and a pile driver of negative thinking was pounding me into the muddy bottom too.

Cindy has a husband, I thought, and children, a big house, an art studio just for herself. Justin had seemed like a good man; I had daydreamed of children with him. But he's gone.

On top of all her other blessings, Cindy is getting accolades and affirmations of her talent as an artist. The governor himself is celebrating her. I have none of that. For years I've yearned for a happy marriage and kids and recognition for my work. Why don't I have these few things? An answer occurred to me: because you're not enough. The idea landed in my gut with a punch.

To add to my desolation, I began to batter myself over my writing. I don't have the talent to write a novel that will rise to Cindy's level of success. I will never get her kind of affirmation—an interview on Good Morning America, for Pete's sake—neither for my fiction nor for my journalism. It's pointless to aspire to write for *The New York Times.*

The battering ram turned its attention to me personally. Justin has dumped me for good reason, I thought. I am not funny and interesting and feminine and slim enough. I'm just a bag of hopeless envy and yearning. All I want is to rise above myself, to be more talented as a writer than I am, to be a wife and a mother and a *success.* Why can't I do that? What's wrong with me?

I was pinned by my negative thinking under the pile driver; I was sucking up the muck at the bottom of the pond in great gulps.

It tasted awful. I felt terrible. The June sun's glare gave me a headache, doubly so because it was reflecting off the pond straight into my eyes. Every joint in my body ached from the verbal beating I was giving myself.

Some dark green grass in a shady patch under an oak tree appeared to be an oasis, and I trudged over to it, seeking relief from the sun. There, hunkering down to sit on the silky grass, I continued to examine myself.

I didn't give enough to charity, nor work on my novel enough. I didn't chase down Matt Morgan's mother to double-check his alibi but instead just accepted his complaint about her spaghetti dinner as sufficient proof. Therefore I wasn't a good enough reporter.

And now I was failing to be a good aunt and daughter. I should be at my mother's at this moment, helping out.

The Lower Power was having its way with me, and I was going along with it, agreeing with every accusatory statement, adding my voice to the chorus of condemnation.

A big motorcycle rumbled its way down the hill into the parking lot, backfiring the whole way. A stocky man in black leathers dismounted and put his helmet on the seat. He stripped off his jacket and gloves and tossed them over the handlebars. The paniers on his bike were huge, capable of holding all that was needed to go cross-country.

If only I could leave with him, ride off, glide westward forever. Leave this useless me behind, intractable problems with myself, a heart that's a pit of envy and self-condemnation. Instead I'd be the envy of the world, floating free down the roads and byways, camping next to clear waters.

The biker walked to the pond's edge. He ambled around it in his heeled boots, and little frogs jumped in as he approached their sunning stations. He went to a picnic bench and lit a cigarette.

Eeeuuuw. I could taste the sour nicotine on his tongue. It woke me up from my dream about taking "a geographic cure," that deceptive option we debunk in the Twelve Steps. I would only take me and my stinking thinking with me.

I raised my head to peer into the sunlight toward the pond. I couldn't be with my niece and nephew in this state, but I had to at least let my mother know I couldn't make it. Come on, Trish, get yourself together enough to drive home and call her, so you can be less of a disappointment to her, to the kids, to yourself, to the world.

CHAPTER 65

I had that urgent story deadline to think about. Instead I spent the evening ghosting from room to room in my house, noticing the dust bunnies but refusing to go find a cloth and round them up. Cindy and Susan and Meg had cleaning ladies, but can Tricia Maguire afford one? No, of course not.

I needed a Twelve Step meeting—it would interrupt this freight train of condemnation, it would lift my spirits. My favorite group was tonight. But I refused to do that too.

In spite of years of therapy and recovery, my mind was a swamp of negativity. I'd heard in the Steps that a mind is a terrible place to explore alone. I needed to talk to Catherine or my sponsor—when *would* she get back from Europe?—or somebody.

But I preferred to "compare and despair," with Cindy as my main point of comparison. Tonight I would just wallow.

Staggering to bed early, I didn't pray but just sprawled, insensate. I may have brushed my teeth, I don't remember, but it seemed as though nothing I did would make any difference to me or anybody else.

When I woke up, I cajoled myself into going to the *Sentinel*. I had to work on that story, and I needed people around me even if they didn't talk to me, especially if they didn't talk to me. To be home alone with myself any longer was unbearable to contemplate.

A beam of sunlight streamed through the newsroom's grimy windows and lit the top of my desk. Pens of all colors lay scattered, papers with scribbles on them too. They needed straightening up.

But I was still in my funk. I refused to do it.

Getting a story written was the top priority of the day. The deadline was imminent. The voracious maw of the printing presses on the other side of the newsroom wall demanded to be filled with stories.

I tried to settle down to writing an introductory sentence, or any sentence, just to find a way into the story about a new curriculum the School Board planned to launch. Instead of focusing on this, however, my mind imagined Cindy in her studio this morning, doing what she wanted, playing with her paints, sunlight shining through her clean windows, bringing with it visions of the peonies that her husband had planted for her. Her advantages and blessings and my envy at them sent me clawing and scrabbling on the gravel path like that frog in the swamp caught in a snake's mouth.

My shoulders were tight, my neck hurt even though it was still early in the day. I tapped in a few words, and they felt ugly. Sounded bitter. I finished a sentence only by boxing with the words. Instead of the usual pleasurable flow of ideas and words, today each syllable landed a punch on me as it emerged onto the page. I knew what Mike Tyson felt like when he was on the ropes. No, on the mat. I re-read what I'd just written and thought it was ghastly. Horrible. There was no song underneath the words, just the sound of body blows of envy and self-condemnation landing with an angry thud.

My hands slipped from the keyboard as I continued to obsess. Cindy has qualities that I don't have, that people recognize and promote. There she'll be on Saturday, walking up to the governor on stage to get her medal, queen of children's books, celebrated by people in power, while I work hard, apply myself with dogged perseverance year after year, and people completely overlook me. Why does she get so much recognition? What is the *je ne sais quoi* she has that I don't? I wasn't born with it and don't know how to cultivate it in myself, so it's hopeless, I'm stuck here for the rest of my life, at this level. There is nothing I can do.

With a huge effort, I pecked at the curriculum story, transcribed quotes I'd gotten from parents who were supportive or skeptical of the School Board's new strategy. A scrap of progress on my assignment.

But each word was soaked in bitterness.

CHAPTER 66

The next morning, still glum, still at the bottom of the pond, up against the deadline for the curriculum story and still in no mood to finish it, I dragged myself out of bed and made coffee, not that I wanted to but out of sheer habit. The caffeine perked me up a bit. I had the thought to take my journal and coffee to the pond. It was the least a useless person could do, write a few words before starting her useless day. Pouring the rest of my coffee into a travel mug, I drove there. I could have walked but felt exhausted.

Sitting under the same oak tree, watching how a breeze riffled the surface of the pond, the thought occurred to me that I once again needed to be saved from myself. Desperately so. I asked God to do it. The breeze reached me and lifted the hair at my neck. I decided to write down my thoughts and look at them. That would help me be cognizant of what was happening inside me.

I rustled through my pocketbook so I could write in green ink today, green for envy. I was sour with it and with the great swamp swirling around at the bottom of my pit of discouragement.

With the side of my hand, I swept a small, winged bug off a fresh, blank page. Honey, I wrote, what are you doing to yourself? You're ruining your life with negativity. We—meaning HP and I—gotta turn this ship around.

I could see my themes of envy, comparing and despairing, and negative thinking still slithering in the grass around me, readying themselves to pounce on me, their prey. Help, I begged. I watched the reeds at the pond's edge sway in the morning breeze.

And a short while later I remembered what I'd learned in church and in the Twelve Steps. God loves you, Trish, just the way you are. You will never succeed enough with your novel or your journalism, you will never have enough money in the bank, you will never give enough to charity, to deserve God's love. That's not what his love is based on. He loves you totally already, just for being a human being, just because he's God.

Want proof he loves you? First, you believe he stretched his arms wide to provide forgiveness. And remember how he gave you the strength to take care of Tommy those last agonized six months? You felt God—at times a warmth, at times a refreshing breeze—like a pillar of fire by night and a cloud that blocked the searing sun by day, come to think of it. Tommy's dying was the darkest pit of your life, and your HP got in the pit with you and helped, minute by minute.

Yes, he loves you totally, Trish. Even though the feeling comes and goes. You walk by trust, not by feelings.

A young mother with two small children came down to the edge of the water. My heart ached to be in her shoes. The boy threw in a stone, and I watched the concentric rings spread away from the spot where the rock had entered the murky water.

And the Psalm I'd read two mornings ago came back to me—my rock, my fortress. I paraphrased: my God with whom I can rest, cuddled in his lap, exactly as is. A puff of fresh air entered my dank prison. I noticed that the door to my cell now stood ajar.

A crow flew from one tree and gave a caw as it penetrated the canopy of another. I hoped he would find a friend on a branch there.

And then I remembered what Catherine had said to me at the shore a week ago: "Trish, just get with your Higher Power." That Catherine! She nailed it days ago. Silly me to have gotten overwhelmed in ocean breakers of negativity.

I scribbled in my journal: You don't need to be like Cindy Pierson, you are loved ravishingly as you are. Remember the warmth, the light, that you've felt grow over the years of doing Step Eleven.

Let go of the envy that's killing you, that kills your ability to do your best. Ask HP to give you the love you need to be happy for Cindy and her accolades, for Catherine and her new car and the way she turns heads.

Gradually the freight train of my downward thoughts was slowing.

From my spot on the grass, I watched as more children arrived at the park. They ran down the incline to the pond and scooted around it, sending frogs leaping from the reeds into the depths. A little girl tumbled in, and her mother rushed to pull her out. One minute later the child was back at the edge, as close as she could get, her fairy tutu muddy and bedraggled.

She didn't seem to have learned her lesson. I felt reasonably sure that learning mine—that HP loved me enough to die for me, that in his eyes I was worth it whether I gained accolades or not—would gradually become more real to me day by day, over a lifetime.

I said a prayer to love God and myself and others better. The breeze riffled some pages in my journal, turning it backward a few days. I read a few recent entries. Turns out I'd actually been a good sister to Susan, a good friend to Meg (except for alerting Dennis, but I made up for that—by the skin of my teeth—thank God). I'd been a good investigative journalist. I jotted down some affirmations: with HP's help, in the future I could and would help my family and friends more, investigate and write news stories better, be a good aunt. I scribbled, you *are* enough, as you are now, simply because God loves you. Gradually the chemistry of my brain was turning from negative toward positive.

After a few more minutes of hopefulness in Higher Power and what I could do with his help, I got up from the grass. I felt lighter, stronger, more courageous for the day. The sun seemed to be gilding the pond and reeds and frogs with honey.

Speaking of frogs, mine was gathering strength to hop free of the snake's grasping mouth.

I jumped in my car and drove to the museum.

At a stop light, a shiny black Porsche Carrera 911 convertible pulled up next to me. It had a beige leather interior. I loved those cars and wanted one for myself. Here was a test of all I'd scribbled in my journal this morning— HP, a test, already? I glanced at the woman in a pink baseball cap who was driving the car, tanned arms draped over the steering wheel as she waited for the light to change. I couldn't say I felt much love for her. I pondered that. How could I love her like I loved Catherine or my sister? Impossible. That's why I needed grace.

Maybe I could just say what my father used to say when people had cooler stuff than him: "May you enjoy it in good health." Perhaps that was sufficient.

CHAPTER 67

I
n my new, more positive mood, I was hoping to connect with Elspeth, to rack our brains together for clues as to who killed Samantha. As I checked in at the front desk with Virginia, however, who did I see disappearing around the corner of an exhibit but David May. Was he avoiding me, or had he simply spotted something fascinating among the exhibits that he'd never noticed until this minute?

I hadn't planned any questions for him, which maybe as a journalist I should have done. Then again, not preparing had worked well with Matt Morgan, while preparing had not worked at all well with Dennis. If I pursued a spur-of-the moment interview with David here instead of at his mansion, at least I would not get envious of all the help he could afford to hire and be tempted to spin gravel on his bushes again.

Elspeth was at her desk tucked under the wrought iron staircase to the balcony, just outside Samantha's former office. I lifted my index finger to signal "one minute," and followed David.

I found him staring with convincing concentration at an exhibit that focused on spinning and weaving. He looked up from the placard he was reading, and his blue eyes bore into me.

"Yes, Tricia, what is it?" His voice had a note of sadness, of resignation in it. Was he sad that his wife was so ill? Or any one of a host of other mysterious reasons that I couldn't guess at.

"I'm trying to get to the bottom of what happened to Samantha—which is my job, actually, as an investigative journalist." That seemed a bit presumptuous of me. My editor had not given me the title "Investigative Journalist." I was just claiming it for myself, partially to pre-empt any objection on David's part to my questions. "I found Samantha on Wednesday morning, wounded. The Tuesday evening before, did you have a meeting with her? Did you see anybody else here that evening?"

"You may consider yourself an 'investigative reporter,'" he said with a sneer. "But you have no right to accuse me of murder."

He'd seen right through me. But I'm nothing if not perseverant. "I'm not accusing you. Just asking if you saw anybody here that night."

"A veiled accusation then." He pointed a long, tapered finger at me. "Why would I have a separate meeting with Samantha? Being here for Board meetings once a month is quite enough for me." He shifted his weight, from one long leg to the other, and I caught myself flinching, preparing for a blow. But he leaned on an exhibit glass case. It occurred to me that he was tall and strong and could have hit Samantha hard enough to kill her. I screwed up my courage and stood straighter.

"I'm speculating here," I admitted, but it sure was a great theory, and I would witness how it landed with him. "You met with her because you wanted to convince her to change her plan about describing slavery in the exhibits. She had read in a book of hers, that I've read too, that your ancestor, the first president of Princeton, owned slaves. It calls into question the legitimacy of your family's fortune—made on the backs, on the blood and sweat, of slaves."

He stood very still, very silent. His eyes continued to bore into mine. I tried not to blink, but I felt compelled to break the unbearable intensity of his gaze. I darted a glance at a spindle instead. I let him win that round. But I wasn't going to let him go without answering me.

"My dear Tricia, all of my set made their money on the backs of others, either slave—" and here he arched his eyebrows and leaned toward me for emphasis— "or paid. I couldn't care less if anybody knew it."

The arrogance, the indifference to injustice, to exult in using not only slaves but people like me who needed jobs, to pay the slaves nothing and the rest of us low wages, and to ruthlessly fight every attempt to escape or unionize, hit me like a blow. He might as well have socked me with one of the iron farming tools on display in a case nearby. Yet why had I expected anything different? Dumb middle-class me, thinking honor might be important to David.

Dogged perseverance. Though flustered, I plunged on.

"Where were you that Tuesday night?"

"You have a hell of a nerve."

"So?"

"To put your stupid speculations to rest, I have drinks with my set at the Black Horse Tavern in Somerset Hills on Tuesday nights. Except Board meeting nights. You can ask Kiki."

Which was cruel, since David and I both knew she could no longer form words.

"Not that it's any of your business," he added in his most American-aristocrat tone. He knew, like so many people in his "set," born to money and privilege, how to make people feel insignificant. He had a lifetime of sharpening his skills at it.

But I wasn't going to let him make me feel small. He could try to drive as many stakes into my heart as he'd like, but I was going to bounce back with the superior energy of the middle class, with resilience. What David and his ilk might call impudence—or an amusing swing and a miss by the inferior working class.

"You know Kiki can't speak," I said, being careful not to blink as I met his gaze, not to give an inch of ground.

His comeback was fast.

"Then ask my servants." He smirked, enjoying his privileges.

"Who wouldn't risk their jobs to be honest about their boss," I snapped back. "I will tell the police about your shaky alibi, however, and make sure they have you squarely in their sights."

I whirled around to make my escape, having said what I hoped would be the last word, having spun some gravel on him and his privilege (though the impulse was unworthy of HP). But David, experienced in put-downs, got in his final dig.

"By all means," he drawled with infuriating complacency.

And with that complacency, he seemed innocent of Samantha's murder. Or maybe just unafraid of any consequences reaching him in his moneyed mansion in Somerset Hills.

CHAPTER 68

I stopped by Elspeth's deserted workstation to leave a note that something unexpected had come up, that I'd consult with her soon. I needed to go back to my little house to lick the wounds that always seemed to get inflicted when I dealt with the upper crust.

In my kitchen, Ninja stropped my ankles as I plunked down my bag with its weight of camera, rolls of film, notebook, a spare, and an array of pens. Pouring a cold glass of water from a pitcher in the fridge, I stepped out on my screened porch and took a moment to regroup. Cicadas began to clack in the trees. New Jersey was heating up for the summer.

The phone rang, and I sighed that my bit of respite had been interrupted already. The phone was in the dining room on a serving table, so I had to go back indoors and leave the cicadas behind.

"Hello?"

"I have great news!" my mom said. "Susan's back. The kids are in school, they don't know it yet, but she says she's given up on Robert. I am so thankful. Glad she's even alive after going back to him like that."

"Did she say what happened? What drove her out of there?"

"She's wearing long sleeves, even in this heat, so I'm suspicious. But she says she's done, and that's all I need to know."

"Thank God!" I felt overjoyed. Couldn't talk for a few moments.

"She's making job search phone calls now. She'll be okay. Come for dinner?"

"Great idea, thanks, Mom, I'll be there." And I knew I'd been forgiven for not showing up the night before to help.

We hung up, and I got out my journal and a purple pen. My sister had left that killing marriage. I rejoiced for a while in writing. As I wrote the words "she's left her abusive husband," I wondered if she'd ever have a good one. And me too, for that matter.

I prayed to HP for wisdom, quieted myself, pictured Justin as I'd seen him on our handful of dates, and listened to my gut instinct. Because he had been busy, Justin had not reassured me after my slip as quickly as would have been beneficial. Maybe I'd seen another character flaw—he didn't communicate when things went wrong. But no, Justin was not an abuser. I decided not to wait any longer for a call from him. I'd take the risk of reaching out. I wrote down in my journal what to say, then lifted the handset. He could be out of the office, out in the field hammering on something, I thought, as the phone rang on and on. I despaired of reaching him. At last he picked up.

"Hi, Justin."

There was a long moment when I thought my plan had failed miserably. Then he jumped in and the conversation began.

"Tricia! I just got in and heard the phone ringing. Nice to hear from you."

"Thank you."

"I should have called sooner. I've been in front of a planning or zoning board every night."

"Your projects get approved?"

"Some. Not all, at least not yet. Listen, about our last date—"

"—I want to apologize. My behavior was out of line," I said.

"I want to apologize for not talking about it with you sooner," he replied.

"Me, too. I felt so awkward, I didn't know what to say." Relief was tumbling through me like acrobats in a circus. It seemed as though things were okay between us.

"I didn't know what to say that night," he continued. "But now I do." He paused.

"Yes?" I asked hesitantly. Uh-oh, maybe I'd felt happy too soon. What was coming next?

"I enjoyed seeing you dance in your living room. If I'd been at a rock concert and had a cigarette lighter, it would have been lit. I would have waved it back and forth and sung along, that's how great I thought it was."

Wow! I was stunned, thrilled. The acrobats were on trapezes now, swinging back and forth in exultation.

"Tricia? Are you there?"

"Yes, I'm here. I'm just glad you feel that way."

"I wondered all these days if I should call you and just say the first thing that popped into mind. Like, 'Dance like that again!'"

"Oh, I'm so happy." It wouldn't hurt to admit it, would it? But I had a crushing need to slow down. "Of course, friends first."

"Yes, easy does it. Go for a burger tomorrow night?"

"Definitely. Say seven o'clock?" I asked.

"Why waste time? Let's say six."

"Got it. Looking forward to it."

"Me, too." And he signed off.

I just about staggered back onto the porch, into my grandmother's wicker rocking chair. What a completely marvelous turn of events! My heart was singing, my body joining in. Oh my, the joy a good man could give a girl. I wanted this happiness for Susan and Meg. Though it would be many days, months, years before they recovered enough from their current marriages to get into another one.

CHAPTER 69

I wasn't expected to work on Saturdays, but I felt so much remorse for not leaping to double-check David May's alibi that I drove out to the Black Horse Inn. It was housed in a Revolutionary War-era building, with low ceilings that made it feel snug. It was not a white-linen-tablecloth sort of place, which I half expected it to be for David May and his "set." Instead it was a comfortable, upscale pub, with polished wooden floors and wooden tables and chairs that matched.

The ranks of liquor bottles behind the bar were reflected in a mirror behind them. The translucent vials, their distilled liquids, and their promise of happiness, all gleamed, backlit and glowing in a way that reminded me of an altar in a house of worship. Living with Tommy and attending the Twelve Steps, I'd lived through and heard hair-raising stories about abuse of alcohol, and how easily people slipped into it and stayed in it—for years, long past the time that the ship of sanity had sailed from their shore. It was a seductive substance. Which didn't stop me from having a glass of wine now and then, but I would forever be on my guard. I hoped.

I approached the bartender, a tall, slim young man with brown hair, beard, and mustache. A traditional long white apron—sparkling white—was wrapped around him, with its strings tied in front. It contrasted with his black shirt and pants.

"What'll it be?" he asked.

"Well, I have to drive," I said, "so maybe just a seltzer and lime?" When he brought it, I slid onto a stool, hearing my grandmother say that doing so gave women the look of a floozy. Things have changed, granny, I thought to myself, and yet I glanced down the length of the bar to see if any men were reaching for their wallets, ready to buy me a drink. But I had the entire mahogany length to myself. I handed over my credit card and spoke in a friendly voice, hoping to win him over as a source. "Besides, I wanted to ask you a few questions."

He gave his head the tiniest sideways twist that might have been a nod.

I gave him my journalistic credentials, then launched a trial balloon. "You see a lot of life as a bartender, I'll bet."

He paused, not unfriendly and yet not friendly either. "Yeah, some," he said reluctantly.

"Are you here on Tuesday nights?" A swipe of his towel was his response this time.

My hopes of meeting a garrulous bartender died. There was nothing I could do now but forge ahead. "As I understand it, there's a group of friends who come in Tuesday nights to have a drink together."

He simply regarded me with his eyes locked on mine.

"Do you remember ten days ago, if one of those regulars, David May, was with the group?"

He burnished the bartop with his white towel. The entire length gleamed with furniture polish and elbow grease. I waited. And waited.

Finally he cleared his throat. "I never, ever, comment to anyone on who was here or who wasn't, or what was said. These are my clients, and I don't talk about them. You want another drink?"

"I see. No, thanks." This had turned out much as I'd expected, with the bartender protecting his clients, his job. But at least I hadn't made an assumption about David May's alibi. At least I'd tried to confirm it.

I slipped off the barstool, and my skirt caught on the round seat. My legs were exposed from top to bottom. So my grandmother was right, women weren't meant to sit at the bar. My eyes darted around the sparsely populated room, but nobody seemed to have noticed.

I dashed to my car and drove out of the Somerset Hills thinking that the bartender hadn't let David May off the hook—he was still a suspect, but not because he wanted to cover up the slavery in his monied background. I was going to have to dig for some other reason. Why had Virginia said he seemed distraught the day he was packing up his office?

CHAPTER 70

I was sitting on my front steps in the early afternoon, waiting for Meg so we could go for a walk, when she arrived in my driveway in her red Audi. I noticed with satisfaction that all its tires were nicely inflated.

"Hey!" she said, stepping from the car. She walked toward me, and I thought I detected the heaviness of grief in her posture. But she smiled gently, with a glimmer of hope in her eyes. It occurred to me that maybe she was hoping to solidify friendship with me. That was gratifying.

"Ready?" I asked.

"Yep."

"Got some bug spray? If not, I do."

"Can I borrow some? 'Borrow' being a euphemism."

I smiled, liking to be with someone who could bandy about the English. Even words that had been borrowed from Greek. Borrowed, never to be returned.

We drove to the swamp in her Audi. The leather of the interior was buttery and luxurious and probably forever outside of my financial reach. Oops, it was starting up again. I could feel myself on my path with the black hole of envy opening up before me. Crap! I mustn't jump in it and make myself miserable again. I gotta love Meg and be happy for her.

"So what's been going on?" I asked as we headed up and over the hill. Our windows were rolled down in the balmy June air. My hair was being fluffed in the wind. Meg's was tied down firmly in a chignon again, but the wind was loosening wisps that flew around her head.

"Dennis relinquished the car, obviously." She turned to me with a smile. "He's moving to New York City so he won't have such a long commute. My name is on the deed to the house, by pure luck—I wasn't smart about stuff like that, I thank my lucky stars it's worked out this way—so when it sells, I'll be in good shape."

"Fabulous!" I clapped my hands. "He'll be out of the state and won't be bothering you." Even after splitting the income from the house with Dennis, Meg would be a millionaire, something I'd always wanted to end up being. Be happy for Meg, Trish!

"I'll also extract alimony from him. He can afford it."

"Smart move." Looked as though Meg would be way past my income level, as were Susan and Catherine. Get out your wee little violin, I thought.

She gave me a sidelong glance. "I have to thank you, Tricia. Your support helped me break free."

"I'm glad." I appreciated being thanked. Her first appearance at midnight—and subsequent Meg and Dennis stress—had not been easy. But yes, I had helped this fellow sojourner.

"Sometimes I'm euphoric to be free. Then a moment later I crash into the worst despair over losing him."

"Yeah, it's called the rollercoaster. Well-known phenomenon for newly divorced people. Your emotions will become more even. You just have to ride this period of your life out. The only way through the grief is through it."

We'd arrived in the swamp parking lot at this point. We clambered out of the car. Meg was so enviably slim, cute in shorts and a sleeveless top. After applying bug spray, we set out on the path between the ponds, towards the woods. Beyond the woods was the swampiest part, where dead trees standing in dark waters lifted bare black branches to the sky. That's where we headed.

"Dennis has moved into a place in the city," Meg said. "I think he already has another lover."

"I know, it's so difficult," I murmured.

"It overlooks New York Harbor, he told my lawyer. I think he was gloating, rubbing it in that I'm living in a shelter." She touched her cheekbone, still slightly yellowed. "If he can afford to look out over the Statue of Liberty, he can afford plenty of alimony."

"He was dumb to give that fact away. And dumb to lose you."

Meg's expression had changed from upbeat to crestfallen. Her shoulders slumped.

"When I see women holding hands with their man, their relationship working out…" She choked up and wiped a tear away with her index finger.

"I know," I said.

We had traversed the woods and now stepped onto the boardwalk that led through an area of the swamp called "The Boondocks." At our approach, dragonflies that had swarmed onto the boardwalk to take a moment's rest now zagged away and darted over the murkiness. Our footsteps thumped on the wood boards even though we were wearing sneakers. The water below the boardwalk was muddy and dense.

"What's happening on the job front?" I asked.

Meg's face brightened. "I started Monday. Looks like a good team I'm on. My degree opened the doors—my work experience sure didn't."

"Bravo! Well done!" But I was thinking of my degree, earned at night at a community college, while working as a secretary, until Tommy helped me finish up at a state school. One good thing that Tommy had done. But Meg had had the support of her family to go to a prestigious private university straight out of high school, when being in college was more fun. The envy hole in my proverbial path was widening—I was near to falling in. I had a decision to make.

"I haven't worked in a long time," she said, "not since I had a summer job in college. At Burger King."

"Yeah, but you went to the University of Chicago. You're smart. You'll get the hang of your new job fast. When do you have to leave the shelter? You can stay with me, if you need to."

"Thanks, Tricia, that's beautiful of you!" Meg turned her face toward me and the sun revealed that she had a lot more healing of her eye and cheekbone to go. "But probably it won't be necessary. I have weeks left that I can stay at the shelter. By then I think I'll have my own place. I've started to look. My lawyer asked Dennis for the security deposit and first month's rent. He seems to be onboard."

We rounded a bend in the boardwalk and emerged from between two huge clumps of reeds on either side. Some wood ducks were already paddling away from us, quacking softly.

"Meg, this is all marvelous stuff! A new start! And you're young, you have many good things ahead of you."

She looked at me with sorrowful eyes. "Will I ever make love again?"

Oh, *that* question. I didn't have the answer for myself, much less anyone else.

"I know, it's painful. We just have to stay positive. With God, anything is possible. Think about coming to a Twelve Step meeting with me. It's where I get help for my negative thinking." I remembered my struggle with envy. "And for my negative character traits."

The ducks had paddled furiously and disappeared behind another clump of reeds. The breeze riffled the surface of the swamp's waters.

"Thanks for the invitation, Tricia. I'll think about it."

Knowing she'd blown it off, I sighed inwardly. Then thought I ought not to be negative about it. She could still be a friend, though people with the wisdom of an HP and the Twelve Steps behind them made exceptional friends.

Meg stopped on the boardwalk, so I stopped too. "I don't know if I can ever forgive Dennis. He ruined something beautiful."

I reached out and touched her elbow in sympathy. "My husband did too." We started to walk beside each other again. "The resentment was killing me—finally started the process of forgiving him. I would forgive, and the resentment would come back. I'd forgive again, and again. It was a long process. It didn't happen in one fell swoop. But it's happening. My Higher Power helps me."

"I'm going to need a lot of help forgiving that bastard." She pulled a tissue from her shorts' pocket and wiped under both eyes. The yellow of the bruise, in this angle of sunlight, glowed under the layer of make-up she'd applied.

Tucking the tissue back into a pocket, she said, "Can we go to a meeting together?"

I grabbed her hand and gave it a happy squeeze. "Of course! And wait 'til you meet Catherine!"

CHAPTER 71

L ater that afternoon Catherine and I went for a walk-and-talk in the cemetery. We paused just inside the black wrought-iron gates to contemplate a small family plot marked off with a low iron balustrade strung between foot-high concrete pillars. Mother, Father, several offspring and their wives. It inspired me to get to work writing, to leave something of myself behind before it was too late.

Catherine stirred first from contemplation of this family. "They're all gone. It tells me there isn't much time," she said.

"I know what you mean." I had proposed this walk with no idea what we were going to end up talking about today. And then I surprised myself.

"I wish I knew more about what I want out of life," I said. "Sometimes it's family more than anything. Sometimes it's career. I'd like to figure it out before it's too late."

"What's going on?" Catherine stuffed her hands into the pockets of her shorts as we began to move along the cemetery path. Good open-ended question.

"I want the joys of marriage and a family. And I'm also ambitious. I want so badly to be a success, to receive acclaim for my journalism, my novel, to distinguish myself in the world."

Catherine gave me one of her sidelong glances. "What's the yearning behind the yearning? The desire behind the desire?"

That Catherine! She sure could ask great questions.

I stopped walking, quieted down within, looked at my feet in their sneakers on the cemetery path, and consulted my gut. Catherine waited next to me. And I realized that I wanted to receive acclamation so I'd feel appreciated. Affirmed. Even more than that . . .

Loved.

Bingo.

What a miracle to be with a close-enough friend to think and talk about these things. Thanks to HP, who had brought us both to the Twelve Steps.

"To bask in love," I said. We began strolling again, past a grave monument shaped as a spire. "To be deeply loved and appreciated."

"I have the perfect quote for you," Catherine said. "I read about John Winthrop yesterday, a governor of the Massachusetts Bay Colony. 'To love and live beloved is the soul's paradise,' he wrote to his wife."

"But you and I both know that husbands might help with that—and might not."

"HP is the best one to rely on," Catherine said, flinging her red hair behind her shoulder. "He loves us the most deeply. And it's a relationship that will never end in crazy control—"

"—or divorce or death," I completed her sentence. "Deep, Catherine!" I said, suddenly uncomfortable with the mention of death. Which is strange for a person who'd suggested a walk in a cemetery.

We passed a mausoleum that dominated the neighboring tombstones with its size and eminence. The name carved across the lintel meant nothing to me. Perhaps that family had died out and had no offspring in Passaic anymore. All their dreams and plans were buried in this tomb with them. The birth and death dates on one plaque fastened to the wall showed that at least one person, a woman, had died at the age of forty. In her day, she would not have been allowed to have a career. I was thankful for mine. And I wished Justin would call.

"Speaking of deep dives, how's it coming with the envy?" she asked, as we walked through a stand of white pines with straight, tall trunks. A breeze was tossing their needled branches far above, and together they made a sighing sound so appropriate for place where the dead were mourned.

I had to admit the truth. "Yeah, it still crops up."

"Some people say envy is only human, it's natural, not a big deal," Catherine said. "But it's listed by the Church as one of the seven deadly sins. Left to fester, it has big consequences."

I thought of Louis, starting his art school, who said most people he met in prison were there as a result of envy. I'd been in prison too, resenting

Cindy's advantages, nearly spoiling potential for friendship with her, with Meg, even with Catherine. Big consequences. That snake certainly did want to devour me.

"I have a Puritan for you," Catherine said. "John Owen. People dump on the Puritans, as if they did everything wrong for this country. But they did some things very right."

"What's the quote?"

"Be killing sin, or it will be killing you."

Whoa, that was a meaty one. It sank in through many layers and landed on my core with the ring of truth. Yes, entertaining envious thoughts was deadly for me. "Yeah, I think that's true," I said. "I used to think envy was a positive seed that spurred me to better accomplishment. But I've gotten more aware. Instead envy boomerangs instantly. It sows a harvest of self-doubt: aren't I as good as, as deserving as, as talented as? It kills me from doing my best."

Catherine blew her nose again. "And it blocks us from God—it raises something in idolatry as being more worthwhile than him. It blocks us from loving that person as ourselves because we harbor hard feelings for the advantages they have."

Yes, I realized, as if a red Audi or a blue BMW convertible could intimately help me day by day the way HP did. I didn't tell Catherine how envious I'd felt about her new car. My courage flagged at that point. I'd tell my sponsor—if she ever got back from Europe.

"Well, we've just about figured things out today," I joked, as we reached the far end of the cemetery. "Shall we head to the Italian place for a soda?"

So we did.

CHAPTER 72

After sipping our refreshing drinks, Catherine and I walked back to my house, where she popped into her BMW, its top down, and drove off, red hair captured from tangling in the wind by a blue scrunchy that matched the color of her car. Saturday afternoon was advancing, and the museum would close soon for the rest of the weekend, until Tuesday morning. I had some more questions to ask there. Until I knew more about how things would go with Justin, I would work to beat the police at solving the crime so I could get the professional credit. They were good at what they did. I had to be better if I wanted to make my journalism dreams come true. Yeah, I thought, and what about your growing awareness that you're doing all this to be loved?

Even though Justin and I had a rapprochement, I still didn't know how things would turn out with him. It was a good life strategy simply to be the best reporter I could be in the meantime. I didn't want to drive to Trenton to cover Cindy Pierson receiving her laurels. So I drove to the museum instead. Benjamin Long sat behind the reception desk.

"Virginia's taking a day off, so you're stuck with me," he said with smile. "What can I do for you?"

"I wanted to ask you—were you around on the day that David May was packing up as curator of the museum? That was a Friday, and Samantha Scarborough started the job the following Monday." I didn't describe what Virginia had said about David May's behavior on that day because I wanted Benjamin's impression unalloyed.

"I think Virginia and I split our hours that day, because that's what we do most Fridays. She was on the desk in the morning, and I did the afternoon shift." He rose from his chair behind the desk. "Sorry, I've got to stand up pretty often. These old bones of mine object to sitting too long. If you don't mind."

"No problem. Did you notice anything about David May that day? Did he look different, behave different?"

Benjamin came around the desk and leaned on the public-facing counter next to me.

"You know, something did strike me as odd. He was boxing up his books. He had a wall of them to get through by the end of the day. I thought I might help, so I went to his office. His hair was all askew as if he'd been running his hands through it. I saw him flip through each book real fast, but real thorough, before he put it in a box. I asked if I could help. He stared at me as if he'd never seen me before, like I was an alien. Then he said no, he preferred to do it himself."

"Did he say what he was looking for?"

"When I left the doorway, to let him do it himself, I heard him mumble something like, "Where? Where is it?" And a swear word. But no, I don't know what he was looking for."

David May had denied being distraught and disheveled that Friday, when I'd asked him about it. But here it was, confirmation from a second source. I could try asking David about it again, but that felt futile. I would get with Elspeth about it, but damn, what had taken me so long to ask her for another chat? Too much going on, my head swirling with personal and journalistic questions.

Time to ask Benjamin a repeat question. I got a different answer from each person, each time, so I launched it again.

"What did Samantha talk about in that staff meeting, what changes did she say she was going to make? Who objected?"

"You asked me this before, and I thought of something afterward. She wanted to get more docents on the team. She said the museum relied too heavily on just Virginia and me. It was okay by me. I could use more time to myself, to take care of business."

"What did Virginia say about it?"

"She was a bit miffed. She told me later that she didn't like being written off as old. Samantha—well, I didn't know her long, but I got the impression that she discounted people. Maybe looked down on them—that's the right expression. Something about her attitude made me suspect she came from money. I don't know that for sure, of course, but she had an expensive education, including two advanced degrees in museum management and art history, a house in the pricey part of Somerville—how could she do all that on a curator's salary in a little museum like this?"

I'd had no idea about any of that. Don't ever stop asking people questions, Trish, I thought. Even in old age. Be as gentle but as persistent as you must. It's amazing what you find out, how much more connected you are to people—to life—as a result.

"What else did Samantha say or do in that meeting? Or with you, later?"

"Nothing else springs to mind right now."

"If anything else does, please do call me." I gave him my card again. "I'd like to go find Elspeth now, if you don't mind."

"Sure thing." And he sat stiffly down in the wooden chair, which groaned. "My bones creak as much as the joints in this chair. What time is it? I'm looking forward to closing up."

"Just half an hour to go," I said. "Enjoy your weekend."

"I'll have time to do my yoga stretches."

"Good for you!" We smiled at each other. I sure did like that man. Then I disappeared from his view, around the corner, past the wrought iron staircase that led to the upper level of the old library, to Elspeth's desk, just outside Samantha's office. Elspeth was holding her hands in front of her, admiring her nails. When she saw me, she turned and began tapping away on her computer, concentrating full force apparently.

Then she pretended to catch sight of me, and her hands stilled.

"Hi, Elspeth, how's it going?"

"Good, nearly done here for the weekend. We work Tuesday through Saturday, you know." She brushed her curly brown hair back from her face. Her pink-colored nails looked so pretty. How did she type so much and keep them looking so great? That had never worked for me, and I'd nearly given up trying.

"Watcha working on so studiously?"

"I'm sending a batch of resumes to the search committee of the Board."

"After you finish that, want to grab coffee or tea? I'd love to talk with you. Strategizing, you know." I knew from experience that someone in an assistant's position might leap at the opportunity to strategize.

"Yeah, give me a few more minutes." She turned back to her computer, and her fingers flew. I wandered to an exhibit and read the placards yet again, looking for clues. I was grateful Elspeth was willing to stay after hours at the beginning of her weekend to talk with me. Maybe she was single and didn't have anything lined up for the evening other than popcorn and a movie at home alone. Speaking of having things lined up, I was due to meet Justin at six. I was torn between making the most of my time with Elspeth and getting home to get cute for my date.

The clacking of Elspeth's keyboard stopped. Rounding the corner of the exhibit case, I saw her putting pens and papers away. After a few minutes of fidgeting, she grabbed her pocketbook and said, "Let's go." I followed her down the wooden spiral staircase to the basement. She was wearing a flouncy, floaty short skirt again today, and a sleeveless pink silk top that showed off her tanned and toned arms. How much time did she spend in the gym? Her legs were long, and the skirt complimented them. I looked nice in my straight skirt, but she looked better. I could feel myself once again walking down the road toward that black hole labeled Envy. She's ten years younger than me, with all the advantages that conveys in the dating market. She looks great in that near-transparent skirt—I could never carry it off. Her nails look great, even her toenails in those strappy, high-heeled sandals. I don't have time to sit around waiting for wet polish to dry, but she does, apparently…

Whoa!

With my growing awareness of envy as a snake trying to ruin me, I caught myself sooner than ever before. Let go of all these despairing comparisons, I told myself.

In the break room, Elspeth flounced up to the counter where the electric teapot stood, and when she arrived at it, her skirt flared. Her legs were muscular too. What all did she do in the gym? Weights? Was she among those rows of women doing "dancercise"? Well, I could always go too, I counseled myself. Though there was hardly time as I dashed all over Central Jersey looking for stories. Oh well, set your priorities, I thought. And make a decision to avoid the pit of envy! Just get with your HP. God, save me from myself!

The frog caught in the mouth of the snake made a desperate effort, scrabbling with his webbed feet against the gravel path—and at last escaped. But he'd have to be vigilant in the future.

Elspeth and I sat at the white break table after making mint tea. Even at close quarters, her nails were perfect.

"Thanks for your time," I said, picking up the mug to ward off the chill of the air conditioning that had flowed downstairs. I tugged my skirt down over my bare legs, which were objecting to the cold. "Gotta ask you about David May. Two people who were here on his last day said he was disheveled—distraught. Did you see that?"

"Yeah, I noticed it too. He was looking for something amongst all his books."

"What for?"

"I asked. But he didn't tell me. Of course not, I'm just the assistant."

That had an edge of bitterness, I thought.

She sipped her tea, which was sending a plume of steam up into the chilled air. "Maybe some sort of stock or bond? Could have been a letter—maybe a historic letter? That's my guess."

Was this slated to be another one of those myriad mysteries I would never get answers to? Damn! There were entirely too many of them in this world.

Perhaps there was one mystery I could clarify: Elspeth's reaction to Samantha's staff meeting.

"Something else to ask you: in that meeting Samantha held, what stood out to you?" What new information was going to emerge this time? I wondered. Every time I had asked the question, people revealed something new.

"You read the minutes, right?"

"Yes, but—"

"I put everything in there," she said, smugly crossing one tanned leg over the other. Her polished pink toenails, pointing toward me, chipless, accused me of neglecting mine.

"But what was most important, to you personally?"

She ripped open two packets of real sugar and teased them into her tea. Not only was she gifted with admirable slimness, but also she could maintain it while putting lots of sugar in her tea.

"Oh, I don't know," she said, leaning to the side, slowly uncrossing her legs. "Nothing jumps out at me."

Damn! Asking the same question didn't work this time. Employ another tactic.

Just then Benjamin Long descended the spiral staircase, only far enough to duck his head below the ceiling and call, "I'm leaving now. Locking the door after me. Good night, ladies. Have a good weekend."

We called good night to him. He stiffly ascended the staircase.

"Well, let's brainstorm," I said. "Solve this puzzle."

"For a few minutes. Then I gotta go. My Dad's picking me up."

"Oh, plans tonight?" It was a friendly inquiry, I thought. But she looked up at me, startled at my question. I had assumed too much familiarity between us, it appeared. I had hoped we were collaborators, but that didn't seem to be her feeling, at least not yet. Work for rapport, I urged myself.

"Well." I was scrambling to cover for the awkward fact that she had no plan to answer my last question. "Don't forget I'll give you credit in the newspaper for your help."

She tucked her hands under her legs and crossed them, at the ankles this time. "Yeah, so watcha got?" she asked.

"I'm still trying to figure out who was here that Tuesday night, who attacked Samantha. Everybody I've talked to denies being here, and I haven't been able to confirm their alibis." Though Matt Morgan's offhand comment about his mother's spaghetti still seemed alibi enough. "I think David May could have been here. Maybe he had a private meeting with Samantha. But the police still have her calendar, right?"

Elspeth had been stirring her tea, staring deeply into it.

"I remembered, after you asked about him the last time, that I did put a meeting with him on Samantha's calendar."

With my rising awareness that she was not quite the ally I'd hoped for, I wanted to confront her with why she hadn't said something sooner. But I didn't. People were busy, preoccupied. She probably forgot.

"A meeting that Tuesday night?" I said.

"Yeah, I'm pretty sure." She brought her hands to her mug and stared into it like she'd find the Oracle of Delphi. "Yeah, I'm really sure."

I was exasperated. But had to hide it.

I could have asked, "Do you know what they planned to discuss?" But that required only a yes or no answer, and what a dead end those were. So I rephrased it to elicit more information. "What did Samantha want to discuss with him?"

"Something about the transition."

Having been a reporter for ten years, I had a sixth sense for prevarication. Elspeth was being so vague. Of course, as an assistant, she might not be privy to knowledge of the topic to be discussed in an after-hours meeting and was making something up to please me. I'd give her the benefit of the doubt on my suspicions of her obfuscation.

Her gaze came up to mine, and she said, "What do you think of this idea: were David and Samantha having an affair?"

I shrugged. "It's a possibility. Why do you say that? Did you notice something?"

"Look, Tricia, it was just a feeling I had. You know how you can tell that people are attracted to each other. Women are especially tuned to that kind of thing, at least I am. Look, I have to get going now."

I sat there pondering. Would David be interested in Samantha? I pictured David and Kiki and how they had seemed together. I'd never seen them so much as touch, but if I had to come up with a single word to describe their relationship, I'd say "devoted." My bullshit meter was waggling in the red zone around Elspeth today. I looked at her toned arms and legs, strengthened by hours every week in the gym. She also had the height to leverage a strong blow.

And at that point my instincts told me who had attacked Samantha.

Elspeth's gaze was locked on me, and I think she saw the idea register on my face.

But then I doubted myself. This couldn't be true. Elspeth was devoted too, to the museum, probably to her boss Samantha, even though she was new. Besides which, I simply couldn't be sitting alone in a deserted museum with a killer. It just wasn't possible. It was unacceptable. Elspeth had been a disappointing collaborator but could not be a murderer. She dressed in pink, for Pete's sake.

I swam up to the surface from the depths of these thoughts, having rejected my instincts thoroughly. Time to go.

"Well, I won't keep you. I have plans tonight too," I said and pushed my chair back from the table.

"I just remembered!" Elspeth stood up, her skirt swinging around her long legs gracefully. "I wanted to show you something. A new iron tool came in. It's got a good story behind it. You're going to love it. Follow me." She strode off in her sandals, nary a wobble in her ankles. "It's in the vault. Come on! David May ordered it a few weeks ago. It arrived today and it's down here for safekeeping."

She pulled open the heavy black iron door, with "Vault" stenciled in chipped gold lettering that had clung to it since the 19th century.

"Why did the guy who built this place put in a vault?" I said. "Can't think why a town library would have rare books to put in it."

"Not sure, but look at this!"

She clicked a light switch on the wall and went in. I felt wary of her, but curiosity compelled me to follow her. Maybe the tool was a clue to David May, who had ordered it. He was once again my main murder suspect. And the tool had a story—irresistible: I could put the story in the newspaper and feed the printing press's voracious maw. I looked around for the implement she was so excited about and spotted an adz on a shelf. Was this it? The museum already had several adzes on display. This wasn't adding up.

And in two quick steps she was past me, out of the vault, and pushing the door closed while I froze in horror. And then the door was shut. I threw myself against it, jolting my body. My forehead snapped against the cold metal. The locking disc spun. It was flush with the door—there was no way to get fingers under it to grip it and turn it from the inside.

I was awash in horror.

Then the light went out.

"Elspeth! No!" I screamed.

The vault's iron walls formed an intense echo chamber, and my cries were earsplitting.

I screamed again. To be locked in a small space terrified me. But before the panic could completely overwhelm me and lessen my chances of survival, I pushed it back down. Be silent so as not to use up oxygen.

Though what were the chances I had enough oxygen in here to survive until Tuesday morning? Oh, Lord.

"Help!" I yelled, both at God and at Elspeth. And then the panic rose up, through my stomach, my lungs and windpipe, and took over my entire body. Its arrival was a plane crash into a mountain—fire, explosion, destruction everywhere.

But at least a fire would illuminate. Instead, it was black inside the vault. I passed a hand before my eyes—I'd read about these scenarios—and saw nothing. Not even a shadow. I shook from head to toe.

"No!" I screamed, over and over, pounding my fists on the door. But there was no answer. I felt short of breath. Was I running out of oxygen already? I gasped for air. "Help!"

An idea came up in my horror-soaked brain. I felt along the shelf, looking for the adz that had seduced me into stepping into this hell. I groped for the door again, and once I'd located it and oriented myself as best as possible while completely blind, I lifted the adz above my head with both hands and brought it down on the door with all my might. The clang in my ears of iron striking iron was excruciating. Then I thought that it would be a bad idea to damage the locking mechanism.

I turned and leaned against the door, hands against the cold iron. Leaning, panting, despairing, shaking with fear. What a horrible way to die. "No!" I screamed at God and at Elspeth.

Then I felt the locking disc tug at my blouse as it turned. I could hardly control myself, but I forced myself to wait until the door was open a crack, and then I used the element of surprise. Putting my womanly weight to work, I used my hips and butt to shove the door open with all my might, and I burst out. The lights in the breakroom dazzled me. Blinking, I saw Elspeth stepping backward briskly because of my shove, but she was sure on her feet, even in high-heeled sandals. Damn that dancercise!

She planted her feet.

And trained a small revolver on me.

CHAPTER 73

N ow that was an iron tool.

But would she use it? The look in her eye warned me not to test her. So I wouldn't. At least not yet. I struggled to get my breath back, to calm my pounding heart. Tough to do with deadly iron aimed at me.

"I had to lock you in while I went to get this." She pointed at the revolver with a free, pink-tipped finger. It was an explanation but most certainly not an apology. "You sure are nosy. Who cares who killed Samantha? Why didn't you butt out?"

I had no answer—too busy gasping for breath. And starting to plot. Grab one of these plastic bucket chairs to ward off bullets? Throw it at her and disarm her? The aura of violence clinging to that pistol terrified me almost as bad as that vault.

I spent too much time thinking about it and missed the opportunity, because she stepped further back, out of reach of me swinging a chair.

"Go upstairs. We're going to your car now. I *will* shoot you if you don't obey me. Go!"

I stepped slowly toward the wooden spiral staircase that led to the main floor of the museum. Think! I commanded myself. I was near the door to another basement workroom, one that housed the beginnings of an exhibit on barrel making. On the wall: light switches. Let *her* get a taste of darkness.

Just as I scrabbled to turn the lights off, I spotted a nice big barrel to hide in. I swiped at the wall switch. Darkness encompassed us in the windowless basement. I rushed to the barrel, removed the lid, clambered in quickly even though the century-old staves felt rough against my bare legs. I hunkered down inside the barrel and lowered the lid above my head.

Oh damn, this wasn't going to work. I was not thinking clearly. Her eyes would adjust, she'd peer into each barrel, and she'd shoot me, right within my shelter.

Here I was in another small, black space. Panic rose up again. Better to stand and take the consequences from Elspeth than be cramped in this barrel a moment longer.

No, just wait. Please, just wait, Trish. You don't know how violent she'll be.

The quiet outside the barrel was eerie. The floor was carpeted in this room, so her footsteps were silent. The sound of my breath—lurching, irregular—also masked Elspeth's location amongst the barrels. Maybe she was changing her mind, realizing the wrongness of what she was doing, heading to the police station to give herself up. Or at least just giving up and going away. I would wait here, with my knees against my chin, as long as it took for her to leave. Then move the lid to see if the coast was clear. Already I was impossibly cramped, in pain, my legs no longer circulating blood, my hips aching. How could I last a moment longer? HP, help.

I felt a puff of air as the lid was moved aside. Elspeth had turned the lights on. I craned my neck to look upward. If I could make eye contact, maybe she wouldn't shoot me.

Elspeth looked in at me, revolver pointing right at my forehead.

"You will get out of that barrel now, slowly," she said in a low, commanding voice.

"I'm sorry," I said. Uh-oh, Stockholm Syndrome, where the kidnapped identify strongly with their captor, had already shown up. I amended that apology to, "I'm sorry, I can't stand up actually. Give me a minute."

The room suddenly spun as Elspeth shoved the barrel onto its side. The ceiling and walls flashed past, I felt dizzy and floating, then landed with a thunk on my back. I could push against the bottom of the barrel to extend my legs and slide my body, bit by bit, free of the barrel.

"You will stop doing crap like that," she said and brought the revolver down on my left hand, which was resting on the barrel. The pistol smashed my knuckles against the wooden staves. The pain blinded me—explosions in my eyes, my hand. I cried out.

"Do you hear me?" she demanded.

I could barely hear her for the pain. Finally, "Yes," I gasped.

"See that knothole in the paneling?" She pointed to a darker spot in the paint on the opposite wall. "You try anything else, this is what will happen." The revolver fired and the knot turned into a black hole.

Where did she learn to do that? At the gym?

"We're going to try this again. Get up and walk to your car."

So I eased myself to my feet. At gunpoint she forced me up the wooden spiral staircase to the main floor of the museum. We left the building, that sweet, humanizing building, except it hadn't worked on Elspeth. She stalked far enough behind me so that I couldn't turn and attack before she fired off a shot.

She kept the revolver pointed at me as I unlocked the doors of the Toyota. With that nasty bit of metal pointed at my head, we got in. She never let the pistol waver.

"We're going to the swamp. Drive."

I got the car in gear, my throbbing left hand not helping much to steer, and pulled out into the light Saturday evening traffic. The dashboard said it was near six. What was Justin going to think of my missing our date and not calling him? And damn, I realized, I'd double-booked myself. My mother expected me for dinner too. By threatening me, Elspeth was making a lot of people unhappy with me.

And by the way, I sure could use Justin's help right now. Where was a man when you needed him?

As usual, I had to deal with the mess on my own. If I wasn't really clever, was I going to end up moldering in the murky waters of the swamp? Trust your instincts this time, Trish.

My aching left hand couldn't grasp the wheel, and my right hand was trembling, like the rest of me, with fear. My right hand's grip slipped on the wheel, and we swerved into the oncoming lane. I righted the car, more scared than ever.

Think! Or you will die, Trish.

What were my options? Lash out at Elspeth's right hand, the pistol-holding hand, that was on the far side of the car, resting against the door handle? Take the risk of losing control of the vehicle and crashing into some innocent family on their way for ice cream on a warm June evening?

Think! Think harder!

What were my tools? My pocketbook was in the basement of the museum. I had nothing else but my body parts, which were each individually terrified of taking a bullet.

Think! Difficult to do when you're shaking from cranium to toes.

Well, I had my journalistic tool of being able to quickly establish rapport—at least with normal people, at least with people who weren't psychopaths. For I was beginning to suspect that was what I was dealing with here. Cruel. No remorse. Narcissistic. Lying. And lucky me had already crossed once. But I was good at asking questions, at bringing out the best in people—if they had a better side—at developing a human connection. At making it harder to shoot me in cold blood.

I would position myself on my kidnapper's side of the issues. I would be sympathetic. I would put Stockholm Syndrome, where the kidnapped identify strongly with their captor, to good use.

"Elspeth, what was Samantha like?" I said, pumping sympathy into my voice despite the galloping pace of my heart. "What kind of person was she? How did she harm you?"

"Why should I tell you?" Scorn heaped on the "you."

"Because I sympathize?" Now I was the one lying, but maybe it would save my life. "Might feel good for you to talk about it." Except she had no typical feelings. Well, I had given it my best shot.

Elspeth twisted. I watched out of the corner of my eye with fear. But she positioned herself to lean her back against the car door and face me. Maybe she was settling in for the revelatory chat I'd been asking her for up until tonight. A chat with the business end of a pistol. "Yeah, I guess I can tell a dope like you. She was a rich snob. She had a big education at Ivy League schools, two master's degrees in museum management and art history. And she had the nerve to look down on me. I was just the daughter of a flat-footed mailman, I was a peon who didn't have a degree."

Wow, I knew the sting of the rich looking down on me. Was it enough to kill over? Quit speculating and build rapport. "Yes, the wealthy have a way of letting you know. I've felt it too. I sympathize."

She grunted.

This was going pretty well. More gentle questions. "What happened that night?" I could barely think straight but managed to choke that one out.

"She asked me to stay late because she was new and needed to get familiar with things. I didn't like her much—she'd already been snooty—but I love that museum, I love old things, I said I would stay." Elspeth sounded relaxed, her tone of voice confirming that she thought I was a dope. Maybe I could use her underestimation of me against her at some point.

"We unpacked Samantha's books and organized them on the shelves. She wanted me to show her the filing system. We did all that. Then she asked to see my resume."

I pulled into the parking lot by the path that led through the swamp, swung into a space, and turned the engine off. We were the only car there. There were no concerned citizens around. This was on me. And HP. Though my nerves were jangling, I reminded myself that building rapport meant looking for the good in Elspeth so I could give her a compliment, a truthful one, and strengthen our human connection.

"Don't move," she said. The pistol was trained on my face just as steadily as ever. Finding something good in her was going to be more difficult than with most of the people I interviewed.

"I want to roll the window down," I said. "It's gonna get hot in here."

"Okay. Slowly."

With the window down I could hear the cicadas clacking in the trees. Soon the frogs would be croaking in the ponds. Summertime in the Great Swamp in Central Jersey. Was this my final resting place?

Think!

"You showed Samantha your resume?" I prompted.

"She had the fucking nerve to laugh," barked Elspeth. "'No college?' she said."

Ouch.

"I was so pissed off. I couldn't afford it, even with loans, especially with loans. I went to work right out of high school."

"Me too. No shame in that," I said, despite my anxiety.

And it all came pouring out. "So there she is being condescending, something I hate more than anything in the world. I hated her and her attitude and her privilege. I envied her education and her position at the museum, the choices she was empowered to make. I wanted all of that so badly for myself. I love artifacts and caring for them and figuring out how to display them. Though I was thinking I'd love to be in human resources. But I need a degree to do any of that. All I could be was an assistant, locked out of doing what I love to do.

"Then Samantha says, 'We're going to need someone with more education in your role.' So smug! After all the help I'd just given her. She was setting my resume aside, just like she was going to set me aside. I thought of how I'd scrimped to get a year of college credits together—and here she was, so privileged and getting ready to fire me.

"She said, 'I see on your resume you worked for the Post Office for a few years.' I said, 'Yes, my father was a mailman too,' to show I'm from honorable stock.

"'You may have to go back to that job,' she said. You should have seen the smirk on her face. She was dissing my daddy too, not just me. I got even madder. She had everything I wanted, and she was taking away the little I had. I grabbed a tool from a bin by her desk and smacked her."

Her face was fierce, her lips drawn back exposing her teeth—a grimace, not a smile. She was still angry with Samantha, who died because of the expression on her face. And aristocratic arrogance. Then again, maybe she had just been stifling a burp at that moment, and our little psychopath here had misread it.

"Which tool? From the bin of uncatalogued stuff?

"Yeah. A mattock."

"Where is it now?"

"Under one of the boardwalks in there," and she waved the pistol toward the swamp. She swiftly turned it back on me. "Same place you're going to end up."

The coldness of her eyes made me shudder from head to toe. Elspeth noticed it and grinned. A death's head grin. Build rapport, Trish, quick! Try to evoke some feeling in her. Look for the good in her. "Uh, you regret what you did?"

"Sure. Just like I'll regret shooting you in the swamp. You're a pain in the ass."

Not much to commend in Elspeth with that comment. And I had thought, up until half an hour ago, that we'd be collaborators. I guess *I* misread that one. I gave up on finding good in her.

It occurred to me she might get away with her crimes. The police didn't seem to suspect her for the attack on Samantha, and what if my body was never found, here in the 8,000 acres of the swamp? Most of it watery. She could push my body under a boardwalk, and nobody walking on it would look through the cracks between the planks and notice me, my nose pointing up at them, underwater just inches from their feet.

"Get out of the car."

Giving it a split-second's thought, I decided to take my chances in the swamp rather than inside my Toyota. My left hand hurt too much to operate the door latch, so I reached across my body with my right hand and then eased myself out of the car. Elspeth put her cloth purse over her shoulder and hid the pistol inside it, keeping it pointed at me.

"Walk."

She had the iron tool, so I did.

We walked down the path between the two ponds, heading toward the woods and swampland beyond. To anyone who saw us, one woman ten paces ahead of another, we would look odd. But it was a Saturday night, people were in their homes or in the pubs, and we were alone. *I* was all alone with a murderer who had already pistol-whipped my left hand. Which throbbed. It would go through all the stages of discoloration that Meg's and Susan's bruises had. That's if I survived.

The pond to the right of us caught my attention. Trees stood on the opposite shore, offering cover. The muddy, opaque water might protect me. My instincts said it was now or never. This time I would listen to them.

I vaulted over the low chicken-wire fence that was supposed to keep people from doing what I was doing—running through briars to get to the water. The thorns tore at my bare legs and vines snagged my feet. I ran for my life.

"Aw, shit!" Elspeth shouted. A whine went past me, near my ear. Yes, Elspeth meant it when she said she'd shoot.

Not knowing how deep the pond was, not knowing if I'd break my neck in the mud lurking somewhere below the surface, I dove in head first in a shallow dive. The pond was pretty deep. I stayed underwater, swimming furiously, zigging and zagging, trying not to send any bubbles up to the surface that would give my location away. I got disoriented—what if I'd turned completely around and was swimming right back to Elspeth? I couldn't get my left hand's damaged fingers to touch each other and form a paddle, so I might be going in circles.

I swam below the surface past the end point of my endurance. I urged myself to stay submerged longer. My left hand struck firm mud as the pond became shallower and I nearly gasped with pain. I popped to the surface spluttering, blinded by a curtain of brown water and green duckweed pouring over my face. Through the film over my eyes, I spotted a big tree and staggered to it for cover. A bullet whizzed by me and smacked into it right next to my face, scattering splinters.

She was a great shot. And she was a nut. A killer nut.

I paused behind the tree, panting, laboring to catch my breath. I was among many mature trees, with spindly young ones and thin bushes standing between them and, always, vines.

Now what?

The keys were in my skirt pocket. So, get back to the car—before she does.

I darted from one big tree to another, deeper into the woods. As I left the pond behind, I became disoriented. I wanted to circle around to the car, but where was it in all this greenery? So I just ran in the direction I thought best, and the wiry branches of the spindly trees whipped me from head to toe. Vines grabbed my ankles and lacerated my skin. I was going to be afflicted with poison ivy if I ever got out of here. I hoped Elspeth would be too. From head to toe.

I couldn't move silently because my waterlogged shoes squished. And the ground under my feet was deep in dried leaves from last fall. They rustled as I ran. I looked down at myself: I was covered in little green dots of duckweed, streaks of brown pond water, and red welts. I wondered what Justin would think of yet another attempt on my life. Then I decided my bigger priority at the moment was survival.

I turned toward where I thought the parking lot might be. Hurry, Trish! Brambles and vines tore at my arms and legs—red scratches and green duckweed. A veritable walking Christmas ornament. Everything stung. I swallowed gnats as I ran for my life. They caught in my throat and made me cough.

This was the most unpleasant time I'd ever had in the swamp. I used to like it here.

I didn't know where Elspeth was. I couldn't hear any footsteps over the sound of my own ragged breathing and squelching shoes on rustling leaves. I tried to hold my breath to listen better, but my lungs wouldn't cooperate. I just had to have more air.

Where was she? How could I get to the car, open its door, get the engine started, back out of the parking space, and drive away without giving her one hundred chances to put a bullet in my brain? She knew as well as I did that the car was the key to my survival.

Darkness would help me if I ever found the parking lot. Dim light wouldn't be much camouflage as I crossed the white gravel to my car, but it would be the only cover available when I approached the Toyota. Where was the damn car!

And I saw a clearing in the trees ahead. This could be the parking lot! I approached the edge of the woods slowly, as quietly as I could, and hid behind a mature tree. Peered around it. Fifty long yards between me and my Corolla. Never had I appreciated my downscale little car more.

But the gravel would be noisy under foot. It would signal my movement to Elspeth. Instead of running straight to the car, I was going to have run around the edge, on the verge, which was short mown grass. That made the trip from my tree to the car into one of maybe seventy-five yards. At that point, I acknowledged that there was too much open ground between me and my getaway vehicle.

I lowered myself, terrorized, to the foot of my tree, somewhat hidden by brush. I tried to catch my breath and think.

The evening had cooled off, and within minutes I was shivering in my dripping clothes. I toughed it out, shaking harder and harder. Hungry Central Jersey mosquitos whined in my ears, landed on my bare arms and legs. I brushed them away, but they were so insistent. I shook more violently.

Suddenly I felt that urge that hunted things sometimes feel—I'd read about it—the urge to have it over with, to be found, to be captured no matter what happened.

I coached myself against that urge. Trish, remember her smile—her grimace—when she talked about Samantha? She was angry at Samantha then, and by now she must be mightily pissed at you. Fight! Fight the urge! You won't survive her wrath. HP! I whispered. As usual, I had to do the legwork in that relationship. Think!

Where was Elspeth? Spooked, I darted my eyes back and forth, peering through the underbrush. I watched and waited. No, she didn't seem to be creeping up on me. Not yet.

Suddenly I had an alternate plan. I needed help escaping Elspeth. I needed human beings, ones willing to get involved. I remembered that a few people lived on the edge of the swamp, in houses that moldered in the dampness. There were several, maybe one-half mile from the parking lot. I just had to edge toward them, staying in the woods parallel to the road, and there would be a house, and maybe two others not far beyond it if the people in the first place weren't home. Or kept the door shut on me.

To move toward other human beings felt like so much better a proposal than sitting at the base of this tree shivering, waiting for darkness. In June, that would mean a long, long wait. And lots of itchy mosquito bites.

I'd do it! Speed and silence, as much as I could muster, would be my best strategies.

With a short, ungrammatical prayer, "Safe," which I knew didn't always get answered the way soldiers hoped when up against bullets and an implacable enemy, I left my tree and began to move away from the parking lot and toward those houses. If only the leaves underfoot wouldn't rustle so much! I walked as quickly as I could, dodging behind mature trees at first, then realizing that I didn't know where Elspeth was, so hiding on one side of a tree or another was pointless. At that point I broke into a trot, to make it harder for her to hit me. I splashed through muddy ground, slipping in swamp goo, sliding, nearly losing my footing.

I righted myself. And heard rustling in the leaves, behind me and to my left. I ran, those damn spindly trees whipping me head to toe with their wiry branches.

Give it everything you have, Trish. This is your last chance. I sprinted like an Olympian. Despite stumbling over grasping vines, I pushed myself harder to escape. But it wasn't enough: judging by the noise, Elspeth, with her longer legs and her dancercise, was getting closer. Through the trees I caught a glimpse of a light far ahead, too far away to be of any use to me. Still, I ran as though my life depended on it, took one second to turn and look behind me, and slipped in a patch of swamp mud. Elspeth was upon me in a split second, revolver once again so close, holding within it the power to kill or maim me.

"You're an idiot," she panted. She was gasping too, legs and arms streaked with red welts where saplings and vines had done their work. I just lay on the wet ground wheezing, trying to recover my breath. Why hadn't she shot me?

"Listen. Listen good," she panted. "Change of plan." She gasped for air. "I don't know how to drive. So you're it." She pointed the pistol at my forehead. Not that again. Then she once again took me by complete surprise. "Not just you but David May. Pain in the ass." She tried to catch her breath. "Take care of both of you at once."

I was out of breath, I was in pain, I was frightened out of my wits, but I was a journalist—I had a question, of course.

"Why him?"

"He was just as bad as Samantha." She stepped back. "Go to the car."

I stood, muscles and bones aching, looked longingly at that light, far away through the woods, and turned back the way I'd come, slowly this time, pushing aside the spindly trees that had afflicted my running just moments before. I hoped they snapped back behind me in time to further afflict Elspeth.

Trying to recover my breath, I urged myself to think. It seemed that maybe my effort to create rapport had helped—I didn't have a bullet in me yet. Though possibly that was just because I was the designated driver. Should I build more rapport? I was unable find good in someone who had taken a shot at me before she remembered she needed me to drive her out of the swamp. But I could still make an effort to sympathize with my captor. Anything to raise the level of humanity in this relationship, even if it was impossible considering all the running away I'd done and how crazy she was.

I would still go for camaraderie with Elspeth, but it was tough. I said over my shoulder, "He's made it evident to me too—" I gasped for breath— "that I'm just from the middle class."

"Drive to his place now. I'll get my revenge on him *and* you."

I was sorry that David May would now be embroiled in this mess but glad I wasn't going to be alone at gunpoint in the swamp with Elspeth much longer. This change of plan bought me time. And it meant she was much less likely to get away with her crimes. Though I was careful not to point that out to her.

We got back to the parking lot, and I crunched diagonally across the gravel toward my Toyota. I reached for the door handle with my left hand and gasped as its bruises bumped hard into the car. Damn! Wrong hand!

I reached again with my right hand, but it fumbled the door handle because it had the keys in it. They fell to the gravel with a clank. I ducked to pick them up but couldn't manage to keep my swollen, stiff, hurting left hand around them. They fell again.

I stooped to pick them up with my right hand this time.

Elspeth was next to me, that deadly iron tool aimed at my head.

"Idiot! Unlock the damn door!"

Even if she needed a driver, she was crazy. Who knew when she'd change her mind again? I was terrified of getting a bullet in my brain.

Or my spine.

But here goes. Element of surprise and all that.

I launched myself from my crouch with all my strength and gave Elspeth a mighty shove. She landed with a crunch on the gravel. I ran as fast as I could back to that same tree on the edge of the parking lot, feet digging into the white stones. With dismay I realized that my body had stiffened up in the evening chill and wasn't moving as fast as I needed it to. A few more footsteps on gravel, and then I heard a "pop" and felt a searing pain in my left calf. The loss of all strength in that leg was immediate, so that I tumbled instantly to the gravel.

She had fired and this time hit me.

One second later Elspeth was standing above me, that damn revolver trained on my head once again.

"What a pain in the ass," she spat out.

I just lay there, hands wrapped around my calf, in terrifying pain, feeling warm blood seep between my fingers, flowing onto the white stones.

"Get up!"

I groaned.

"I said get up!"

I stared into that barrel, where a new bullet was just waiting for the slightest excuse to burrow deep into me and wreak havoc.

"Believe me when I say you are not going to get another chance. I'll just leave you rotting wherever. I'll fucking walk home."

I looked at her. Evaluated her once again. In the dying light I could see that her eyes held no hint of warmth, of humanity. I decided she had come too close to putting a bullet in my brain already. I'd better not aggravate her any further.

Yes, Trish, believe your gut instinct. "Gotcha."

"Really? 'Gotcha'?" she said bitterly.

I rolled to my knees, the sharp gravel puncturing them. I took a deep breath and rose up to stand, keeping my weight solely on my right foot. My left calf ached and felt on fire, all at the same time.

She kept the pistol aimed at me while she took a few steps to pick up a long, thick stick lying among the ferns at the edge of the verge. She handed the far end to me, then immediately stepped back to be out of range.

My left leg useless, I hobbled with the help of the stick to the car as fast as I could, Elspeth not far behind me. She grabbed the stick from me and threw it in the back seat, well out of reach. In the driver's seat, I bled onto my sweet little car. Mud on my skirt and legs was soaking into the seat. My left hand throbbed, my hundreds of red welts stung.

I was beyond exhausted, trembling, clothes wet, body aching, but adrenaline kept me alert driving. A few miles past the Great Swamp we were in old-money territory again. Lights twinkled in the mansions, set to advantage on their hillsides. They were so remote. There was no help for me in any of them.

I drove up David May's long driveway and parked. The bushes I'd sprayed with gravel looked none the worse for wear. Unlike me.

As Elspeth kept the pistol pointed at me from several feet behind me, I hobbled down the flagstone walkway, leaning on the stick. What was my obligation to protect May and his wife from Elspeth? I turned to look at that revolver, held out of reach of my stick, and realized, ashamed, that I was all out of the courage necessary to interfere for their sakes. I seemed to have used mine all up.

I was reluctant but nevertheless rang the bell, and the maid, Anita, answered.

As she opened the door, she gasped at the sight of me. I could only imagine what the swamp and a bullet had done to my appearance. Elspeth pushed me in with the pistol digging into my spine. I stumbled over the doorstep, past Anita, and fell to my hands and knees. My stick clattered on the floor.

"Get up!" Elspeth barked at me. "Where are they?" she shouted at Anita, who gulped, maybe wanting to protect her employers but now in the same dilemma I was.

"Who is it, Anita?" came David's voice from the solarium.

"Go." I got up painfully. Elspeth herded us, waggling the pistol impatiently. We lurched through the living room to the solarium. Through the doorway I caught a glimpse of David sitting next to Kiki, who was strapped in her wheelchair. When I burst in, Anita behind me, and Elspeth last, he dropped Kiki's hand and stood up.

Elspeth strode to stand several feet in front of him. "Sit!" she commanded. He remained standing. Was it foolishness or was it courage?

"I said sit down!" Elspeth pointed the pistol at a small Tiffany lamp—it had to be real. It was warmly glowing on the far side of the giant room. She squeezed the trigger. The lamp exploded into a million stained-glass pieces that pierced the air like shrapnel. I felt several stings on my cheeks. Thank God the shards didn't fly into my eyes. Colored glass lay scattered all over the black-and-white diamond tiles. The roar of the gun was excruciating. Anita screamed.

For a person who loved old things, Elspeth sure was destructive.

"That leaves enough bullets for the rest of you," she said.

David sat slowly down.

"Now, we're going to have a discussion about class." Elspeth waggled the pistol close to his face, and he reared back. "Just because I wasn't born onto a pile of money does not mean that I am somehow 'less' than you."

David just stared. Kiki was raising her head to watch Elspeth; she had to drop it when she ran out of strength to hold it up any longer. Then she would struggle to gather the strength to raise it again.

I was in a tense confrontation—and unlike my much-admired Margaret Bourke-White, I did not have my camera with me. It was in my purse back in the museum's kitchen, where I'd sat down with Elspeth for tea before this nightmare started. Not that it would have survived the pond and the mud I'd plunged into in the swamp. I would just have to notice as much as I could with my own two eyes and tell the police later. If I survived.

Elspeth lengthened her arm to point the pistol directly onto David's forehead. "Do you agree?"

While she was so focused on David, maybe I had a chance to tackle her. But she was so damned strong, and my calf crippled me…I'd probably just cause her to put a bullet into David's brain. I didn't move. It was up to him to stand up for himself.

"Agree? Dammit!"

"You're quite right," he mumbled.

She paused over that answer and the tone in which it was delivered. She shook her head and waved the pistol impatiently. "That's not good enough. You are now going to pay for all your condescension to me. David May, born to money, you may kiss my feet." Then she cooed, as if cajoling a small child. "It won't be so bad. I had a pedicure. Aren't my toes pretty?" Talk about condescension. Talk about crazy.

Besides, her sandals, feet, legs, and flouncy skirt were splattered with mud. Heavily.

"Maybe not just kiss but lick." She gave a light laugh. "Let's see where that takes us!"

David was frozen in his wrought-iron chair.

"Do it!" She pointed the revolver at the Tiffany lamp's twin, on the far side of Kiki.

Then she corrected herself and aimed at Kiki. David's face went white.

He lowered himself out of his chair, to his knees. Slowly he advanced one knee toward Elspeth.

I watched in horror. Who wants to see humiliation? Human dignity is sacred. This was awful. My calf throbbed. The blood from my bullet wound dripped a scarlet puddle on the black and white tile floor. The glass of the solarium's walls and ceiling trembled with the tension of the humans within it. Anita was crying. I felt faint. The plants were pulling back in horror.

And Kiki made her move. She pushed the driving lever of her electric wheelchair forward. Elspeth swung the pistol from her to David and back. Kiki nevertheless advanced steadily, her head drooping again but her chair right on target. I wanted to intervene in this mess but couldn't. And besides, Kiki was taking care of it. At huge risk. She raised her head again, her lips compressed in a thin line, her face full of determination. Maybe she didn't care if she died—or maybe even wanted to. Maybe she was thinking only of David's pride. Another mystery I'd never know the answer to.

Elspeth had the pistol pointed at Kiki's heart.

But she evidently couldn't make herself pull the trigger to kill a handicapped person.

I'd finally found something good in Elspeth.

The wheelchair's foot supports rammed Elspeth's shins first. She shrieked and began to tumble as Kiki's knees and the chair's arms crashed into her thigh muscles. She dropped the pistol as the two bodies—one fit, one failing—tangled into each other.

The black revolver spun toward my feet. I picked it up gingerly by the barrel—I wasn't letting my fingers get anywhere near that trigger.

David savagely pulled Elspeth off of Kiki and grunted as he shoved her backwards into a potted palm. Her footing in those heeled sandals finally failed her. The slick black-and-white diamond tiles were her undoing. She fell back onto the palm's blue ceramic pot with a sickening crunch. It all tipped over and the pot cracked, splintered upon impact with the floor. Dirt scattered everywhere. Shards of cerulean blue went skittering across the slick floor. The palm's deep green fronds were silhouetted against the black and white. And there lay Elspeth, wild-eyed.

David took the pistol from my hand and pointed it at her.

"Anita, call the police." He sounded as imperious and aristocratic as ever.

He turned to his wife. "Darling, are you okay?" He now sounded tender.

He patted her shoulders, then remembered himself and trained the gun on Elspeth again. She had lost that brief chance to get up and attack again, dazed as she was by the force of David's shove.

She moved to get her feet under her. David brought his other hand up to support his pistol-bearing arm.

"Unlike you, I *will* shoot." His voice was firm. Convincing. At least I was convinced.

Elspeth looked wary, alert, though she didn't move her legs another inch. Which was amazing since she was sitting on tiny shards of Tiffany glass and potsherds.

I collapsed in my muddy clothes onto a wrought-iron settee softened by a cushion covered in green and blue Dior fabric.

Oh my. I felt like I'd been strafed—actually, I had been, just like Margaret Bourke-White, first woman photojournalist to be shot at by the Luftwaffe.

What a Saturday night.

Which reminded me. I really needed to give Justin a call.

CHAPTER 74

"Tricia, hold this pistol on Elspeth."

I had thought the crisis was over, everything under control, David keeping Elspeth at bay. And here he was pulling me back into the maelstrom.

"I can't shoot it." My voice shook. "I-I-I can't shoot a human being. I know this."

"Oh for the love of Mike!" David said, his condescension to the "weak" middle class evident again. But if he was so sure that he was a higher-quality person because he felt confident he would pull the trigger on another human being, that was fine with me. I didn't want Elspeth in control of the situation, but I was loathe to touch that pistol ever again.

Before the police arrived for Elspeth, and an ambulance for me, I had to ask some questions. Might be a story in the answers. My shoulders drooped with exhaustion. The mud drying all over me, the scratches, and the mosquito bites, all itched, but I persevered. "I have a question, David. Three people have told me that you were in distress your last day in the office. What were you looking for amongst your books?"

"You ask far too many questions! And at a time like this! You're nuts!"

I thought there was someone far nuttier amongst us but let it go. He didn't realize that he'd gotten off easy as far as my questions were concerned. I hadn't asked him a huge percentage of the ones that came to my curious—nosy—mind. Like, did Kiki not care about being shot and killed because she'd be relieved of her weakening body? Or, to be really outrageous: How did your family make its first pile? It must have been in industry of some sort—something you look down on others for doing now. What does your personal balance sheet show? Just how rich are you? It would be fun to know. And one I've asked you before but got no answer to: why are you selling some of your land?

Mysteries, all of them! Never to be answered. I'd never know. For the love of Mike!

While we waited in the solarium, it got so quiet I heard the air conditioner click on. In the lull, I remembered that Higher Power had answered my prayer and helped me. I was trembling, I had a hole in one leg, but I was okay, and so was everyone else who'd been threatened.

"Thank you," I breathed.

Then Justin tumbled back into my mind.

"I need to use your phone," I told David. He nodded. I reached for the phone sitting on one of the nearby glass-topped, wrought-iron tables. I would stay in this room because I wanted to keep my eyes on the culprit, in case Elspeth tried anything. I would have no privacy for my conversation, but then again, I really didn't care what any of these people thought. None of them was going to pay my taxes, were they? So they could kiss my mud-encrusted toes. Not the best attitude, Trish.

"Justin," I said to his answering machine at home, "I'm so sorry I missed our date. I was truly held at gunpoint—tell you about it soon. I'm safe, the police are coming—call you tomorrow." Then I remembered I'd double-booked myself—my mother had expected me for dinner tonight too. I called her but didn't mention the gunpoint problem.

Elspeth remained sprawled on the floor. She had tugged her floaty skirt down with a hand whose manicure needed work, but lots of toned, though sapling-lacerated, leg still stuck out. Was she remorseful? Look where envy had taken her. It wasn't a harmless indulgence or a minor character flaw. It went to human beings' deepest problem: a sinful nature. Be killing it or it be killing you.

The solarium was glorious, the furnishings beautiful (except for the ruined lamp and the mud I was leaving on the Dior), the view over the hills stunning, though by now most of the June evening light had faded from the sky. Kiki's head was down while David caressed her shoulder with his free hand.

They had a lot.

I had a lot. I had me and my Higher Power, with whom all things were possible.

Just get me home to Ninja, I prayed.

It was many hours, many questions from a cop grilling me in the emergency room about Elspeth and my bullet wound, before that prayer was answered.

CHAPTER 75

When I got home in the early morning hours, long after the newspaper had gone to press for Sunday's edition, I washed the swamp off me, careful of the bandages on hand and calf. Then I snuggled Ninja to within an inch of his life as I tried to settle myself down. I sat on my porch with a candle and a cup of tea, the screens keeping the bugs off, the cicadas buzzing and whirring in the night, and talked in a disjointed whisper to HP for a while. "Thank you for helping me." And "I'm sorry for the time I've spent in envy." And "Please forgive me and help me to love people enough to be happy for their blessings." I rested with HP to be reassured, to be comforted, to be filled.

On Sunday, bandaged and exhausted to the core, I went to church and gave thanks again, then wrote up my eye-witness account of Saturday night. The weekend editor read it and approved it, along with one of my photos of the museum. I got both my byline on the article and my name in the photo credit. Cool.

Justin came over that afternoon—his first time inside my house. I hoped we wouldn't have to open the microwave. Before he had arrived, I hobbled to my bathroom and took the card with my affirmations off the mirror. I wasn't willing for him to see those vulnerabilities that I was trying to strengthen. We sat on the porch, me with my calf elevated, sipping lemonade and eating the Italian sandwiches he'd brought for us. He kept looking at me with an expression that, if I had to find a word for it, seemed to be awe.

"You sure do take risks for a story," he said.

I smiled. "That's what a real journalist does to get the truth."

He leaned back in one of my grandmother's wicker chairs, making it creak, and a frown crossed his face. "Maybe too big of risks?"

"Well, I had no idea Elspeth was the culprit until it was too late. I really couldn't have avoided the situation."

He sighed. "True."

I hoped risk wasn't going to be an issue between us.

"You're ambitious. I admire that about you," he said.

And I finally realized that there are men who cherish women's dreams. It's just some men who don't. Discernment needed.

My story appeared above the fold Monday morning. The photo, the photo credit, the story, my byline: it felt so very good. I love being a journalist.

From my back porch, where I was recouping, I called Chief Bognavian. He told me that, under questioning Saturday night, Elspeth had revealed herself immediately to the police as somebody who needed to be locked up in a psych ward. Her façade had disintegrated more than the Tiffany lamp she'd shot up. Funny how no one at the museum had suspected she was a psychopath (my diagnosis). But they're known for their façade of normalcy. And my encounter with her in the vault supported my diagnosis. And the one in the swamp. And in David May's solarium.

What had been the hint that Elspeth was a psychopathic killer? Something subtle. I pictured Elspeth and pondered. Her beautifully painted nails leapt to mind. I poo-poohed that idea. A great mani-pedi was not a clue to a killer. Instead, I should have known when she said she'd like to get into human resources. Since so many people in HR are manipulative, unempathetic psychopaths, that should have alerted me.

What else?

Well, hadn't she been narcissistic? I had caught her admiring her nails. To me, as a person who never had both her mani and her pedi up to date at the same time, it seemed that perhaps Elspeth's twenty aggressively perfect nails might actually have been a clue. Then again, I took time to admire mine, too, when they were finally done.

In any event, we now had the truth about Samantha Scarborough's killer. I hoped my account on the witness stand of Elspeth's confession to me in the swamp would help justice to be done. Surely Lady Justice would help. Samantha's rich family could probably pull levers in New Jersey to make sure that happened.

As the day heated up and the cicadas whirred in the trees, I thought of the role envy had been playing in my life. I had been miserable. It had killed my ability to write—my livelihood. I had hated myself and everyone who had more than me. Envy cost me. And look what it cost Elspeth, and her victim.

Monday afternoon I fielded calls from both the Associated Press and Reuters, two wire services who watch regional newspapers for interesting stories. They double-checked the facts with me before sending the story around the world. I waited for a call from *The New York Times*. What I got was a call from my counterpart at the state-wide newspaper. Monica Bodinsky double-checked the facts and seemed completely unimpressed. Hmm, competitors.

I waited on the *Times* another two days, and it became apparent I had not captured their interest. I felt frustrated at that and thought of calling them and introducing myself as the investigative journalist who had uncovered the killer at the museum in Central Jersey (a place that was usually of no interest to those editors). I wanted to—and I didn't want to. Put myself forward? Maybe wind up at the *Times,* my lifelong dream? Or wait and see what happened with Justin?

The professional success I was currently enjoying—a killer nabbed, a big story on the front page—felt great. But I imagined Mike Tyson in his mansion in the Somerset Hills, with his violent parties where the police kept turning up. He'd made his professional goals a vivid reality while falling apart on the inside. His life was the perfect demonstration that relationships bring more well-being than achievements. That the journey, not the destination— a world heavyweight championship, a published book, a job at the *Times*— is what gives us the fulfillment we need so deeply.

Maybe having dear people surrounding me was more important.

I took my resume out of my purse, where I'd stowed it the day Samantha Scarborough was attacked. Grabbing a red pen, I added my scoop on discovering her killer. I stared and stared at it. I could get accolades, like Cindy. Like Margaret Bourke-White.

What about Justin? Was this going to work out? Was there some way my professional dream and personal life could be combined? Would I be alone the rest of my days?

I dithered about calling the *Times*. For five long days. I felt angry at the *Times* and at myself for not calling for each of those five days. I picked up the phone. I set it down. And then it felt as though the news had cooled off, the world had moved on, new headlines had buried mine, the opportune time had passed. Maybe my procrastination was lack of courage, fear of the *Times* saying no. Or was it wisdom, giving myself more of an opportunity for the joys of marriage and babies?

Maybe someday soon I would know.

Until then, it was a whole other mystery.

If you enjoyed this book, would you help other readers find it by posting a review? Mention what you liked about a specific character, and Amazon will be happy. Thank you!

ALSO BY THIS AUTHOR

Numbers Count (Book I in the Tricia Maguire romantic mystery trilogy)

Why Spy? (Book III in the trilogy)

Want more romance and intrigue? Join my readers list and get a free, humorous prequel set in this world! **https://sendfox.com/nhop1234**

The Paris Writers Circle

The Traveling Writer, a photo journal with insightful captions at NormaHopcraft.com.

READ THE FIRST CHAPTER OF THE NEXT BOOK IN THE TRICIA MAGUIRE TRILOGY, WHY SPY? (BOOK III):

Justin and I strolled the boardwalk in the Great Swamp Wildlife Refuge where, just a few inches below our feet, frogs, mosquitoes, and snakes steeped their eggs in the brown waters. The swamp felt creepy. The dark water reflected the cumulus clouds in the summer sky. Could the woods around us harbor the legendary Jersey Devil, ready to spin and rage toward us?

In my ten years as a single, ever since Tommy died when I was 27, I had walked here alone often. I'd been lonely at times, but I had learned to love the total freedom of singleness.

Justin's hand brushed mine, and we both pulled away self-consciously. I glanced at him, wishing I knew how he felt. My eyes traveled up his lean frame to his face. His strong cheekbones and angular nose and jaw sported a sheen of sweat—in the late June heat, mine probably did, too. His sandy hair was damp and dark at his temples. The sun had bronzed his face and arms because he often worked outdoors.

He was a developer—one with a conscience. He left more trees than most. And he dated me with style—we had dinner recently in New York City, with a show afterward. Next week we were going to the Museum of Modern Art and then out to dinner. His interests and mine dovetailed nicely. He also liked ice hockey, but I could overlook that.

As we walked I enjoyed the upside of dating Justin: I hoped for his love and companionship in marriage, for the joys of sex, and for the baby or two that I wanted and didn't have much longer to conceive.

But there was a downside: new fears. What if I made a bad choice? Soon after the wedding, Tommy had started looking at his drinks as if they would love him back. I couldn't go through a descent into alcoholism again.

Just as bad, would Justin try to squash my dreams—or, worse, influence me to squash them myself—as Tommy had? Would he help or hinder me? Two armed and warring Greek choruses within me, one that hoped for a husband and one terrified of marriage, pounded on their shields with battleaxes.

We ambled along the boardwalk.

"Why are there no ducks in this swamp?" Justin asked. "That sign we passed said Duck Marsh."

"Maybe they didn't read the sign?" I answered with a smile.

Justin chuckled, and I was pleased.

It was just after the solstice. Iridescent damselflies—or were they dragonflies? —alighted on the boardwalk ahead of us, then zagged sideways as we approached. Even though it was early evening, the sun burned my neck, and the air felt hot and muggy. I was eager to walk into the cooler shade of the woods.

"Ready to appreciate what you see at MoMA next week?" he teased with a mischievous glint in his eyes.

"Some of it will be very interesting. But some of it will look like a child had a tantrum and threw paint." I sounded prim in my own ears, and I groaned inwardly.

He winked, and my heart lifted.

"Jackson Pollack wasn't having a tantrum. He was having a delight fit."

"Hmmm."

He stood before me on the boardwalk, blocking progress, and gazed at me with a lopsided grin.

"Tricia Maguire, I'm going to teach you to appreciate modern art," he said with satisfaction. He spun and we walked on, our footsteps sounding hollow on the wooden planks.

"And what's with Picasso, breaking women up into little pieces?" I said.

"You couldn't do what he did."

"Stick a nose on a breast?"

"See the world in a whole new way, and express that vision on a flat canvas, yet give it depth."

"Maybe that's what he did in his art, but he was terrible to women. I don't admire him as a man, so I have trouble admiring his work. When I look at his paintings, my eyes are intrigued, but my ears hear women sobbing."

We'd reached the edge of the marsh, and before we re-entered the woods I looked back. The gentle cumulus clouds were quickly building into thunderheads. A moist wind stirred the trees and turned the silver undersides of the leaves up and made them tremble. The only way to the car and safety lay through the woods. We took a few steps into the trees' shade, and the temperature dropped two muggy degrees. The dragonflies preferred the marsh, so here we were, a man and a woman, alone in the woods, as far from civilization as you can get in Central Jersey, our only witness a squirrel that raced along the fallen trees rotting on the ground.

We walked in silence for a while, our feet now scuffing the mossy path. It's nice when you reach that stage in a relationship, when you're comfortable enough with your companion to be quiet, and each person has his own thoughts for a minute or two.

"Tricia, come to dinner Sunday after church. You can meet Mike."

I heard thunder far away, and my heart lurched.

"I'd love to," I said. I dreaded meeting his 14-year-old son. Justin had told me the bond between father and son was very tight since Mike lost his mother, and Justin his wife, a year ago. Mike probably thought of me as an unwelcome intruder.

"He has a practice later that afternoon. You're welcome to come," Justin said.

"Let's see how the day goes," I said, not looking forward to watching teen boys kick up dust in a field. That did not seem to me like the relaxing Sunday afternoon I needed in order to gather my strength to face the challenges of the week ahead.

But I was looking forward to sitting with Justin in church. He started coming to my small church shortly after we met and so far hadn't gone back to his very large congregation. He hadn't yet put his arm around me protectively, the way many of the men did to their wives during the sermon. But at least he was there, his body throwing off heat that I could feel an inch away through my thin summer clothes.

I was nervous about meeting Mike, and also about seeing Justin's home for the first time. Would it be disorganized? Decorated in bad taste? Dirty? I was going to learn a lot about Justin on Sunday.

We'd reached the edge of the woods, and the pond came into view. Just before the pond, the path forked. One way led past the pond and through a meadow, to the parking lot and civilization, and the other led to a bird blind. At the fork stood a huge dead oak, stripped of bark and scorched by the lightning of a prior storm. The wind whipped the neighboring trees—their branches and leaves danced. A cooler breeze brushed my arms and face with a splash of rain. In a crevasse in the tree, I saw something silvery glinting.

"What's this?" I stood on tiptoe to reach. I hoped I wasn't invading a squirrel's territory and going to be bitten. My hand closed on the object, an aluminum cylinder that had slipped halfway out of a black nylon bag. It had a screw top, so naturally I unscrewed it. Inside was a slip of paper.

"Port Elizabeth—Pier 31—12 a.m.—June 30." I read it aloud to Justin, who stood silently.

"I wonder who wrote this," I said.

"Who was supposed to read it?" Justin nervously looked over his shoulder. "Not us, that's for sure. We're minding someone else's business here."

"I know, but it's fascinating," I whispered, consumed with speculation. "Why is this note here?"

"Illicit lovers?"

"The time is romantic—midnight—but not the location so much," I pointed out. "I'm wondering if it could be the Mafia. There've been rumors for years that those gated, stucco houses in Floral Park belong to Mafia dons. It's just the other side of the swamp."

"Then why would they use a tree on this side?"

"Good question."

"Besides, Mafia thugs doesn't use drops like this. They're city guys, they use telephones."

"Which get wiretapped. Maybe when they moved to the suburbs and saw chipmunks and rabbits in their yards, they got interested in nature?" I couldn't help smiling at my own remark.

"Tricia, let's go," Justin said. "There's a thunderstorm coming."

"Maybe there's a story in this!" I said, waving the slip of paper in the air. My editor at the Central Jersey Sentinel was always clamoring for stories to feed his news-hungry printing press.

"Don't get involved," Justin said.

"But this is so intriguing! I wonder what's going on. The 30th is Saturday night." I dared to brush his tanned forearm with my fingers and smiled beguilingly, trying to win him over. "Will you go with me?" I wheedled.

"Right. I take risks every day—with my money, not my life."

"Just because this is mysterious doesn't mean it's Mob-related." But if it was, what made me think that I, who had worked at a weekly until three years ago, and now was newly hired at a daily and just out of probation, could write a story that big? I didn't know. But I had to find out.

"I'll make a dry run in the daytime," I said, mostly to appease him. "I'll find a safe spot where we can watch what happens."

"Tricia. I don't think so."

I smiled winsomely. "We'll probably find out it's just Boy Scouts trying to earn a badge in…in scavenger hunts, or whatever."

"And we could just as easily find out there are scary people behind that note." He had told me on one of our first dates about his own experience with the Mob, who in his early days in Hoboken, across the Hudson from Manhattan, had threatened to burn down his contracting office if he didn't walk away from a land deal. He'd assumed they'd meant it.

"Okay. I get it. Mike needs you. So I'll scope out a safe place before Saturday night, and then…"

"—Tricia—"

I heard an angry edge to his voice, and he rubbed his elbow, massaging vigorously.

I plunged ahead. That's what reporters do, though maybe not brides.

"—we'll see what happens without too much risk," I finished breathlessly.

Justin was silent. Would he help or hinder? I had to be a great reporter and get a shot at the Pulitzer Prize. That's what I wanted most out of life. At the same time, I wanted a shot at marrying Justin—if my risk-taking and my personal terror of marriage didn't sabotage me first.

Another clap of thunder shook the ground. Shook my bones, too.

"We'll be electrocuted!" I said.

Justin stood massaging his elbow.

"Nothing bad will happen. Come with me," I wheedled.

He let go of his elbow, shrugged has muscular shoulders, then nodded.

"Okay. But if I say, 'Let's get out of here,' then you have to run like a track star."

"Okay," I said, wishing he weren't so ambivalent, that he would get into the spirit of the chase. Although it was possible that one cautious person in a partnership wasn't a bad thing. Then again, maybe Justin's reluctance was a sign that he wouldn't support my goals. There was no way I was dragging a reluctant man along as I pursued my dreams. It cost too much energy and time; I had learned the heartbreaking way. Though I suspected I was too fond of him at this point o walk away. My conundrum.

"Look, I guess you need to get a good story." He guessed? Well, that would do for now. My heartbeat doubled at the possibility that he would support me in the pursuit of my goals. I'd be happy to help him with his. What I needed was to see his support in action, not words.

I memorized the information on the little slip of paper in my hand because I hadn't brought my purse, with its ever-ready pen and notebook, on my stroll through the swamp. Then I carefully put the cylinder back into the nylon bag and put both into the crevasse.

We racewalked past the pond and through the meadow toward the car. Wild yellow birdsfoot trefoils and yellow and white daisies bounced at our feet in gusts of wind. Thunder resounded over the swamp. Bees zagged among the blossoms, at work despite the threatening storm. My mind buzzed like bees' wings, wondering if Justin would help or hinder.

Order Why Spy? from online bookstores like Amazon, Barnes & Noble, Apple, Kobo, Tolino, and more.

www.ingramcontent.com/pod-product-compliance
Lightning Source LLC
Chambersburg PA
CBHW030525120726
47904CB00005B/1635